Praise for Denzil Meyrick and the DCI Daley thriller series:

'Absorbing . . . no run-of-the-mill tartan noir'
The Times

'Good atmospheric writing . . . moments of chilling horror
. . . a fine example of tartan noir'
Allan Massie, *The Scotsman*

'You'll have a blast with these'
Ian Rankin

'A top talent, and one to be cherished'
Quintin Jardine

'If you favour the authentic and credible, you're in safe hands'
LoveReading

'Spellbinding . . . one of the UK's most loved crime writers'
Sunday Post

'Universal truths . . . an unbuttoned sense of humour . . .
engaging and eventful'
Wall Street Journal

'Satisfyingly twisted plot'
Publishers Weekly

'Touches of dark humour, multi-layered and compelling'
Daily Record

A note on the author

Denzil Meyrick was born in Glasgow and brought up in Campbeltown. After studying politics, he pursued a varied career including time spent as a police officer, freelance journalist and director of several companies in the leisure, engineering and marketing sectors. The bestselling DCI Daley thriller series includes: *Whisky from Small Glasses* (Waterstones Scottish Book of the Year, 2015), *The Last Witness*, *Dark Suits and Sad Songs*, *The Rat Stone Serenade*, *Well of the Winds*, *The Relentless Tide*, *A Breath on Dying Embers* (longlisted for the McIlvanney Prize, 2019) and *Jeremiah's Bell*. Denzil lives on Loch Lomond side with his wife, Fiona.

Also available in the D.C.I. Daley thriller series

FOR ANY OTHER TRUTH

A D.C.I. DALEY THRILLER

Denzil Meyrick

Polygon

First published in Great Britain in 2021 by Polygon, an imprint of Birlinn Ltd.

Birlinn Ltd
West Newington House
10 Newington Road
Edinburgh
EH9 1QS

www.polygonbooks.co.uk

1

ISBN 978 1 84697 571 4
eBook ISBN 978 1 78885 454 2

British Library Cataloguing-in-Publication Data
A catalogue record for this book is available on request from the British Library.

Typeset by 3bType, Edinburgh

Dedicated to the memory of
Alec Monteath

'What we observe is not nature itself,
but nature exposed to our method of questioning'
—Werner Heisenberg

PROLOGUE

MI5 HQ, London

Where once oak-panelled walls echoed to the sound of exclusively male upper-class accents, tobacco smoke hung heavy in the air and the old school tie was as good as any badge of office, all had changed. Sleek, low-lit corridors in glass and steel made the place look more like a futuristic space from a dystopian novel than the offices of the organisation tasked with protecting the UK from its enemies.

Today – and long overdue, many considered – things were very different. Kazia Omar, in her position as head of operational contingencies, was frowning at the large screen in front of the long black glass table.

'You tell me he's super-glued himself to the carriage?' she said, watching the footage of a young man wrestling with half a dozen uniformed police officers.

'Yes, and he's not the only one.' Iolo Harris's deep Welsh baritone resonated round the room. 'It's a co-ordinated operation. We have sixteen such incidents here in London. It's affecting both rail and underground networks. I'm afraid the place is grinding to a standstill.'

Omar looked across at a young man in a hoodie and expensive dive watch, whose gaze was fixed on a computer screen. 'Fabian, what about the rest of the country?'

'It's hard to say just what is happening,' he replied in a St Lucian drawl. 'But we have incidents flagged in Birmingham, Manchester, Glasgow and Cardiff.'

'They're closing the UK down!' Tabitha Saley-Brown blinked at Omar through her thick glasses, her face pale as a ghost. 'I think we should recommend that the army be deployed.'

Omar was always surprised how quick her head of implementation was to take the most strident action possible. Though she looked like a nervous sparrow, Tabitha was probably the most hawkish person in the room.

'Far too soon,' said Harris. 'In any case, it's our last card. We put the army on the streets, and they've won the argument. *We live in an oppressive, top-down society* – I can hear the bloody spokesperson now.'

Omar sighed. 'It's our job to work out what's going to happen next. It's clear the police are struggling. Goodness knows they've enough to do without people gluing themselves to trains all over the place.'

'Not only trains. One woman has chained herself on top of the empty plinth in Trafalgar Square. She's calling herself *the living embodiment of a tethered world*. She's been nominated for the Turner Prize, and it's only just a quarter after nine.' Tyrone Selnick, from Elizabeth, New Jersey, was on exchange from the FBI. His job was to gauge the global situation. 'But there's nothing anywhere else in Europe or back home. This must be a UK phenomenon,' he said, rather dismissively. 'Like a Chinese fire drill.' His eyes darted across the table. 'Oh, sorry, Zhan. No offence intended.'

Zhan Wei scowled at him. 'I'm from Dudley. What would I know about Chinese fire drills?'

'Gentlemen, please!' Omar didn't like raising her voice. Her mother had taught her that it was an intimation of defeat. But the pair didn't like each other and were forever bickering. In any case, Selnick had been rather forced upon her and she found his abrasive character at odds with the way she preferred to run things.

Clashes within various factions of MI5 were legend. It was her job to end all that. But every day she saw examples of little federations sprouting up within this supposedly united service. She was determined to do all she could to extinguish them before they took hold. But one had to be careful.

Omar stared at the screen again. The man glued to the train had been stripped of his clothes. He appeared to be desperately grabbing his private parts as officers looked on, scratching their heads. 'What's happening now?' she asked Harris.

'It looks like they thought he stuck his clothes to the train. Turns out it was his bare back. He must have cut a hole in the back of his jacket or something.'

'That's got to hurt,' said Omar.

'I would imagine so.'

She bit her lip for a few seconds, trying to work out the best course of action. She was under pressure from the director general. He was one of the last of the old guard and Omar knew that if, in time, she wanted to replace him she had to prove her mettle. The job as his deputy was already up for grabs, but she faced stiff competition.

She looked round the table. 'Can you give me the room, please, guys?' As they all scooped up laptops, tablets and papers, she turned to Iolo Harris. 'Can I have a few minutes of your time?'

'Sure. Nothing much I can do until we have some more intel anyway.'

Finally the room cleared, leaving the Welshman and his boss alone.

'We can't go on like this, Iolo. It's the fifth time in two months. They're under pressure upstairs from the politicians, and that pressure is now on me.'

'Pass the parcel, eh? And now it's time for the shit to roll my way, I suppose?'

'You should know me by now. We've worked together for two years.'

'But we're rivals, mark you.' The Welshman smiled.

'The old man isn't going anywhere soon. You know that. Public support's our only crutch these days.'

'With this climate brigade, you're right. Everyone imagining their grandkids being drowned, or consumed by forest fires. I'm not sure about the dissident terrorists over the water, though – and those from further afield. There's no doubt there are some mounting problems to face down. But one thing's for sure: we can't go on like this. And while the climate protesters look like a rag-tag bunch, they're tight as a drum. We have very few viable assets amongst them, and even those we have are way down the chain of command.'

Kazia Omar walked across to the window and stared out at the grey January day. It made her feel depressed but, despite the weather, this country was her home. It had been a haven after a troubled childhood in Iran and she owed the country much. She turned to Harris. 'These organisations are much more careful with their vetting since the Met undercover boys ran about shagging everyone, the stupid bastards. But we need to do something. Rivals we may be, but we'll both be in the Min of Ag and Fish if this carries on.'

'Oh, that doesn't sound too bad. Bags me the fish part. I love the sea. You can't come from Port Talbot and not love it. Our little piece of heaven, it was.'

'Ha! I'll do my best, Yol. Meantime, while we're still here, let's get our heads together.' She hesitated. 'Have you applied for the deputy post?'

'You make it sound like the wild west. But yes, I have. First working-class lad from Wales as deputy director. Now that sounds good.'

'Not as good as first Iranian.'

'May the best minority win!'

Harris was smiling, but Kazia Omar could see the steel behind his blue Celtic eyes.

1

Six months later

From the Kintyre peninsula, the great ball of the setting sun appeared to hover above the straight line of the horizon as though reluctant to make its passage beneath the waves. The glowing orb seemed desperate to cling on to its hold over the white sandy beaches, the mountains, fields and rolling hills, desperate to hang on to the day. It shimmered above a molten sea, still flecked by its fading sparkle. It called across the great expanse of time to all those who had witnessed this spectacle, for nowhere else did it set with such majesty – or so the good folk of Kintyre would tell you.

Across Islay and Jura settled a purple fringe, framing the islands in a luminescent glow, while to the south the sliver of land that was Ireland shimmered in the remnant of heat from what had been – for this part of the world, at least – a stifling day. The flash of the Antrim light was no more than a glint now. But soon, against the velvet curtain of the short night of stars, already embarking upon their twinkling dance across an unsullied sky, it would shine brighter than the sun.

Mandy Roberts first heard the aircraft while walking her dog on the Isle of Gairsay. She scanned the golden summer evening sky and noticed a small plane flying low over the North Channel.

Aircraft of all shapes and sizes were common in the skies above the island. But few flew at that altitude. As the plane banked to the right her eyes followed its likely flight path. She reckoned it was making for Machrie airport near Kinloch. Mapping out the terrain between Gairsay and there in her mind's eye, she supposed that, with no major obstacle in the way, it would be okay to fly so low – but still the journey would be nip and tuck.

Mandy pulled her mobile phone from her pocket and considered reporting what she'd seen to the authorities – but who?

She looked down. Craig, her Scottish Terrier with an insatiable appetite, was tucking into what looked like dung. Quickly, she slid the phone back in her pocket and pulled the dog away, chiding him for his disgusting behaviour. Thoughts of the low-flying aircraft soon disappeared with the waning tone of its engines as she knelt down and tried to clean the dog's muzzle with her handkerchief.

'Bad boy, Craig! How many times have I told you? I'm fed up cleaning shit out of your mouth.'

The little black animal looked back at her knowingly, head cocked to one side, caring little for her opinion – or anyone else's, come to that. He liked the taste of horseshit and was already scanning their likely route ahead for more as his owner wiped away the last vestige of mess from his muzzle.

Next to notice the plane was Sam Armour. He heard the high whine of the single engine as he emerged from the cake store located not far from his farmhouse on the very tip of the peninsula.

He removed his flat cap and rubbed his forehead free of sweat with the back of his hand. The opening to the cattle feed store, it seemed, became narrower every year. He patted his belly with a shake of his head as the plane flew past, almost at eye-level as viewed from his position on the mull.

'Are you seeing that?' said his wife Karen, walking towards Sam across the yard, her hands white with flour.

'Aye, she's low, eh? Must be landing at Machrie.'

'I hope so. If they go any further, they'll crash into the town hall spire at Kinloch! I thought the airport would be closed at this time.'

Sam looked at his watch. 'You're right: it will be by now. Och, who knows? Everybody and his friend has one o' they planes these days.'

'We don't. Mind you, the bother you've got getting in and out that cake store, I'd hate to see you trying to fit into a wee plane like thon.' She smiled. 'I've got scones jeest about to come out the oven. I know how you like them warm wae melted butter.'

'Aye. That's why I canna get in the cake store.'

The pair trudged back to the farmhouse as the sun began to sink into the ocean in a flurry of rainbow colours ranged across the sky. Soon, the whine of the aircraft's engine faded on the still, sweet air.

Wilma Cairns was driving too fast on the little single-track road that was a shortcut from her boyfriend's house back home to her parents' on the outskirts of Kinloch. Loud music thumped in the small but powerful red Mini as she swung the car into a long bend in the narrow road. She and Colin had been at the beach all day, and her tanned skin radiated the warmth of the sun. There was sand between the toes of her bare feet, but she liked the feeling, as she did that of driving with no shoes. The summer was heaven.

So loud was the music in the car that she jumped in her seat and slammed on the brakes as a plane, seemingly only feet above, filled her windscreen.

Wilma looked to her left. The plane was rocking in the air, its wings swaying like the pole of a tightrope walker, desperately seeking balance ahead of landing. She could see along most of the length of the runway at Machrie airport. There were no landing lights, which was unusual. She gasped, hand to her mouth, as the plane touched down. It bounced a couple of times, then rose back into the air once more before landing again, this time its wheels firmly planted on the tarmac but slewing to the right. It bumped across some rough ground – an emergency run-off area – before being brought to a halt by a chain-link fence, which it all but demolished.

Hand trembling, Wilma took the mobile from the tray just under the gear stick and dialled the emergency services.

2

DCI Jim Daley was lying back on his reclining chair enjoying the view across the loch from the large picture window of his home, high on the hill above Kinloch. It was well after eleven, but still light. Such were midsummer nights on the west coast of Scotland.

He reached for his glass of cranberry juice as he followed the line of the ben opposite. As the sun sank lower in the west, it was adorned with a crown of purple and a hint of green that matched the heather on its slope: truly beautiful. He'd been marvelling at the sight for several days now, for they'd been blessed with fine weather in his small corner of the world for weeks.

His wife Liz and son James junior were on holiday with his mother-in-law. Secretly, he was pleased to have the place to himself. He loved his son, of course. He cared for Liz, but not in the all-consuming way that had once been the case. Their relationship was more perfunctory now, seemingly rehearsed, like a play on a long run at a provincial theatre. There was nothing new for the cast of this little drama – everyone knew their lines and cues and there was little in the way of surprise. They merely followed a life of repetition, which seemed to vary only with the seasons and the passing moods of all involved.

With his son about to start school, Daley wondered how this change would play out in the family dynamic. Certainly, Liz seemed happier now, the effects of her attack at the hands of an erstwhile boyfriend less apparent, though he could see the times when she stared into space and could only imagine the horror of the thoughts running through her head.

Was it a marriage of convenience now? He didn't know. Daley did what he'd always done through good times and bad: immersed himself in his job. But he could see that his philosophy on life was changing from one of clinging desperation to a resigned inevitability. That his illness had altered his outlook was true. But though his heart condition was well under control, something else inside him had changed, and he couldn't put his finger on it – despite his best efforts. Tiring of self-analysis, he had resigned himself to the fact that this must be the normal passage of the human condition, the ageing process at work.

These thoughts didn't engender any feelings of melancholy until his gaze settled once more on the rows of gravestones that stood across the still waters of the loch. Though he loved the view from this room, he wished that it didn't feature the local graveyard so prominently, a constant reminder of his mortality.

He placed the glass back down on the table just as his mobile phone buzzed in his trouser pocket. Daley dragged out the device and stared down at the screen. *Brian* was described in bold letters; he clicked on the call.

'Jimmy, what are you up tae, big man?' Acting Detective Inspector Brian Scott's voice would have sounded normal to most, but knowing him so well, Daley could detect an edge of concern, stress even.

'What's up, Bri?'

'There's been an incident out at the airport. A light plane's crash-landed. Did you no' hear the sirens?'

Daley, who until a few minutes before had been listening to Mahler with the volume at eleven, answered in the negative. He sat forward in his chair, which groaned into place with him. 'Fatalities?'

'Aye, looks like it. Potts is out there, and I've just been talking to big John the fire officer. We've two dead males, by the sound of things. I think we should get going. You want me to pick you up?'

There followed a pregnant pause.

'Hello?' said Scott.

'I can drive myself; it'll be quicker.'

'Aye, right, Jimmy, nae bother. If you're sure an' that?'

'What does *sure an' that* mean, Brian?'

'Well, you know . . .' Scott's voice tailed off.

'No, I haven't been drinking, if that's what you mean. I'll take a picture of my glass of cranberry juice and send it to you, if you want?'

Scott's tone changed. 'Never crossed my mind, big man. Nope, not at all.'

'I'm not sitting here every night getting boozed up just because Liz is away. Anyway, we'd better get a move on. I'll see you out there.' Daley ended the call abruptly and immediately regretted it. He knew that Scott was just concerned for his wellbeing, but the notion that his best friend clearly thought he had a drink problem irritated him. Yes, he'd had spells of over-indulgence, but he'd never descended into the pit of despair, the true depths to which Scott himself had plummeted due to his misuse of alcohol; well, he didn't think so. In any case, for him, because of health issues, his days of excess were over.

As he quickly changed into a fresh shirt and jacket, he tried to focus on the incident at the airport. Tragic though it clearly was, there could be all kinds of reasons why a small plane would crash-land at a rural airport. But for Jim Daley, the hairs on the back of his neck told him that there was more to this. Too many years and too many suspicious deaths almost made this sixth sense inevitable.

3

As Jim Daley was jumping into his car at Kinloch, miles away on the banks of the river Clyde on the outskirts of Glasgow Carrie Symington was breathing deeply of the night air on the balcony of her apartment. She swirled the big glass of red under her nose, enjoying the aroma of the expensive wine. As the skies darkened, the lights of the city began to take hold. As she looked to her left towards the busy city centre their many colours twinkled in the dark river.

Symington loved her home. Though it was small – only one good-sized bedroom, and a smaller version for guests – it was an expensive riverside property, perfect for her. She could come back here, close the door and leave behind the troubles of the day. She heard her phone buzz on the coffee table in her lounge, padded back inside and picked it up.

Though Symington didn't recognise the number this was nothing unusual. Colleagues were always calling her from mobile numbers she didn't know. Casually she clicked on the call.

At first, she thought it was yet another sales scam, or a nudge from her network provider, anxious to punt phones she didn't need, or new payment plans that her work covered.

But it only took a few words from her caller to turn her blood cold.

'Hello, Carrie. It's a lovely evening, isn't it?'

The sound of the voice stunned her: Harry Chappell, her old tormentor. 'Why are you calling me?' Suddenly Symington's voice was only a whisper.

'Oh, you know, must be the summer air. Takes me back, that kind of thing.'

Symington clenched her jaws involuntarily. Though her hand was shaking, she was determined that this dragon from the past would remain slayed. 'Fuck off, Chappell! Never call me – ever!' She would have ended the call then, but his next words stopped her cold.

'Still enjoying a tipple or two, I see.'

'What?'

'You with your wine on the balcony, pretty as a picture still.'

Symington swung round to face the window. 'Where are you?' she shouted, a sudden tremor in her voice.

'Oh dear, the big boss losing her nerve, eh?' His Cockney accent sounded strange now after so much time spent in Scotland.

'No, I'm not losing my nerve. Listen to me. I don't want you to call me again, do you understand? I thought we'd covered that last time.'

'Not got your Scotch bodyguard with you tonight? I thought not. But before you put the phone down, this isn't what you think, Carrie.'

The very sound of her name on his lips made her shudder. 'What is it then?'

'You'll have heard I retired, yeah?'

'No. How on earth would I hear that? Why would I be interested?'

Her caller carried on undaunted. 'I'm in the private sector now – corporate crime, as it happens. I don't know why I stayed in the job for so long. This is a licence to print, believe me, kid.'

The knowledge that her long-time tormentor was no longer a police officer somehow calmed her. 'So you're a private investigator, big deal. Now fuck off!'

'Wait. You remember Larry, don't you? Larry Bower? He's retired now, too.'

Symington flopped down on the sofa, red wine sloshing on to her jeans. 'What is this, a walk down memory lane? Well, I don't want to go. And to disabuse you, I don't remember him.' This was a lie. Symington had a vague memory of a big, unpleasant man.

'You'll want to hear this, so hold on. Larry and me, well, we was at my retirement party. Sad you never made it, by the way. Anyhow, I'd had a few sherbets by that time, and – well, you know how hard I find it keeping my gob shut with a drink, eh? We gets talking – about our time in the job, and that. I don't know what came over me, it just all spilled out. Guilt, I suppose.'

'You, guilt? Don't make me laugh. I'm ending this.'

'No, wait a minute. You've not heard the best bit yet.' Symington could hear the sneer in his voice. 'He just looks at me and says, "Well, what a thing! Little Carrie, fuck me!" So, we gets to talking some more. He's been up here on this fraud case. We're partners now, you know. Harry and Larry – fabulous, isn't it?'

'I don't care!'

'Well, this company – private bankers they are – they don't want plod involved, big reputation to keep intact, that sort of thing. That being the case, as it goes, we're in for a massive payday if we get a result. And I mean massive!'

'What has this to do with me?'

'Well, you know, before, it was like just a little secret between you and me, wasn't it?'

Symington didn't reply but swallowed hard.

'You'll remember that Larry was on that shift? Remember, the night you offed that kid on the bike?'

Symington could feel her throat constrict and tears fill her eyes. The old, familiar shame and misery only heightened by the unwanted call.

'Larry's going to speak to it, isn't he? He's going to say he knew all along. About our little secret, I mean. So, I think the landscape has changed considerably compared with a few years back, wouldn't you say? It's nothing sordid, don't worry. We just need a bit of information, that's all. You know, with us being ex-job, it's stuff we can't get our hands on. But you, up here, a big chief super, and that. It'll be at your fingertips.'

'It's not that easy. You must know what I mean.'

'Oh, I understand. But we both know how good you are at covering your tracks, don't we? I'm willing to bet you'll think of something, eh?'

Symington thought for a few moments. 'What do you need?'

'Tell you what, best not do business over the phone. I'll meet you tomorrow – in public – any place you like. We can have a coffee, go over old times.'

Symington was thinking. 'There's a Wetherspoons – Hengler's Circus at the top of Sauchiehall Street. I'll meet you there at noon. I'll be in one of the booths. But I warn you, any shit and I don't give a fuck any more.'

'I love the way you said the name of that street. A right little Jock you're becoming.' He paused. 'Okay, that's fine, it's a date. But one more little favour.'

'What?'

'Get back on that balcony. I'd like to have a proper gander at you again.'

'I'll ask again. Where are you, Chappell?'

'Close enough to blow you a kiss, darling.'

Symington clicked off the call and threw the mobile phone across the room on to a leather sofa. Tears were streaming down her face now. She reached for the bottle of red wine on the coffee table and filled the big glass to the brim. Gulping at the wine like a man dying of thirst, she looked back out across the balcony. On the other side of the river sat a big hotel. She scanned the windows she could see from her chair, but they were too distant to make out anyone looking back across the river, though her every sense told her that's where he was.

She got to her feet, locked the door to the balcony and pulled the curtains, then curled up on the big chair and cradled herself in her arms. She thought she'd seen the last of Chappell, the man who'd haunted her for so long. Her last sight of him was with a broken and bloody nose, Brian Scott standing over him in the darkness of the car park outside the little hotel on Gairsay.

But her tormentor was back.

4

Daley arrived at Machrie airport. It was darker now, and lights from police and fire and rescue vehicles flashed red and blue, illuminating the sky like a fairground. To his right, across the runway from the terminal, he could make out the shape of the small plane embedded in the chain-link fence. A fire appliance was nearby, an officer on a ladder spraying white foam on the aircraft, under powerful LED lights.

As Daley pulled up in the car park on the other side of the terminal, Scott appeared in his headlights.

'Hi, Jimmy, I've just arrived myself. Are you ready?'

'Aren't we always ready, Brian?'

'Aye, true, big man. Well, most of the time.'

As they walked across the road in front of the terminal Daley turned to his old colleague and friend. 'Do you know any more?'

'Just what Potts told me on the blower on the way out. Two men, DOA: one was the pilot, the other a passenger. That's all I know. The CAA accident investigators are on their way. The ambulance guys are here, though there was nothing they could dae. But the scene has been disturbed. They had to get the guys out of the plane and reduce the risk of it going on fire. I'm sure they'll tell us more.'

The police officers were ushered through the airport and out on to the tarmac by a member of staff. There was a strong smell of aircraft fuel, and what looked like smoke or steam rose from the plane under the powerful lights.

A man in the uniform of the airport's fire service approached.

'Desmond Dewar. I'm the duty airport fire officer tonight.' He removed a padded glove and shook both Daley and Scott's hands firmly.

'I bet you were expecting a quiet night, eh?' said Scott.

'Absolutely. We're always here, just in case of emergency, but nothing like this has ever happened before and I've been in this job over twenty years.'

'No warning at all?' said Daley.

'Not a thing. We'd normally be alerted by aircraft control if there was going to be an emergency landing, but they had nothing. They reckon these guys must have flown really low – you know, under the radar.'

'You're worried the thing's going to go on fire?' Scott asked, watching white foam still being poured on to the plane.

'With a landing like that, there's always a danger. Big John and the Kinloch boys have come out. They've been great. We have joint exercises for this type of thing, but you never think it'll happen.'

'How close can we get?' said Daley.

'This is it – well, until we're sure it's not going to go up.' Dewar looked over his shoulder. 'I'd better get back to it. I saw you arrive; just thought I'd give you the heads-up. The ambulance paramedics have the bodies over there, well out of the way.'

Daley watched as Dewar hurried off. 'Once they've finished

spraying all that foam over the plane, I don't give forensics much of a chance.'

'Likely get bugger all,' said Scott.

They made for the ambulance sitting near the terminal at a safe distance from any danger posed by an exploding aircraft.

'George, how are you?' said Daley, shaking hands with a paramedic he recognised from his visits to the hospital.

'I'm sorry, Jim. We'd no choice other than to remove the occupants of the plane. The fire team did it. There could have been a chance they were still alive. I know it won't play well with your crime scene people – if it's a crime.' He shrugged apologetically. 'Needn't have worried, though. They've both been dead for a while, though we'll have to wait for a doc to arrive to do the official time of death stuff.'

'Why? We know when the plane hit the ground, poor bastards,' Scott observed.

The paramedic was looking puzzled. 'No, they were dead before that, Brian. There's not a scratch on them – well, from what I can see. Quite possibly there are broken ribs from the impact, but it wasn't the crash-landing that killed them. Here, come and see.'

The back doors of the ambulance were open, and Daley leaned in to have a look, careful not to get too close when he noticed that the ambulance personnel were wearing gloves and masks. George's had slipped down over his neck, and he replaced it before pulling a green sheet from the face of one of the dead passengers.

'Blue, you see?' he said.

'Yes,' said Daley, as Scott fumbled in his breast pocket for his glasses.

21

'Oxygen deprivation: gas or engine fuel, most likely. But it'll take a PM to confirm that.'

Scott assessed the body. 'So how long have they been deid?'

'A couple of hours, judging by the rigor mortis, I guess. But it *is* only a guess.'

'But they landed just over an hour ago. How did that happen?'

'I'm a paramedic, not a pilot,' said George.

Daley looked at the dead man in the back of the ambulance. He had dark hair, well cut. While death aged anyone, the DCI had seen enough to put him at no more than thirty years old, probably less. 'Can I see the other guy?'

The other green sheet was pulled back to reveal another blue-tinged face, the black spread of death already showing around the nose and mouth. Despite this discoloration Daley noted this man was older – middle-aged. His hair – what was left of it – was red flecked with grey. It was short, and had receded well back from his forehead. His face was heavily pockmarked, and there was what looked like a puckered scar on his right cheek, a darker blue than the rest of his face. 'Are they wearing the same clothes?' Daley had spotted the collar of a grey suit jacket over a white shirt on both corpses.

'Yup. And I've more odd news. We had to search them before we examined them. Procedure, just to make sure there was nothing dangerous – needles, corrosives, that sort of thing. We wore gloves, Jim.'

'You did the right thing, of course,' said Daley. 'Safety first.'

The paramedic handed Daley a small plastic bag. 'We normally use these for tablets. I thought I'd better bag this for you. It's the only thing I found on either of them.'

Daley took a small torch from his pocket and looked at

the contents of the clear plastic bag. Inside was a crumpled piece of paper. He could make out a few scribbled words, but not their meaning. 'Which of the deceased was this found on?'

'The younger man. It was in his right trouser pocket.'

'And that was it?' Scott looked bewildered.

'Not another thing: no keys, wallets, money, mobiles, credit cards – nothing else.' He leaned over both corpses, replacing the green sheets over their faces, affording them at least some dignity in death. He removed his mask before talking to the detectives again. 'I know it's not normal procedure, but we had no choice. The fire officer just wanted the plane doused with that foam as quickly as possible in case the whole lot went up. If we'd left them in there . . .' He shrugged.

'No, that's what anybody would have done – should have done. At least SOCO have something to work with,' said Daley.

'I'll tell you something else – not medical, just an observation.'

'What?' said Scott.

'As far as I can see, the labels have been cut off their clothes. Obviously, I only checked their jackets. But in both cases you can see where the manufacturer's name has been removed from the collar and inside pockets. Good quality, mind you. I like a good suit, but I couldn't afford those, I'm willing to bet.'

'How can you tell? A suit's a suit, is it no'?' said Scott.

'Huh, no way, Brian. There are suits, and there are suits, if you know what I mean,' said the paramedic.

'I'll take your word for it. Ella buys mine. Jimmy here gets his fae Asda. As many as you want for a tenner.' He laughed. 'Is that no' right, big man?'

Daley was too busy squinting at the note in the plastic bag under the bright light of his torch to reply.

'You'll see that better in the terminal, Jimmy,' said Scott.

'You're right. Come on, we'll take a wander. I'd better get the ball rolling up the road.' He turned to the paramedic. 'Thanks, George.'

'We have to wait here for the duty doctor to arrive. Any chance you could grab us a couple of coffees?' George asked.

'Aye, nae bother,' said Scott. 'I'll get young Potts on it pronto.'

Back in the bright terminal building, Daley made a few calls on his mobile before taking a seat beside his partner, who was examining the note in the tiny plastic bag. 'Here, Jimmy, are you sure big George did the right thing – taking this oot the guy's pocket, I mean?'

Daley shrugged. 'Under normal circumstances no, but these are hardly normal circumstances. He has his team's safety to consider, and we've no reason to believe this is a crime scene.'

'No' yet at least, big man. Are the cavalry on their way?'

'Yes. I tried to get Symington, but she's not answering her phone.'

'She'll be in her bed!'

Daley looked at the time. It was almost one in the morning. 'I never know what time of day or night it is at this time of year. Especially when the weather's like this. I remember I could never sleep in the summer when I was a boy – too light.'

'I cannae sleep at all just now,' said Scott.

'What's up?'

'My boy arrived off the late bus yesterday.'

24

'Willie?'

'*Will*, now. Plain Willie's no' good enough any mair.'

'He's not home often. I thought he was travelling round the world?'

'Supposed tae be in South America at the moment. Came home early. Och, just you wait, Jimmy. They're a mystery at that age, you'll see wae wee Jamie.'

'No doubt. What age is Willie – Will – now?'

'Twenty-five. Aye, an' still nae job in sight. Has his uni course tae finish.'

'I remember being that age. It's hard – you don't know where you are.'

'We did. We were doing this.'

'Huh. Look where it got us, eh?'

'Oh, I don't know. Lot o' guys never made it to the heights we've reached, Jimmy boy. I certainly never expected to.'

'I suppose so.' Daley gazed out of the terminal windows. Though it was still bright under the lights, the fire appliance was no longer spraying foam. He reasoned that they were happy now that the aircraft wouldn't suddenly ignite. It just sat there amid the wreck of the fence like a badly iced cake. 'I wonder what this is all about, Brian?'

'I cannae understand how dead men managed tae land.' Scott looked wistfully out at the plane.

'How much do we know about flying?'

'I've been flying before now. A bottle o' Whyte and Mackay and I'm on my way.'

'That's not happened for a while.'

'No.'

'They have all kinds of stuff now – tech. Planes can probably land themselves.'

'No' very well by the look o' things, Jimmy. I can just imagine the pilot o' my next jaunt tae Majorca. "Good evening ladies and gentlemen. We'll be flying at a height o' three feet then crashing intae a fence."'

'I'm sure the investigation team will be able to tell us how they landed. Question is, what happened to them before that?'

'Aye, and I've another question for you. Where did you get that dinky wee torch fae? See, if they're new standard issue and I never got one, I'll want tae know why. Great, they wee things.'

Daley looked at his old friend. 'Good to know your mind's working overtime on this, Brian.'

5

Carrie Symington checked her watch. It was well after midday, and she'd been sitting in the pub waiting for Chappell for over half an hour. Her mobile phone was on the table in front of her, and the more she stared at it, the less it seemed to do.

Was this all some kind of game? she wondered. She knew only too well that mental cruelty wasn't beyond the man she'd hated for so many years; she expected it, almost.

Symington eyed the clientele. It was a big room, but sparsely occupied. Only one other table could boast any customers – a young couple, clearly in the midst of a row – and just a few ragged men were standing at the bar, taking advantage of the cheapest booze in any pub in Glasgow's city centre. One man was gazing round the room, mashing his empty gums together, a half-empty pint glass in one hand. For no apparent reason, he'd burst into short paroxysms of laughter every few minutes, though what he was laughing at was unclear.

Symington had purposely dressed down for the occasion. She was wearing a faded cord jacket over a polo shirt and denims. In her experience, the people of this city seemed to have an unerring knack of spotting police officers in or out of uniform. She was doing her best to remain as anonymous as possible, huddled into a corner of the high-sided booth on a raised section at the end of the long room, well away from the bar. Nonetheless, she kept her eyes open for any unwanted advances. Symington knew she was vulnerable. She'd booked time off with the excuse of a visit to her GP. She was more than aware that nobody knew her whereabouts, and it made her cautious.

Just as the toothless man at the bar burst into another gale of laughter the mobile phone on the table rang, making her jump. She read the caller ID and swithered as to whether she should answer the call. In the end, she put the mobile to her ear. 'Hello, Jim. Sorry I haven't had time to get back to you. I know about the accident last night. Any news?' She could hear the rushed nature of her words and was annoyed with herself.

'No problem, ma'am,' said Daley, his voice loud in her ear. There have been a couple of developments I thought you should know about.'

'Oh, right.' As Symington replied the man at the bar laughed again. 'Listen, can I get back to you, asap? I'm at the doctor's.' As soon as she said it, she realised how ridiculous it sounded. The couple at the table in front of her had chosen this moment to recommence their argument, and the barman was busily throwing empty bottles into a bin that clinked and clattered in a way familiar to anyone who regularly inhabited licensed premises.

'Yeah, no worries, ma'am. When's the best time to catch you?' Daley sounded surprised.

'Give me an hour or so. Sorry about this. Everything happens at the wrong time, doesn't it?' Symington tried to inject some levity into her voice, but she realised that it sounded forced.

'Okay. Speak to you shortly.'

'Yes, as soon as, Jim.' Symington ended the call and grimaced. Jim Daley was no fool, and she knew he'd have picked up on her mood, not to mention her surroundings.

She checked her watch. There was still no sign of Chappell. She held the mobile in her hand and thought for a moment. Making sure she blocked her caller ID, she dialled the mobile number he'd called her from the previous evening. Even though she felt understandable trepidation about meeting the man who had preyed on her for so many years, at the same time she was irritated by his tardiness. She just wanted to get this meeting over with as quickly as possible.

The mobile was ringing out, and she was about to end the call when it was answered.

'Hello, who is this, please?'

Though Symington didn't recognise the voice, she knew it didn't belong to Chappell, and was pretty sure it wasn't his partner in crime, Larry Bower. Though she recalled little of the man, she remembered he had a strong Cockney accent. Whoever was on the other end of this line had a distinct Scottish twang. Before she thought about it, Symington said hurriedly, 'Sorry, wrong number,' and ended the call, cursing herself for saying anything.

For someone who had spent a career catching criminals, she was aware that she wasn't very good at clandestine behaviour of her own.

As Symington wondered who had answered Chappell's phone, she made up her mind to give it another half an hour before leaving. Was it all a ploy to pull her further into whatever it was he was doing? She couldn't be sure, but she knew that he was capable of anything.

The man at the bar burst into idiotic laughter again, further fraying Carrie Symington's nerves.

'What was all that aboot?' Scott asked. He was sitting across the desk from Daley in the glass box. As they'd both had information to impart to their divisional commander, Daley's mobile had been on loudspeaker.

'Your guess is as good as mine, Brian.' Daley shrugged.

'Doctor's, my arse. That was a pub she was in, nae danger.'

'Well, if anyone knows what a pub sounds like, it's you.'

'Huh, listen tae the boss o' the Temperance League o'er here.'

'She might be out to lunch with someone, you know?'

'A bloke, you mean?'

'A bloke – anybody – who knows?'

'Well, why be so furtive aboot it? Nah, that was the voice o' somebody wae something tae hide.'

'You've been in this job too long, Brian. There's not a problem round every corner. She's a private person. Everyone deserves a life away from this, don't they?'

'Oh aye, but have you ever had one? Because I haven't.'

'I'm sure she'll get back to us soon.' Daley was staring at the magnified image on his computer screen. It had been taken by the SOCO unit still working alongside officers from the accident investigation team trying to discover why the plane had crash-landed at Machrie the previous evening, and, more important, why it contained two dead men.

The paper had been very crumpled, and the writing, in pencil, was faded. Though it was open to interpretation, both Daley and the SOCO officers reckoned that they knew what it read.

Ian Macmillan. CH.

But Brian Scott wasn't convinced. 'It doesnae matter how often you stare at it, Jimmy. That could be Jan, or Joe, even.'

'But the surname is clear enough.'

'You think? It could be MacAllan, MacMullen, a whole pile o' names. I know what you're thinking. But we'd better tread carefully, big man.'

'I think it's *Ian Macmillan, County Hotel*, CH. Surely that's obvious?' Daley stared again at the writing. It was of the old copperplate style, similar to his mother's hand. It looked nice but was often hard to decipher.

'Aye, it's obvious tae us 'cos we're aware o' him; it's too convenient, Jimmy. He's a guy we know, but we don't know. Naebody else in Kinloch really knows him, either. It's colouring oor thinking – well, yours. Before we storm doon there and start asking questions, we should ca' canny.'

Daley laughed.

'What's so funny?'

'I think this is the first time in our career working together that you've counselled caution.'

Scott looked unimpressed. 'You know that's no' true, my friend.' He nodded knowingly.

'Okay, maybe not.' Many incidents suddenly flashed through Daley's mind, times when he'd happily, or unhappily, thrown caution to the wind. 'But more often than not it's the other way about, Brian.'

'Aye, I'll gie you that. But I still think I'm right this time.'

'Okay, he arrives here, and seemingly on a whim shells out on the County.'

'It's been in his family. He's got piles o' dosh. You've got tae remember that. Money means nothing tae folk who've got

31

plenty o' it. You cannae condemn the man for buying a hotel his grandfaither used tae own.'

'Maybe not. But how do we know where all this money came from?'

'I'll take a look this afternoon. He's supposed tae own this big trucking company in Canada, right?'

'Yes.'

'Okay, so I check his credentials wae they Mounties, and we keep an eye on him, just in case – aye, and any other Ian Macmillans in the area. If he is up tae something and we give him the heads-up – well, who knows what could happen.'

'You're right. I've had Potts ready to go keep an eye on him. But, conveniently, he's out of the country. He's due back soon, though; that's why I wanted to talk to Symington. We could do with some more bodies.'

'So you're determined. Oh well. Oor dead aviators have nothing tae worry aboot.'

Daley shook his head at Scott's attempt at humour. 'Do we know anything more about them?'

'As far as their identity, no. We'll get the results o' the PM later, so at least we'll know how they died. I know a bit more about their suits, by the way.'

'What?'

'We can't fix a tailor yet, but we know the material of the suits and shirts is Italian. Just had the call from up the road when you were out getting lunch.'

Daley pursed his lips and looked at the enlarged image once more. Though he was sure he knew what was scribbled on the crumpled piece of paper, he also knew Scott was right. They'd have to be watchful, but careful.

'I'll away and get in touch wae the Mounties, then.'

'Do you know where he's from in Canada? There's more to policing there than the Mounties, you know.'

'Aye, I've always kind o' wondered aboot that. I mean, would you put oor horse branch in charge o' anything – apart fae landing great piles o' shite in the street, that is?'

'I'll take a note of your thoughts on equine policing and send them to the chief constable. I'm sure he'll be all ears.'

'Aye, on you go.' Scott smiled. 'I'll gie Annie a visit – casual, like. She'll know where he's fae. We can take it from there. She likely knows what type o' knickers his mother used tae wear by now. You know what they're like here.'

As Scott left the glass box, Daley stared once again at the magnified image of the note on his screen. Then he thought about Symington.

6

Carrie Symington was walking quickly through the Glasgow streets to the multistorey car park. It was a hot, sticky day, but grey and overcast. She could have done without the oppression of this weather. As her mother would say, they needed a good thunderstorm to clear the air.

As Symington paced briskly towards her car, she was alert. Chappell hadn't turned up. He hadn't answered his phone, though someone else had. The man had toyed with her for years. But she was determined that this persecution was at an end. That he was no longer a police officer gave her an advantage. But she knew the animal cunning the man possessed. He'd arranged a meeting then not turned up just to unsettle her, of that she was sure.

Well, Carrie Symington wasn't a wet-behind-the-ears beat constable any more. The burden of her past hung over her every day, but she'd learned to cope, to survive, despite the guilt she knew could never be banished.

She was just about to enter the car park when she spotted a man leaning against a wall a few feet away. He was watching her intently, as he drew slowly and deliberately on a cigarette. Symington stared back, anxious not to appear intimidated. She didn't recognise the man. He was lean, tall and probably in his early thirties, dressed casually, but smartly enough. The more she stared, the more he gazed back, no particular expression on his face.

She wasn't sure if it was her frustration at the reappearance of Chappell in her life, or irritation at the fact he'd been a no-show, but Symington's dander was up. She changed direction and walked towards the man.

Stopping within a few feet of him, she addressed him in a manner best described as 'confrontational'.

'What's your problem? Do you like my jacket, or is it my haircut?'

Suddenly he looked bewildered. 'Sorry, I didn't mean to upset you. I was just – you know – thinking.'

He opened his mouth to say something else, but Symington beat him to it. She dipped into her handbag and flourished her police warrant card in his face. 'I want to know who you are and what you're doing?' She spat out the question.

The man held up his arms in mock surrender. 'It's my wife. She's in that clothes shop across the road, ma'am.'

It took a split second for Symington to register the title. She must have looked puzzled, because he spoke again.

'I work in your division, ma'am.' He gestured to his pocket and with finger and thumb drew out his own warrant card. 'Constable Connolly from two-shift – I'm on annual leave. I thought it was you, but wasn't used to seeing you dressed casual, like. I'm sorry if I unnerved you, ma'am.'

'No, it's me who should apologise, Constable Connolly. It's just been one of those days. I'm sure you know what I mean.' Symington felt the blush of embarrassment on her face.

'Absolutely, ma'am.' He smiled. 'In our job, is there any other kind of day?'

Taking her leave of the off-duty police officer, Symington entered the dank cool of the car park. The warm weather had made the smell of piss even more prominent. Though the young constable had been more pleasant than she deserved, she knew well that the divisional HQ would soon be buzzing with news of their awkward encounter.

Daley was in the AV suite at Kinloch police office. On the screen pathologist Marion Forbes loomed large as she explained the findings of the post mortem on the two mystery aircraft passengers.

'They suffocated, right? A problem with the plane, perhaps?' said Daley.

'It happened tae thon Ron Denver – you know, the country and western singer,' said Scott, as he tucked into a burger roll.

'John Denver,' said Daley.

'Him tae? Fuck's sake, makes you wonder aboot setting foot on a plane for your holidays – especially if you're called Denver, eh?'

A large chunk of burger was propelled in Daley's direction, but he managed to avoid it with a swift move of the head that would have made a cricket batsman proud.

'The asphyxiation didn't happen on the plane, gentleman.' Forbes's voice was authoritative.

'How do you know?' said Scott.

'Because had they been alive in such a small aircraft for any time at all, there would have been traces of aircraft fuel residue in the lungs. That wasn't present in either man.'

'Have you ever watched that *Silent Witness*?' Scott asked. 'You'd be a star on there, by the way.'

'I'm really flattered.' The sarcasm was palpable. 'As I said, it is normal to have a trace of aircraft fuel in the lungs. Without the slightest residue, there's a problem. I looked carefully at the images taken by those first on the scene and by my SOCO colleagues. Using these as a guide, together with the condition of the cadavers when I was carrying out the PM, I'd say they'd been dead a short time before take-off.' She turned to a laptop at her side and typed something on the keyboard.

A large image flashed on to the screen. It took Daley a few moments to realise that it was a close-up of one of the dead men's necks. He could see a livid bruise just above the shoulder. 'What's that, signs of strangulation?'

'No, they weren't strangled – all the wrong pathology. I think they were suffocated. These bruises are consistent with something – a plastic bag, for instance – either being held, or more likely tied in place, over their heads and impeding breathing.'

'And this is present on both individuals?' said Daley.

'Yes, almost identical. At a guess some thick rope or constricting band. The former, if you want an opinion. A rope tied or pulled tightly caused the bruising.'

'Wait,' said Scott. 'How the hell did they manage to take off when they were both deid?'

'That's something you'll have ask the experts in aviation, DI Scott. Something I'm not. I can tell you that the shorter man was in his forties and drank a lot judging by the condition of his liver. Liked sugar, too – or perhaps not dentists. His teeth were in poor nick, even for a man his age.'

'The other man?' said Daley.

'Younger, most certainly fitter. I'd put him at anything between twenty-five and thirty. No signs of morbidity.'

'Apart fae being deid,' Scott observed, much to Daley's chagrin.

'He was fit, inspector. Clearly looked after himself, his diet and fitness. You'd be surprised how many young people I see here who've killed themselves with poor diet, alcohol and drugs.'

'No, I wouldnae. Where I come fae, the average life expectancy is twelve.'

Forbes sighed. 'Another interesting fact: both men were vegetarians. At least the content of their stomachs showed no sign of meat or fish. Generally, there are indications that this was the case for some years, at least in the older man.'

'So, the one wae the red hair wouldnae eat meat, but he liked a good bevvy? Cannae understand how he managed tae keep his hands off a kebab at one in the morning when he was pished.'

'I assure you, he seemed to be able to.' Forbes glared at Scott, this expression emphasised on the large screen.

'Anything else unusual?' Daley asked.

'Very little else to go on, I'm afraid, DCI Daley. Both men wore watches on their left wrists that had been removed. I could tell by the lighter skin tone where they would have been. Also indicates both deceased men were right-handed.' She turned her attention to the computer again. 'Only one other definite clue to ID.' This time the image of a forearm was clear. On it, amongst the thick pelt of red hair, was a tattoo.

'What is it?' Daley asked.

'Might not be quite as clear as it is in the flesh, so to speak. It's a representation of the planet, I reckon. Not very well rendered and been there for a good few years.'

Daley squinted at the screen. 'Yes, I think I can just about make it out. I'd be grateful if you could send me a hi-res image. Any other thoughts?'

'Whoever killed these men was very careful. The bodies have been scrubbed clean, and very thoroughly. No dirt under fingernails, clean teeth. A great effort has been made not to give any indication where they were from – or had been, at least. And most certainly no pointers to who killed them.'

'But we've still got prints and DNA,' said Scott.

'No, actually, you don't have prints.' Another image appeared on the screen. It was a close-up of a fingertip. The end of the finger was a blackened mess. 'This applies to both sets of prints. The surface has been removed – by some corrosive material, acid I'd guess.'

'Bugger me. Lucky the poor bastards were deid. That would be agony,' said Scott.

'I think this was done before they died, inspector.'

Scott grimaced as Daley thanked the pathologist.

'I still have many tests to carry out, and of course the analysis. But I thought you'd like my first impressions, gentlemen.'

'Thank you,' said Daley.

Forbes smiled before the screen flashed to the image of Police Scotland's emblem, the jaggy thistle.

'Shit, I'm glad we can do this down the line since we're so far away,' said Daley.

'Aye, you were never keen on the post mortems and that, Jimmy, right fae the start. They never bothered me.' Scott belched loudly, the after-effects of his burger.

'So, we have another murder case on our hands.'

'Didnae happen here, big fella. We must be able tae work out a radius of where the plane could have flown from, using her theory of time o' death, combined with the likely speed of the aircraft and fuel consumption, I'd say.'

'Hercule Poirot, where have you been all my life?'

'The guy wae the bowler hat and the lisp fae the seventies? Aye, he was funny.'

'That was Freddie Parrot Face.' Daley shook his head. 'The murders might not have happened here, Brian. But however it was done, this was a sign – a warning for somebody.'

'Might no' have been intended for Machrie. We'll have to ask the CAA investigation team how they managed to fly the plane. Aye, and if it was supposed tae land here.'

'Still not convinced by Ian Macmillan, I see.'

Scott shook his head. 'Not until I'm proved wrong, Jimmy.'

'Fair enough.'

'Gangland – has tae be. And what gangs dae we have here, apart fae the Women's Rural?'

Daley nodded silently. He took the phone from his pocket and checked it again.

'Still nothing fae herself?'

'Nope.'

'Maybe she didnae get on very well at the doctor's.' Scott winked.

'It's not like her. I mean, John Donald, you expected him to disappear now and again.'

'Aye, but we never realised why.'

'No, true.' Daley stared out of the window as the afternoon sun beat down over Kinloch.

7

The bar at the County Hotel was busy. Since the change of ownership, business had definitely taken a turn for the better, despite the general trend in the trade. Macmillan was creative when it came to bringing in customers. There were games nights, with pool, cribbage and darts. Intimate ceilidhs on a Saturday afternoon in the bar rather than the function suite upstairs, appealing to the older generation, who no longer liked late nights at the weekend. The bar itself had been spruced up: nothing too drastic, a lick of paint here, prints of old images of Kinloch there. There was a regular quiz night, as opposed to the ad hoc events of the past. And a host of special promotions, including wine tastings, and even curry evenings.

Upstairs, one by one, the guests' rooms were being given a much-needed facelift, though Macmillan was keen not to lose the traditional feel of the old hotel. A new chef had been hired. Though he was young, he'd worked in some Michelin-starred restaurants, and cooked up a storm. Some of the local clientele were at first wary of the foams, jus and foreign names. But very quickly, the County had become *the* place to eat out in Kinloch.

Amidst it all, Annie toiled happily away, not only glad the place had survived threatened closure, but delighted to see it returned to the bustling hotel she remembered in her early days of her employment. All of the staff, bar her, had new uniforms, consisting of shirts embroidered with the County Hotel logo, neat trousers and skirts, even branded aprons. Annie herself was resplendent in a well-cut trouser suit, her name and designation of 'General Manager' displayed proudly on a brass lapel badge.

In her time in the Kinloch hotel trade, Annie had seen many new brushes sweep clean; but while the County was undergoing a long overdue facelift, it had lost none of its old charm.

On the bridge of her command, behind the bar, she checked a sparkling tumbler under a pin-spot light. Happy that it was up to snuff, she returned her attention to the first customer of the day: one thing unaltered by the subtle refurbishments. Hamish was sitting at the table nearest the bar, his perch for more years than most could remember. He was swilling the last few drops in the bottom of a glass when Scott appeared round the door.

'It's yourself, Brian,' said Hamish with a broad grin.

'Aye, once seen, never forgotten,' the police officer replied. He took a seat on one of the stools at the bar and had a look at the basket of filled rolls available. 'A ginger beer and lime for me, and whatever your man's on,' he said, nodding to Hamish.

'Nae bother, Brian,' Annie replied jauntily. 'You'll be wanting a roll, or are you after something mair substantial?'

'What's falafel?'

'Oh, here, they're jeest fantastic. Like wee spicy balls o' chickpea, deep-fried and served in a wee pitta bread wae a smashing tangy sauce. I canna get enough o' them.'

'Is this mair bright ideas fae your new chef?'

'Young Michael? Aye, the boy's a genius, so he is.'

'He still canna get his heid roon a good plate o' mince an' tatties,' said Hamish witheringly. 'Aye, and I'm no' too keen on his batter, neither. There's nothing that ruins a good piece o' fish like inferior batter.' He downed the last drops from his glass.

'Och, your arse!' said Annie. 'You don't like the mince because he'll only use steak, no' the floor sweepings you like. And you only took against the batter when you found out he made it wae a special lager.'

'Lager's place is in a glass. And even then it's poison. Noo if he was using a decent beer tae make it, it would make all the difference.'

'Michel Roux! Sorry I didn't recognise you,' said Annie sarcastically.

'And don't you call me names, Annie. You might be in a posh suit wae a fancy new title, but as a customer I have the right o' it. And I'll no' be called a lassie, neither!'

'Hang on, the pair o' you, I've come here for some late lunch and a bit o' sanity. I get plenty hysterics up the road,' said Scott.

'And no wonder at it,' said Hamish. 'Planes landing themselves in the middle o' the night, so I hear.'

'How do you know that?' Scott quickly thought better of asking the question, remembering what the Kinloch grapevine was like. Resigned to defeat, he waved his hand dismissively.

'It's taken a while, but you're getting it, Brian. There's no' much goes on here that the whole toon doesna know aboot in jig time. They tell me the poor people on board were mangled beyond recognition. One o' their heids was cut clean off.'

Hamish shook his head as Annie handed his dram over the bar via Scott.

'It just shows you how much crap you hear, tae,' said Scott.

'Cheers!' said Hamish indignantly.

The detective turned to Annie. 'Things seem to be going well in here, eh?'

'Aye, it's a pleasure tae be at work, Brian. Ian's done a marvellous job, so he has.'

'You're jeest crowing because you got a big pay rise and some fancy trouser suits. Not forgetting the new title, of course. You were insufferable enough when you were jeest plain manager. You weren't much better when you were a barmaid, come tae that.' Hamish sipped at his dram.

'Tell me, 'said Scott, doing his best to ignore the old fisherman. 'It's a lorry business he has over in Cananda?'

'Aye,' Annie replied. 'Though he calls it "trucking".'

'Must be doing well judging by what he's doing here, eh? Fancy chefs and all the work on this place don't come cheap.'

'He doesna stint on anything, Brian.' Annie smiled proudly.

'And he's no' often back in Canada?' Scott looked for her reaction over the top of his glass.

'He's got a general manager in charge – like me, though o'er there. He tells me things work themselves, mair or less. He's back at his roots. I've got tae say, sometimes he reminds me of his auld grandfaither. This place was his pride and joy. He was a lovely man.'

'He was a miserable auld bugger,' said Hamish. 'He wisna averse tae wringing oot the bar cloth intae a glass and selling it for a penny tae the poor pensioners that were short on funds but desperate for refreshment.'

'You mean the alkies,' said Annie.

'Here, I mind seeing that,' said Scott. 'Can you imagine, all the fag ash and bugger knows what in your glass.' He shivered at the thought. 'Makes a pint o' slops sound like champagne.'

'Och, there's still those that get a wee benefit, here and there.' Annie stared at Hamish.

'Like whoot?' he returned.

'Every week I clean the beer lines, I know who'll appear tae drink the run-offs.'

'My mother telt mc that waste was a sin. I've always lived by that motto.' Hamish searched out his pipe and puffed determinedly at it, unlit.

'He must have mair than just trucks,' said Scott. 'Have you heard him on aboot any other businesses?'

Annie bit her lip and narrowed her eyes, deep in thought. 'No, I cannae mind o' him mentioning anything aboot any other businesses, to be honest. I think he's fair sick o' the lorries. He's a man that's worked hard, and now he's enjoying the fruits o' his labours.'

Scott nodded as he took a bite of the falafel wrap. He coughed and took a gulp of his ginger beer. 'What's he got in this, gunpowder?'

'He likes his spices, does oor Michael. It took me a couple o' goes tae get used tae the falafels, but as I say, I cannae get enough o' them noo.'

'It'll be the toilet roll in the fridge the night, Brian.' Hamish beamed at his own joke.

'So, he's done well for himself. Good for him.' Scott took another tentative bite.

'He has that. The rumour in the town is that he's worth millions.'

'He'd need tae be wae all that's being done in here.' Scott took another glug of his drink to banish the burning spices in his mouth. 'And family? He's not married, is he?'

'They're separated. She's a right bitch, apparently.'

'Huh, but you would say that,' said Hamish. 'You've got a right crush on the man. It's as plain as the nose on Eric Duncan's face. And man, that's a record breaker.'

'Don't be ridiculous!' Annie glared at her elderly customer. 'She fills his kids' heads full o' nonsense – wicked, so it is.'

'Like what?' said Scott.

'He was talking aboot it one night it was just me an' him in the bar. You know, after hours, like.'

'Oh aye,' said Hamish with a knowing look.

'He's a perfect gentleman. Any more o' that and you're barred for the rest o' the day.'

'What age are his kids?' said Scott.

'The eldest – his lassie – I think she's twenty. At college studying tae be a nurse.'

Scott nodded. 'And the boy?'

'Still in school, I think. He's no' got long tae go, but he doesna seem tae know whoot he wants tae be at.' She leaned into Scott. 'A bit o' a problem child, if you know whoot I mean.'

'I know that feeling,' said Scott, thinking of his own son. 'He's from Toronto, isn't he?'

'Aye, that's right. A lovely big hoose, tae. He showed me pictures, Brian. Och, you jeest dream o' places like that. It overlooks this great big lake.' Annie stared dreamily into the middle distance.

'Nice.' Scott wiped his face with a napkin. 'I'd better be back off up the road. We're busy, as you already know.' He winked at Hamish. 'All they headless bodies.'

'Sarcasm isn't your strong point, Brian.' The old fisherman puffed again on nothing.

'You've no' finished your falafel, Brian,' said Annie.

'A bit too hot for my taste, Annie. Anyhow, I had a burger earlier.'

'It's mair falafels you're needing. A man o' your age should be steering clear o' the burgers. Did you no' hear aboot that writer that died o' eating burgers? Och, he had as many pen names.'

'Aye, I'll live for ever and just burn my backside off instead. I'll see you later.' Scott took his leave.

'Do you no' think he looks stressed, Hamish?'

'Maybe. But he's no' stupid.' He stared into space.

'What's on your mind?'

'Och, you know me, jeest wondering aboot life.'

'Wondering where your next dram's coming fae.'

'No, mair like why Brian is so interested in your new boss.'

'He's jeest being friendly. Brian's always the same.'

'In that case, why have you jeest been in receipt of a gentle probing?'

'Eh?'

'You might be the *general manageress*, but you don't know subtle questioning when you see it. He was on a fishing exercise, and he's oot tae catch your boss by the sound o' things.' Hamish nodded serenely, like an oriental deity.

It was after two p.m. when Carrie Symington got back to her office. There were various notes, memos, emails and phone messages awaiting her attention. That was the trouble about taking any time off, as far as she was concerned. When you commanded the division, work was all-consuming.

As she flicked through her emails, one in particular caught her eye. It was a widely circulated message from a detective inspector on Glasgow's Southside. The subject box was entitled *Any Info Gratefully Received.*

Reading the body of the message Symington gathered a man had been found in the underground car park of a hotel. She was lost as to how she could be of any help in this until she read on.

The victim, Charles Chappell, has been identified as a former member of the Met Police's Special Branch. Now retired with his own private investigation company, he was in Glasgow with his business partner on a corporate fraud case involving a hedge fund with offices here in Glasgow.

Symington pushed her seat away from her desk, as though trying to put distance between her and what she'd just read. Her mind was working overtime now. Phone records would be checked – her number was bound to be on Chappell's call register. And what about his partner?

The chief superintendent did her best to calm herself. She took a drink from the large bottle of water she always kept close by and forced herself to read the email again, noting the name of the DI – Cox – and his mobile number. She knew that she had to be careful, but why wait for her colleagues to uncover a call made by Chappell to her mobile the previous evening, and hers to him just over an hour ago? Better to play it straight, she thought. .

Her hand trembling, she dialled DI Cox's number.

8

Experts from the Air Accidents Investigation Branch had made a preliminary investigation of the light aircraft at Machrie airport, and while his team was preparing to transport the plane to their facilities at Farnborough the senior AAIB investigator, Dan Adley, made his way to Kinloch police office. Daley stood and shook his hand as he strode into the glass box.

'Well now, you're the man who can tell us how this happened, Mr Adley,' he said. 'I have to say we've no idea. Of course, I've been on the internet, but I realise that could be wildly misleading.'

Adley, dressed in a smart suit with an open-necked shirt, sat back in his chair and scratched his head.

'I have to say, DCI Daley, this is a puzzle. While Autoland, or cheaper Eastern European and Chinese variations of the system, are by no means uncommon, take-off is another matter. We have found some unusual kit on board. We'll have to take it down south and analyse it before I can give you a definitive answer as to how this was done.'

'Oh, I see.'

'You look rather crestfallen, DCI Daley.'

Daley shrugged. 'I suppose I thought you'd be able to give us instant answers. I know that was naïve.'

'Well, to be fair to you, this is rather unusual.' Adley paused for a moment, as though considering whether or not he should say something. 'Up until three years ago I was doing this job for the RAF.'

'I rather assumed that. You have a kind of military aspect.'

'Hard to shift after thirty years, I suppose.'

'Don't worry, it's the same in this job.'

'Crosses to bear and all that old stuff, eh? I'm proud of my time in the RAF. Made me the man I am today. I hadn't a bloody clue what to do when I left university.'

'I was much the same – minus the university bit.'

'I'm going to be candid – for your ears only, DCI Daley.'

'Nothing goes beyond these glass walls.' Daley gestured around his box.

'There has been take-off tech available to the military for some time. It's there in case pilots take a hit and getting out of a bad situation is essential. You know what I mean, I'm sure.'

'Absolutely.'

'It's there, but it's bloody expensive. I don't know how it would have leaked into the private sector – well, not at this level. Trials are in place with the big aero companies – Boeing, Airbus and the like. But we're well away from your holiday flight to Tenerife doing the business all by itself. And a small aircraft like this – well, unbelievable.'

Daley's brows were knitted. 'Could it have been some military experiment gone awry? Machrie used to be an RAF base.'

'I know. Flew in a good few times. I was nearly posted here, in fact. I wish I had been – looks beautiful.'

'Oh, it is. Glorious. I just love it in Kintyre.'

'But to answer your question, given the deaths of those on board, there's no way this is military. Even the black ops chaps wouldn't risk a stunt like this. Though you didn't hear "black ops" from me.'

'Don't worry, I've already come across them.' Daley remembered the odd aircraft in the huge hangar from a few years before.

'Ah, so you'll know what I mean.'

'Sort of.'

'I'm sorry to be so vague, but you'll have to leave the whys and wherefores of this flight and how it got here to us. I should have something concrete for you in a week or so. I know you'll be carrying out investigations as far as the deceased are concerned. I've had a copy of the interim PM.'

'Yes, I thought we'd have to wait.'

'I can tell you one thing, however.'

'Yes?'

'The Cessna didn't land here by accident.'

'No? I thought maybe – well, just an emergency landing. I realise I sound like an idiot.'

'No, not at all. In a real emergency it would be any port in a storm. But that's not the case here. Off the record, the navigation device was set to land at Machrie. Not only that, but the flight path was calculated to fly deliberately under the radar. At least, that's my first impression. We'll be liaising with aircraft control at Prestwick. But it looks pretty clear to me, though once they do a proper analysis they may find something we missed.'

'Right, thank you.' Daley stood up and shook Adley's hand again. 'You'll have a long journey home.'

'Yes. Thankfully I'm flying. I feel sorry for the poor buggers on the tow truck. But rest assured, as soon as I know more, so will you.'

They said their goodbyes and Adley bounded out of Daley's glass box.

Symington was staring from her office window. Her head ached and her mouth was dry.

DI Cox had displayed no indication that he was suspicious of what she'd told him. But Symington of all people knew how the police worked. She'd admitted that Chappell was an old colleague from her time in the Met over a decade and a half ago. He'd called and they'd arranged to meet for lunch. When he hadn't turned up, she'd called.

It turned out that Cox himself had answered the dead man's phone. Symington repeated the excuse of thinking she'd called the wrong number to explain the fact that she'd put down the phone so quickly, though she worried that this hadn't sounded as credible as she wanted it to.

Cox had appeared happy with what Symington had told him, and they'd arranged to meet at her office the next day. He'd asked her bits and pieces about Chappell and she'd told him about the incident on Gairsay, when he'd appeared with Special Branch officers. She didn't mention his dealings with Brian Scott.

On firmer ground, she was happy that she sounded so convincing about having seen or heard very little from him over the last few years. That was the truth, and the truth was always easier to tell than a lie, as bitter experience had taught her.

When she asked about Bower, Cox revealed that he was missing and wasn't answering calls to his mobile. Again,

Symington was happy to relate that, though Chappell had mentioned that he was in partnership with Bower, she didn't know the man very well, since they had only worked together very briefly – the truth again.

Now all she had to do was wait for houses to be searched and computers and phones taken apart in order to find out what secrets they contained. These were all matters of routine when a murder was committed. She knew the playbook off by heart. She also knew that because he was a former colleague, a huge effort would be made to discover who'd killed her erstwhile tormentor.

When she'd asked Cox to send her the SOCO images he'd hesitated.

'Pretty gruesome, ma'am, I'm sad to say. Maybe with you being a friend of his it would be better if you refrained?'

She'd chided him, making sure he knew who was boss. Of course she'd be upset, but she was a professional: how dare he!

Symington surprised herself when the crime scene images arrived in an email attachment. She knew she should have recoiled at the detailed photographs of the man with the livid slash across his throat, lying in a dark pool of his own blood. Instead, if she felt anything it was relief; she was glad he was gone, glad he was out of her life for ever.

Then she wondered about Bower. If Chappell had told him about the accident so long ago, surely now it would be revealed. But it was her word against his, and the fact that he was missing pointed to the possibility that he may have had something to do with Chappell's death, or indeed was himself a victim.

Symington had never thought she'd want to hear news of a murder. But despite herself, she was subconsciously willing the phone to ring with the news that Bower's body had also been found. She knew it was wrong, but the primal part of her didn't care. It was all about self-preservation.

Only then did the old flashes of memory return.

She was in a pub car park with colleagues. It was near Christmas and she could smell the smoke from coal fires on the frosty air of the Essex village. Symington remembered the feeling of camaraderie, of knowing she was part of her own tight-knit community, her team. She was little more than a girl, but at last she'd found her niche in life, many miles from her rural Yorkshire home, doing the job of which she'd always dreamed.

She should have realised he'd spiked her drinks. She should have known she was intoxicated. She had seen him stare at her at work, looking her up and down, sizing her up, imagining what lay beneath the bland uniform. But that was the way some men were, right? Wet behind the ears she might have been, but not so much so as not to realise that she turned heads. But she was a police officer now, a police officer safe amongst her own.

Symington stared again at the murdered man in the dark underground car park. She'd been in one not unlike it only hours before. She gazed absently at the pool of blood that framed him, subconsciously trying to discern a recognisable shape, as the brain is wont to do.

Only then did she see the dead boy on the mortuary slab. Only then did she feel the old pain, the desperate guilt and sadness.

Carrie Symington ran into the lavatory next to her office and vomited into the toilet pan.

9

Ella Scott stared at the sleeping figure on the couch. Though she was pleased to have her son home, she worried about the change in him in the few months since she'd last seen him. He was thin, painfully so, and his skin was pale and marked by small spots and blemishes. She remembered that he'd managed to stay mercifully free of acne as a teenager, and how careful he'd been about his appearance. But the young man lying in front of her looked, at best, dishevelled.

Most troubling to her was the resemblance he bore to his father after one of his many bouts of heavy drinking. The tired eyes, the puffy face, the lack of personal care. She'd always been there to mitigate this for Brian, at least to some extent. But she couldn't help but feel that her son was a lost, lonely soul.

'Willie, I've brought you coffee.' She tried to cajole him into movement.

Instead, the response was a feeble one. 'Right, Ma. Just stick it down there.' He turned his face further into the cushion.

'Come on, son. It's the middle of the afternoon. You should be up and aboot. It's glorious oot there!'

He rolled over to face her. 'What do you want me to do, go and play in the sand?'

'No need to be sarcastic. I get enough o' that fae your faither. Surely you've got things to do?'

'Och, give me a break, eh? I thought I was coming here for a wee holiday to see my folks, not to get hassle from you all fucking day.'

'Don't you use language like that to me!'

'Don't dare say that I never heard *language like that* when I was growing up. We know that's shite.'

'Och, I gie up.' Ella Scott threw her arms in the air. 'If you want tae waste the best days o' your life lying aboot, that's up tae you!' She stormed out of the lounge, tears of frustration in her eyes.

He was taking drugs, she was sure of it. On reflection, she supposed that this shouldn't be a surprise. His cousins – on her husband's side of the family – were into all sorts. But somehow Ella had never worried that her son would take that path. He'd been a bright, energetic child who turned into a studious, enthusiastic teenager.

Where had that all gone?

Ella picked up the mobile phone on the kitchen table and dialled her husband's number.

'Aye, what's up?' Brian Scott replied.

'Your boy, or hadn't you noticed?'

'Willie? What's he up tae now?'

'That's just it, he's not up tae anything. He didnae get up until gone twelve, and he's been asleep on the couch ever since.'

'He's likely going through one o' they growth spurts, Ella. You know fine how that tires them oot.'

'He's twenty-five, Brian, no' some teenager! Any growing that's he's going tae dae has been done.'

There was silence for a moment, then Scott spoke. 'Listen,

Ella, I'm in the middle o' a big inquiry. What do you want me tae do? He's still no' telt us why he arrived out o' the blue. I tried tae gee him on wae some old Rangers DVDs – you know: "Twenty of the Best from Super Ally". He used to love that, but he went to his bed in the middle o' it.'

'Faither o' the year!'

'I'll have tae be honest wae you here, Ella. If I'd been like that when I was his age my faither would have toed my arse doon the street.'

'Something for him tae get on with on his way tae the pub, I dare say.'

'I don't have time for this right now. Throw a bucket o' water o'er him or something.'

'And ruin my good couch? No' likely. It's obvious what's up wae him, Brian. You of all people must know.'

'*Me o' all people*? What's that meant tae mean?'

'He's on the drugs! Look at the nick o' him. I've seen smarter beggars on Buchanan Street.'

'He's no' got a wee dug. They beggars always have the wee dugs tae make you feel sorry for them.'

'Fine. What a relief. Here's me thinking my son's a druggie, but my detective husband has put my mind at rest because of the absence of a wee dug. Fabulous, thank you!'

'Och, I'm away.'

The line went dead. Ella slammed the mobile down on the kitchen table. This was typical of her husband. He might be a good policeman, but when it came to his family there was a blind spot – certainly as far as his son was concerned.

She walked back across the hall and peeked round the lounge door. Her son just lay there, his mouth gaping open, snoring quietly, his coffee untouched.

One way or the other, Ella was determined that this would not continue.

Symington decided that she'd had enough for the day. She'd taken a file containing information on the incident at Machrie airport with her in order to get to grips with what was happening in Kinloch. Though she knew that Jim Daley was more than capable of handling the situation as it stood, perhaps a trip to the furthest-flung part of her little empire would be welcome, especially in light of recent events.

She took the lift to her apartment and followed her usual routine after arriving home and closing her front door against the world. Slowly, she walked into her bedroom removing every stitch of her uniform, down to her underwear, and slipped on her silk dressing gown, mercifully cool after the heat and stress of the day. She decided she'd have a long soak in the bath but would wait a while and have a couple of glasses of wine to soothe her soul first.

Without bothering to tie the dressing gown, she padded into the lounge. Bright light flooded through the French windows that opened out on to the balcony. She blinked into it, her eyes adjusting after the relative gloom in the bedroom.

On reflection, she wasn't sure whether she'd sensed or seen him. But some instinct made her turn her head swiftly to the right. There, sitting on her favourite chair, was a man clad head to toe in black.

She screamed and turned for the door. But in a flash he was up and had grabbed her by the wrists, forcing her arms painfully behind her back.

'There's an easy and a hard way to do this. I don't care either way, but I'm guessing you'd prefer the former.' His voice was cold and calm with a hint of estuary. If this man wasn't from London, it was from somewhere nearby.

She did her best to relax in his grip, but her voice spoke of anything but ease. 'How the hell did you get in here?'

He didn't answer the question. 'If you promise to behave, we can sit down and talk about this like adults. But if you give me any trouble, I'll hurt you, got it?'

They were still for a while, like two dancers motionless in a pose. But soon she nodded her head and whispered, 'Yes.'

He pulled her away from the door and pushed her on to the sofa, retaking the seat on which he'd been sitting. He crossed his legs and stared at her.

Symington sat as far into the corner of the sofa as she could, her arms folded across her chest. She pulled at the folds of her dressing gown to cover her thighs.

'Modest little thing, eh? I remember you vaguely.'

'Mr Bower, I take it. I don't remember you at all,' she said as calmly as she could.

'Yeah, that's it, boss. Pleased to make your acquaintance again after all this time. Though I must say, Chappell never shut up about you.'

'You know he's dead?' Symington raised her chin defiantly.

'Yes, I do, as it goes. Well, I would, since I cut his throat.'

'What?' The colour drained from her face.

'Did you think me and him had been bad boys and somebody had caught up with us? I bet you'd have loved me to be lying on the floor of that car park too, eh? Well, I'm sorry to disappoint you.'

'You know you're going to get caught, don't you?'

'That's a bit clichéd, if you don't mind me saying. We've all seen that fucking movie. This is real life, darling.'

'And I'm a real-life chief superintendent. Work it out!'

He looked around the room, seemingly unconcerned by anything she had to say. 'Was that why you came up here to Jockoland, then? To get away from Chappell?'

'None of your business.'

'No, don't suppose it is, really. You know what it's like being a copper. I just like asking questions. It's how I make sense of the world.'

She stared at him, seeing Chappell in another body. The same glib sarcasm; the same demeaning cruelty, hidden behind what would seem to others like nothing more than dreary conversation – the same implicit threat. Well, Carrie Symington had had enough of that.

The last time Chappell had appeared, it was literally out of the blue, on a helicopter on Gairsay when he was working for Special Branch. She remembered shaking uncontrollably, crying, almost collapsing in on herself. But somehow this was different. Despite Bower's breaking into her home, despite his threats and the fact that he was a self-confessed murderer, she felt somehow emboldened. Perhaps it was the image of the man who had taunted her for so long lying dead. Maybe she'd just grown up. In any event, she didn't feel the paralysing fear that Chappell had instilled in her. 'I don't care what you think you know. Whatever it is your dead pal told you, it died with him. It's my word against yours – hearsay. If you want to kill me for some reason, well, what am I going to do about it?' She shrugged, doing her best to look as unconcerned as her current predicament would allow.

'Nah, it's not as simple as that, sweetheart.' He reached into the inside pocket of his jacket.

Symington flinched and braced herself on the sofa, fully expecting him to produce a weapon. Instead, he pulled out a mobile phone.

'Something tells me you're not as confident as you pretend. Did you think I was going to off you there?' He laughed.

'Get on with it!'

'Okay, hold your horses.' He pressed the face of the phone a few times then held it out in front of him, his arm straight. The mobile looked tiny in his big hand. 'How's your eyesight?'

Symington felt her heart sink as the face of Chappell appeared on the small screen. He was chatting easily, obviously relaxed. She recognised Bower's disembodied voice as he encouraged the man who had died in the car park earlier that day to tell all he knew about her past. While the tale was all too familiar, he'd embellished it in parts. She recoiled at his sordid descriptions of what he'd made her do, his obscene jokes about how he'd taken advantage of her.

'He was a great storyteller, was our Chappell. But you know that already.'

'Fuck you! If you think you're going to pick up where he left off, you can think again!'

'Wait a minute.' Bower waved his hands in a calming gesture. 'You're a pretty little thing, no doubt about it – bonnie, they say up here, isn't it? But my tastes in the bedroom – well, let's say you're not my type.'

She cringed at the look on his face. 'What, then?'

'Kinloch. I'm interested in that place. On your patch, yeah?'

She nodded.

'Good. All I want you to do is go down there. I'll be in touch.' He saw the defiance flare in her face once more. 'I understand. You've got choices here, no doubt about it.

61

Well, two at any rate. But you'll go down if the right people see my little film, you can bet on that.' He hesitated, a puzzled expression on his face. 'You know, I'm a bit disappointed in our Chappell. I thought he'd more in him. Okay, he had his end away with a nice piece of skirt, but what else did he get out of it, eh? He should have put his resource to better use, if you ask me.'

'Better use how?'

'Plenty of time for that. Just you get yourself down to this Kinloch.' He pronounced the name as though it ended in a k.

'You realise that the whole of Police Scotland is searching for you, don't you?'

'I do, as it happens. No wonder, is it? In fact, I'm going to go and speak to the detective in charge of your pal Chappell's murder. You know the story: they set upon us; I got scared, got my head down. Heard that poor Chappell copped it on the news.' He rubbed an imaginary tear from his face. 'I'm distraught.'

'You'd better be convincing.'

'Oh, don't worry about that. You and I both know how to lie to police officers, don't we?' He stood and loomed over her. 'Chappell was right about you.'

'What do you mean?'

'No fucking backbone.' He turned on his heel and made for the door. 'I'll be in touch – in Kinloch.'

Carrie Symington heard the door slam. She tried to calm down, though her heart was pounding and her mouth was dry. She had thought her years of persecution were over. They were back – and this time it was worse. Much worse.

10

Hamish sucked at his pipe as he chugged through the channel that took him past the island at the head of the loch, and out into the sound. Ahead, the Isle of Arran was bathed in light, with only a promise of the evening to come. Seagulls soared in the fading azure sky, above the still, blue, oily sea that looked as thick as custard.

'My, this is the life,' he said to himself, as a cloud of smoke issued from the bowl. Hamish wasn't sure how often he'd made this journey – most likely thousands of times – but his passage out to sea from the harbour at Kinloch never lost its allure. He'd seen this part of the world in all its many guises, but for him, in the shimmering heat of an evening in high summer, it was at its best.

His mind turned to thoughts of the past. He could see the face of Sandy Hoynes puffing on his own pipe as he scratched his head at the paucity of catch, way back in the summer of 1968. They'd blamed everything from supersonic planes to the malign intent of the fishery officer. Little did they know it at the time, but they were presiding over the first signs of the long rape of the sea. A resource once considered infinite proved to be anything but. And it was always with great sorrow that Hamish now looked across the harbour in Kinloch,

63

where only a handful of fishing boats bobbed when once there had been dozens.

The thought made the old man sad, but he did his best to banish any notion of misery by remembering the good times he'd had on the waves, first with his father and then with Hoynes, and a cast of other characters now gone but not forgotten.

He tended his lobster creels morning and evening at this time of year, in the hope that luck was on his side. Though in truth, his nautical meanderings were now little more than a hobby, designed to keep his mind and body active, and more important, out of the County Hotel.

Still, for him, fond as he was of a dram and convivial company, without the sea his life would be as nothing. He drew a deep breath of the tang of the air, listened to the gulls' squawks and wails and was lulled into an almost meditative state by the gentle lapping of water at the side of the boat as the diesel engine chugged a counterpoint.

He was alongside the island when a flash of something bright caught his eye. He turned to see a small group of men surrounding a big RIB on the boulder-strewn shore below the lighthouse. One of them looked up, no doubt distracted by the thud of Hamish's engine. The old fisherman doffed his Breton cap and hailed the small party with a shout of 'It's a fine evening', but was slightly disappointed when his call was met with a less then friendly silence. Instead, all of those gathered around the inflatable boat simply turned to stare at him.

He placed his greasy cap back on his head and sucked again on his pipe. After pondering yet again on the ill manners of folk these days, he pushed the throttle forward slightly and built up a knot or two in speed as he made for his scattered archipelago of lobster creels, all marked by faded fluorescent orange buoys.

Behind him now, back on the island the men were hurriedly pushing their RIB back into the waves that lapped the rocky shore.

Brian Scott was making ready for home when his mobile phone rang. Noting the caller's name on the screen, he very nearly ignored the call, but decided, on the balance of things, it was better he answered.

'Yes, ma'am,' he said, placing some files on the passenger seat of his car.

'Brian, are you alone?' Symington's voice was tense.

'Aye, I'm just about tae drive home. If it's about the plane, we know it was stolen from a small airfield in Hampshire six months ago. They'd tried tae strip it of any identity by filing down serial numbers and the like, but they weren't clever enough for they boys doon in Farnborough. Anyway, Jimmy – DCI Daley – will fill you in, ma'am.' He was about to ask if there was anything else when Symington silenced him.

'Brian, I need your help.'

'Oh aye, what with?' There was silence on the other end of the line. Scott examined the screen of his phone to make sure the call hadn't dropped out. 'Hello?'

'You remember Chappell?'

'Aye. How could I forget that bastard? I hope he's not bothering you again?'

'It's more complicated.' She swallowed hard against her dry throat. 'I'm on my way down – at Inveraray. Can I have a word with you when I arrive? I shouldn't be more than a couple of hours.'

Scott thought of the brooding presence of his son and his agitated wife. She'd been on to him again about doing something about Willie, and he'd promised to speak to him later that evening. 'I've a wee bit o' trouble at home. Nothing serious, mind. My son's come tae visit – well, to lie aboot, basically. Kids. Never have any – trust me. Will I ask big Jimmy to come and meet you?'

'No!' The reply was instant, with more than a hint of desperation. 'Just you, Brian. Please don't tell anyone else – including DCI Daley.'

'So, there is bother, eh?'

'You could say that, yes.'

'Okay, what time, where? In the office?'

'No, I'll meet you down by the pier. We'll be anonymous enough there.'

'In Kinloch, are you kidding? They'll have me and you up tae nae good, and no mistake.'

'Where then?'

'You could come to the hoose, but it's no' the most restful o' places at the moment.'

'No, just me and you, Brian.' She thought for a moment. 'What about the airport car park? Surely there'll be nobody about by then? And with recent events in mind, even if anyone did see us, they wouldn't think anything of it.'

Scott sighed. 'No, I dare say. See you in a couple of hours, ma'am.'

'Thanks, Brian.' Parked near the pier in Inveraray, Symington ended the call, took a deep breath and started the car. Soon, she was back on her way to Kinloch, to the one person she could trust.

Hamish was hauling in yet another empty creel when he heard the distant thud of a powerful engine. It was nothing unusual in the summer: first it had been speedboats; now – in the main – fast RIBs were the order of the day for tourists and hobby sailors. 'It's no wonder I canna catch a bloody lobster,' he said out loud, irritated by the racket.

The engine noise grew as the craft neared his little boat. By this time, Hamish had tossed the creel back overboard, in the hope of better luck the next day. Only when the tone of the approaching engine lowered to a putter did he turn round.

A large RIB with four figures aboard was cruising towards him at low speed. Shortly, they were almost athwart the old lobster boat.

'It's yourselves. No' enamoured wae the island, I see. Man, it's fair rocky roon the edges. No' much o' a place for a picnic or the like.'

As he finished speaking, one man jumped from the RIB on to Hamish's vessel, quickly followed by another.

'Here, whoot dae you think yous are at?' Hamish turned to face them defiantly. 'In this part o' the world it's courtesy to ask permission before you set foot aboard a craft other than your own.'

Without bothering to reply, one of the men lurched forward and grabbed him by the collar of his jumper. Hamish opened his mouth to protest, but before he could say a word a heavy blow to the head sent him tumbling to the deck.

'What now?' The taller of the two had a County Antrim twang.

'Take him across to the RIB and tow this old wreck,' said a smaller, sharp-featured individual.

'Why don't we just tie him up and sink the old bastard? We could leave the boat adrift. No bugger would be any the wiser. Doddery old man falls off his boat. Fuck's sake, I can smell the whisky on his breath from here!'

'Do what I say, not what you think, you stupid arsehole.'

The larger man deferred to his companion, and soon Hamish's unconscious figure was being hauled aboard the RIB.

11

Jim Daley was already at home. He was mildly annoyed that his wife hadn't seen fit to call from their holiday in the sun to let him know how his son was faring. But such was the state of their relationship he wasn't surprised. Daley had resolved to leave it until tomorrow and call them instead.

Before him on the dining-room table was a large map. He'd tried to do this job on his laptop, but as an analogue man in a digital world he was much more comfortable doing it the old-fashioned way. There was nothing like a map on real paper to help orient oneself as far as he was concerned, despite the bells and whistles offered digitally.

Daley remembered a recent chat with a retired journalist who'd been the bane of his life when he'd been a DC in Glasgow. Now free from having to bring recalcitrant police officers to the attention of the public – or so Daley hoped – Tommy Mearns was able to indulge in his passion for American baseball. He'd written a book on the subject. The pair had kept in touch over the years, and Mearns assured his old adversary that he could stare at his typescript for hours on a computer screen and find little fault. Only when he bothered to print it out on old-fashioned paper did myriad mistakes become obvious.

Mearns reasoned that this was something to do with the nature of how an electronic screen was viewed: subtly flickering, though this wasn't apparent to the eye. This flickering, he maintained, meant that if you stared at your laptop screen for half an hour, in fact you only actually saw it for a fraction of that time.

Without putting this theory to any kind of test, Daley was convinced. He demanded to see the many documents, reports and pages of evidence that made up the bulk of his job on paper now, not just as email attachments.

He leaned over the map with a large magnifying glass. He was glad to be doing this at home and not in the office, as it would have been an open goal for some of Scott's sarcastic comments, despite the acting DI being even more analogue than himself.

Daley had drawn a red circle around the airfield in Hampshire where the Cessna had been stolen. Then, from the few sightings of the plane he'd managed to compile from locals, he'd tried to plot the trajectory of its likely flight path. Though he knew that the forensic teams in Farnborough would come up with a much more accurate plan of the aircraft's movements, his own calculations were aiding him in the mysterious realm of instinct.

Like a computer algorithm, his brain seemed to piece together random facts. And – more often than not – make sense of what had happened and finally discover the truth. Daley had solved umpteen cases from very little hard evidence, just through instinct. But instinct never held up in court; proof was all. Nevertheless, he was sure that instinct was something a detective honed as his or her career progressed. He knew Brian Scott was of the same opinion.

When something wasn't right, it wasn't right. It was a feeling, a tug at the gut. Who knew how it worked?

Daley stared at County Antrim, the closest part of the island of Ireland to the Kintyre peninsula. All the evidence he'd heard, from locals, and the initial theories of the man in charge of the air investigation, brought him back to this part of the world.

He scribbled down a note which would prompt him to ask one of his detectives to find out about airfields or possible take-off points in the area. He also reckoned that a chat with his appropriate opposite number in the PSNI would be prudent. He added this to his aide memoir.

He was just about to begin the task of folding the large map back into its appropriate form when his mobile rang. Hefting it from his pocket, he fully expected to see *Liz* emblazoned across the screen. But he was wrong.

'DCI Daley? Martin Wishart from the Police Scotland press office. Sorry to bother you in the evening.'

Daley sighed. His opinion of the force press office was not a high one. In fact, he was surprised that anyone from that department was working outside their habitual nine-to-five routine. 'I hope you've got your overtime sheet handy,' he said less than respectfully.

'I think you should look out yours, too.'

Clearly Wishart wasn't easily cowed. 'What's up now?'

'Your dead men on the plane, DCI Daley. Despite our best efforts, our friends in the press have got hold of it.'

'How could that possibly happen?' As he said it, the number of ways this information could have reached the fourth estate quickly dawned on him. 'Tell me the worst.'

'They have it in remarkable detail: two men, well dressed,

carrying no identification in an unmarked light aircraft. Somebody on your patch has been talking.'

'My patch? Are you even a police officer, Wishart?'

'No, I'm a journalist. Just what you've been missing, as far as I can tell.'

'Well, you're right there, at least.'

'Of course I asked . . .' He hesitated as though looking for something. 'I asked this Nathan Sidley where he'd got his information, but as usual he was tight-lipped.'

'I haven't heard that name before, and I'm no stranger to the gentlemen and women of the press.'

'No, indeed – I've seen your file.'

'Super.'

'This hack is from London, a real old tabloid man. I met him once, when he was pissed. But he's bloody good at his job – a proper investigative journalist. There aren't many of those around these days.'

Daley thought for a moment. 'But surely, if the tip came from here the initial contact would have been in one of the Glasgow papers?'

'You have a point. But however he came upon the information, he has done. It's my job to keep him off the scent until we have something to say – let's just say "manage the story", for clarity. I take it we *don't* have anything to say?'

'No, we haven't got a clue. A lot will depend on what they can find from the plane at Farnborough. Please don't tell me I'm about to be deluged by a pack of journalists.'

'Only two.'

'Eh?'

'Sidley has an exclusive. It's in his interest to keep it quiet. It's quite interesting, actually.'

'What is?'

'Well, in the last few years he's concerned himself with climate issues. You know, like car manufacturers pretending their vehicles run on flowers, when they pollute like buggery.'

'So he's branching out,' said Daley.

'Could be. But if so it'll be the first time he's written about anything else in more than a decade. These guys get so deep into their subject matter that it becomes an obsession.'

Daley's mind was working overtime now. 'Do me a favour. Before Nathan Sidley was obsessed by climate issues, what did he specialise in?'

'I'll dig about a bit. I know he worked in Northern Ireland during the Troubles. He's no spring chicken. In fact I was surprised to find he hadn't retired.'

'Okay, if you can find out what else he's spent his career doing, maybe we can pin down his interest in this. It can't be climate change, surely?'

'I'll have a look.'

'Who's the other hack on their way?'

'Sorry?'

'You said there would be two journalists.'

'Oh, of course: it's me. I'll see you tomorrow, DCI Daley.'

'I'll look forward to it, Mr Wishart.' Daley ended the call. He was staring again at the circle he'd made around County Antrim. Was it any coincidence that the journalist who'd scooped the story used to specialise in the horrors that place had faced for so long?

Deep in Daley's brain, connections were being made. But whether they were right, or merely the result of coincidence, he couldn't say.

Then he remembered his old mentor's dictum. 'In this job, there's no such thing as coincidence, son.'

There was an icy silence over the dinner table where the Scott family were eating salad. Ella stole anxious glances at her wan-faced son as he picked at his food. Seemingly oblivious of any of this, Brian Scott tucked in heartily to the summer vegetables, chicken legs and crusty bread.

'You need tae eat, Willie!' Ella's voice was as strained as her expression.

The young man put his fork on his plate and leaned his head on the palm of his hand. 'How many times, Mum? I'll eat what I want!'

'Ho!' shouted Scott, ignoring a reasonably large chunk of un-masticated chicken that flew from his mouth. 'You'll eat your dinner, or you'll wear it. I've nae time for this nonsense. Can't you see your mother's worried sick?'

'Aye, your faither's right. I'm sick o' you just lying on that couch all day. The only sustenance you're getting is fae mugs o' tea. You've hardly touched your salad, and your chicken's all piled up on the side o' the plate!'

'I don't do meat! I can't understand why you find that so difficult to get.'

'What dae you eat then?' said his father.

'Don't you start. I get enough from her.'

'*Her* is your mother. And if she wisnae here, I'd stick my toe firmly up your arse for your cheek!'

'What model parents I have.' Will sighed and pushed his fork into a plum tomato.

'You'll remember that it was these model parents who paid for you tae go tae that fancy school, when you should have been oot earning your ain living!' Brian Scott's patience was being severely tried.

'It's university, not school.'

'Well, whatever it is, why the fuck are you not at it?'

'Doh, it's the summer.'

'Your mother tells me you've dropped oot.'

'Yeah, I have.'

'Well, see when the summer's over, just you busy yourself and drop right back in again.'

'I don't want to.'

'So you've no' officially left?' Ella looked relieved for the first time since Will had arrived.

'No, I haven't told them yet. But I'm not going back.'

'Aye, you are,' said Scott.

'What is this? I'm twenty-five years old. I can decide what the fuck I do, and what the fuck I don't!' Will slammed his fork on to his plate.

Scott sat back in his chair, wiping his mouth with a paper napkin. 'Aye, true. You're an adult – it's up tae you what you get up tae.'

Ella looked at her husband askance.

'At last! Some common sense.' Will laid his knife beside his fork. 'If you'll excuse me, I've had all I want.'

'You never let me finish,' said Brian Scott. 'Yes, you're an adult. Yes, you have the right tae make your ain decisions. But with power comes responsibility. You get a job and you pay your way if you're staying in this house, understand?'

'Fine. I'll pay you what I owe you and I'll be off tomorrow.' Willie turned to his mother. 'Exactly how much is that, Mum?'

'Wait!' Ella held her hands in the air in a gesture of submission. She turned to her husband. 'Well, ask him.'

'Ask me what?'

Scott eyed his son for a few seconds. 'Are you on the drugs?'

'Oh, this is priceless! My alcoholic father asking me if I'm on drugs.'

Scott lurched to his feet, sending the kitchen table scraping across the floor and a mug of coffee flying. 'Stand up!' he shouted.

'Why, are you going to hit me?'

'Nah. I'm going to catch you by the collar and throw you out the front door. You cheeky wee bastard!'

'Don't worry, I'm off. I'll come back and pick up my stuff tomorrow, Mum.' Will Scott pushed back his chair and shot from the table, leaving his father standing with his fists bunched.

The front door slammed.

'Congratulations, Brian. Well handled,' said Ella, a look of despair on her face.

'Och, he'll be back. And if he doesn't, I'll get the boys on the night shift tae round him up.'

'Then what? Lock him up?'

'Ella, I don't know what you want me to do. If I'd spoken to my faither like that . . .'

'We know. You don't need tae tell me again.'

'Anyway, like he said, he's coming back tae get his stuff. You can talk to him then.'

Ella picked up her handbag from the floor beside her chair. 'I found this. It was in a sock in his drawer.' She produced a large roll of banknotes held together by a thick elastic band.

Scott stared at it for a moment. 'Money. So what?' He shrugged.

'I thought you were the detective? I counted it. Do you know how much is here?'

'Don't hold me in suspense.'

'Almost eight thousand pounds.'

'Maybe he's pawned that guitar that cost him a fortune?'

'Don't be ridiculous! It was expensive, but it wasn't a tenth o' this.' She threw the bundle of money on the table.

'So, dae you want us to arrest him, is that what you're saying?'

'Do something, Brian. Just do something!' She held her head in her hands and tears spilled down her face.

Scott set the coffee mug upright on the table. 'I'll need tae think aboot it. While I'm away, I want you tae go through everything he has. Aye, wae a fine toothcomb, tae.'

'So you're going to fetch him back?'

Scott shrugged into his jacket. 'No, I've got tae go back tae work. It's the chief super.'

'Fine, just fine. She clicks her fingers and you come running like a wee dog. It's no wonder your name is Scott: lapdog by name, lapdog by nature. Come over here and I'll tickle you behind the ear.' She folded her arms defiantly.

'Unlike your son, I've got a job o' work tae do. If you hadn't mollycoddled the boy in the first place, maybe it wouldn't have come tae this, eh?'

'He wasn't mollycoddled!'

'Oh no, not at all. When all the other boys his age had jobs delivering newspapers or working in a supermarket on a Saturday, he was glued tae they computer games. When other lads were oot cutting the grass, he was inside watching you dae it. I never said much at the time, but I wish I had!'

'You were too busy running aboot the place trying tae keep big Jimmy's arse oot o' trouble tae notice what was happening tae your ain family.'

'Ach, gie it a rest. The boy's a lazy bastard, just like they brothers of yours.'

'My brothers have been unlucky. Illness, redundancies – you should try it.'

'Ha! Always an excuse – you sound just like them, Ella. I'm off. You know where to get me if you've any mair bother with our son and heir.' Scott brandished his phone in the air and walked out of the kitchen.

'And why's it you and no' Jimmy Daley that's away out at this time? Tell me that?'

'It's police business. I'll see you later.'

Ella heard the door slam for the second time in a few minutes. 'I hope your next police business isn't dragging our son oot o' the sea, Brian Scott,' she whispered to herself.

12

Scott drove in the golden light of evening through the streets of Kinloch. It was quiet, and he hoped that he'd catch sight of his errant son before meeting Symington. But after driving around for a while, he reasoned that Willie would probably be in a pub somewhere. Certainly, it appeared as though he had plenty of cash to splash around. Scott very much doubted the money Ella had found was the whole of his stash.

As he took the road to Machrie airport, he recalled the many lives he'd seen ruined by drugs. Far too many, he considered. He also reflected on the nature of having children. He was proud of his family. As children – even teenagers – his son and daughter had been very little bother.

Now things had changed. While his daughter was on a scholarship at a university in New York, doing really well in her quest to become a doctor, it seemed his son had gone backwards.

The sight of Willie at the dinner table had brought back memories of his father slumped over a plate of stew that his mother had managed to pull together from the pittance her husband gave her with which to run the house. It was the same grey, unhealthy pallor, dull eyes, resentful tone.

The trouble was, despite years of experience in the police,

he didn't really know what to do. The last thing he wanted for his own child was the hell of drug addiction, or the blight of jail and ruination.

Then Scott thought of his own struggles: the power that alcohol had over him. He wasn't stupid enough to believe that he was beyond sinking back into the bottle. He knew that the rest of his life would be spent resisting the urge to drink his problems away. Though he rarely thought about it, over dinner he'd smelled the whisky on his son's breath, and for a split second the old yearning was back. For what was only a moment in real time, he experienced the memory of the warm spirit as it slid down his gullet, and the gentle embrace of the drink as it did its job: a buffer against life's ills.

Soon he arrived at the small terminal outside Machrie airport. Symington was behind the wheel of her big black SUV. She waved at him feebly.

With a sigh he parked alongside, conscious of a guilty feeling that instead of solving the problems of other people, he should be addressing his own.

The old man stirred on the hard wooden floor. His hands were bound, and a chain around his right ankle was secured by a rope to a stake rammed firmly into the ground nearby. It was only with a massive effort that left him gasping for breath that he was able to rise into a seated position.

He was in what appeared to be a large shed. Most likely on a farm, he thought, judging by the stench, though he could see no sign of animals via the many little slits of golden light that issued through the wooden walls. It was stiflingly hot. A memory took him back to his boyhood, when he and a friend had been locked inside a shed by older youths. The bullies had threatened to burn them alive, holding flaming matches up against the dirty old windows in order to terrify the younger boys inside.

But it wasn't the fear he remembered. It was that airless summer long, long ago, when inside the shed it was so stuffy that breathing was difficult.

He felt the same panic rise in his chest now, felt his throat tighten.

The strips of light picked out dust motes in the air. Again he was reminded of his youth. Long afternoons at the local cinema, with the likes of Bogart, Burt Lancaster, Cary Grant and Bette Davis towering on the big screen.

But this was no old film. It was real.

He closed his eyes and tried to control his breathing. He could hear his heartbeat in his ears. His mother had warned him about that when he was little more than a child.

If you can hear your heart in your ears, you'll die.

That saying had terrified him then. But now the thought was much less frightening. He'd had a relatively long life, much longer than his father's. He'd even surpassed the age at which his mother had died. Strangely, the thought of letting go seemed to appeal.

He was startled when he heard a heavy bar being removed from the door.

Hamish blinked into the light.

Brian Scott was sitting in the passenger seat of Symington's big SUV. She'd told him everything about the trials and tribulations she'd suffered in the last couple of days, and the detective was staring out of the window trying to make sense of it all.

'I thought you of all people would have something to say, Brian.' She looked at him pleadingly.

'Ach, I'm just scunnered. I thought we'd put all this tae bed back on Gairsay.'

'We did. This is different – worse, maybe.'

'And do you think this Bower bastard knows aboot me?' She shrugged. 'He never mentioned it.'

Scott thought back to the hotel car park on Gairsay and his fight with Chappell on the rough ground in the darkness. From what he'd seen of the man, he appeared to be beneath contempt. He could picture the boastful, swaggering bully who had persecuted a young woman in the worst possible way for so many years. 'He won't have said anything, ma'am.'

'How can you be so sure?'

'A man like that would never dredge up a tale of being battered by some country cop like me. Think aboot it – does he seem like the kind o' guy that's going tae boast aboot that? Nah, no way.'

Symington bit her lip as she pictured Scott astride her nemesis, throwing punches at his face. 'You're right. He'd want to keep that quiet.'

'Bower – well, he's another kettle o' fish.'

'He's a murderer. He told me quite calmly what he'd done.'

'But why does he want you doon here? Let's be honest, he could have been intae you for all sorts.'

'I don't know. I can't work it out, Brian.'

Scott turned in his seat to face her. 'We've got two choices here.'

'Please don't say that none and fuck all thing that you usually do.'

'No. I mean we can approach this one o' two ways.'

'I'm listening.'

'We either play this bastard along – me in the background, like. See what he's after, or whatever, then decide how tae handle it . . .'

'Or?'

'We come clean and tell oor Jimmy.'

'No! Brian, we can't do that. Jim's a good cop. He'd never be able to overlook what I've done.'

'He's a pragmatist; he taught me what that word meant, tae. Anyway, he doesnae need tae know everything.'

'About the accident, you mean?'

'Aye. Carrie, you were only a lassie. They slipped you the booze and the boy on the bike hit you. You didnae do anything wrong. If you'd held your hands up you'd have got off wae it, likely.'

'I'd have lost my job at the very least.'

'There are mair jobs aboot than the polis, you know.'

She swallowed hard. 'I know – I've known it for years. But it was like being on a plane. I couldn't get off in the middle of the flight just because I wasn't enjoying the experience.'

'What's done is done. Here's what I think: we lift this bastard, and I gie it tae him auld style until he breaks.'

'Auld style?'

'Aye, a wee bit o' gentle persuasion, you know.' He smiled.

'He's too cool to be flustered by that. And anyway, how could we keep that away from Jim?'

'I'll have tae work on that bit. Anyway, you'll be aware that Jim Daley doesn't exactly have a squeaky-clean record either.'

'Shit!' Symington swore loudly. 'This isn't fair on you. I should take this to the bosses. I'll think of something. After all, this guy's a killer. It's too dangerous.'

'What aboot the video of your old pal Chappell telling all?'

'He's not here to back it up, is he? I'll just discredit it.'

'You think? This Bower killed a man and openly told you he'd done it. Dae you not think that perhaps he's no' telling you everything? You have to be pretty confident tae tell a chief super that you've offed your mate, then try to blackmail her, wouldn't you say?'

'You mean things could get worse?'

'In my experience things can always get worse.' Fleetingly, Scott thought of his troubled son.

'In that case, I'm definitely going to take this upstairs.'

Scott sighed. 'That's a last resort. If he'd killed some innocent member o' the public, I'd have said aye, report it. But that's no' the case. Depending what this clown's after, we can hold off. Might be the case that he's all talk.'

'Chappell wasn't saying much on the floor of that car park.'

'No, but that's his Achilles heel. He's a murderer, and we know it.'

'He could just deny it. I mean he even handed himself in as a witness.'

'Listen, there's no' a bastard alive who doesnae make mistakes.'

'I'm certainly in that category.'

'I've seen them all – big men, invincible. They have it all sussed oot. Until they're being carted off in the prison van, shaking their heids. But promise me. If it gets heavy, and we cannae handle it. Before you go running tae the ACC with your letter o' confession, we tell Jimmy, right?'

She stared at him for a few moments. 'Okay, I promise.'

13

Symington had opted to stay at the hotel in Machrie, rather than one in Kinloch. So, after a final agreement on how they'd approach her dilemma, she and Scott parted.

Scott drove back home as night slowly descended over the town. He drove round a bit, partly in search of his son, and partly to clear his head. He'd tried to keep calm and measured in front of Symington, but it hadn't been easy. That she was in trouble was putting it mildly.

He had a decision to make, and he had to make it quickly.

Scott pulled up outside the County Hotel and dialled Ella on his mobile. 'Any sign of oor boy?'

'Aye, he's back.' Ella sounded weary.

'What's he saying tae it?'

'Nothing. He just came in and went straight upstairs.'

'Did you get a chance tae have a look through his stuff?'

'Aye, quickly. I didnae find any mair money.'

'Well, that's good, is it no'?'

'But I found a notebook.'

'What was in that?'

'Just names and mobile numbers. Surely kids these days keep that stuff on their phones, eh?'

'Aye. Och, it'll be something and nothing.' As Scott said

the words, he tried hard not to betray the lie to his wife. Phone records were easy to find and easy to track. Old-fashioned pen and paper was favoured by criminals – at least those with half a brain. 'Listen, I'll be home in half an hour or so. Did you put all his stuff back where you found it?'

'Aye. I'm no' daft, Brian.'

'Good. I'll take it fae here. Me and him need tae have a talk. Aye, and no' just an argument o'er chicken legs.'

'Okay. I'll see you shortly.'

Scott ended the call and looked at the door of the County Hotel. There was a lot on his mind, but one thing dominated his thoughts: whisky.

The man stood before Hamish with an expression that spoke of toughness tinged with pity. He was above average height and middle-aged. But somehow his lined, leathery face was redolent of someone who worked outdoors, a hard man in every sense of the word.

The old fisherman returned his gaze with rheumy eyes. 'I canna think why I'm here. I was jeest checking my creels. Whoot harm can I have done tae you lads, eh?'

His captor knelt on one knee before him. 'Wrong place, wrong time, my friend.'

His accent was that of County Antrim. Hamish recognised it immediately. He'd fished with men from across the North Channel since ever he could remember. Most of them were fine, upstanding exponents of their trade. But as in the Kinloch fleet, there was the odd exception: men taken by drink or ruined by the wicked master of gambling. 'Are you a Ballycastle man?'

'Now that would be telling, so it would.'

'Aye, I recognise the voice. Some fine men sailed oot o' the harbour there.'

'Some no' so good ones too, eh?'

'Aye, but that's life.' Hamish lowered his head, suddenly wondering how much of his own life was left.

'Listen tae me, old man.'

'You can call me Hamish.'

'Aye, well, Hamish it is then. You pay attention tae what I've got tae say and you'll be away in that boat and sailing back into the harbour at Kinloch.'

'Oh aye. And when will that be?'

'When we've concluded our business.'

'Wae thon big RIB?'

'Never you mind. It'll be over when it's over.'

Hamish nodded. 'That's the normal way o' things, right enough.'

'You'll be hungry and thirsty, eh?'

'Aye, I'll no' deny it. Despite my precarious position, I could fair go a bite tae eat and drink, right enough.'

'Okay. I'll send the lad in wae some scran for you.'

'Would you mind untying my hands? It's no' as though I'll be sprinting off anywhere wae that big chain roon my ankle. And at my age, the chances o' breaking through the walls are dismal at best.'

The Irishman snorted a laugh. 'At least you're being realistic. No doubt you wouldn't say no to a whiskey or two?'

'I certainly would be more than happy tae take you up on that kind offer, even if it's that Bushmills poison. No offence intended, by the way.'

'Ha! None taken, auld fella. You're a bold one, right enough.'

'Och, nothing wrong wae the whiskey. But I took a right scunner at it when we were berthed at Cushendall for a week wae the hurricane way back in the sixties. I had more than an elegant sufficiency, you might say.'

'Aye, I did the very same thing with Southern Comfort when I was a lad. The smell of it still makes me boke. But if you can manage some Jameson's you should be okay. In any event, that's all we have.'

'That would be very kind.'

The man worked on the bonds around Hamish's wrists, setting his arms free, at least. 'I'm sorry the boys were rough with you, Hamish. They're an uncouth lot, so they are.'

'I had noticed. But whoot's done is done.'

'Aye, well, I'll away and make sure you get fed and watered. It'll no' be cold the night, so you should be comfortable enough. But I'll see to it you get a blanket.' He stood and nodded his head at the older man before turning on his heel, leaving the big shed and locking the door firmly behind him.

He crossed a muddy yard, scattering some protesting chickens, and kicked an old wooden door that opened on to a kitchen where two men sat playing cards, a bottle of whiskey sitting between them. Across the room, a younger man stood over a stove, tending to a frying pan of bacon, eggs and beans.

'Here, you, make a plate o' ham and eggs for our guest, and a mug o' tea. Aye, and gie him a bumper o' a dram into the bargain while you're at it. It'll help the poor auld bugger get some sleep, at least.' He turned his attention to the two men at the table, and walked towards them. Without warning, he raised his foot and kicked the smaller of the two off his seat, sending him sprawling on the floor, his hand of cards tumbling through the air like old feathers from a burst pillow.

'You bastard, Sean!' shouted the stricken figure as he tried to get back to his feet. But before he could do so, a vicious kick to his stomach saw him double in two, coughing and yelping in pain.

Sean kneeled over him in much the same way he had over his captive in the shed. He thrust out a big hand and grabbed the fallen man round the neck. 'You make me a killer of old men now, you fucking gobshite!' He tightened his grip. 'Why could you not just have left him be?'

'Hold on, Sean.' The man sitting at the other side of the table spoke timidly.

'Don't you tell me to *hold on*, Bobby! Am I the only man here wae any brains? What harm was that auld boy in his boat doing us?'

'He saw us on the island.'

'So why didn't yous just wave tae him and wish him a good evening? He'd have thought you were a team o' arseholes out for a jolly, so he would. But no, no' yous; you storm aboard his boat like the fucking SAS in front of bugger knows who, knock him unconscious and bring him back here.'

'There was nobody about, I swear, Sean. There wasn't another boat tae be seen,' the man on the floor spluttered.

'Oh aye? Could you see up intae they hills? There's a coast road running right past the bloody place. Did you see anyone there, Fergal?' He kicked him again, making him howl in agony.

'We can just blindfold him and get him back on to his boat. A few threats and he'll be brand new, so he will,' said Bobby.

'No bother – great news. He'll just jump aboard, thank us for the ham and eggs and wave us a fond farewell. Shit, we could tell him it was a case of mistaken identity.'

'That's a sound plan, big man.'

Sean made his way round the table and leaned into Bobby's face. 'When the time comes, you and that useless bastard on the floor can decide who does for him, got it? For I tell you something, I'm not sinning my soul with another innocent man's blood.' He stormed from the room muttering oaths under his breath.

As Brian Scott walked through the doors of the County Hotel, there was only one thing on his mind. He wanted a drink, and not a ginger beer and lime. He knew Annie would object. But if necessary, he'd remind her that he was the customer and she wasn't. It had been a bad day – bad days – since his son had arrived. And things looked nothing like changing for the better.

The bar had a decent number of customers from whom buzzed a background of chatter. Scott took a stool and sat down heavily. 'Annie!' he called, and in moments the general manager of the County Hotel emerged from her tiny office behind the bar.

'Right, before you say anything, don't,' said Scott. 'I just want tae sit and have a few drams: nothing overboard, just a couple o' whiskies. I've had a bugger o' a day.' He massaged his temples, eyes closed, waiting for the onslaught from the woman who knew how hard he'd battled against alcohol. But nothing came. Scott looked up. 'Are you okay, Annie?'

She was standing, ashen-faced, wringing her hands. 'No, I'm no' okay, Brian.'

Scott sighed. He'd toyed with the idea of going to the Douglas Arms, or any other of Kinloch's many bars, knowing that the host here would be less than happy to fulfil his order.

'Listen, you don't need tae worry. It's a one-off. I just want a wee something tae relax. You know how it is, dear.'

'It's no' that, Brian. It's Hamish. He hasna been seen since he left tae check his creels earlier this evening. Folk at the quay saw him go, but nobody's seen him come back. They're sending the lifeboat oot.'

Scott looked bewildered. 'But he only just goes out intae the sound. The water's like a millpond. He's likely got a great catch o' lobsters and he's just taking his time.'

'Nah, no' Hamish. He's a creature o' habit. Since he came off the boats and started at the creels, I've never known him be late. He's sitting there by half seven, and nae danger. He's only got a few creels tae check. The boats coming in saw no sign o' him or the boat at the back of the island where he has them.'

'It's the summer. Could he no' just be holed up in some cove? Maybe he's sitting eating lobster beside a right good fire under the stars.'

'He knows how things work, Brian. He'd never think o' such a thing, no' without letting someone know. His radio's dead.' Tears were now flowing down Annie's face.

'Right, I'm sure there's an explanation. They boys on the lifeboat know their business. I know, I've had the pleasure of being oot wae them.' Scott grimaced at the memory.

'I won't be able tae take it if anything's happened tae him,' Annie wailed.

Scott reached into his pocket.

'What are you going to dae, Brian?'

'What I always do in times o' crisis. I'm going to see oor Jimmy.'

14

Daley stood with Scott on the new quay at Kinloch and watched the lifeboat speeding out of the loch, a great bow wave at its head. It was nearly ten in the evening, but the golden light was still shining on the blue water that now had a deep metallic hue.

'There's bound to be some explanation,' said Daley, noting the strained look on his colleague's face. This was unusual, for no matter what they'd faced in their long time together, Scott was normally able to strike up a laugh in the darkest times. Now, in the light of the low summer sun, he looked older – tired. Worn out, somehow.

'I'm worried aboot the old boy, I'll no' deny it.'

'Me too. But what else is it, Bri?'

'What dae you mean?'

'How long have we known each other?'

'Aye, a long time.'

'Well, I can read you like a book.'

Scott sighed and shaded his eyes with one hand as he watched the lifeboat disappear past the island and out into the sound. 'Och, it's that boy o' mine. I don't know what's got intae him. He's like a stranger, Jimmy.'

'Takes some longer than others to find their feet, Brian.'

'Aye, just like we spoke about. But when he's in the glums, so is his mother.'

'And therefore, so are you, eh?'

'That's just about it, right enough. This wae Hamish – well, that's the last straw.'

Daley was about to reply when his phone pinged with a message. He took it from his pocket and scanned the screen.

'Have they found him?' Scott asked hopefully.

'No, but we have an ID on our dead red-haired guy from the plane. Come on, there's nothing we can do here. Potts has been to Hamish's cottage – no sign of him. I've got a constable down there in case he turns up.' He patted Scott on the back companionably.

'Aye, you're right, big man.'

The pair trudged off to Daley's SUV parked at the head of the quay.

Will Scott sat in his bedroom looking up at the ceiling. He could hear the television blaring out downstairs, so was sure that his mother was fully occupied. He hated the way she was wasting her life staring at grim soap operas, or pointless reality shows. She was clever, but he supposed the decision to do nothing with her fine mind was her business. He'd checked the drawer in which he'd hidden the cash and various other bits and pieces. Nothing was missing, meaning his mother hadn't found it, so at least that was something.

His mobile phone was sitting beside him on the bed. He reached for it and scrolled through his contact list. Soon, he heard the ringtone. He could feel his heart thud in his chest as he waited for the call to be answered.

'Hello, Will. Is everything okay?' The voice was quiet, as though deliberately speaking in hushed tones.

'Des, this is hard. Real hard.'

Hesitation. 'I know. I feel it too. But there are more important things than just us. You know that – we spoke about it. Are you still worried about your parents?'

'No, they're the least of my worries.'

'You said your father might be difficult.'

'I'm not talking about that! Fuck, you said it. There's more to this than our relationship!'

'Don't speak about it on the phone. You know what Linda said.'

'Linda. That's all I ever hear from you – Linda this and Linda that. Linda's the reason I'm sitting in the hell of my parents' house and you're in Edinburgh.'

'It was handy. You know that.'

'Aye, handy for Linda – handy for everyone else – but it's a nightmare for me.'

'Just hang on. Linda says that she can sort things out.'

'Okay, Desmond, just like she did the other night?'

'I'll put the phone down if you say anything about that. And you know I hate it when you call me Desmond. It always means you're angry with me.'

Will shook his head in frustration. 'I'm not angry with you. I'm pissed off because of the situation. I'm frightened, Des.'

'You know Linda has this sussed, don't you? You have to learn to trust her.'

'You mean the same way our *friends* trusted her?'

'Don't say any more!'

Will adopted a loud whisper. 'Do I have to remind you that I'm in my father's house? He's a police inspector.'

'Yeah, but that's good, right?'

'Oh aye. Good that I can try and find out what the local cops are up to. My father's not stupid, you know.'

'Huh. You always said he was a pushover.'

'As a father he was. Not as a policeman.'

'Well, you shouldn't have told Linda that he was.'

'Here we go again, bloody Linda! It wouldn't matter what I said to her. She hears what she wants to hear. You must have caught on to that by now?'

'She does what's for the best. You know she does.'

'I know at least two people who would disagree.'

'Okay, I know what kind of mood you're in, Will. I'm going.'

'Don't end the call like this. I won't be able to sleep. I'm bad enough as it is.'

'Well, don't be like this! Sit tight. Linda will come up with something.'

'Yeah, I suppose.'

'I love you, Will.'

'Yeah, I love you, too. I just want to come back up the road. This place makes me feel trapped.'

Des's voice was suddenly a whisper. 'I need to go.'

The line went dead.

Ben Houston was back home in the room he reserved for what had once been a hobby but was rapidly becoming his main source of income: photography.

The beautiful spell of weather had been a blessing, and over the last few days he'd been able to capture large parts of the Kintyre peninsula at its very best, adorned by a summer sun that cast the hills, sea, skies and beaches in a colour palette that could have sprung straight from the pages of a Caribbean travel brochure.

He loaded the memory card into his desktop computer and began reviewing the shots he'd taken earlier that evening. He gazed at an image of Arran pictured from Kintyre's east road. Having used a large lens, the island stood out against a golden sky like a behemoth, and he was sure that once he'd applied some of the many filters available to him via his photography tech these images would make great centrepieces for the exhibition of his work planned for the Christmas period in a Glasgow gallery.

Houston had captured twenty-two images earlier that evening, each from a slightly different angle and perspective. As he worked his way through them, two caught his eye. Frozen in a long strip of sea turned pink by the fading evening light he saw two small vessels. He zoomed in on this part of the first image and stared at it.

Almost instantly, via the high resolution of the photograph, it was obvious to him that something didn't look right. He zoomed in further, losing some definition, but it looked even more wrong, as though a man on one of the boats was being grabbed by someone else. In the next frame he seemed to be being dragged off the boat on to what might have been a RIB.

Ben Houston took three screenshots of the various enlarged images and viewed them again. Though he tried to convince himself that nothing was awry, instinct told him otherwise. He picked up the phone and called the police.

15

Daley and Scott were sitting side by side looking at the large computer screen on Daley's desk.

From it stared a younger version of one of the dead men who had been found in the light aircraft at Machrie airport. He was standing ramrod-straight in the uniform of the RAF, his cap tucked under the crook of one arm. The shadow of a smile could be seen across his face, and a woman in a floral dress hung on to his other arm, leaning into him affectionately.

'An RAF boy then,' said Daley.

'Aye, and he's a lot slimmer than he was when he copped it, Jimmy.'

'Eric John Reynolds, from London. Funny, I thought he was a Scot.'

'Lots o' redheads in my family. I can see why you thought that, big man.'

'No, I mean *a Scot*, as in his nationality. There's no shortage of red hair here, is there? Just shows how dangerous it is to assume anything.'

'I was lucky. I missed oot on the carrot top. Oor Willie wisnae so lucky.'

'But he had his head shaved to the wood the last time I saw him.'

'So would you if you were ginger like that. I cannae think o' anything worse.'

Daley, who could think of many things worse, opted to change the subject. 'We have his records here. This was taken nineteen years ago.'

'It'll be his passing out parade. That'll be his wife or girlfriend. Ella was at mine at Tulliallan.'

'Big day. How did you celebrate?'

Scott shrugged. 'I passed oot. End o' story.'

'No, after that, I mean.'

'I'd tae go to the hospital. I gave my heid a right dunt on that parade square. It was the middle o' June – one o' they roasting hot days. You know fine what it was like, Jimmy. Kind o' temperatures we've got just now. I looked o'er at Ella and that's the last thing I remember.'

'So you literally passed out at your passing out parade.'

'Aye. We had the booze-up the night before. Ella was there tae. She said I made a pig o' mysel'. We had this Aberdonian inspector, teeth like Bugs Bunny. He was always pulling me up for something or other.'

'I can imagine,' said Daley.

'Anyhow, me wae the drink, an' that. I got a hold o' some orange peel, turned it roon tae the pith and shoved it in my gob – you know, like his teeth.'

'I bet he was chuffed.'

'I cannae mind, but Ella says he wisnae happy.'

'So no passing out day photo of you in your best uniform with Ella, then?'

'Och, we took one later on, but it was outside my mother's hoose.'

'Well, that was okay, at least.'

'Okay? Are you kidding? You know how popular the polis were where my dear auld ma stayed. We had tae get in an' oot quick smart before Frank MacDougall clocked me.'

'Right.' Daley grimaced. 'I hadn't thought of that. But at least you had something to remember your big day by.'

'It wisnae until we got the photos back fae the chemist that we realised that two dogs were shagging in the background o' every shot. You've seen them, Jimmy. You must remember.'

'Yes, I do now you mention it. Better focus on this.' Daley pressed a button on the keyboard and Reynolds's RAF record was displayed on the screen. 'He did two tours of Iraq as crew on a supply aircraft. No coward, anyway.'

'Strange the poor bastard made it through all that just tae die in a wee plane oot at Machrie.'

Daley stared at the image again. 'It's funny.'

'What is?'

'Well, the air investigator told me that while the kit needed to take off and land the plane automatically was rare in the commercial sector, the military had been testing it for a long time. In case they had to take off and land without a pilot, that sort of thing.'

'Why would any bugger dae that?'

'Pilot injured or killed – makes sense when you think about it.'

'Aye, I dare say. So you reckon this Reynolds swiped the kit fae the RAF before he left?'

Daley shrugged. 'It's a reasonable line of inquiry, if nothing else. I'll call Farnborough tomorrow. It's over my head. He served for just under seventeen years, so he wasn't on civvy street for long. Though I can't see how he could have got away with something like that.'

'He'd have been better off staying in Iraq.'

'We'll need to go through everything we can find out about him. I'll get Potts on it first thing.'

'And what about the lassie? Is it his wife?'

Daley scrolled through Reynolds's service record. 'Nope. He was single the whole time he was in the RAF.'

'Girlfriend, maybe?'

'Could be his sister for all we know. Another job for Potts and co.'

'She didnae get the red hair if it is his sister.'

A sharp knock sounded on the door of Daley's glass box, and Sergeant Shaw's head appeared round it. 'Sirs, a Mr Houston here to see you. He's a local photographer.' His face was pale.

'You need tae stop burning the candle at both ends, buddy,' said Scott. 'You look right unhealthy. You're here first thing in the morning, and last tae leave at night.'

'I'm re-rostering the holiday detail. We're four down, for various reasons.'

'Well, at least that's one thing I don't have tae worry aboot any mair.' Scott looked relieved. His time in charge of the subdivision during Daley's illness and suspension had been notorious for shifts in double figures one day and two or three the next. The job had since passed to the ever-reliable Shaw.

'What's up with this Houston?' said Daley, his brow furrowed at the troubled look on Shaw's face.

'I'll let him explain, sir. But I don't think you're going to like it.'

The bar at the County Hotel was closed. With Hamish missing, few of the regulars were in the mood for revelling, and they had drifted away in dribs and drabs. When the last guests, a quiet couple from Manchester, had headed back up to their room, Annie decided to call it a night.

She was busying herself with little tasks in order to take her mind off Hamish's disappearance, but no matter how many tumblers she polished, her mind drifted back to thoughts of the old man and where he might be.

The last glasses back on the shelves, she decided to attack the two big drawers under the bar. It had been a while since she'd last cleared them out, and everything from discarded lighters and old pens to unclaimed jewellery was piled high.

Having fished out a signet ring, watch and bracelet from one drawer, Annie resolved to place anything of significant worth in a box on the bar so those to whom the pieces possibly belonged could have a look. Otherwise, she'd arrange to have it all sold for charity. During her time behind the bar, she'd never ceased to be amazed by the things people appeared happy to lose and not try to find.

With the top drawer in some kind of order, she turned her attention to the one below. It was so full she had to pull hard to drag it out. Again, she discovered more rubbish: old laminated menus, four golf balls, a worn pool cue chalk, assorted darts, with and without flights, and a broken calculator. As the drawer emptied, she pushed her arm to the very back and felt something wooden and smooth to the touch. Gripping it gently, she pulled it out.

Annie blinked at the briar pipe for a few moments before her eyes filled with tears. 'You daft old bugger, you were looking for this for weeks.' She stared over at the table at which the old fisherman was normally to be found.

Swallowing back tears, she reached under the bar and

produced a newly polished stemmed glass. She pushed it three times up against a quarter-gill optic under a bottle of gin and gulped the spirit down.

'Where are you, Hamish?' she wailed to nobody.

Through her lamentations, Annie heard the lock in the big front door click. She was sure that all her guests were in their rooms, but someone who had a key was about to enter. She reached under the bar for the old golf driver she kept there just for emergencies, and peeked through the serving hatch just as the front door swung open to reveal the tall, dark figure of Ian Macmillan.

'Hey, Annie!' he shouted in his Canadian accent. 'It's quiet tonight. Who's died?'

She looked at him for a moment then burst into tears.

Daley's expression was serious as he stood over Scott, who was examining the computer screen again. 'What do you think, Brian?'

'Aye, I think it's Hamish's boat. I can just aboot see that blue flash that runs along the side o' it. It would maybe help tae get some fishermen to help in the search. They'll likely recognise the lines, or whatever fishermen see in their vessels.'

'Good idea. Will you give the harbour master a shout, please, Sergeant Shaw?'

'Yes, no problem, sir.' Shaw bustled off to do as he'd been bid.

'So we're certain of the time here, Mr Houston?' said Daley.

'Absolutely. The camera is synced with my smartphone. The time adjusts automatically. It'll be right to the second.'

Scott squinted at the numbers at the top of the screen. 'So, seventeen-fifteen – it fits, Jimmy.'

Daley stared again at the image of both vessels, and what looked very like one man being dragged from a smaller boat to a larger one. He sighed. 'Mr Houston, thank you for bringing this to our attention. I take it we can keep the memory card?'

'Yes, it's a copy. I knew something didn't look right. That's why I called.'

'And you're sure you've nothing else? Maybe another shot wae the boats on it?' said Scott.

'Yes, I'm absolutely certain, inspector. But I've no problem with making the other images available to you. I don't know Hamish very well. I'm not a local yet – I've only been here for twenty-seven years.' Houston chuckled. 'But I know him well enough to realise he's a bit of an institution in Kinloch.'

'Aye, you can say that again,' said Scott, looking glum.

'I'd be grateful if you could email the rest of the images you took this evening, Mr Houston,' said Daley. 'Our forensic teams can work miracles at times. You never know.'

'Oh, I'm sure. They'll have equipment far in advance of mine. I'll send them to you as soon as I get back home.'

'Thank you. And I'd be grateful if you would keep this to yourself for the time being,' Daley added.

'Of course. You needn't worry on that score, Mr Daley.'

Scott showed Houston out of the glass box, while the chief inspector stared again at the enlarged fuzzy image. 'Bastard!' he yelled, throwing an empty mug against a filing cabinet and turning it instantly into smithereens.

16

Daley stood before a large group of fishermen and other volunteers who had access to boats. Scott was at his side, and both men regarded the early morning light with grim expressions. It was only just after six a.m., but when the harbour master had been asked the previous evening to round up some volunteers to search the seas around Kinloch for any sign of Hamish's boat, the response had been overwhelming.

'Now, you all know what you're looking for?' Daley shouted over the cries of gulls and the gentle wash of the sea against the pier steps.

A general murmur in the affirmative came from the gathered mariners.

'That's good!' Daley paused. 'You all know Hamish. He's one of the first people I met when I arrived here in Kinloch. I'm sure he has a place in all your hearts.'

'Taught me all I know about the fishing!' Robbie Paterson, skipper of one of the few fishing boats left in the Kinloch fleet, called out. 'There's no' one of us he's no' helped in one way or another. You needna worry, Inspector Daley, we'll give it all we've got!' At this, a cheer rose from those gathered.

'Thank you, all. The police helicopter will join the search shortly, alongside the Royal Navy, as soon as they can. I won't delay you any longer. Jock McKinven the harbour master will be your first point of contact by radio.'

Daley and Scott watched as men and women hastened to fishing boats, yachts, small cabin cruisers and RIBs under a light blue sky. There was a cool breeze off the loch, but if the recent spell of glorious weather was anything to go by, it would soon be banished by the warmth of the midsummer sun.

'I swear I saw a tear in Paterson's eye there, Jimmy.'

'Yes, I saw that. I was nearly there myself.'

'Who'd want tae harm the auld fella, eh?'

'I don't know, Brian. It's not as though we're plagued by pirates, is it?'

'Don't say that. We've encountered everything else since we came here, right enough.'

'True.'

'I was thinking. Hamish's disappearance couldn't have anything tae do wae oor men in the plane, could it?'

Daley shrugged. 'Right now, we can't rule anything out. That journalist is due here this morning. That'll be another problem.'

'This is the guy wae the bee in his bonnet, eh?'

'You could say that. The good thing is that he's keen to keep everything to himself – an exclusive. Hopefully, there will be things he can tell us.'

Scott looked unconvinced. 'Help fae the media? That'll be a first.'

As he spoke, the first vessel, a RIB, purred out of the harbour over the smooth water. Fishing boat diesels chugged into life, and a sleek yacht slipped her mooring under the power of her inboard engine.

'Just shows you what they all think of him,' said Scott. 'Pity we cannae tell them the truth.'

'It would be akin to letting loose vigilantes, Brian. If they find the boat, great – if not, well, we're back to square one.' As Daley looked up the pier, he saw a large black SUV driving slowly towards them. 'That looks like Symington's car.'

'Oh aye. I forgot tae tell you. She arrived last night. Right knackered so she was – just turned in for the night.'

Daley studied his colleague's face. 'You and she had a nice chat, did you?'

'Just a wee call. It completely slipped my mind, what wae Hamish and that.'

Daley had known the man beside him for too long for a casual lie not to be obvious. Brian had never been a good liar, and yet again he was proving it.

'This reminds me a bit of the time back on Gairsay. I always felt you and she knew something that I didn't.'

'Eh?' said Scott, mustering all the innocence he could. 'If you're suggesting anything is going on, be sure no' tae say anything tae oor Ella. Bugger me, things couldnae get mair icy back hame. It's like thon exhibition all they guys died on. I'm buggered if I can mind the name o' the bloke who was in charge.'

'Scott,' said Daley.

'Eh?'

'His name was Captain Scott, and it was an expedition.'

'Well, whatever it was, he made a right arse o' it. He'd have been better sticking tae an exhibition.'

Before Daley could reply, the SUV came to a halt before them. The driver's window rolled down and Chief Super-intendent Carrie Symington blinked into the early morning sunshine. She looked pale and drawn, with dark rings round her eyes.

'Gentlemen, good morning.' Though she smiled, it was forced. Her eyes flicked nervously between Daley and Scott.

'Morning, ma'am,' Daley replied. 'My able assistant here forgot to tell me you were in Kintyre with us.'

'Oh, last minute thing, Jim. I decided to drive down last night. Obviously, your business with the plane is attracting much interest up the road.'

'Not much we can do until we have more from Farnborough, ma'am. I do have the identity of one of the dead men.' Daley looked around. 'I'll be able to fill you in when we get back to the office.'

'What's all this?' Symington gestured to the exodus of boats from the harbour.

'Long story, ma'am. Again, I'll fill you in back at the office.'

'Of course, DCI Daley. I'm just heading there now.'

As her window closed slowly, Daley saw Symington flick Scott another nervous glance.

Hamish was miserable. He'd spent a cold, restless night under a blanket on some straw. His hips were sore, as was his neck. And cold as the shed that was his prison had been during the night, now the sun was shining it was beginning to become hot and stuffy again.

The door swung open and his captor came in. He was carrying a plate and a large plastic bottle. 'This will keep you going until we get back, Hamish.' He presented the old fisherman with two bread rolls from which slices of bacon protruded.

'I've no' much of a stomach for it, to be honest. I didna sleep well at all.'

'I suppose you wouldn't, under the circumstances.'

'Aye, and I'm in dire need of your facilities, if you know whoot I mean.'

The leathery-faced Sean looked around. 'The best I can offer you is this.' He walked through the shafts of sunlight and returned with a bucket.

Hamish regarded it with distaste. 'Och, if you're going tae do with me as I suspect, you'd be as well to get it o'er wae.'

'I don't know what you're talking about. We spoke about things last night. You have to spend a wee while longer as our guest, then you're free to go, so you are.'

Hamish looked at the straw that had been his bed for the night. 'I'm no' a stupid man, Sean. And apart fae that, I've seen enough tae know when I'm being strung along like a fish. You men are up tae nae good, of that I'm certain sure. And whether or no' you achieve what it is you're at, I can identify you. Now and until the day I die.' He turned a steady gaze on the man standing above him.

'By that time, my friend, everyone will have more to worry about.' Sean pulled some old rags from the corner of a shelf above Hamish's head. 'You can clean yourself with these. I'm sorry this is happening to you, but as we discussed last night, things are the way they are.'

Hamish watched him march off and regarded the bucket and the rags with a sinking feeling of disgust. He had more on his mind than what he'd chosen to reveal to the man who'd imprisoned him: dreams. And what he'd dreamt during the night was fuelling what promised to be a miserable day. Hamish closed his eyes and remembered the nightmare.

He'd been back aboard his boat, sailing into the sound. He glanced back only to see the waters of the loch boiling blood-red. He called out, and one by one the faces from his life he'd loved most and lost emerged from the sea, skin plastered in crimson gore.

Terrified, he'd put his hand to the throttle of the vessel, but as he did so he was aware of a woman standing on the prow. Like the others she was bathed in red, and she was staring down at him with a look of sadness and great pity spread on a face that bore the shadow of a mournful smile.

'Annie!' he'd called out, holding out his hand to help her down from the prow. But in an instant she was gone, and as he looked round to try to catch a glimpse of her, the boat began to sink into the dark depths of a bloody sea.

Hamish opened his eyes, firmly back in the here and now. He'd been having dreams like this for years, some when he slept, the others like passing thoughts: feelings, pictures in his mind he couldn't explain. All he could do was try to draw some sense from them. It was like reading the runes, challenging the fates to give up their secrets.

But this one didn't require a great deal of analysis. Without realising it, the man who had left him lying tethered on fetid straw in the mouldering shed had helped him make sense of it all.

Clearly, judging by his reckoning that *everyone will have more to worry about*, something terrible was going to happen. This was clearly represented by the blood-red sea, and the gory forms rising from it in his nightmare.

The second part was easy.

He'd come to think of Annie the way he supposed some men felt about their daughters. The County Hotel was like a second home, and the lass he'd watched progress from a weekend waitress to the manager of the establishment had become a friend. Yes, they bickered and squabbled, but it was all done in jest, and he was very fond of the woman who, as well as pouring his drams, was also his confidante.

In the dream she was clad in red, her shade of mourning. Every funeral they'd attended together – and there had been a few – she'd always worn the colour. Annie hated wearing black. The sea that had opened up before him was his grave.

Hamish stared again at the bucket and rags. Now, if he had been unsure before, he knew he was going to die.

17

Will Scott was driving the old Nissan Micra his mother had reluctantly loaned him. The car either had a tiny engine or was on its last legs, for it struggled to make the twists, turns and spiralling heights of the country road.

He'd lost any guidance from the satnav on his phone, which was now showing a clear *No service* notice on the screen. He cursed it as he eased round another tight bend, the engine complaining with a high whine and a puttering noise. He pulled it into first gear, and it revved frantically.

Now on a mercifully straight, level piece of road, overhung by trees thick in leaf, he spotted a layby ahead and pulled in to consult the map he'd bought from a newsagent in Kinloch. Even that had been difficult. He'd been bombarded with questions as to who he was, where he was from, where he was going, and why he needed a map. The middle-aged woman behind the counter had offered personal directions to anywhere he wanted to go, but he'd made the excuse that he was just on holiday and wanted to identify points of interest as he casually meandered around.

Reluctantly, the shop assistant sold him what he wanted. It was now spread across the bonnet of his car. He was looking for a small cove. His instructions stated clearly that he'd pass the ruins of an old castle and the place he was looking for wasn't far ahead. He followed the route with his forefinger. Sure enough, about a mile away there was the castle, depicted in typical OS style.

Will jumped back in the car and revved the reluctant engine back into life.

Nathan Sidley was a sharp-faced man who wore his grey hair long, pulled back off his face in a ponytail. His chin was peppered with grey stubble that was probably more of an outdated fashion statement than lack of personal grooming. Indeed, everything about the lean, tall man in the T-shirt and frayed denims spoke of a period thirty or more years before. It was as though, for him at least, time had stopped somewhere between the late seventies and early eighties. He stared at Daley across the desk with narrowed gimlet eyes.

'You're more than aware that there's a limit to what I can tell you, Mr Sidley.'

'In my experience, it's me that normally keeps you detectives right.' Nathan Sidley spoke with an accent toned down slightly from his native Liverpool. 'In my time I've come across some decent cops, but on the whole, they're just marking time until retirement.'

'We all know people like that – in many professions.'

'I'm sure. The question is, are you one of them, DCI Daley?'

'I'd like to think not. But I'll leave you to work that out for yourself. In any event, you're welcome to your own opinion. I don't particularly care either way.'

Sidley's laugh was the crackling one of a heavy smoker. 'A bit of spirit, eh? I like that. Used to find it in the RUC, back in the good old days. Good lads, but some right bad apples amongst them.'

'Not that good, then?'

'No, bloody awful. I got out of there by the skin of my balls. But it's not the most dangerous thing that's ever been in the world. You know that.'

Daley nodded. He opened a file and produced images of the men found dead in the light aircraft at Machrie. 'Do you recognise either of these people?' he asked, having decided not to allude to the fact that one of the dead men had already been identified.

Sidley removed a pair of modern-looking spectacles from a case and hung them over the bridge of his nose. Of expensive design, they were at odds with his 'vintage' look. He squinted at the corpses, pictured in situ in the aircraft. 'No, can't say I do, sorry.'

'What about this?' Daley produced a blown-up image of the tattoo on the arm of the man with red hair.

Sidley stared at it, his nose almost touching the photograph. 'Now, that I do recognise. It's not well wrought, but that is the mark of LWS.' He took off his spectacles and smiled broadly at the policeman across the desk. 'Just as I'd hoped!'

'I don't know what LWS is, so I'm not sure if it's good news, or not.'

'The League of World Saviours, DCI Daley. What's the best way to describe them?' The journalist asked himself the question, chewing at one arm of his spectacles. 'They were climate extremists. You know the kind of stuff: chaining themselves to railings, disrupting public transport, blocking roads – that type of thing.'

'You said *they were*. What are they now?'

'Ah, now there's the rub, eh? It all started with one woman.' Sidley reached for a mobile phone in his pocket. With his glasses perched back on his nose, he scrolled through some images. 'Here we are. Linda Alton – or Delaney, that was. Though I think she's back to that name following separation from her husband.' He held the phone up in front of Daley's face.

Daley saw a woman with straggling long hair, grey in parts, dark in others. He placed her in late middle age. Strangely, from this picture, at least, her dress sense came from the same fashion era as Sidley's own: post-hippie.

'Things changed at LWS when she appeared.'

'Why so?'

'She's very charismatic, especially for young people. You know the type: students, failing exams and searching for a reason to ignore that. Wasters, desperately trying to discover why the world's been so unfair to them. She became a lecturer in environmental issues when she was made redundant from her first career.'

'And what was that?'

'Terrorism.' The reply was straight to the point.

'In Ireland?'

'Oh, yes. But what's a girl to do when the guns fall silent? In her case, marry a businessman with lots of political influence, bag some peripatetic posts lecturing at universities across the country, and make some money.'

'I thought her issue was with the climate?'

'Oh yeah, it is. But she's not forgotten her old pals – and some old enemies, too.'

'You've lost me.'

'This is where my reasoning becomes somewhat speculative, Mr Daley. My theory is that she wasn't the only terrorist left high and dry by the Good Friday Agreement. And we all know how these groups made money in various ways – right across the board, I mean. One side was as bad as the other. Don't think it all ended up in the coffers of whichever organisation it was intended for, because it didn't.'

'No, I know all that. It's old news.'

'But environmental terrorism isn't. You've no idea the zealots that are out there.'

'Environmentalists? They want a better world, not one plunged into chaos.'

'But young people are impressionable. And when money's at stake, well . . .'

Daley stared again at two dead men in a light aircraft, deep in thought.

Will made his way down a short rocky incline on to a white sandy beach. The air was thick with the tang of the sea mixed with the earthy tones of the sun-drenched land: a rich cocktail for the senses, the sweet scent of high summer. He placed his hand over his eyes to shield his view out on to the sound. The only vessel to be seen was a yacht. Distant, its slanting sail was propelling it past the tip of the Isle of Arran.

He sat on the sand and thought about his life. There was no chance he'd complete his qualifications. The prospects were much bleaker than those he'd painted for his parents. In fact, he'd all but been asked to leave the course. At first, he'd been enthusiastic about a career in electrical engineering, but the real world of tertiary education had filled his mind with other ideas – other ideals.

Then he'd met Des.

Will thought about his mother. In his opinion, she had wasted a good brain looking after her children and her wise-cracking, heavy-drinking husband. Now he and his sister had moved out of the family home, to him she appeared listless and bored, just making her way through life in a dwam of cigarette smoke and trash TV.

Will had mixed feelings about his father, too. He'd been a good dad when they were kids – well, at least what they'd seen of him. The police had eaten away at large parts of the time serving fathers spent with their families. But still, he'd been easy-going, playful and funny. Though now, staring out across the sea, he found it hard to believe that his father was the guileless jack-the-lad he'd known when he was young. He'd seen more than a hint of Brian Scott's hidden depths and was glad – for his mother's sake at least – that his father was now sober.

But everyone had hidden depths.

In many ways it was because of Des he was sitting on this beach in the middle of nowhere. His passion for the 'project' that Linda always referred to was much greater than his own. Yes, he cared about many things, agreed with many of the points his lover made. But he couldn't help feeling that he was getting further and further out of his depth as everything escalated ever more quickly. It was like being on the bike he'd had as a kid. At first the thought of hurtling down the long hill without touching the brakes was thrilling. But as the bicycle speeded up the urge to stay safe, to slow down, became greater and greater.

He'd watched with the rest of his friends as Johnnie, a boy he went to school with, was taken away in an ambulance after losing control of his bike and crashing into a wall.

He'd been lucky, but still bore the scars as a testament to his recklessness.

It was hitting the wall that scared Will Scott.

He felt his eyes closing, the restless nights he'd experienced over recent days catching up with him. He was on the edge of sleep when he heard the modulating roar of an engine. He got to his feet and looked again out across the sound. A boat, a wash of white water at its prow, was arcing towards the cove at high speed.

Will's throat was bone-dry. There were three figures aboard the RIB. He felt his stomach churn as they slowed near the waterline. Leaving one of their number aboard, two of the crew waded to the shore.

A middle-aged man with a rugged, leathery face looked him up and down. He had a canvas satchel slung over his shoulder. The other man was younger and taller, with a forbidding look.

'So, you'll be Linda's boy, then?' The leader's smile was a sarcastic one. The man behind him snorted.

'Have you got what she wants?' He could hear the tremor in his own voice.

'Aye. If you've got the money, you can have it, so you can.'

Will delved into his pocket and pulled out a wad of high-denomination bank notes curled together and held in place by a thick elastic band.

'You're not short of a bob or two, are you, son?'

Ignoring him, Will continued to count until he got to three thousand pounds. He stuffed the remainder of the money back into his pocket without bothering to secure it with the elastic band. He handed over the bundle of notes and the man counted them, squinting under the bright sun.

'Three thousand pounds, bang on. You're good at your numbers, eh?'

Will nodded, aware that his legs were shaking.

'Aye, well, the price has just gone up, so it has.'

'What? You agreed the cost with Linda. I've given you the money, now give me what she wants!'

In one quick movement, the man grabbed Will by the throat and began to squeeze. His grip was powerful, and Will quickly struggled to breathe.

'Now, I'd say you've another grand, maybe more, back in your pocket there, eh?'

Will tried to speak, but so constricted was his throat that the words wouldn't come.

'Get it out!'

Feeling his world start to spin, Will thrust his hand in his pocket and pulled out the remainder of the money he'd brought with him.

With his free hand his attacker grabbed it and then pushed Will to the ground. He fell awkwardly, gasping for breath. The satchel landed heavily just beside his head, making him start. His face was cast in shadow as a face appeared close to his.

'Let this be a lesson to you, my boy. You're not in Asda now, so you're not. When you come to make a transaction like this, don't bring any spare change.'

The sunlight was back, bright in his eyes as he heard the two men walk back to their boat, laughing as they went.

Will coughed and spluttered. He massaged his throat with one hand, but other than that he didn't move until he heard the roar of the RIB's engine fade as it hurtled away across the still waters of the sound.

Painfully, he sat up on the sand. He could still feel his attacker's tight grip round his neck, smell the stale alcohol on his breath.

He reached for the satchel. It was heavy. Will hefted it on to his lap, undid the buckle and pulled at the stiff leather. Sunlight flashed off the unmistakable object inside: a well-oiled, gleaming pistol.

18

Daley and Scot were sitting in the office Chief Superintendent Carrie Symington used when she was in Kinloch.

Their conversation was more stilted than normal, and Daley noticed that his superior was ill at ease. He also noticed that Symington was trying her best to avoid Scott's gaze. To a man who'd been observing people and the way they behaved – reacted to certain situations – for so many years, the fact that all was not well was more than obvious.

'So, Jim, no word on the whereabouts of Hamish, I take it?' said Symington stiffly.

'No, I'm afraid not, ma'am. I've just been on to the harbour master. So far there's no sign of him or his vessel. The Royal Navy are searching too, but haven't come up with anything.'

'Where's the main focus of the search?'

'Well, there've been no reports of him in the sound, so they're now out in the North Channel, ma'am.' Daley hung his head for a moment.

'Jim, I know how much you and Brian think of this man. I like him, too.'

'Yes. He saved my life not long after I arrived here. I owe him a great deal.'

'Me tae,' said Scott. 'The old boy's a gem. If anyone's hurt him . . .' He left the rest unsaid.

'Regardless of our feelings, we behave professionally. I'm sure I don't need to tell either of you that.'

Daley noticed Scott looking at Symington with a raised brow but decided not to comment. 'As far as our dead aviators are concerned, we've managed to identify one man,' he said.

'Yes, I read the report,' said Symington, clearing her throat.

'Hot off the press, ma'am: oor man was unmarried,' Scott put in. 'He's been studying at a college in Glasgow for a couple of years – after his service in the RAF ended. No previous – clean as a whistle, in fact. There's nothing linking him tae any criminal activity. No' even a parking ticket.'

'Okay, Brian, thank you.' Symington glanced at Scott for the first time in the meeting. Quickly she averted her gaze, shuffling some papers on her desk as an excuse.

Daley had had enough. 'Right. Pardon me, ma'am, but just what's going on between you two?' He looked between Scott and Symington.

'Sorry, Jim?' The chief superintendent was all innocence.

Scott folded his arms across his chest and sat back wordlessly.

'Listen, I've seen the pair of you like this before – at the time of the disappearances on Gairsay. I didn't say anything then, but now's the time. If you are involved personally in some way, well, that's your own business. Though from bitter personal experience, let me tell you, that's no cakewalk – not in this job.'

'What are you suggesting, DCI Daley?' Symington looked astonished.

'Tell him, ma'am.' Scott's arms were still folded, and his expression was grim.

'Okay, that's enough. We're all tired. I think the stress around Hamish is getting to us,' she croaked.

'It's got nothing to do with what I'm asking,' said Daley. 'If this is something between you and him, I've nothing more to say.' He glared at Scott. 'Tell me, Brian. I'm not judging anyone here. I've no right to.'

'It's no' my place tae say anything, Jimmy. But it's not what you're thinking.' Scott turned to Symington. 'I'm asking you, ma'am. Tell Jimmy. I promise you can trust him.'

'Tell me what?' Daley shouted in exasperation.

'Okay, okay.' Symington stood, arms outstretched. 'Let's not attract the attention of the whole bloody station.' She looked at Daley. 'I'm going to tell you something, DCI Daley. When you've heard it, I don't want you to feel compelled to do anything other than what you think is right. If that involves problems for me, then so be it.'

'I'd just get on wae it if I were you, ma'am. It's a long enough story as it is,' said Scott with a sigh.

Daley massaged his temple. 'Right. Whatever this is, it has to come out now.'

'Not here,' said Symington. 'I hear Liz is on holiday with your son, yes?'

'She is, why?'

'We'll meet at your house, if that's okay – in an hour or so? I'll need something to drink to get through this. And this isn't the place.'

Daley shook his head. 'Whatever you say, ma'am.'

*

Hamish woke from another troubled dream. Unusually, he could remember little of it, but was sure that Annie had featured in some way. Perhaps it was because he hadn't had a chance to say goodbye, he reasoned. When his mother had died, he'd been out on a fishing boat. By the time the message had reached him and they'd made it back to port, it was too late. The woman who'd raised him, bullied, cajoled and dominated his young life, desperate that her son wouldn't turn out like his father, was gone.

But in his dreams, she remained.

The old man wiped a film of sweat from his brow. He was finding it hard to breathe in the shed. Bright flashes of light, beaming through its ill-wrought walls, confirmed that it was again a bright, sunny, very hot day. Hamish reached for the large plastic bottle of water that Sean had given him and drew deeply at it. It was warm, but he gulped it down greedily nonetheless.

He was screwing the lid back on the bottle when he heard footsteps. He was sure that the men in the house had gone out earlier. He'd heard snatches of their conversation before they departed in two separate vehicles.

Holding his breath, Hamish put one eye to a gap in the wall of his shed. He had to twist and turn painfully, but eventually, he managed to manoeuvre himself into an angle that afforded a limited view of the run-down yard outside. Sure enough, there was a man in a suit carrying a briefcase, looking over the house as though trying to spot any life about the place.

Hamish's heart pounded in his chest as he agonised over what to do. Was this a member of the gang who captured him, a better dressed companion? When he put his eye back to the slit in the wall the man was still there.

Figuring he had nothing to lose, Hamish called out. His throat was dry and his voice was rough at first, but soon he was able to make himself heard with a loud 'Help!'

He watched the man turn on his heels, a puzzled look on his face. He was young, no more than a boy, Hamish thought.

'O'er here, man! In the shed.'

For good or ill, the man in the suit had identified the source of the cry for help and was making his way towards Hamish's place of confinement.

Hamish felt a stirring of hope, tempered with fear and caution. After all, he couldn't be sure of the sympathies of this unexpected visitor.

He whispered a silent prayer to himself as the man neared the door of the shed.

Carrie Symington was perched on the edge of the long leather sofa in Jim Daley's lounge, Scott at the other end. They both looked sheepish as the man of the house paced to and fro, muttering to himself. Symington leaned across and lifted a glass of wine from the low coffee table in front of her. She took a long gulp, emptying the glass of its contents.

'Well, say something, Jimmy,' said Scott.

Daley turned on his heel. 'I don't know what you want me to say.'

'Jim, you must do what you think is right,' said Symington. 'All I ask for is a day or so to get things in order before you go to the bosses.'

'What do you take me for?' Daley's eyes flashed with irritation. 'You stood by me when . . . well, we all know when. You both knew what I did to that bastard.'

'Still, this is different. Nobody died, did they?' Symington's voice was little more than a whisper.

'Listen, I know the accident wasn't your fault. I know you'd had your drinks spiked, but when it happened what else could you have done? It would have been your word against Chappell's.'

She shrugged. 'Who knows – who'll ever know? I wasn't speeding. I was on the right side of the road. But . . .'

'But what?'

'If I hadn't been drinking maybe I could have reacted more quickly. Come on, Jim, how many RTAs have you attended over the years when a drunk driver could have saved a life if he or she had been sober – even if the accident wasn't their fault?'

'It was a long time ago,' said Scott. 'Look what Chappell put you through. There's no' a court in the land that would find you guilty presented wae the facts. You're a victim here as much as the lad who died.'

'But no court was ever going to hear the facts, were they?' Symington filled her glass again, leaving the bottle of white wine half empty.

'You should have told me, Brian.' Daley glared at his old friend.

'Aye, and you should know me by now, Jimmy. When I give my word, I keep it!' He looked defiantly back at his boss.

Daley stared across the loch. Again, his eyes passed over the dead stones of the graveyard on the other side of its still waters. How many times he'd stared at them deep in thought, he wasn't sure. All he knew was that they never came back with any answers to his problems. But he was at heart as decisive as he was loyal. Scott may be reckless and lacking in caution at times, but Daley knew he'd been right to help Symington. The story of Chappell's abuse of her over the years made him sick to his stomach. Yes, she should have come clean, faced the music, and reported the facts behind the accident so many years ago. But Daley knew what being a policeman was all about. He was more than aware of the cliques that existed amongst officers, especially going back to the years before the old stagers had all but disappeared. Right or wrong, they would have stood together to make sure that none of their own faced censure. What chance did a young rookie cop have? None, he reasoned. Regardless of Symington's innocence, the likelihood was that she'd have – at the very least – lost her job. More than likely she'd have been found guilty of some serious misdemeanour.

The face of Ian Burns, his mentor and friend, passed across his mind's eye. Not the whip-thin figure in the beige raincoat with the never-ending cigarette, but the corpse lying in the ditch below Dumgoyne hill. Though he'd been dead all these years, his words still echoed round Daley's head like a mantra: 'Always do what's right – follow your heart and you'll know what to do.'

Daley turned to Symington. 'This Bower, do you know where he is?'

She half closed her eyes before answering. 'No, but I know he concocted that story for the police about being with Chappell when he was killed.' She wrung her hands. 'I never thought I'd meet anyone more despicable than Chappell, but Bower is worse – he's a cold-blooded killer.'

Daley turned to Scott. 'Brian, I want you to find out all you know about this Bower, but discreetly. He was a cop, so there must be plenty on file. He's a witness, so they're bound to have contact details for him in Glasgow. You know what to do. Use my office, my own laptop, got it?'

'What am I to do?' asked Symington.

'You're going to carry on as normal. I know that's easier to say than do, but please try. Meanwhile, we're going to do the impossible: save your arse, find Hamish and get to the bottom of these dead guys in the plane.'

'And what then, collar Lord Lucan?' said Scott.

'We focus, we do what we need to do, and we work the problem like always. How many times have we done that, Bri?'

'Too many, Jimmy. Aye, and you're forgetting something.'

'What?'

'This time it's personal.'

'It's always personal, one way or another.'

Symington sprang to her feet and embraced the big detective. 'Thank you, Jim. Thank you.'

'Who's in there?' said the man with the briefcase.

Hamish could detect the County Antrim burr, but this time much less apparent. 'I'm a captive here. I want you to call the police.'

'What?' The man sounded shocked.

'These buggers kidnapped me off my boat. Och, it's a long story, man. Get your mobility phone oot, or whootever you call they damned things, and get them!'

Hamish watched as his potential liberator fumbled in the trouser pocket of his suit and brought out a phone. He pressed the screen and placed it to his ear. 'Damn, no bloody signal! It's always the same around here.'

'In that case, you'll need tae break this door doon!'

'I work for the council. I'm not in the habit of breaking doors down.'

'Aye, well, there's a first time for everything, and this is it. Man, a wean could just aboot blow this place doon. Put your shoulder tae the bloody thing and be quick aboot it!'

Hamish lost sight of the man. Soon he heard a thud against the door of the shed followed by a yelp of pain.

'You'll need tae gie it a better dunt than that,' Hamish implored.

'Shit! I don't think I can do this.'

Again there was a thud against the door. Alongside the moans and profanities, Hamish heard the splintering of wood. 'You're nearly there. One mair go should see the job done.'

'I think I've broken my shoulder.'

'Aye, well, you've got another one right handy. This is a mission o' mercy. You'll likely get a medal.'

Hamish heard the man outside swear loudly. The next second, amidst the clatter of cracking wood and a squeal of broken hinges, he flew headlong through the door and landed face down on the hard earthen floor.

Hamish felt a rush of relief. He scrabbled as close to his saviour as his tether would allow. 'Right, find something tae cut me free and we'll get going, quick smart.'

When no answer was forthcoming, Hamish sat on his backside and managed to prod the prone figure with the toe of his boot. 'Come on, we need to get oot o' here!'

But the man lay still, out cold.

19

Daley arrived back at Kinloch police office, mind racing, desperate not to let any of the information to which he was now privy show. As always, Sergeant Shaw was busy at the front desk. He lifted his head and beckoned the DCI.

'Someone here to see you, sir. Mr Macmillan from the County Hotel. He says he thinks you might be looking for him.' Shaw shrugged. 'I put him in the family room.'

Cursing Kinloch's bush telegraph, Daley made his way straight to the hotelier. He closed the door behind him. 'Right, I think we owe you an apology, Mr Macmillan.' Daley had just discovered that the Canadian perhaps had some inkling as to the name on the scrap of paper found on the dead men in the plane, and he'd had to think on his feet.

'Oh, how so?' Macmillan replied innocently.

'I suspect the local gossips got carried away. We're investigating a rather unusual crime, and being a stranger to the town, your name was mentioned in despatches, so to speak. I'm sure you're getting used to Kinloch.'

'Wow! I had no idea. I heard one of your guys was at the hotel asking a few questions about me *without* asking – if you know what I mean?'

'Yes. The reason for his evidently not so subtle questioning was that we realised quite early on it was the local rumour mill. Again, you have my apologies.'

'Well, that's a weight off my mind. I'm busy trying to create the right impression, and all the time folks apparently think I'm a potential killer of some sort. These guys in the plane were murdered, right?'

'As I'm sure you appreciate, I'm not at liberty to comment on the incident. The last thing we want is to get barred from the County.' Daley forced a laugh he hoped was convincing.

'Hey, don't sweat it. I'm no stranger to gossip – and not just here. When you have some money people are all too ready to believe the worst about you. My pop said it was jealousy at work, though sometimes I think it's sheer vindictiveness.'

'Thank you, Mr Macmillan. You've been away, I understand?'

'Yeah, I went back home for a few days. You know, family, kids – it all takes work. You'll see that for yourself when that little boy of yours gets older. Trust me, it gets harder the bigger they get.'

'Oh, I'm ready for that. If he's anything like his mother, it's bound to be fun and games.' The prospect of James junior sharing Liz's many foibles suddenly replaced the worry over Symington's dilemma in his head.

'I thought that too. But I gotta tell you, there's nothing like a kid of your own to make you see your younger self and all the dumb things you got up to.'

'Ha, I'm sure.' Suddenly Daley felt guilty for thinking only his wife's shortcomings would be passed on to his son. He was well aware that he had many of his own.

'Okay, I'll get back to Annie.' Macmillan stood, ready to leave, but hesitated. 'Say, do you mind me asking about old

Hamish? The hotel is like a morgue. People are so worried – especially my manager.'

'Nothing new to report, I'm sad to say. We have an extensive search on the go at the moment and we're hoping something comes out of that. He's important to us all.'

'Sure, he's a great guy. Those stories he tells – what a character. I'll leave you to your day, Mr Daley. And I thank you for being so candid. It's a weight off my mind.'

'Thank you for your understanding.' Daley watched Macmillan leave the room before making his way back to the CID suite. 'Potts, my office,' he said as he strode into his glass box.

'Sir,' said Potts a moment later, standing stiffly opposite Daley.

'I want you to do something for me as quietly as possible.'

'Yes, no problem, sir.' Automatically, Potts was willing and keen, as always.

'Don't write this down, son. I want you to arrange for taps on Ian Macmillan's mobile phone, and any calls to and from the hotel that he takes. Okay?'

'I'll need to follow procedure, sir.'

'Absolutely. Initiate the process with the bosses. The reason is ongoing investigations into the air accident the other night. I'll do the forms and sign it off. I'll leave you to do the donkey work.'

'Yes, straight away, sir.'

'And this stays between us – well, as far as this office is concerned, okay?'

Potts nodded and left to go about his clandestine work.

Daley stared at the closed door for a few moments. He didn't know what it was, but there was something about the suave, good-looking new owner of the County Hotel he didn't like. But then, he reasoned, perhaps it was just those qualities in a man almost his own age that piqued his jealousy. Daley – despite the best efforts of his wife – had never been one for sharp dressing, either at work or in his private life. He shrugged, and tried to work out what he'd use as an excuse to listen in to the telephone calls and internet use of a man who, ostensibly, had done nothing wrong.

Though the distance between Hamish and the unconscious figure of his erstwhile liberator was no more than a few feet, the old man knew his aim would have to be true. He pressed down hard on the plastic water bottle, and a stream of water arched through the air, landing on the unconscious man's back and soaking his shirt.

Hamish said a silent prayer that he thought unlikely to be answered, until he saw the man's right eye twitch. 'Here, son, wake up!' he shouted as loudly as he dared. He hadn't heard anyone return to the farmhouse, but he didn't want to make too much noise, just in case. In a way, he was lucky. The shattered shed door wouldn't be immediately apparent to his captors when they arrived because of its angle in relation to the yard. But he knew it wouldn't take long for them to see the shed had been broken into.

'Shit, what happened?' The man was stirring. He tried to ease himself off the hard ground but gave up and slumped back into a prone position.

'You'll need tae turn oot quick smart, or this'll be the worst rescue in history,' Hamish hissed.

'Okay, okay.' He forced himself into a seated position on the floor and squinted at Hamish through narrowed eyes.

'I feel as though I've been hit by a lorry.' He rubbed his head where it had connected with the ground. 'Wait, are you tied up?'

'Top marks, son,' said Hamish. 'If I hadn't been, I'd have broken doon the door myself, wouldn't I? Whoot's your name?'

'Terry, Terry Johnstone. Who are you?'

'Hamish is the name. But we don't have time for pleasantries, Terry. You need tae get me untied and oot o' here.'

'Aye, fair play. But I don't carry a knife on me. I'm with the council rates department. This place is supposed to be abandoned, but we had reports of lights and comings and goings. We can't be having folk not paying their dues, can we?'

'I'd get back tae the office an' tell them tae send the SAS if I were you. Take a look aboot, son. This is a shed – there's bound tae be a blade o' some description lying aboot. Quick!'

Terry got to his feet slowly and painfully. 'Oh, you bastard. I've not long bought this suit and look at the shape of it now, eh?' Though he was in shirtsleeves, doubtless because of the heat, his trousers were filthy, ripped at the right knee, where a trickle of blood showed from a wound sustained during his fall.

'Come on, shake a leg, Terry!'

The young man looked on one shelf, but only found some rags and an old pot of paint. The next shelf was bare, apart from a broken wooden ruler and a jam jar, festooned inside by a complication of spider webs. Moving on, he almost tripped over a wooden box on the floor, recovering his balance in time to bend over it and root through its contents. 'Here, what about this!' he said, brandishing a worn hacksaw blade.

'Aye, that'll dae fine. Gie it here and I'll get tae work on this rope, son.'

Suddenly a wary look crossed Terry's face.

'Come on! We've nae time tae waste, man!'

'How do I know you're not the dangerous one? Whoever's camped out up here might have you trapped ready for the polis to arrive. I've seen this kind o' thing before.'

'Right, so you're in the habit o' finding auld fishermen tied up in sheds. Good stuff. You'll know exactly whoot tae be at, then.'

Terry was still looking at Hamish with no little suspicion. 'Dae I look like a danger tae the public?'

Terry bit his lip and thought for a few seconds. 'Okay, I believe you. But I want to go straight to the police when we get out of here.'

Hamish sighed with relief and sawed away at the tarred eye of the rope through which the chain that shackled him had been passed. Though the blade was no longer capable of the use for which it was intended, it was still sufficient unto the task of slicing through his bonds.

With the rope severed, Hamish was left with the chain around his ankle. It would have to remain there, but he was sure it wouldn't be much of an encumbrance, and they didn't have time to try to prise off the small padlock that held it in place. He tried to force himself to his feet, but it wasn't until Terry offered a hand that he managed to stand. His knees were stiff, and his ankles were throbbing. Nonetheless, he knew they had to get as far away from this place as quickly as possible. Then another thought crossed his mind. 'Where exactly are we, son?'

'Eh? You mean you don't know where you are?'

'I widna have asked if I did!'

'We're about six miles outside Ballycastle, just off the coast road.'

'Aye, I thought as much.' Hamish was limping towards the ruined door. 'I hope your car's nearby, Terry.'

'It's down the bottom of the lane. There's no way I was bringing it up here – it's like the surface of Mars. I'd have done in my suspension.'

'And how far away is that?'

'I don't know – about two hundred metres give or take.'

'Bugger,' said Hamish.

'What?'

'We canna risk it. These cutthroats could be back any minute. It'll take me too long tae hobble doon this lane o' yours. We'll have tae hit the hills and take a trip across country.'

'In these shoes? You must be joking.'

'Come on!' Hamish squinted into the bright light of the day. He was tempted to stand and take in the fresh sea air, a relief after being trapped in the hot, stuffy shed, but instead he crouched round the corner of the decrepit building, beckoning Terry to do the same.

A low hill was in front of them. Hamish eyed it, his back pressed against the shed walls. 'What's over the other side o' that rise?' he whispered.

'How should I know? I'm not from round here, and I tend to get about the place in my car, not over the hills and far away.'

'Which way to Ballycastle?'

Terry looked around, trying to work things out through the throbbing pain in his head. 'Aye, well, I reckon if we get over that we'll be going in the right direction. I can't say what's on the other side of it, mind you.'

Having heard enough, and not bothering to reply, Hamish took off up the hill via a gap in a fence where a gate should have been. Terry shook his head as he watched the old man half crouch, half scramble away.

'Shit. I thought this was going to be an easy morning, too,' he muttered to himself. Though he'd been taken aback by what he'd experienced since arriving at the farm, he realised that there was something far from right about the old man being held prisoner in a shed. But that was for the police to work out. He followed Hamish through the opening, cursing as the dust of the dry earth under the sun-bleached grass coated his best pair of shoes.

20

Carrie Symington was back in the hotel at Machrie. She lay on her bed fully clothed. Though she was relieved by the attitude Daley had taken when presented with her difficulties, she felt huge guilt and remorse. To involve Scott way back on Gairsay had been bad enough, but then she thought her troubles were at an end. She'd always known Chappell was a coward and was pretty sure he'd relent in his persecution of her when it was clear that she'd confided in Brian Scott.

She'd been wrong.

Part of her wanted to confess – to unburden herself of the shame she'd carried for so long. But she knew what she was likely to lose: her job, her pension and, more than likely, her liberty. This wasn't how the young, keen Yorkshire lass had envisaged her future. She was happy that she'd risen through the ranks so quickly. But with each promotion she had dreaded what she feared was to come – the revelation of her deceit for all to see.

Symington couldn't count the times she'd turned this over in her mind. She processed it every day. And always, just when she thought things were getting better, Chappell reared his ugly head. She could still feel his weight pressing down on her, the stench of stale beer on his breath, the sheer pleasure he took at having her in his power.

But he'd paid the price for what he'd inflicted on her over the years: he was dead. Now, though, she faced circumstances worse than any presented by her deceased colleague. Bower was a killer, she knew that, and twisted as Chappell had been, he was only a bully, albeit a wicked one.

She had heard his rasping voice coming from Bower's phone. She shivered at the thought.

She'd had time to think about it all since Brian Scott had battered him in the dark car park on Gairsay. She'd been determined to call his bluff, to tell him to do his worst in the pub in Glasgow where they'd been scheduled to meet. Little had she known that as she waited for him he was lying dead.

Suddenly, Carrie felt the walls of her room close in about her. She jumped off the bed, put on a flat pair of shoes, hefted her handbag over her shoulder and was soon on the stairs leading to the ground floor of the hotel.

She walked into the bar, catching the eye of the man serving behind the counter. 'I'm sorry, I'm due to visit a friend this evening, and I forgot to buy a bottle of wine.' She smiled ruefully. 'My head's all over the place – must be this heat.'

'Aye, I know whoot you mean. I'm roasting in here all day. The sun fair pours through these big windows.' The barman was young and friendly. He had *Jed* printed on a badge on his shirt.

'Can I buy a bottle from here to take out, Jed?'

'It'll cost you. It's no' supermarket prices in this place.'

'Oh, that's okay. Better than going empty-handed.'

He shrugged. 'You're the guest, and guests are always right.'

Symington smiled. 'A Chardonnay – anything white and half decent will do. A screw-top, if you have one, please?'

'You don't like corks either? Bane o' my life in this place, they are. I'll away and have a quick look at what we've got. I'll no' be a minute.'

As she waited Symington gazed out at the still sea. It was adorned by a fading blue sky, tinged with peach and the odd straggle of thin, wispy cloud. It would be hours before the short dark night descended over the village of Machrie. But she'd heard all about the sunset's magnificent display here, and she reckoned that there was no better time to experience it. Perhaps, along with the alcohol, it would help banish her fear of the immediate future, if only for a while.

'Here we are, an Australian Chardonnay.' He presented the screw-topped bottle. 'It's thirty-five quid, I'm afraid.' He grimaced.

'No problem. Can you put it on my bill?'

'Aye, sure I can. Room twenty-two, isn't it?'

'It is indeed. Thanks, Jed.'

Once she was outside on the steps of the hotel, Symington placed the wine bottle in her oversized bag. She cursed herself for not bringing one of the glasses from her room, but she figured that the wine would taste just as good from the bottle.

Instead of making for her car, she turned left out of the hotel gates and walked through the village.

Hamish was tired. His feet were aching and the chain on his right ankle was chafing his skin. It hadn't taken long for Terry to discover that his mobile phone had fallen from his pocket when he crashed through the shed door.

'That was a bloody expensive one,' he lamented. 'Aye, and it wasn't insured, either.'

For Hamish, it was just another blow. They'd been up hill and down dale and spotted only one remote farmhouse.

They'd knocked at the door, then looked around, but their search had been a fruitless one.

'No sign of the coast road, never mind Ballycastle, Terry. I think you have me away on one o' they wild goose chases.'

'I don't understand it. We've been walking for ages.'

'Aye, that's right enough, but no' in the direction o' Ballycastle, I'm thinking. You might be up tae date wae all the latest in tax, rates and the like, but you've the sense o' direction o' a drunk fisherwife.'

'You can't say things like that now.'

'Why ever no'?'

'It's sexist! You older folk have no idea how to behave. My grandfather's the same. I'll no' even tell you the stuff that comes out of his mouth.'

'So, you'd call them fish persons, eh?'

'Aye, that's much more like it. If I was to be casually sexist in my job, let me tell you, I wouldn't be in it for much longer!'

'You can report me tae the authorities when we reach civilisation. Though by that time I'll likely be deid o' exhaustion, so it'll no' be a problem.'

'Come on, Hamish, you're doing great. I hope I'll be as fit when I'm your age.'

'You will be my age by the time we make it to Ballycastle.'

They'd stopped for a rest under the sheltering branches of an old oak tree. As Hamish looked around, he saw the sun lowering in the west.

'Wait, if that's the sun setting o'er there, we should be going that way if we're tae catch the coast road.' He pointed a gnarly finger roughly towards a steep hill.

'I thought we were making for the town?'

'Och, I've lost all hope o' that notion. I'm sure we've been walking aboot in circles. I think we've had a drink twice oot o' the same wee burn.'

'You're a fisherman, you say?'

'Aye, what of it?'

'I thought you had to be grand at the old navigation to go to sea.'

'As any man with a head on his shoulders will tell you, there's a queer difference between plotting your course on your natural element and trying to circumnavigate the globe overland. If we were at sea, I'd have had us at oor destination a long while ago.'

'You can't say that either.'

'Whoot, circumnavigate?'

'No, queer; you said a *queer* difference. It's better to say gay or something.'

'The mair I get to know you the mair convinced I am that I was better off tied up in that bloody shed.' Hamish rose stiffly to his feet with the aid of the stout tree trunk.

'Here, would it not be a better idea for me to boost on up that hill and take a look about? If the coast road is nearby like you think, I'll be quicker getting to it and I'll flag somebody down. If I don't see it, I'll just come back.'

Hamish thought for a few moments. 'Aye, there's sense in that. The good Lord knows, my feet are fit tae drop off at any minute. But how will you know where tae find me?'

'The chances are that whoever I flag down will have a phone. If the road's over that hill, I'll just point and say *he's on the other side of that hill*.' Terry spoke the last words in a slow drawl, alluding to the fact that he thought Hamish thought him stupid.

'There's no need tae get sarcastic. But the plan seems sound enough tae me. I canna think that there's no' folk oot searching for me, so the polis in Ballycastle will more than likely know fine who I am.'

'Right, job done! I'll be off. Mind, if I don't come back, I've made my way down to the road.'

Hamish sighed as he watched his new friend scale the hill, thankful it wasn't him. He had the tree for shelter, and a small stream nearby if he needed water. 'God bless you, son,' he muttered as he settled back down on the rough ground, his back against the trunk.

Symington had to admit, the combination of the wine, the wash of the sea and the shimmering vistas across it had calmed her. The pink hues in the sky were becoming ever deeper, the blue sky fading as the hour of sunset approached. Across the islands to her right, purple hues offset by hints of green settled in a glorious multi-coloured canopy. Symington was well travelled, but she had never seen the like.

It's true, she thought as the first stars appeared in the darkening sky. We're of so little consequence, just tiny specks. Our lives mean nothing in the great scheme of things.

Her troubled mind was being soothed by the comforting balm of the fruit of the vine, and the power of nature.

She closed her eyes and breathed deeply.

'Such a lovely evening, isn't it?'

The unexpected voice came from behind. Symington twisted round, letting the bottle spill its contents in the sand.

Towering above her, Bower looked like a malevolent colossus.

21

It was beginning to get dark when Daley walked from Kinloch police office and headed for the County Hotel. His visits there had become less frequent of late, mainly because he was trying to keep his alcohol consumption within limits. He'd never been able to understand those who could spend time in licensed premises drinking coffee or a soft drink. He admired Brian for the way he'd morphed from a heavy drinker into a teetotaller almost seamlessly, though he was sure the process had been nowhere near as easy as Scott had made it look.

In truth, the big detective was low in spirits. He'd asked Brian to accompany him, but his sidekick had pressing matters at home to attend to, namely the continued brooding presence of his son. So Daley was alone as he walked through the familiar grand front door of the County, and into its inner sanctum.

Though there were a few customers dotted round the bar, they all seemed to be in a quiet, reflective mood. Daley was in receipt of the odd 'hello' here, or a simple nod of the head there, but of anything approaching revelry there was no sign. He realised that Hamish's continuing absence was the main reason for this, and for Annie's darting from her office behind the bar just as he arrived.

'Any word, Mr Daley?' Her expression of wide-eyed hopefulness soon withered to one of keening despair when Daley shook his head, eyes downcast.

'The Navy and the lifeboat are still out there, but there's no sign of him or the boat. The local flotilla was ordered back to port by the coastguard. The last thing we need is an accident in the dark. But they're all raring to go out first thing in the morning again.' Daley leaned on the bar and ordered a large glass of red wine. He wasn't sure if the apocryphal tales were true, but red wine was supposed to be good for the heart – in moderation, he reminded himself.

As Annie was pouring his drink, a man with the tanned, gnarled face of someone who had spent a lifetime at sea sidled up to the bar.

'Mr Daley, good evening to you,' he said, staring straight ahead.

'Fraser, how are you?' The newly retired fisherman was a familiar face in the County and around Kinloch. Daley had enjoyed his tales of the fishing and the way he and Hamish sparred with each other over their relative seafaring experiences. But it was all good-humoured, and the policeman realised that they were old friends.

'I could be better, and no mistake.' He lowered his voice and leaned in to Daley, so that Annie wouldn't hear. 'My hopes were fair raised this morning. But I have tae say, from whoot I hear, there's nothing tae justify that this night.'

Daley shrugged. 'It's a lot of sea. Hamish could have had problems with the boat and been forced to hole up in some remote cove somewhere.' As he said it, Daley realised how lame it sounded.

'This is true.' Fraser sucked air in through his teeth, as

though he knew what the detective had just said was far from the whole truth. 'I've been around this coast for many years, Mr Daley. No' as long as Hamish, I'll grant you. But enough time to know that a search like the one that's been on the go since the auld fella went missing should have turned something up by now– aye, for good or ill.'

'Meaning?'

'Well, meaning that if he's safe and well he'd be sitting right at that table there.' Fraser nodded to Hamish's usual seat, now empty.

'And if things aren't all well?'

'In this weather – barely a decent wave to be had, never mind a heavy sea, the sun splitting the sky – I think they'd have found something.'

Daley considered this as he took a long sip at the red wine, feeling guilty that he was in possession of facts unknown to most people in the town. His drink was sour, not the quality he kept at home, but it would do. 'Do you have a theory, Fraser?'

The fisherman watched Annie disappear back into her office before offering a reply. 'I heard something strange yesterday. I was up at Tarbert. An old shipmate o' mine was having his seventieth birthday, so we all gathered for a dram wae him to help him through the trauma o' it. I get free on the bus now – a great thing, right enough.'

'I'm sure. But what did you hear?'

'Och, I never paid much heed tae it until today. I was lying in my bed – no' jeest as quick on the go this morning after my wee jaunt tae Tarbert, you understand – when it crossed my mind. In fact, if you hadna appeared the night I had made my mind up tae take a wander up the brae and have a word with you tomorrow.'

Impatient for Fraser to finish his preamble, Daley nodded enthusiastically in an attempt to move the story on.

'Since I can see you're fair champing at the bit, I'll cut tae the chase, so tae speak.' Fraser raised his eyes at Daley's apparent reluctance to listen to anything more than the unembroidered facts. This was not the Kinloch way.

'Please do.'

'Some young Tarbert lads – off a boat called the *The Gael* saw something unusual earlier in the day – before Hamish disappeared.'

'What exactly?' Though they hadn't made the information available to the public, Daley was thinking of the images taken by Houston.

'Under the lighthouse on the island it was. They saw some men busy wae crates and the like, hauling them aboard one o' they big RIBs. Och, we had a yarn aboot it and it was put doon tae maybe somebody renovating the old lighthouse keepers' cottages there for holiday homes, or the like. No mair was said on the matter. But I took a wander intae Campbell's the lawyers this afternoon, and it appears that the cottages are still up for sale.'

Daley nodded thoughtfully. 'What else could the men have been doing? Hobby fishing?'

'If they were, they'd be the first hobby fishermen I've seen getting the fish caught wae crates. Unless, of course, they were expecting a much better catch than they were likely to get.'

Daley's interest was definitely piqued. 'What was the boat's name again? The one belonging to the Tarbert fishermen, I mean.'

'It's called *The Gael*. A bonnie vessel she is tae.'

'Sounds as though I'll be taking a trip to Tarbert tomorrow.'

'Then you'd be wasting your time, Mr Daley. They were setting sail for Lewis this morning. But if you like, I can try and get hold o' a telephone number for you. Every bugger and his friend has the mobiles these days.'

'Thank you, Fraser. It's much appreciated.'

'It's a bit late now, but I'll be on the job first thing tomorrow, rest assured. Of course, it may be nothing at all. But then again . . .'

'What aren't you telling me?'

'The island is riddled wae caves – aye, fair teeming wae them, so it is. It's no secret now, but many a cargo was hidden fae the Excise there in years gone by. Man, they say that there's still unclaimed booty tucked away by some poor buggers that either got the jail or died before they could enjoy the fruits o' their labours. No' that I would have any truck wae anything unlawful, you understand,' said Fraser quickly, remembering who he was talking to.

'No, I understand. I had every intention to send someone over there tomorrow anyway. But thanks for the nudge.' Daley smiled, though remembering Houston's enlarged images, his heart sank. What could Hamish have stumbled into? On the other hand, he reasoned, maybe it was all pure coincidence. Had it not been for Fraser's story, he would never have considered the island.

Then a thought struck him. Excusing himself, Daley walked out into the corridor outside the bar and grabbed his mobile phone from his jacket pocket.

The scene chez Scott was one that had become familiar over the last few days. The stony silences were broken only by stiff conversation, apropos of nothing. Though Brian, Ella and Will

147

were gathered around the kitchen table together, they might as well have been on different continents for all that passed between them.

Ella and Will were picking at their plates, while Brian's was almost empty. It took more than frosty silence to dampen Scott's appetite. He was just scraping the last of the gravy and a few peas into a tiny pile that could be easily propelled to his mouth when Ella caught his eye. At first the nod of her head and the furtive glance at their son confused him, but casting his mind back he remembered the conversation they'd had earlier in the day. Ella was of the opinion that her son needed a man-to-man talk. She'd reasoned that there were likely to be things a young man would rather share with his father than with his mother.

Though Scott doubted her logic, he was the first to admit that whatever was wrong with their son, it had to be addressed as quickly as possible. His sullen behaviour was one thing, but the wad of bank notes that Ella had discovered hidden in a sock was something else entirely, and the policeman was worried. Though he had spent a career upholding law and order, that occupation – going back through the generations – was by no means a Scott family trait. In fact, almost the polar opposite was true. He feared that his son may have taken the easy path to money, and it troubled him.

As agreed, Ella yawned, held her hands above her head and declared how tired she was. 'I'm off to bed. Aye, and it'll no' do you pair any harm tae clear up and get they dishes washed for a change. I'm no' the hired help, remember.'

With that, and her dinner left virtually untouched, she left the table, and was soon to be heard padding up the stairs.

'Aye, right,' said Scott. 'You get that scran doon you. It's one thing your mother no' eating – she's likely on one o' her diets. But you're a growing lad. You need your grub.'

'Dad, I'm not ten. If I want to eat, I'll eat, if I don't, I won't. Did your father tell you what and when to eat when you were my age?'

'No, he didnae. But if he'd been sitting at the table and no' doon at the pub, he would have, trust me. Your grandfaither wasnae a man for holding on to his opinions – aye, on any subject.'

'I don't remember him.'

'No. He saw you, though. Held you in his arms, so he did. He was very fond o' you, that's for certain sure.'

'I thought he disappeared for days after I was born.'

'Aye, well, he did go on a bender, right enough. But it was well intentioned. He'd always wanted a grandson. And much as he loved your sister, you were the apple o' his eye. Men are like that; they see themselves going on for ever through their sons and grandsons.'

'He was yellow. I remember the photograph of him holding me.'

'Aye, he wisnae in very good shape by that time. Life had taken its toll.'

'Booze, you mean.'

Scott raised his chin, as though taking a blow like a man. 'It's no secret my faither liked a drink.'

'Liked? He devoted his whole life to it!'

Scott's face flushed. 'At least he devoted his life tae something! All you seem to be at these days is hanging aboot like a wet Wednesday. I'm telling you, Willie, you've got me and your mother fair sick wae worry.'

'About what?'

'Ach, you used tae be a bright wee boy, full o' fun. It's like having a stranger in the hoose these days.'

'I've got things on my mind. I'm sorry to say, I'm not like you and granddad. I don't head down the pub and drink myself into oblivion to forget them.'

'Good for you.' Scott folded his arms. 'These things you've got on your mind, would it be anything tae dae wae all that money you've rolled up in a sock?'

Will's mind was working overtime now. He was glad he'd taken the precaution of hiding Linda's money in various places round his room. He'd had a good idea his mother would be on the prowl. Luckily, she'd only found a fraction of the cash he had stashed away. 'I was working in a pub for a while when I was away. Cash in hand. I converted it into sterling when I got back. Just haven't got round to putting it in the bank.'

'Oh, right.' Scott seemed mollified by this news. For all his experience as a police officer, the part of his mind that was anxious to believe that his son was still on the straight and narrow overcame the immutable rationale of the detective who'd seen just about everything. 'Well, do me a favour and tell your mother. Maybe she'll get some sleep and eat something.'

'Okay, I will. Though I shouldn't have to explain where I get my money. And my mother shouldn't be searching through my shit to find things that are none of her fucking business!'

Scott shook his head. 'See me, son. I'm quite a simple bloke. I don't have the best education in the world – no' a degree like you're going tae have. But me and your mother have managed tae keep a roof o'er your heid and food in your belly for a long time. So when you're in this hoose, if your ma wants tae check your heid for nits, she can do it. If you don't like it, you know where tae go. But it seems tae me that your options are limited on that front just noo, eh?'

'Oh, fuck this! If you don't want me here, I'll pack right now and be on my way.'

'Hold your horses.' Scott realised that it was time to calm things down. 'Listen, you and me, we're more alike than you think.'

'Oh aye?' Will looked doubtful.

'Aye. You know, the best thing that happened tae me was meeting your mother. But I tell you, I'd mair than one broken heart along the way – other women, like.'

'You and Mum were together from when you were kids.'

'Aye, but we was earlier on the go in they days. Folk had less time tae have families and suchlike.'

'Because they wanted to spend more time in the pub? Great.'

'No, because where I come fae you'd be on your last legs by the time you were fifty. You wanted tae make something o' yourself before it was too late.'

'Oh, this is blowing my mind. Don't hit me with your Glasgow socio-economic deprivation shit as an excuse for you and Mum's lifestyle.'

'Eh?'

'Never mind! Listen, enough of the pep talk. I'm tired too. I'm going to bed.' Will stood.

'Hang on. Hear me oot, son. You can talk tae me. If this moping aboot is over some lassie, let me tell you, it's no' worth it. It's an old saying, but there's plenty mair fish in the sea.'

'Dad, for a detective, you're pretty slow, aren't you? So is Mum – for all her clandestine spying into my stuff.'

'Slow at what? Are you telling me you're on the drugs?'

'No, I'm not *on the drugs*. I'm gay, Dad. I have a boyfriend and I'm missing him. Happy?' Will stormed out of the kitchen, slamming the door behind him.

Scott sat. His mouth opened and closed, but no sound came. Then his mobile rang. It was Jim Daley.

22

After such a long time marooned in his airless prison, hot and thirsty, Hamish was now experiencing something entirely different – he was shivering with cold. The dark loom of the sky had all but banished the sinking sun, and a quiet darkness, a thinning out of the day, was now well advanced. The muted calls of roosting birds sounded more akin to a piper's laments than the joy of the morning chorus. Unseen creatures flitted through the tall grass on the banks of the small stream that Hamish had visited more than once to quench his thirst during the long wait for Terry's return.

He'd looked about for something with which to cover himself against the chill of the late, late evening. But any kind of shelter, apart from the canopy of the great oak under which he sat, was all he could find, and it wasn't very insulating. At least it's no' raining, he thought to himself.

The old fisherman tried to keep his mind occupied with thoughts of home, his life and the many people who had shaped it – for better or worse. Images of his father, body wasted by alcohol, stood against an angry sea. For Hamish, it seemed like yesterday, though many tides had ebbed and flowed since he'd last set eyes on the man. He recalled his mother's old saying: if someone's in your heart, son, they never die. Both she and his father were firmly lodged there and would be until the day he drew his last breath.

This thought made him even more melancholy. He feared that the fateful hour of his demise might not be far off. The young lad who'd come to his rescue was plucky enough, but Hamish doubted his directional sense, and wasn't entirely sure he appreciated the true gravity of the situation. Remembering how they'd gone round in circles following his escape from the farm, Hamish knew he should have been able to place himself in the landscape and at least find the road. After all, one way or another, he'd been navigating all his life, though as he told his rescuer, finding his way overland proved a much more complex task than doing so at sea. He recalled the time he and Sandy Hoynes – his old skipper and the man who'd taught him what his father hadn't had time to, and much more besides – had found themselves in Glasgow. They were in search of a radio for the boat, a matter forced on Hoynes by the powers that be after he became hopelessly lost in a blizzard. Though Hoynes had baulked at what he saw as an unnecessary expense, and something likely to terrify any sea-dwelling creature within range, he'd had no choice other than to submit. Hamish recalled the pair of them standing at the top of the city's Hope Street, staring down on to a mess of shops, traffic and busy pedestrians. To men used to the quiet, more sedate ways of Kinloch, it looked like an unimaginable chaos. A place where pedestrians appeared sanguine when it came to pitching the fleet-footed skills of their fragile bodies against those of a thundering lorry, or a large diesel-chuntering omnibus. Of course, in the process of searching for the radio vendor, these two who made their way seamlessly across the sea became hopelessly lost in the broiling, incomprehensible march of the city.

Hamish smiled at the memory.

Now, as the stars twinkled in the encroaching darkness, he wished for nothing more than to be at his usual table in the County Hotel, enjoying the playful jibes of fellow customers and the gentle admonitions of Annie, as she flitted hither and thither making sure all was well in her little fiefdom.

Though he was feeling the chill, he knew that the night would be warm enough to mean he should come to no real harm. So, abandoning himself to chance and the elements, as all good fishermen are wont to do, he settled down with his back against the unyielding trunk of the tree and tried to encourage sleep, all the while cajoling himself to believe that however uncomfortable he was now, it was preferable to being caged in a musty old shed, tethered by rope and chain.

He was just drifting off when something made him open his eyes. He struggled to his feet and took in his surroundings through the gloaming. Sure enough, making their way as though by their own volition down the hill that Terry had climbed came two wavering lights. Torches, he reasoned.

He cleared his throat and shouted for help.

Daley was back behind his desk when Scott appeared, ready for an impromptu nightshift.

'Right, Brian, I've been on to the harbour master. He's managed to find us a boat that'll take us out to the island at dawn.' He waited for Scott's inevitable protestations about having to take, yet again, to the sea. But none came.

'Aye, whatever, Jimmy,' came the muted response.

'Everything okay, Bri?'

'Aye, aye, everything's fine. Och, family stuff, you know.'

'Anything I can help with?'

'Nah. Me and Ella will have tae figure this one oot.'

'Ella not happy?'

'She doesnae know yet.'

'Oh.' Daley looked mystified. 'Something to do with Will, I take it?'

'Aye, it is.'

Daley decided that whatever was bothering his old friend it wasn't something Scott wanted to talk about. And, unusual as this was, he opted to press on to what he considered to be the matter in hand. 'It should be getting light in about four hours. I'd like to have gone now, but McKinven tells me that the shore there is no place to land at night.'

'He's gay.'

'Eh, big Jock McKinven? Well, I'm surprised, but—'

'No, oor Willie.'

'Sorry?'

'Willie – my son – is gay, Jimmy. He just announced it oot o' the blue. Just before you phoned, in fact.'

'Okay.' Daley shrugged. 'I hope you did the right thing and supported the lad. It can't have been easy coming out – not to you anyway.'

Scott squinted at Daley. 'Supported?'

'Yes. You've said he's been subdued since he came back. He's obviously been trying to build up the courage to tell you and Ella. Though these days, he shouldn't be.'

Scott looked at Daley as though he'd never seen him before. 'If I'd telt my faither I was gay he'd have knocked my teeth oot! I doubt he'd have known what *gay* was!'

'And he was a fine example of the best that humanity had to offer, wasn't he?'

'Steady on, big man. You cannae be saying that aboot a man's faither.'

'But you're happy to behave as though your son just cut off somebody's head? Come on, Brian! It's the twenty-first century. Leave all that macho nonsense where it belongs, back in the dark ages.'

'They weren't up tae a' this gay stuff then, Jimmy.'

'When?'

'In the dark ages! Men had tae be men back then – oot hunting mammoths, repelling invaders and the like. No place for jessies when you were getting tae grips wae a boatful o' Vikings or roundheads. Aye, no' tae mention a' that business wae Bonnie Prince Charlie; there was nothing gay aboot him.' Scott paused. 'He only wore that dress tae escape alongside that MacDonald lassie – Fiona, I think her name was.'

'They must have been shit scared of bumping into any of those mammoths, eh?'

'Och no, they weren't sailing as far north as that. They were on their way tae Skye, remember. The big mammoths were up in Russia, and the like. I saw a documentary about digging one oot the snow on Dave the other night. They must be right secretive bastards, because I've no' seen a photo o' a live one.'

'What about the Greeks?'

'Too far south for mammoths. Anyway, how would they have time tae be gay when they were busy thinking up all that stuff? That Plate guy – nah, he had his mind on greater things.'

'Brian, I'll never understand how you managed to pass the entrance exam for this job.'

'Well, if you remember, ancient history wasnae part o' it. As I recall, it was a bit o' adding up, taking away, some reading stuff and answering questions. Anyway, the recruitment sergeant was in the same lodge as my auld fella, so it was kind of a foregone conclusion that I'd pass.'

'Modern policing in action.' Daley sat back in his seat and massaged his temples. 'You know, if you push him away, he might not come back.'

'Aye, I know. I was thinking that, Jimmy.'

'We've come across all sorts in this job – bad, evil bastards, gay, straight, the lot. Are you really telling me you can't get your head round the fact that your son might be in love with someone of the same sex?' Daley shook his head. 'You've surprised me plenty over the years, Brian, but you're not the man I thought you were if you can't come to terms with this. Remember, he's your son, and it's his life!'

Scott sighed. 'It's a shock, that's all.'

'Well, get over it!'

'Aye, I will. I just need a wee bit of time.'

'My arse!' Daley looked at his watch. 'Get back up the road, wake up Ella, get Will and talk the whole thing through. Be back here in a couple of hours.'

'You said we might find Hamish.'

'Well, we won't find him until it gets light. Go and sort out your family, Brian.'

'You're right, big man.' Scott shrugged. 'I'm like one o' they dinosaurs.'

'Just as well Will never ran into one of them.'

'You think I'm stupid, Jimmy?'

'No, I was only joking.'

'The dinosaurs died oot hundreds o' years before oor Willie was born.'

Daley stared at his DI, a number of questions going through his mind, to none of which he intended to give voice.

*

The lights got brighter the further down the hill they came. Soon, Hamish was able to make out the rough shapes of two dark figures, torches in hand.

'O'er here!' shouted Hamish, waving his arms like someone guiding an aircraft into land.

'You'll be Hamish, then.' The voice belonged to a woman and had the local lilt about it.

'Aye, that's me. And fair glad I am to see you, that's for sure.'

They were beside him under the oak tree now. 'Are you okay to walk? If not we can organise something – a stretcher, maybe?'

'Och, I'm fine. I've had plenty time tae catch my breath since Terry left. How is the young lad, by the way?'

'Terry? Oh, he's just fine.'

'You'll be the police?'

'No, nothing o' the kind!'

For a moment, the indignation in her voice made Hamish's chest tighten.

'No, we're the mountain rescue, so we are.'

'Oh, right.' Hamish thought for a second. 'You canna be very busy, mind you. I don't recall seeing many mountains hereabouts.'

'You'd be surprised. The number of tourists that get lost in these hills would amaze you.'

'Aye, well, you're doing a fine job, right enough, then.' He looked at the tall man at her side. 'You don't say much, do you?'

'He's dead shy – aren't you, Declan?'

The man nodded his head and grunted a reluctant hello.

'Right, we'd better get you to the police in Ballycastle.

If you come with us, we've got an SUV not far away. I'm afraid your Terry wasn't too precise as to your whereabouts.'

'No, I kind o' thought he wouldna be, right enough. But he got the job done in the end and that's the main thing. I've got tae say, I thought I'd breathed my last. We can tell the polis in Ballycastle,' said Hamish. 'By the way, I don't know your name. I owe you both a great debt of gratitude.' He held out his hand.

'It's my absolute pleasure.' The woman directed the torch beam into her face as she shook Hamish's hand. She was of late middle age, with long salt-and-pepper hair. 'I'm Linda, by the way.'

23

Scott stood at the end of the bed, while his son hugged Ella. He'd done as Daley asked and woken the house. It hadn't taken long, and he'd been impressed by the way his wife had not for one instant questioned Willie's sexuality.

They were both in tears. But being something of a west of Scotland unreconstructed male, Brian Scott remained dry-eyed, though his throat ached with the effort of remaining so.

'I cannae understand why you didnae just tell me straight off, son,' said Ella, now dabbing her eyes with the edge of the duvet.

'I don't know.' Will glanced at his father. 'I suppose the time was never right.'

'There's nae time like the present. That's what my faither used tae say.'

'Aye, but he was always talking aboot his next drink – there's a difference, Brian,' said Ella. This made Will laugh.

'Well, noo we know where we all stand, I need tae get back tae work. I'm off on a boat again.'

'Oh, where to?' Will asked, suddenly interested.

'Och, it's a bad business, son.'

'Something aboot Hamish? I hope you find him,' said Ella.

'Aye, well, fingers crossed, and that.'

'How far away?'

'Just the island at the head o' the loch. We've heard a tale that things aren't all they should be there. Though likely it's the usual chit-chat o' this place. But if it helps us find the auld boy, I'll take tae the Atlantic in a tea chest if necessary.'

'While you're away I'll find out when we can meet Des, eh?' Ella beamed at her son.

'Whoa, steady, Mum! Let's not burst into a sprint just when we've started walking.'

'But you have to admit, son. I bet you were dreading this moment – well, telling your faither, at least.'

'Come on, cut me a break, Ella. I did my best,' Scott protested.

'I suppose.' She smiled at her husband. 'You'd better get your skates on. It'll be getting light soon. But this is a night I won't forget, that's for sure.'

'Me neither,' said father and son in unison.

'I have to get my head down. I can hardly keep my eyes open.' Will kissed his mother on the cheek and got up from the bed. 'I hope all goes well for you and you find your friend, Dad,' he said as he slapped his father on the shoulder before making for the door.

'Aye, son, me tae. You get some kip.'

Brian and Ella waited until they heard their son's bedroom door shut.

'I'm so relieved,' whispered Ella. 'I thought he was ill or on drugs or something, I really did.'

'Big Jimmy put me right, I'll tell you that. He's always good wae this personal stuff.' Scott lowered his head. 'Sad tae say, I've got too much o' my faither in me.'

'Come here, Brian.' Ella Scott embraced her husband. 'You're nothing like your father. He wasn't half the man you are, and that's the truth.'

'Are you being serious?'

'Yes! Now get going and find Hamish.'

Biting his lip in the darkness of his room, Will heard his father's footsteps on the stair. He reached for the mobile phone on the nightstand by the bed. 'Come on,' he implored as he listened to the ringtone. Finally, he heard a tired voice on the other end of the line.

'Will, come on, man. It's like four in the morning. What's up now?' Des yawned loudly.

'It's complicated. You'll have to listen.'

'Okay.' The reply was wary.

'First – and this isn't why I'm calling – I came out to my mum and dad tonight.'

'Wow, awesome! I didn't think you'd ever do it. Why are you whispering, by the way?'

'Because my mum's awake and I don't want her to hear.'

'But you've already told them. What's the problem?'

'This is the bit where you have to listen carefully.'

'Oh, do tell. Is it juicy goss?'

'No, it isn't. Be serious will you, Des!'

'Okay, lover, don't bite my head off. What is this great secret?'

'My father's heading for this island in the loch. Something's been reported, and they're looking for a missing fisherman. Is that anything to do with us?'

'Us?'

'I mean the group – you know.'

'Yeah, right, okay, I've got you now. First off, how would I know? And second, what could I do about it if it was?'

'You can always think of something. And you know so much more about this than I do.'

'I could give Linda a call. But I'll wait until breakfast time.'

'That's too late, Des! They're leaving as soon as it gets light. My dad's just left the house.'

'Shit! Okay, I'll call her. But you'd better hope that it is something, because she'll go apeshit if it isn't and I wake her up at this time in the bloody morning.'

'I'm sure it's better for her to know.'

'Okay, okay. You're a right little spy in the camp, aren't you?'

Suddenly Will Scott felt guilty.

The woman was sitting at a table in a long, empty bar. The dimmed lights over the gantry were all that illuminated the room. She was drawing deeply on a cigarette as she stared into the distance. She reached for the glass in front of her and sipped at the long gin and tonic it contained. 'This is the last bloody way I wanted to spend the night,' she growled.

She saw the hulking figure silhouetted before the gantry lights shrug. 'You do what you've got to do,' he said throatily.

'Aye, but the trouble is, I'm the one who should be calling the shots, telling everyone else what to do. Instead, I'm here having to get on with the heavy lifting. Making good the mistakes of others.'

This engendered only a grunt from her companion.

'You did exactly as I told you?'

'Aye. I followed your instructions to the letter, I swear.' He held his hands up in the darkness.

'Good. You'd better have, or you'll get a dose you'll not wake up from.' She was about to say more when her mobile buzzed on the table in front of her. She looked at the screen and sighed with irritation as she clicked on the call. 'How many times? Don't call me, I call you!'

'But this is serious – or it could be.'

'Stop speaking in damned riddles and just tell me what's going on.'

Linda listened with mounting interest, eyeing the two bodies lying on the carpet in front of her. Ending the call, she addressed the man at the bar. 'We need to get going. There's a problem.'

'Can't your man get on with it?'

'Aye, so he can leave a mess like this behind himself? Not likely!' She gestured to the motionless figures on the floor. 'What are we going to do with these two?'

'Leave them where they are, for now. This place isn't opening any time soon. We're still closed for refurbishment, sure you know.'

'It's on your head, then. Come on, time we got moving. We've stuff to do.'

'It's still dark outside.'

'I don't care if you can't see your hand in front of your face. We've time to make up. Come on!'

'Whatever you say, Linda, whatever you say.' He watched her drain her glass, stand and step over the bodies of Hamish and Terry.

Daley was kitted out in a rain jacket and tying the laces of a pair of stout walking boots when Scott burst into his glass box.

'That's the job done, Jimmy.'

'Good. I hope it went well.'

'Aye, I suppose it did. It's the same as anything else you dread. Once it's over, it's over.'

'Ella and Will?'

'Put it like this: she's much better at this kind o' thing than me.'

Daley nodded, knowing exactly what his colleague meant. When it came to tact Brian Scott wasn't in line for any awards.

'You're looking right smart, big man.'

'There's some kit for you, Bri.' Daley pointed towards a jacket and a pair of boots on the floor beside his desk. 'They should fit you. The foreshore is covered in boulders, so tan brogues won't do.' Daley looked pointedly at Scott's footwear.

'It's no' walking boots I need – a good pair o' flippers would be mair appropriate.'

'It's hardly an Atlantic crossing, Brian. We'll be there in no time.'

'Aye, but it's a boat. Enough said.'

Daley opened his jacket and checked the contents of his shoulder holster.

'We're going in heavy, I see.'

'No choice, Brian. I can't take the chance.' He looked at his watch. 'Okay, we've got time for a coffee before we head down to the pier. Sergeant Shaw will sign you out a weapon.'

Scott looked unimpressed. 'What's the chances, Jimmy?'

'Of finding Hamish?'

'Aye.'

'He has to be somewhere, doesn't he?'

'That's true. But what shape will he be in, eh?'

'Let's not think about that.'

24

Symington ended the call and placed her mobile back on the bed. The hotel room was in darkness, only the weak light of dawn dimly apparent through the thin curtains affording a modicum of illumination. She held her head in her hands.

'What's up with you?' Bower was sitting in an armchair on the other side of the room, his face shrouded in darkness.

'Jim won't swallow this.'

'Your DCI? Why not?'

'Because his friend is missing.'

'Are you the boss or not, love?'

'Yes, but . . .'

'But what?' He pretended to ponder what she meant. 'I know you've said something. That mate of yours who gave Chappell a good hiding – you've told him.'

'What would you have done?' Symington's voice was wavering.

'Just what you did, Carrie. Here, you don't mind me calling you Carrie, do you?'

'I don't want you to call me anything,' she hissed.

'It's that thing about being a cop, isn't, eh? We're all taught to think the same. I don't think it's a good idea, myself. If we all think the same, we all miss the same things. Kind of stands to reason, doesn't it?'

'Why are you talking in riddles?'

'We're programmed, like robots. So when I wonder what you're going to do – under these circumstances, like – it's not a stretch for me to work it all out.'

'I don't know what you mean.'

'I thought back on what Chappell told me about your Scotch cop friend. Now, maybe I'm wrong, but cops stick together – we're famous for it. Don't matter if it's Borneo or Birmingham. If you have your mates around you, you'll confide in them.'

'I've had enough of this!' Through the gloom, Symington saw his face lit up by the screen on his phone.

Bower held the phone to his ear. 'You see, I've always been a belts and braces man, me. I'm over insured right across the board.' He paused. 'Hello, mate, how's it going?' He listened for a while, chuckling at what he was being told. 'You dirty bastard! I didn't know you had a weakness for older women. Here, put her on, will you?' He held out the phone and pressed a button activating the loudspeaker. 'Hello, love, do you want a word with your daughter?'

It was as though someone had taken a knife to Symington's heart. Panic set in as she heard the familiar tones of her mother's voice.

'Why am I here? We've done nothing wrong, Carrie.'

'Mum!' Symington wailed.

'These policemen came in the middle of the night. They've taken your father away. They say I can't speak to a solicitor until later on this morning. I hope you can sort this out, dear. What on earth is going on?'

Bower was out of his chair and holding his finger to Symington's lips. He whispered in her ear. 'Play nice, and tell Mummy you're doing what you can. It must be a mistake.' The menace in his voice was plain.

'Listen, don't worry, Mum. I'll make some calls. As you say, it must be some mistake or other. Try not to worry.'

'Thank you, dear. You don't know how good it is to hear your voice.' Another voice could be heard muttering on the other end of the line. 'They say I've got to go. Do what you can, Carrie. And phone Mr Pinkney, if you don't mind. He dealt with the house for us. I'm sure he can get to grips with this mess – he's a good lawyer.' The line went dead.

Symington looked up into Bower's face. She could make out his features now that he was so close, the enlarged pores on his nose. He was sneering down at her. 'If you harm them . . .' She began to sob.

Bower's face was only inches from Symington's now. 'One wrong move from you and I'll make sure your lovely parents have a very uncomfortable time. Right now they think it's a mistaken arrest. I'll make sure they're okay while you do your bit.'

'Anything!'

'That's the spirit. You see, I know your brave boys know you're in the mire. So they won't take things upstairs if you tell them not to. So, at worst, I've got a few country cops to deal with. At best, they'll be good boys and obey orders. It's your job to keep them on side. I'm sure you get it.'

Symington nodded her head silently. Then she pictured Jim Daley and Brian Scott. The thought of them blindly obeying orders sent her heart thudding in her chest.

Annie had woken early. She was used to being disturbed by the nocturnal sounds of the hotel. Over the years, her ears had become accustomed to the raucous conduct of drunken guests, bickering partners, people in distress, courting couples, the lot. But this night was different. She looked at her bedside clock again: just after four.

Her sleep had been troubled since Hamish had disappeared, but tonight was the worst yet. Her troubled dreams had turned into full-blown nightmares. She was in a bar; it was like the one she called her own, but unlike it at the same time. Bigger, grander, the place was familiar, but unfamiliar too.

The old man held out his hand to her. She hugged him. She could smell the familiar odours of tobacco, whisky and the sea she always associated with him. 'It'll be okay, Hamish,' she heard herself say. 'Trust me, you'll be fine.'

She pulled away from his embrace, suddenly frightened. She stared at his face, expecting to see those familiar slanting eyes, the leathery skin tanned by so many summers at sea. But instead, his eyes were tightly closed, and dark blood was pouring from his mouth.

Annie remembered screaming in her dream. She wasn't sure if she had screamed out loud, but her throat was dry and sore.

Now convinced she'd get no more sleep, she switched on her bedside lamp. Blinking in the light, she picked up a brick of a book by Danielle Steel, desperately in search of anything that would take her mind off Hamish and the nightmare she'd experienced. She'd just opened the book, leaving her bookmark on the bedside table, when she heard something. Now she knew she was awake, and this was no dream. Someone was shouting and doing so very aggressively.

Being high summer, the hotel was almost full. Annie went over the guest list in her mind. Mostly couples, mostly old, apart from a travelling salesman in room twelve and a teacher in twenty-two. They'd all seemed like nice folk when she'd checked them in, served them with drinks and meals, or passed the time of day in the hotel lobby. But from bitter experience, Annie knew that looks could be deceptive. In any case, it was her job to make sure everyone was okay and none of the other guests in the establishment were being disturbed.

She slipped her dressing gown over her onesie and thrust her feet into her slippers. She was irritated by the shouting, which she could still hear. She'd had a bad enough night, and this was all she needed.

Unlike the guest corridors, hers was unlit save for the exit sign that shone brightly just above the stairwell. Quickly, she realised that the shouting wasn't coming from one of the guests' rooms, but from the suite occupied by Ian Macmillan.

She edged her way along the corridor, holding the dressing gown tight at her neck. His door was ajar, and a crack of light cast a bright wedge across the carpet before her. She hesitated a moment, and then put her eye to the gap.

'Don't give me excuses, just get this fucking thing done!'

In Annie's experience, Macmillan had always been quietly spoken, and she was sure she hadn't heard him swear. She thought for a moment, then decided that whatever it was that was incensing him, it wasn't her business. He'd stopped shouting, and for Annie that signalled it was time to go back to her room and leave her boss to it. But as she turned, her foot alighted on one of the many old floorboards that should have been replaced a long time ago, and it creaked loudly in protest. Annie winced.

She'd taken another few steps towards her room when the corridor lights stuttered into life.

'Annie, you okay?' Macmillan was standing in the corridor wearing a shirt open almost to the waist and a pair of dark trousers. His hair was standing on end, and his eyes looked puffy and red under the harsh light. Annie was sure he was unsteady on his feet. In fact, though she'd never seen him take more than a couple of bottled beers, she could have sworn he was the worse for drink. 'Hey, did I wake you? I'm sorry.'

'No, nae problem, Ian. I was just checking everything was okay with the guests.'

'Yeah, sure – of course.' He ran his hand through his messed-up hair. 'It's your job. I should be more careful. Sometimes I forget I'm not at home.'

Annie returned what she felt had been his forced smile.

'Family, yeah? Who needs them?'

'Oh, I know that feeling. Don't think any mair o' it, Ian.'

'That's very decent of you. I apologise, Annie. I suppose I should try and get some sleep. It's all this flying – I'm still on Canada time.'

'Aye, it canna be easy, right enough.' Annie wished him goodnight and headed back to her room. Something about the incident made her uneasy. If he'd been talking to a member of his family, it was someone he wasn't very fond of, that was certain. Perhaps his estranged wife – she knew they were at odds. But if indeed it had been her, the sheer venom with which he had spoken to the mother of his children was surprising.

Och, it's none o' my business, she reasoned.

Suddenly tired, she switched off her bedside light. She

hoped to sleep for a couple of hours before it was time to get up. But now more unwanted thoughts crowded in. Annie tossed and turned as the quiet half-light of the early summer morning encroached round the edges of the thin curtains.

25

The police car left Daley, Scott and Constable Watson at the head of the pier. In the weak haze of the summer morning everything looked bleached of colour: the loch was a dark oily slate as it lapped at the sea stairs, the buildings that housed the offices of the harbour master, the fish buyers, fuel vendors and civil servants appeared grey, and only the fluorescent pink buoys amidst a tumble of nets showed any sign of reflecting the sun's first rays. Across the loch, Daley spotted a terracotta-tiled roof, which marked the house out from the rest of the expensive properties that marched up the hill opposite. A seal popped its head above the treacle-smooth water, disappearing again just as quickly. The detective noticed how the normally strong scent of the sea and the creatures that dwelt within it also seemed somehow diminished.

But to the east the sun was already doing its job, as a salmon-hued sky began to spread out above a layer of thin altocumulus cloud that would soon burn off as the morning progressed, again bathing the town in warmth.

'Red sky in the morning,' said Scott, an ominous tone to his voice.

'Good to see you're staying positive,' said Daley as they walked along the jetty. A fisherman of middle years, with a pockmarked face and a habitual frown that made him look permanently furious, was pulling a large orange net aboard his boat, which was sitting proudly at the side of the pier on the high tide.

'Good morning, gents,' he said as he watched the police officers approach. 'You've picked a fine morning for it.'

'See what I mean?' whispered Scott in Daley's ear. 'This bastard always looks as though he's about tae pull your heid off.'

'Good morning, Mr Duncan. It's very good of you to help us in this way,' said Daley.

'Aye, yous are paying well for my services, so no quibble there.' Then, in a slightly less mercenary tone, 'Of course, if it's Hamish yous are looking for then I'd have happily done the job for nothing.'

'I can't say anything about that, Mr Duncan. But as I'm sure you know, we're doing everything in our power to find him.' The words tripped off the tongue too easily, and Daley felt a sudden ache in his heart. At first, having been ill not long before, he worried that something physical was wrong. But he soon realised that the sensation was more to do with his concern over the old man who had befriended him and saved his life. It was a potent emotion.

Scott eyed the fishing boat with a less than enthusiastic expression. 'How dae I get aboard this thing?'

'How do you think?' Duncan replied.

Scott looked over the edge of pier. 'There's a gap there you could fit a horse through.' He scanned the lapping water between the jetty and the vessel.

'Man, it's coming to the bit if the polis are scared tae jump aboard a boat. I've no' had much experience of trains, but I've seen a bigger gap between them and the platform. Are you frightened o' that, tae?' Duncan smiled thoughtfully. 'It was a bonnie creature, right enough.'

'What was?' Scott asked.

'The train I was on. Och, a while back now – maybe seventy-nine, or thereabouts.'

'You've no' been on a train since nineteen seventy-nine?'

'No, I have not. And I dare say I'll no' be on any mair before my time's oot. But I just had tae get a ride on one, just once. I'd seen them in the comics an' that when I was a boy – went all the way to Glasgow on the bus, special, like.' Duncan reminisced about his short excursion on the rails. As Kinloch was the most remote place on the UK mainland from a train station, he wasn't alone among locals in his interest in a form of transport that was commonplace elsewhere.

'Where did you go?'

'Airdrie an' back. Man, did the thing no' get up a fair move on! Fair skooshing past the cars on the motorway an' that.'

'Where did you go when you got tae Airdrie?'

'You're an inquisitive bugger right enough, Mr Scott. If you must know, I sat on the platform and watched the world go by for a while, then I jumped on another train and came back tae Glasgow. I went intae this wee pub for a couple o' drams tae make the journey home on the bus mair tolerable. Ach, you know fine how curious they Glasgow punters are – especially when they're in their cups. This keelie comes up tae me an' asks where I'm fae, and whoot I've been doing in the city. When I telt him he stroked his chin and telt me that you can see Ben Lomond fae Airdrie.' Duncan shook his head. 'Man, I'm here tae tell you, it made me fair homesick for the toon, so it did.'

Scott looked confused. 'Ben Lomond's nowhere near Kinloch.'

'No, very true. But if you go up Ben Saarnie on a clear enough day, you can see it, plain as the nose on your face. It's a helluva thing tae get your heid around, right enough, but apparently it's true. Imagine that: you can be standing in Airdrie, and on top o' that hill o'er there, an' be looking at the same place. Toons that are miles and hours apart. I'm thinking that Einstein was right enough.' Through his frown, it was clear the whole notion still befuddled Duncan. He bent back over his nets.

Scott looked at Daley and twirled his finger round at his temple. 'Away wae the fairies, this mob,' he whispered.

It was Daley's turn to frown at Scott. But as he did so, the familiar strains of the *Sopranos* theme sounded from his pocket, alerting him to a call on his mobile. He retrieved the phone and squinted at the screen. *Symington* flashed across it.

'Yes, ma'am,' he said brightly, walking away from the small group beside Duncan's fishing boat.

'Good morning, Jim.' Symington sounded tired, but it was still very early, so Daley thought little of it. 'Your trip to the island. I take it you've not left yet?'

'Just about to.'

'Well, you'll have to abandon it, Jim. Orders from above. ACC Hunter.'

'What? But Hamish could be there. You know about the photographs – it's a firm lead, Carrie!' Daley's voice was raised now, attracting Scott's attention. 'In any case, how on earth does ACC Hunter know about this, and what's his reasoning behind aborting?'

'You drew firearms, Jim. He's been ACC in charge overnight. Seems as though he authorised the operation, then had second thoughts. It's connected to our dead aviators.' She hesitated. 'I'm sorry, Jim. I know how anxious you are about Hamish. I've just called Sergeant Shaw. He's expecting you back with the weapons. He'll sign them back in and confirm it with HQ.'

'Come on, Carrie, you can surely go in to bat for us here?'

'I tried. He was adamant. He obviously knows something we don't.'

Daley reflected for a moment; an unpleasant notion crossed his mind. He lowered his voice. 'Carrie, are you okay? I mean, you're not under any duress, are you?'

'Me? No, I'm absolutely fine. I'm still in bed at the hotel, actually.' Suddenly, Symington sounded brighter.

'Okay. If I've no choice, I've no choice, that seems clear.'

'Sorry, Jim. I'll see you about lunchtime. I've some calls and emails to catch up with from up the road. I'll do them here, might as well.'

'Yes, ma'am. See you then.' Daley ended the call unceremoniously and beckoned Scott, who hurried over.

'Problem, Jimmy?'

'That was Symington. Looks like our little jaunt is off.'

'Eh? What aboot Hamish?'

'I know. Hunter, an ACC, has put a hold on it. She says it's because he knows something we don't about the plane.'

'So they reckon Hamish disappearing is something to do wae that?'

'Looks like it.'

'Are you men ready? I've a job tae be on with, you know,' Duncan shouted.

'Give us a moment please, Mr Duncan,' said Daley.

'Are you thinking what I'm thinking? How did she sound?'

'Bit tired, Bri. But look at the time.' Daley bit his lip.

'Tell you what, you an' the boy go back up tae the ranch, check in the firearms. I've got tae go to the doctor – I'm sure you won't mind if I come in a bit late, eh?' Scott winked.

'I can't take that risk. If what she's saying is right, who knows what you could be walking into. You saw those pictures. We've had every boat in Kinloch out looking for him. I've felt guilty about it, but people wanted to do something, and there was always a chance they'd turn something up.'

'You can be over there in a flash if I get intae trouble.' Scott looked Daley squarely in the face. 'I'm no' missing out on saving the auld fella, Jimmy.'

Daley met his eyes, and pressed the screen of his phone. 'Sergeant Shaw, I hear you're expecting us.'

'Yes, sir. I've just spoken to Chief Superintendent Symington.'

'I need you to do me a favour.'

'Of course, sir.'

'Get hold of ACC Hunter at HQ and tell him I'd like to speak to him – urgently.'

'I will. Do you want me to give him your mobile number?'

'Yes, that would be ideal. Oh, and stand down as far as the firearms are concerned. I'll wait until I've spoken to him.'

'No problem. I'm on it now, sir.' Shaw paused. 'And good luck.'

Daley smiled. 'Thank you, sergeant.' Call ended, Daley held down the button on the side of his phone, switching it off.

'Like that is it, Jimmy?'

'What would you do, Brian?'

'I'd probably just have gone and no' said a dickie bird. But then, I'm a reckless bastard.'

'Right, come on. Let's go. And switch off your phone!'

Symington had pretended to be tired for Daley's benefit, but the reverse was true. Every fibre of her being was screaming at her for being so stupid. She'd been living a lie for so long, the lie had become reality. She'd been selfish, thinking only of her own career, her own freedom. But now much more important things were at stake: the lives of her parents.

Bower had gone, but the smell of his aftershave lingered in the hotel room like a dead fish, unwanted. She opened a window and let the cool salty air of the early morning banish its unwelcome stench. Outside, the waters of the Atlantic were lapping on to the white sand. An early morning dog walker was at the other end of the beach, while a cormorant took to the air in a typically low, clumsy flight before settling on another rock, the iridescence of its coat reflected in the burgeoning light of the new day.

Symington had worried how Bower would be able to slip in and out of the hotel without being spotted.

'Hiding in plain sight is my speciality,' he'd replied.

Once he'd identified himself as one of her colleagues, nobody thought anything of his visits. And if they did – even in this tight-knit community – they valued their jobs too much to risk them with idle gossip about a guest. Especially when that guest was a senior police officer.

To Symington, Bower had become the repository of all that was bad. He seemed invulnerable, capable of murdering and kidnapping with impunity. Why the DI investigating

Chappell's murder had swallowed his story, she wasn't sure. Maybe he was in on the whole thing. Suddenly Symington questioned her entire profession. Was it really so easy to commit serious crimes and get away with them? She knew many who had. It seemed that a lie about the simple theft of a car had been enough to free Bower of any suspicion.

She knew Jim Daley would never have taken this at face value, in the same way she knew he'd disobey her order to stay away from the island. She felt guilty about the deceit, but with her mother and father at the mercy of such ruthless people, what else could she do?

Carrie Symington was now actively helping Bower. Not only by doing what she was told but by using her knowledge of people like Daley to help him. She reckoned the big detective would assume she was under pressure to stop him from going to search for Hamish, but the story about ACC Hunter was true. Symington didn't have the time to consider why this was, but when she'd received the call from the man in temporary charge of Police Scotland during the previous night, she'd realised that it presented an opportunity to allow her to do what Bower wanted.

Jim Daley was true to his friends – always. She'd played at being tired badly, and her bright answer to his question about being 'under duress' had surely been nowhere near convincing enough to fool him.

But fool him she had. It had been Bower's idea. Faced with Symington's obligation to pass on the ACC's message to Daley, he'd taken the calculated risk of placing faith in the DCI's integrity, his decency in helping his own.

Bower had been right.

She'd called the office twenty minutes after her call to

her DCI. Shaw was sure-footed, but a poor liar. Daley hadn't gone for an early breakfast; he'd gone to try to find his friend.

Symington supposed that a life of deceit, albeit for what she saw as sufficient reasons at the time, had made her good at it. But all she had achieved was to mislead her colleagues, lie to her friends and family, and place those closest to her in danger.

She took in her reflection in the wardrobe mirror. She had showered and was in full uniform now, complete with braid and insignia. But all the chief superintendent saw was an empty shell, a carapace. She was nothing more than adorned artifice. She'd endangered her own career a long time ago, and had kept it by allowing herself to be abused and manipulated in order to perpetuate a lie. Now she was putting Daley's career in jeopardy.

Symington closed her eyes for a moment. This was surely her end. But in it she could do the right thing at last. She could save her parents and she could set the record straight, tell the truth. But before she could do any of this she had to reel Bower in and catch him, and to do so involved more lies.

Then she thought of the old man with the pipe and the faded Breton cap.

26

With a little help from Daley and Constable Watson, Brian had managed to make his way up the side of Duncan's fishing boat and safely on to the deck. This achievement wasn't something that made him particularly proud, or happy. He was back – however briefly – at sea.

'That's it,' he said sourly. 'I'm putting in for a posting as far away from water as possible.'

'Better to wait for your inspector's post to be made permanent, no?' Daley replied.

'I don't care! I'll go back tae being a beat cop for the rest o' my service.' Scott looked at Watson, a young constable with a string of qualifications. Much had been made of these academic achievements by the senior management at Police Scotland, and it was clear he was being marked out for greater things. No doubt, thought Scott, he'd been sent down to work with him and Daley to discover how things shouldn't be done. In that case, as they sailed out of the harbour, it was clear that they were doing very well by him.

'Here, son, just you gie me that kit o' yours an' you can stand in as the acting inspector o' the aquatic branch, here.'

Watson eyed him nervously. 'I'm not sure Force Standing Orders permit that, sir.'

'Did you memorise a' that guff?'

'Well, yes, I suppose so.'

'See that, Jimmy. The boy knows all aboot it. You're the man for us, right enough, constable, because he cannae remember, and I never knew anything aboot it in the first place.'

'I think what ADI Scott is trying to say is that you won't find it all in a book,' said Daley. 'He's been saying it since he was my gaffer.'

Watson looked between the two detectives. 'That's a joke, right?'

'Bugger you,' said Scott. 'I taught him all he knows.'

'And some,' said Daley. 'But it's absolutely true.'

'Aye, you too can reach the heights o' the DCI. Just you stay close to me, son.'

Scott jumped away from the side of the boat. A long grey shape was arcing through the waters of the loch. 'What the fuck is that?'

'Och, you needna worry, at all. Jeest a big basking shark,' said skipper Duncan. 'Harmless they are. It's a while since I've seen one this close in, mind you. The good weather will have brought them in. Mysterious creatures they are, tae. Disappear in the winter – nobody knows where – then back in the spring. Nothing tae get your knickers in a twist aboot. They've only got teeth like weans.'

Scott looked unconvinced. 'I don't know. That nephew o' mine bit me when he was a wee boy. Broke the skin, so he did.'

'The way you jumped when you saw it, you'd have thought you'd seen a great white.' Duncan laughed.

'Not so much jumping the shark as jumping away from the shark,' said Daley with a smile.

Though Scott and Duncan looked puzzled, Watson laughed heartily.

'One o' they intellectual jokes, I take it, Jimmy?'

'Something like that, Bri.'

'Sir, when should I switch my radio back on?' said Watson, clearly troubled by this breach of standing orders.

'Just you keep your hand on your ha'penny,' said Scott. 'We're going intae a situation where stealth is required. We're no' wanting to be aboot tae sneak up on some bugger just as Shaw radios the beat man tae ask for a pie fac the bakery, are we?'

'No, true. I never considered that, sir.'

'Jeest you leave the considering tae me an' DCI Daley. You'll have plenty time tae get considering as you go. Enjoy the freedom while it lasts – it doesnae last long, by the way.'

'I heard you mention ACC Hunter,' said Watson.

'Do you know him?' Scott asked.

'He's my uncle.' He looked at Daley. 'Not that I'm name dropping or anything, sir.'

'He's a fine man,' said Daley.

'Aye, the kipper's knickers,' said Scott. He threw Daley a doubtful glance.

'It's a pity we're nearly ready tae drop yous off,' said Duncan. 'I've got some great kipper tales.'

'Fuck me, I'm heartbroken tae miss that,' said Scott.

They had just passed through the channel between the island and the straggle of houses that marked the edge of Kinloch. Duncan slowed the engine and glided his small vessel towards the rocky shoreline. 'This is as near as I can get you, lads. It's as well it's a high tide, or I widna have dared go in this close.'

Scott looked over the side. 'Hang on, we'll need tae swim!'

'Not a bit o' it. The water will likely no' even reach the top o' your thighs.'

'Jimmy's maybe, but we're no' all giants like him.' Scott looked back towards Kinloch.

'What's up, Bri?' said Daley.

'Aye, get on wae it,' said Duncan.

'What aboot Jaws back there, eh?'

'Don't be ridiculous. I telt you, nothing tae worry aboot.'

'Tell that tae the assistant chief constable when the bloody thing eats his nephew!'

Suddenly pale, Watson looked over the side of the boat into the clear water at the island's edge.

Sergeant Shaw looked briefly taken aback when Symington appeared in the office. But he quickly regained his composure and greeted her with a polite, 'Good morning, ma'am.'

She smiled. 'Anything happening I should know about, sergeant?'

'Nothing that springs to mind, ma'am.'

'Have you got a touch of the sun, Shaw?' Symington had noticed his face redden.

'Yes – the weather's been brilliant, hasn't it?' He looked down at his work, hoping Symington had nothing else to say to him.

'DCI Daley is back, I take it?'

'No, ma'am, not to my knowledge.' Now Shaw looked nervous.

'Oh. Okay, I'll get him on his mobile. I take it ADI Scott is with him?'

'I believe so.' Shaw was now desperately hoping that

Symington wouldn't ask about the firearms he'd assigned to the pair.

To his relief, she looked through a couple of files absently, checked the daily roster of who was doing what in the sub-division, and made her way out of the bar office.

Shaw sighed with relief. But it was short-lived.

Symington poked her head back round the door. 'Anything from ACC Hunter?'

'Yes, ma'am, he sent an email to DCI Daley. It was for his eyes only. I printed it out and put it in a sealed envelope on the DCI's desk, ma'am.'

'If you don't mind my asking, why didn't you just leave it for him to read on screen? If it's confidential, I mean. And why on earth do you have access to his email messages?'

'It's his instructions, ma'am. He likes to have everything on paper now. Something about flickering screens, ma'am.'

'Good grief! We're going backwards instead of forwards.' Symington marched from Shaw's domain. He held his breath for a moment, but this time she was gone.

Symington made her way not to her own office, but to the CID suite. A couple of young detectives started to stand, but Symington waved them back into their seats before walking into Daley's glass box and closing the door firmly behind her.

Now in her DCI's inner sanctum, she closed the blinds one by one, isolating herself from the wider office beyond. Sure enough, on the blotting pad sat an A4 envelope, marked *For DCI Daley's Eyes Only* in bold red felt-tip, underlined twice.

Symington sat in Daley's large office chair, and again feelings of guilt and shame began to weigh her down. She held the envelope before her face, as though desperate to discern its contents without breaking the seal and opening the missive. But she knew that was a fruitless exercise.

Remembering the plight of her mother and father, she took a neatly manicured nail to the sealed-down portion of the envelope and tore it open. When she peered inside, she saw that two printed sheets of A4 were contained within. She slid them out on to the desk and placed them side by side.

Symington had seen her fair share of redacted documents in her time, but none more so than this. A line of text appeared here and there, interspersed by large blocks of blacked-out information, forming dark, sinister shapes across both pages.

She read what she could, which was basically very little. The make and model of the aircraft that had landed under its own steam while containing two dead men was mentioned. Also noted were the time, location and action taken. She saw the list of attending police, ambulance and fire personnel, including Daley and Scott, and the airfield's own fire and rescue service.

The next five paragraphs were entirely obscured, but by whom it was unclear, as the signature identifying the author of the document had also been redacted. Symington wondered why on earth Daley had been sent this document until she noticed the list of names copied into the circulation at the very bottom of the second page. Daley's name, of course, then that of ACC Hunter, then I. W. Harris, whose designation had been redacted. The name Harris rang a bell in Symington's mind, a bell that connected him somehow to Daley. But she couldn't quite grasp its resonance.

She shook her head at the final line on the page, obviously appended as an afterthought.

For your information.

How bizarre, she thought. She reached for the phone.

'Hello?' Shaw's voice was uncertain, the sergeant no doubt confused by the fact that he was taking a call from Daley's internal line, while knowing for certain that his superior wasn't there.

'This email – I'm reading it now. Why's it almost completely redacted?'

Shaw hesitated.

'Spit it out, sergeant! I am the boss around here, you know.'

'Ma'am, if you look at the sender, it may shed light on that particular aspect of the email.'

Symington looked at the top of the first page but could only see Daley's name. 'Stop talking in riddles, man! Who sent this?'

Shaw cleared his throat. 'MI5, ma'am.'

Symington looked further up the page. Sure enough, in very small text stretched out across the top, she made out *MI5* amidst an indecipherable clutter of hypertext.

It was then that realisation struck her. Of course she'd heard of Harris! He was the MI5 officer who'd been involved in the case of the missing family on Gairsay.

Symington shivered. Now things were truly spiralling out of her control.

Daley was first to ease himself down into the sea. He was surprised that it only reached just above his knees. 'Right, come on!' he shouted to Scott and Watson, who were still peering over the side of the vessel.

'You're next, son,' said Scott.

'Yes, sir,' said Constable Watson, dutifully obeying his superior officer by climbing over the guardrail and slipping

189

down into the clear cold water. 'Oh, shit!' he proclaimed as the sea rose halfway up his thighs. At around six feet tall, he was shorter than Daley. But Scott, at only five foot ten, was shorter still.

'The first couple o' seconds will be the worst,' said Duncan, rather unhelpfully, as Scott made his way gingerly over the rail.

'Until it hits my bollocks, you mean.'

'Aye, something like that.' Rather surprisingly, the fisherman's habitual frown melted into a broad smile and he chuckled heartily. 'Working wae the polis is a much happier diversion than I thought it would be!'

Scott hesitated on the small ledge at the other side of the rail. He scanned the calm sea, looking for the 'harmless' basking shark that he'd spotted a short time earlier.

'Och, is that you fretting o'er thon big fish?'

'Aye,' said Scott emphatically.

'It's no' the basking sharks you should be worried aboot. But they orcas – now they're right dangerous.'

'What's an orca?'

'You'd likely know it as a killer whale.'

Scott was about to abort his dalliance with the waves when he heard a call from the shore.

'Hurry up, Bri, we haven't got all bloody morning!' Daley was standing beside Constable Watson on the rocky shoreline.

'Oh shit!' said Scott as he abandoned himself to the elements. The water was cold, and he had to stand on tiptoes to avoid further immersion than he'd have wished. But in this awkward way, in a flourish of white water, he made his way as quickly as was humanly possible towards the shore. He noticed that the seabed darted up the nearer he got to Daley and Watson. When he was only feet from them he lunged up the slope, feeling very exposed in an element as unwelcome as it was unfamiliar to him. Unfortunately, his walking boot caught on an unseen rock, and he pitched forward into the water.

Though the tide broke his fall, it was a pathetic, dripping creature that emerged from the depths. From behind, he could hear Duncan's throaty chortle, while ahead Daley shook his head and Watson looked as though he didn't quite know how to greet the occurrence.

'Bugger it!' said Scott, shaking his arms to expel seawater from inside the sleeves of his jacket. 'I'll never complain aboot being in a boat again. Being in one's nothing tae being oot o' one.'

The note of Duncan's engine rose as he chugged away in a plume of diesel fumes and billowing smoke.

'When's he coming back for us?' said Scott, regarding the waves with particular loathing as he pushed his soaking hair back off his forehead with both hands.

'We can walk back if necessary,' said Daley, as he took in their position.

'Eh? I know you've got a high opinion o' yourself, big man. But I didnae think even you would reckon walking on water was an option.'

'There's a tidal causeway, Brian. Remember?'

'Why the fuck did we no' just walk o'er here then?'

'Take a look.'

Scott followed Daley's pointing finger. Sure enough, like a serpent snaking just below the surface, the twisting shape of the causeway could be seen below the still waters of the loch.

'Let's not forget why we're here, Brian.'

'Aye, big man, I get it. Right. Which way tae these lighthouse buildings, then?'

'Follow me.' Daley squelched off across the boulder-strewn shoreline, his two, thoroughly miserable companions close behind.

27

Chief Superintendent Carrie Symington was still sitting in Daley's office – desperate to work this problem through, desperate to save her parents.

But she had been given another job to do by the ruthless Bower.

Symington had always been observant – even as a child. She'd spot any change to the house that her mother made: the slightest movement of an ornament, a missing painting, a new radio. Any number of insignificant things that would have passed most other children by, she picked up.

One thing she'd noticed about Daley was now very important. He kept the passwords for his phone, tablet and computer written on a small piece of paper taped to the side of a drawer. She just hoped the drawer was open.

Symington pulled at the handle, and sure enough, it creaked open. She paid no attention to the bottle of whisky or drinking glasses it contained, but quickly took a mental note of Daley's computer password. She didn't doubt that Shaw also had access to the device, but asking him would have been a last resort.

Quickly, she keyed in the password, and looked on anxiously as the computer booted up. Despite being sure that

Daley was off looking for Hamish, the time it took the machine to become operational seemed endless. But eventually a large image of Daley's son filled the screen, and she knew she was in.

Her instructions were specific. She had to remove something from Daley's files and make sure that no copies had been made. Though Symington was no computer expert, she figured that this shouldn't be too difficult. But she realised that she'd have to check with Shaw as to the distribution list, if indeed the images had been distributed at all. It was a risk she had to take. Bower reckoned that she would have a day at the very most to do his bidding before Daley cottoned on. And while she hoped he was right, the irony of the situation wasn't lost on her. Here she was following the instructions of a heartless killer, destroying files that formed part of a major operation.

She saw her mother's kind, open face. The smile that always seemed to play across her father's mouth, as though he could burst into laughter at any time. She was alone in the world apart from them. She couldn't bear the thought of losing that unconditional love to some horror of her own making.

Symington swept a stray strand of hair from her forehead as she searched through Daley's most recent downloads. She found crime scene photos from a number of cases, most recently those from the Doig inquiry. She came across scanned documents of court files and witness statements. She even found pictures of the light aircraft that, by crashing into a chain-link fence with two dead men on board, had somehow kicked off the nightmare she currently occupied. The faces of those men stared back at her with the blank gaze of passport photographs. On mortuary gurneys they looked as they were: utterly devoid of life.

Symington's mind wandered back to her parents. She could see them in her mind's eye, their chest and stomach cavities cut open in post-mortem examinations and then sewn roughly with the thick black thread of the trade. The waxy skin puckered where ruined flesh had been drawn together. That was the problem with being a police officer: you couldn't unsee the seen, couldn't expel the many horrific sights that had passed before your eyes from training right through your career. And you couldn't stop projecting those horrors on to those closest to you.

At first, Symington had thought herself alone in this morbidity. But the longer she worked as a police officer, the more she realised that just about everyone in the job felt the same. You could dismiss it – laugh about it, even. But as the day neared its end and the lights went out, a catalogue of ghouls in a parade of despair crossed the mind of anyone with a heart.

She banged the desk in front of her in an act of frustration that wouldn't have been unfamiliar to the man whose computer she now searched so frantically. She knew Daley had the images that Bower wanted deleted – she'd seen them herself. She just couldn't find them now.

Chief Superintendent Carrie Symington could feel the throb of terror in her chest, and the brim of tears in her eyes. Again she looked through recently downloaded files, email archives, images, trash and spam folders. There was nothing, nothing at all to indicate that the images of Hamish's encounter with the men on the RIB had ever existed.

She held her head in her hands, staring absently at

Daley's scribbled doodles on the ink blotter in front of her. Like him, it was old-fashioned. There he was again: an analogue man in a digital age. Even though he'd learned how to work with computers, she knew that he'd have rather used the methods with which he'd been inculcated as a young police officer. On the other hand, Scott hadn't even bothered to take his dealings with technology that far. He knew the bare minimum about the many IT systems with which police officers had to familiarise themselves in order to carry out their duties in a modern police force. But when it came to instinct, both he and Daley had few peers.

It was then she had an idea. Frantically, Symington rifled through the drawers of Daley's desk. The analogue man who preferred printed emails must surely also prefer photographs to flickering electronic images. She resolved to search every inch of Daley's glass box.

The going underfoot on the island was difficult. The small boulders that had greeted them at the rocky beach on which they had been unceremoniously landed had morphed into ever larger ones the further they progressed. Scott cursed as he slipped and grazed an elbow while trying to traverse a boulder almost as high as himself. But it was the most direct route, and the will to locate Hamish drove all three of them on.

Out of breath and irritated, Scott finally caught up with Daley and Watson who were standing just ahead.

'You okay there?' said Daley.

'You'd need tae be Dumby Dave tae make it safely across this lot,' Scott wailed. 'How come the smiling fisherman didnae set us doon nearer tae these cottages?'

'Because if there is anyone there they would have seen us.'

'Are they no' roon that corner?' Scott pointed the way ahead.

'Yes, they are as a matter of fact.'

'Well, how would they have seen us, Jimmy?'

'Think about it, Bri. If you were up to no good, you'd be on the lookout for trouble, wouldn't you?'

'I've been up tae no good for years, and I've never had tae look out for trouble. It just came my way of its own accord, out o' the blue.' He looked at Constable Watson. 'Don't you go telling your uncle that. I'm only joking, son.'

'Okay, now we have to be more careful. If anyone is in these cottages, we need to flush them out with the least fuss possible,' said Daley, unholstering his weapon.

'Aye, I'm sure you're right, Jimmy. But I cannae get my heid roon this mush.'

'In what way?'

'The guys in the plane, Hamish disappearing, folk up tae no good on this bloody rock. What's the connection?'

'What would you have said if you'd seen barrels of whisky?'

'Smugglers!' said Watson excitedly, anxious to contribute.

'So that's what you reckon is going on? I've got tae say, big man, I cannae see the logic there at all. I mean, what were those poor bastards on the plane smuggling, eh?'

'Who knows? Could have been a message – a warning.'

'Okay, so it's smuggling. Let's just imagine that for a minute. But what's being smuggled, and why would you dae it here, right in front o' a toon?'

'Have you ever heard of the saying, "hiding in plain sight"?'

'If you say so, Jimmy.' Scott re-examined his injured elbow.

'Right, come on.' Daley crouched down and made his way stealthily towards the corner around which the lighthouse and the old cottages built for the men who used to tend it were located.

Above a small escarpment they could see the tall tapering cylinder of the lighthouse, still operational, but automatic now and requiring little human attention. To the right were the grey roofs of the keepers' accommodation.

'There's a path,' whispered Scott.

'We can't just stroll up there, Brian.' Daley scanned his surroundings. Just in front of them was the escarpment, only slightly taller than Daley himself. 'We get up that way,' he said, pointing to the sheer bank of boulders and rough patches of grass.

'We should have brought a rope. Or better still, a set o' ladders,' said Scott.

'Don't worry. I reckon I can get up there quite easily,' said Watson.

'Aye, that's why we brought you, son. Just you get up there an' haul me and big Jimmy up.'

The young constable looked warily at Daley, worried he'd somehow insulted his senior officers.

'And if you drop either o' us, I'll be the first one on tae that uncle o' yours. Aye, quick smart.'

Ignoring Scott, Daley nodded, and the younger man made his way, tentatively at first, then with ease, up the sheer face of earth and rock. He leaned out over the edge and offered Daley his hand. With some grunting and groaning on both their parts, the DCI was up. Daley lay down, and Watson pulled a protesting Scott up on to the rise.

'Fuck me. Deep-sea swimming, sharks, mountaineering – I'd never have volunteered for this if I thought we would need Bear whatshisname wae us.' With a disgruntled expression,

Scott tried to brush his rain jacket clean. But still soaking after his submersion near the shore, he only succeeded in slathering a large stripe of mud across it, then on to his face as he rubbed his chin. 'Just as well my Ella's no' here. That's all I'm saying.'

Daley moved up the rise of rough grass littered with black sheep droppings. Peering over the top, he signalled to Scott and Watson to join him.

From there, the police officers could see down on to the shale ledge upon which the lighthouse and the dwellings had been constructed. The lighthouse jutted tall and proud from a huge concrete base. It looked well maintained, painted in a gleaming white, with only the slightest smear across its lower half, a testament to the rough weather that came off the sound and no amount of maintenance could keep entirely at bay. The three old cottages were another matter. One roof was almost completely caved into the dwelling below, while the others were moss covered and looked as though they could follow suit at any moment. There was no sign of life: no smoke from the tumbledown chimneys or movement behind the tiny dark holes where once windows had protected those inside from the elements.

'If these smugglers you're reckoning on are holed up here, best o' luck tae them,' Scott whispered.

'Come on, we'll go in closer,' said Daley. He made his way over the brow of the small hill, and with his pistol held out in front of him hurried to the broken-down row of cottages.

Scott drew his weapon and urged Watson on. Though the young man moved forward eagerly enough, he bore a doubtful expression.

'What's up wae your coupon?' said Scott.

'I'm just thinking about your firearm, sir.'

'Don't worry, I've all the right certificates, if that's what you're worrying aboot.'

'No, of course. I was just wondering if it'll work – you know, after you falling into the sea.'

Scott hadn't thought of this. And as he watched Daley approach the nearest cottage, he pictured a gang of desperate smugglers appearing round the corner armed to the teeth while his own sidearm wouldn't fire because of water damage. He turned to Watson. 'Och, I've seen it in loads o' films. You don't see Rambo oot wae the towel when he emerges fae some river or other.'

'Who?'

'Before your time, son. But just substitute Captain America – you'll likely have heard o' him.'

'He doesn't have a gun, sir. And anyway, he's not real.'

'Neither is Rambo! Come on.'

They rushed towards Daley, joining him by the gable wall of the first cottage.

'What dae you reckon, Jimmy?'

'Well, given there's no sign of a RIB or any other vessel in the bay down there, who knows?'

'What's that smell?' said Watson, curling up his nose.

It soon became apparent from where the stench was coming. A khaki tarpaulin was spread out over an indeterminate shape, around which flies were buzzing furiously.

Scott looked at Daley. 'You don't think . . .'

Daley's face was pale. He crouched over the tarpaulin, and with the toe of his boot lifted the filthy sheet. Dreading to see Hamish's corpse.

28

Terry Johnstone opened his eyes. The pain in his head was worse than any hangover he'd ever experienced. He tried to swallow, but it took no little effort. He was lying face down on a cold floor. Though the room was dark, he had the sense of being in a reasonably large space. He was cold, his bones ached, and his mind was a jumble of random thoughts, none of which quite made sense.

He tried to push himself up off the floor, but a wave of nausea brought him back quickly to the position in which he'd first awoken. This time, though, his head was turned to the other side. Though his eyes were crusted, he could see a shape through the gloom. Gradually, the reality of his plight dawned on him. He remembered rescuing the old man imprisoned in the shed. Then they'd become lost in the hills and he'd gone to find help.

With a great effort of will, Terry forced himself into a sitting position, his legs crossed. He felt so sick that he had to lower his head and wait for the unpleasant sensation to pass. After a few minutes, he began to feel better, and with another huge effort he reached out and prodded the body beside him.

'Hamish!' he hissed. 'Is that you?'

But if the still figure was that of the old man, he didn't move.

Terry drew his hand back, feeling sick again, and lowered his head. He was tired – exhausted – and he was sure, had it not been for the nausea, he'd have lain back down and surrendered to sleep. But the conscious part of his brain was willing him to stay awake. His instincts were screaming at him to get out of this place.

Just as he reached out again to try to wake the unconscious man beside him, the room was flooded with light. He tried to turn round and find out where the light was coming from, but before he could discern its source he was kicked in the back. He toppled on to the floor, his mind scrambled again.

'So you're the brave boy, eh?'

The voice was low and rough, but Terry recognised the accent, which if not from Ballycastle was certainly nearby. 'Who are you?' he heard himself splutter.

'Never mind that. Who the fuck are you?'

Terry felt another vicious blow to his side, this time knocking the breath from his lungs. He groaned with pain and lack of air. Another man's voice, younger this time: 'Herself's been on the phone. She's on her way back. We've to wait here, so we have.'

Suddenly the clouds that shrouded Terry's mind cleared. He saw the blue Land Rover coming towards him on the coast road. He'd waved frantically, and they'd stopped.

He remembered a big man and a woman with straggly grey hair. Then he felt the pain.

Symington had been through every drawer, nook and cranny of Daley's office and found nothing. She knew she'd have to risk it and ask Sergeant Shaw if he had copies of the photographs. But as she held her hand to the phone on

Daley's desk, the man she was looking for appeared framed in the doorway.

'Ma'am, we've got a problem.'

She looked at him, confused at first, but then managed to focus. 'What kind of problem?'

'Mr Houston the photographer. He was here seeing DCI Daley recently.'

'Yes, what about him?'

'He's been found badly injured, ma'am. The window cleaner found him an hour or so ago.'

Symington tried to stay calm, but the bile was rising in her throat. 'Is this the man who took the pictures of Hamish's boat?'

'Yes, ma'am. He spoke to me first – showed me the images.' Though Shaw retained his professional bearing, it was clear he was looking to the chief superintendent for guidance, and the incident had thrown him off his stride.

'How bad is he?'

'Bad enough – unconscious when he was taken away in the ambulance.'

Symington swallowed hard. She knew she had to put on a front for Shaw, but it took every ounce of her strength and determination. 'Get me DCI Daley and get him now!'

'Ma'am, he's on the island. I'm sorry.'

'And don't tell me, he's switched off his phone.'

'I don't know about the signal across there.' Though flailing, Shaw was still trying to cover for Daley, who had disobeyed Symington's direct order.

'Get him back! I don't care if you've to send the lifeboat for them – or row them back here yourself. Just get Daley back here now!'

Symington watched Shaw rush off. She hoped that she'd been convincing in her affected wrath. But, she reasoned, her own very real horror had made the emotion seem more genuine. The awful truth was impossible to avoid. As she'd been trying to find and destroy the copies in Daley's office, someone else had found the originals. And it was all her fault. She'd passed the information on to Bower.

His wicked face, then those of her parents, flashed before her.

Carrie Symington was alone, and more frightened than she had ever been in her life.

'Oh, that's rancid!' said Scott, turning away from the rotting sheep that lay under the tarp. The decaying animal stank, and the growing warmth of the morning was making it worse.

Daley held his hand over his face. 'Come on, round the front.'

The police officers were more relaxed now, though still on their guard for anyone lurking inside the cottages. Leaving Watson to keep watch outside, Daley and Scott reached the first door. Though it had seen better days, it was still intact until Scott put his boot to it. The door smashed open, and with Daley covering him Scott entered the building, weapon in hand.

In moments, he came back, shaking his head at Daley, and moved on to inspect the house with the collapsed roof. The DCI's task was easier. The big detective only had to step over a few broken timbers to gain access to the third cottage. Inside, an old table was scattered with empty lager cans and a discarded whisky bottle. Cigarettes had been stamped out on the floor, and the remains of crisp packets, a mouldy, half-eaten pie, and other detritus was scattered around. The cottage may be empty now, but someone had been here recently.

Scott appeared in the doorway. 'So they chose this one to stay in. That must mean whatever was in the mair secure cottage was important – delicate, eh? No sign of life under the collapsed roof, Jimmy. And the other hoose had none o' this.' He moved a crisp packet with his toe.

Despite the mess, it was clear that the new occupants had lived a spartan existence. The dwelling consisted of one room. The table sat in the middle, with a broken sink at the back wall. In place of chairs, boxes had been upturned, and a filthy sleeping bag lay in one corner.

'It's not exactly the Marriott, but someone's been here, and not long ago,' said Daley.

'Heavy drinker, tae, by the look o' things,' Scott remarked.

Daley was hunkered down, examining the cigarette ends. 'More than one person, I'd say. There are at least three different brands here. You know what smokers are like, Brian. They always stick to the one brand.'

'But no sign o' any smuggled goods, eh?'

Watson stuck his head round the door. 'Sirs, there's someone coming from further up the hill. Two people, but I can't make out much more than that. They'll be here soon, though.'

'Get in!' Daley commanded. 'Did they see you?'

'I don't think so, sir. I'd taken your lead and I was observing from the corner of the building.'

'Aye, always right tae take Jimmy's advice, son.' Before anyone could comment, Scott was out of the squalid cottage and edging his head round the corner to look up at the steep hill.

'Two folk, right enough. I think one o' them is a woman, but I cannae be certain. Mind you, they can only be coming here.'

205

'Okay, we wait here. This will be a nice surprise for whoever it is. Maybe this is the key to finding Hamish,' said Daley.

Pressed against the inner wall of the cottage, the police officers held their collective breath. Soon they could hear the murmur of two people in conversation. The police officers made no sound as the voices grew louder.

'They've stopped,' whispered Scott.

Daley listened carefully. Sure enough, the conversation wasn't getting louder, but it was difficult to tell whether the newcomers had stopped or were simply moving away from the buildings.

'Okay, Brian, you go out, flash your warrant card. I'll be right behind you. Constable Watson, you keep a watching brief from here. If anything goes wrong, don't hesitate to press the panic button and get on the radio.' Suddenly, despite their weaponry, Daley realised how exposed they were. The cottage had clearly been inhabited recently, and judging by the images of Hamish's encounter with the RIB there might well be a number of other people on the island they just hadn't seen yet, and they could be nearby.

'Sorry, big man.' Scott's voice was genuinely apologetic.

'What's up, Bri?'

'I don't have my warrant card.'

'Where is it?'

Scott thought for a brief moment. 'The last time I remember, it was on the chest o' drawers in oor bedroom.'

Daley sighed. 'Some things never change, eh, Brian?'

Scott shrugged apologetically.

'Here, take mine. They'll not notice at a distance.'

Watson looked horrified.

'Don't worry, son. I'll no' say anything if you don't,' said Scott as he caught the ID that Daley had thrown to him. 'And don't you mention Force Standing Orders.' In a flash, he was through the door and out into the sunlight. 'Oi, you pair, stand still!' he shouted, brandishing his gun and Daley's ID. He was about to identify himself as a police officer when a loud scream echoed off the sheer rock behind them.

29

Symington was suffering a mixture of emotions as she sat in the back of the police car heading up the hill that led from the town to Firdale. Shaw hadn't been able to raise Daley's party by radio or phone. Though attempts were being made to get a message to the DCI, it was clear that as the senior officer she would have to attend the crime scene at Houston's home.

They turned off the road and down a short driveway. Perched on the hill in a similar fashion to Daley's house, though at a lower elevation, sat a large bungalow. Instead of pointing directly across the loch, its large bay window looked over the island and further out on to the sound.

Chief Superintendent Symington stormed out of the car and was handed a paper suit and plastic overshoes to guard against pollution of the crime scene. She shrugged on the suit and shoes, a grim look on her face, and stared across at the island. She could see the lighthouse standing tall, but the cottages below, where she knew Daley and Scott to be, were obscured by a low hill.

'You stay here,' she said to the young DC at her side. 'I'll go in and take a look about. I take it SOCO are on their way?'

'Yes, ma'am.'

'And find out if anyone has managed to contact DCI Daley yet,' she added emphatically.

As Symington walked into the house, she noticed framed photographs of the area adorning the hallway. They were good. There was no doubt that Houston knew what he was doing when it came to photography.

She passed an open door leading on to a spacious kitchen fitted out with the best of appliances and walked into the living room, where she noticed two things almost simultaneously. The huge picture window she had seen from outside was, if anything, more dramatic than Daley's. The other thing she couldn't help but note was the state of the room. Houston had clearly used the space as an office as well as a living area. Drawers had been pulled out and thrown across the floor, along with their contents. A large computer monitor had been smashed and was lying in pieces among the mess. The cupboard doors of a large unit were open, one hanging off its hinges. Some ornaments were smashed on the grate beside the fire, and a cracked crystal vase lay on its side on a table at the back of the room. The dining area was littered with cutlery, and on the wall a canvas had been diagonally slashed.

It was then she noticed the slather of congealed blood on the table and a white wall nearby. It was clear that Houston had faced extreme violence in the search for the photographs of Hamish and the mystery RIB.

As a wave of guilt swept over her, Symington's attention was diverted to the ring of her mobile phone. As she struggled to manoeuvre it from her trouser pocket through the paper suit, she hoped it was Daley. She was ready to give a bravura performance of being pissed off over his wilful act of disobedience until she saw the screen: *No caller ID available*. She was pretty sure who was on the other line.

'Symington,' she answered in a tentative voice.

'You won't find anything, Carrie. We were very careful.'

'How do you know I'm here? Are you watching me?'

'Never mind that!' Bower's voice was unmistakable. 'Do whatever you have to in the house but be quick about it. I want you up at the hospital. Find out where that arsehole Houston stashed the images we're looking for. He must have it on a cloud drive, but the fucking idiot wouldn't tell us where.'

'We? You said we.'

'What?'

'Who else is there?'

'Carrie.' Bower's voice was now calm. 'The last thing you need to worry about is what I'm doing. Your dear old mum and dad, remember?'

'Yes.'

'Get up to the hospital and find out where those images are, got it?'

'I'll have my work cut out. He's still unconscious.'

'In that case, use your initiative, darling! You didn't get to be a chief super without knowing a thing or two. Do it!'

The line went dead. Carrie Symington stood alone in the ruined room wondering what on earth she was going to do to save her parents.

The woman was wearing a red fleece, shorts and stout walking boots over thick green knitted socks. Scott placed her in late middle age as he approached her and her male companion, both of whom were standing with their hands in the air as though extras in a bad movie.

'Please, don't hurt us,' said the man. He was tall, rangy, and almost bald, only a few loose wisps of hair above his ears being tugged at by the warm breeze off the sea.

'Who are you?' said Scott, still wary.

'My name is Arthur Wheen, and this is my wife Esme.' The woman, who looked truly terrified, was now half hidden behind her tall husband. 'We're camping on the other side of the island – off our boat. I'm a retired civil servant.'

Scott eyed the pair doubtfully. 'Campers, you say? I cannae think this is the kind of place I'd like tae spend my holidays, that's for sure.'

The woman was whispering something to her husband.

'What are you saying?' asked Scott.

'My wife would like to see your warrant card – so would I, as a matter of fact.' Mr Wheen stood taller, adopting an almost haughty tone. 'We have every right to, as I'm sure you know. That is, if you are who you say you are.'

'Who else dae you think I am? Are you used tae mad folk bounding about wae firearms?'

'There've been some strange things going on in the few days we've been here. I'd like to see it, please.'

'There's no need. It's mine.' Daley appeared from behind Scott.

'Why on earth has he got your warrant card? I may never have been a police officer, but I know enough to realise this is most irregular,' said Mr Wheen.

'He forgot his,' said Daley. He pulled his warrant card from Scott's hand and held it out while Scott shrugged sheepishly.

'A detective chief inspector, no less. Well, I'm glad to see you – now I know you're not one of the shady characters we've seen on the island. We have to go into Kinloch for supplies today. I had a notion to pay a visit to the police station there.'

'Oh yes? To say what?'

'There have been some rather unsavoury men about, officer,' said Mrs Wheen.

'Unsavoury in what way?'

'Foul language – and we heard gunshots the other day. I suppose they were hunting seabirds for the fun of it. Utterly disgusting, if you ask me – and against the law.'

'Can you describe them?'

'There were six, maybe eight of them. We were near the trig point at the top of the island when we heard the gunfire. I was very careful not to be seen when I looked over the hill. They were milling about on the foreshore down there. They had boxes of some kind – metal boxes,' said Mr Wheen.

'Metal boxes?' Daley looked puzzled.

'Sturdy, metallic. It took two men to each box, so clearly they contained something heavy.'

'Can you give me any kind of description of these men?'

'I didn't want to give myself away, DCI Daley. I had a look through the binoculars, but only long enough to see what was going on. They were dressed casually: jeans, T-shirts, that kind of thing. It struck me at the time that they didn't look kitted out for the environment.'

'The way yous are?' said Scott, taking in the Wheens' almost identical outfits.

'When you're on rough terrain, you make sure that you have the right kit. You both look dressed for the part. Though you do look rather grubby, if you don't mind me saying.'

Scott was about to speak when Daley interrupted. 'You say you were very careful when you came across them the other day, Mr Wheen. Why be so bold now and come striding down the hill?'

'We saw them leave. They had a large RIB. One of the type usually used for ferrying tourists around beauty spots – or moving equipment. Our son is in the Royal Navy. We have a photograph of him at the helm of a similar vessel.'

'When did you see them leave?'

'The evening before last.'

'They were towing another boat,' said Mrs Wheen. 'We were back at our campsite by that time. It had been terribly cold in our tent the previous evening, so we decided to spend the night in the boat. Plus, those men did rather put the wind up us.'

'Holiday o' a lifetime,' said Scott.

'Our boat is rather cramped, DCI Daley,' said Mr Wheen, purposely ignoring Scott's ironic comment. 'And anyway, our goal is to spend the night on as many islands around the Scottish coast as we can. It's been an ambition for many years. Feels like cheating if we stay on the boat.'

'I've always stayed away fae ambitions,' said Scott. 'Now I know why.'

'The boat being towed behind this RIB, what did it look like?' said Daley quickly.

'Oh, it was a little working vessel,' said Mrs Wheen. 'I thought perhaps a scallop boat – maybe crabs or lobsters. We've seen many of their like on our travels, haven't we, Arthur?'

Daley glanced at Scott.

'Yes, indeed,' said Mr Wheen. 'I was rather puzzled by that, too.'

'Why so?'

'Because there'd been no sign of such a vessel when I first

saw the men. The RIB was anchored out in the bay here, but there was no little fishing boat to be seen.'

'I thank you both for your help,' said Daley. 'As it turns out, I think you may have been very lucky.'

'Oh, why so?' Mrs Wheen held her hand to her mouth in shock.

'Well, we're looking for a fisherman missing from Kinloch. You've just described his boat. We were here investigating a report of some odd behaviour on the island. It seems likely the men you saw were involved in his disappearance.'

'Bloody hell!' said Mr Wheen.

'Arthur, language!' chided his wife.

'What should we do? I can't say I'm tempted to spend another night here now we know this. We'd planned to sail to Millport. I hear it's lovely.'

'Aye, if you don't mind sharing a tiny wee island wae loads o' drunk folk fae Paisley,' said Scott.

'I suggest you sail into harbour at Kinloch. Find somewhere to stay the night. I'd like you to give your statements officially at the office, if that's okay,' said Daley.

'Yes, of course. I must admit, I think we'd feel much safer in Kinloch,' Wheen replied.

'You've no' spent the last few years policing the place,' Scott remarked.

Constable Watson came across to the small party, making the Wheens take a step back.

'Yes, Watson?' said Daley.

'Sir, it's the lifeboat. Looks as though they're heading for the bay here.'

Daley looked across the still blue water. Sure enough, the familiar outline of the RNLI lifeboat with its orange superstructure was making for the island, a wash of white water at her prow.

'Symington,' said Scott, throwing Daley a knowing look.

'Yes, I reckon so.' Daley turned his attention back to the Wheens. 'I'll get the lifeboat to take you back to your vessel. I want to see you make headway to Kinloch before we leave you.'

'That's very kind of you,' said Mrs Wheen.

'Oh, one more thing I've remembered,' said her husband. 'The men, I recognised their accents. You know how sound carries out here. I could make out what they were saying – well, most of it.'

'Really?' Daley's interest was piqued.

'Yes. I spent time in Belfast – for work, DCI Daley. If these men weren't from that city, I'll eat my socks. I'd put a wager on it.'

'Bugger me, that would be a tasty snack,' Scott muttered.

Fortunately, his words were drowned by the low rumble of the big lifeboat engines as she anchored in the tiny bay.

215

30

Terry was sitting forward on a chair, his head pounding. The stocky man with the lined face was berating someone on a mobile phone. A motionless figure still lay on the floor in the dim light of the shuttered room. Through his throbbing head and queasy stomach, the after-effects of the drug he'd been given, Terry realised they were in some kind of run-down bar. The place stank of stale alcohol, though the gantry seemed well stocked.

'If you wanted a babysitter you should have found someone more suited to the task!' The man listened for a few more moments before ending the call unceremoniously and turning to Terry. 'Where is it you're from, young man?'

'Originally from Coleraine, but we moved to Ballycastle a while ago.'

'You'll be wishing you stayed put by the time we're finished with you,' said a tall man with a bruise over one eye. 'Eh, Sean?' He then nudged a younger man beside him, and the pair started laughing.

Sean walked across to them. 'Why are you fucking giggling like a pair o' wee lassies, eh? This is all your fault!' He was right in the face of the taller man now, making him take a step back. 'Fergal, come here and give me a hand with the auld fella. We need to get out of here.'

The three men walked over to where Hamish lay, unconscious. Terry tried to discern any kind of movement that would indicate breathing, but peering through the gloom, the old fisherman he'd failed to rescue showed no sign of life.

'Hamish, what about you?' Sean leaned over the old man, shaking him gently by the shoulder in an effort to wake him.

'I think the auld boy's had it, so he has,' said Fergal. 'In a way it's a blessing, for that's where he was going anyway.'

Ignoring him, Sean held two fingers against Hamish's neck. 'He's got a pulse.' He looked up. 'For your information, that means he's not dead. Now shut the fuck up!' Sean stroked his chin for a few moments. 'Right, bring the van round to the back door. We'll get them in there.'

'What are you going to do with us?' Terry asked through his pain.

'Never you mind, superboy. Sure, you're the last person I'd want tae rescue me, you idiot.' He turned to his companions. 'Well, what are yous waiting for, fucking New Year?'

The men hurried off. Briefly, a bright shaft of sunlight shone through an open fire door before it was slammed shut.

Though Terry had never been a rough and tumble type of lad, he realised that both he and Hamish were in real danger. Whoever these men were – whoever the woman who'd abducted him the previous evening was – it was clear they intended harm to both him and the old man.

When he'd been ushered to the chair by the youngest of his captors, he'd noticed a black glass ashtray on the table in front of him. As the men were busy fussing over Hamish, he'd pulled the ashtray towards him. He was now clutching it in his right hand. He knew he would have few opportunities to escape, but with the other two men now outside he felt the bile rise in his throat as he contemplated what he had to do.

Sean had his ear to Hamish's back. He turned to Terry. 'How did she get yous under? Did you eat something?'

'No, I think they injected us with something. The last thing I remember was a pain in my neck.'

'You don't know how well put that is. That woman's been a royal pain in my neck for years. Who was she with?'

'I dunno, some big guy.'

'Thick-looking?'

'He didn't say much.'

'Tell me, how on earth could yous get lost just outside Ballycastle, for fuck's sake? A blind man could find his way to the town, so he could.'

Terry just shrugged. He had been drugged and imprisoned by a gang of thugs. He wasn't in the mood to have his sense of direction – or lack of it – questioned by his new captor.

The thud and rattle of a diesel engine sounded outside the fire door. 'Right, you, come with me,' Sean barked.

Terry's mind was in turmoil. He realised that if he was to do anything, now was the time. 'I don't think I can stand,' he said hesitantly. He made a half-hearted effort to push himself off the chair with one hand but fell back gasping for breath. The ashtray was now concealed on his lap, obscured by the table.

Sean shook his head. 'See you young lads these days! Your father should have put his toe up your arse, so he should.' He wandered over to Terry and held out one hand by way of helping him from the chair.

Everything happened very quickly. As Sean began to pull him off the chair, the fire doors crashed open as Fergal and his friend came back into the bar. At that moment, Terry swung the ashtray at Sean's head with all his force, sending him tumbling backwards with a howl of pain. Something silver flashed through the air and skittered across the hard floor towards Terry.

'Shit!' shouted Fergal as he made a dash towards Terry and the stricken Sean, now flat out on the floor.

Instinctively, Terry bent down and retrieved the pistol that had been dislodged from Sean's waistband as he fell. Clumsily he held it out in front of his face with both hands.

'Hang on now, son,' said Fergal. 'Just you put that down before you hurt yourself.' He was holding one hand out, beckoning Terry to hand over the weapon. 'Come on, don't be stupid. You've just made things worse for yourself. Don't make them terminal.' He edged nearer.

Though he was in a dark, dank public house, with a wounded pensioner at his feet and a gun in his hand, Terry's mind flashed back to a visit to his uncle's when he was just a kid. Uncle Joe liked guns – liked them too much according to his sister, Terry's mother. The pair of them had been left alone at the house on the hill above Limerick when his parents had gone out for a meal.

Fergal was still walking towards him, but it was as though he was doing so in slow motion. In Terry's head, he was back in Limerick on that hot, sunny day, his uncle Joe towering over him.

'Take a shot, son. Your mammy's no' going to know anything about it. Here, mind and pull down on the safety catch, or you'll be right disappointed.'

Terry was surprised how easily this safety catch moved. His memory of the other was of its being really solid. But he was no more than ten years old that day. Now he was a man.

The safety catch snapped open. Fergal was nearer now, his hand still held out. His mouth was moving, but Terry could only hear his uncle's voice.

'Hold the gun in both hands, Terry. Don't pull the trigger. That's what cowboys in the films do. Squeeze it, and make your shot count!'

The flash came before the sound echoed round the bar, before the weapon's recoil forced back Terry's shoulders. Fergal fell backwards, a chunk of bloody flesh erupting from the right side of his stomach and splattering on to the floor. He screamed in agony as he went down with a thud.

Quickly, Terry recovered his senses. It was as though the firing of the pistol had cleared the cobwebs of the drug from his head. Life returned to its normal pace. He turned the weapon on the younger man, who was already backing away towards the fire doors.

Again the gun fired, but this time Terry was ready for the recoil. Instead of another man falling to the floor in a spray of blood, however, a puff of plaster and chunks of wood splintered from the wall beside the doors. He'd missed. Just as he realised this, he saw his quarry slip through the doors and away.

Fergal was now screaming profanities, clearly in agony. Terry ignored him and walked over to Hamish's side. He shook the old man vigorously with one hand, the other still holding the pistol. A sliver of gunsmoke snaked up through the space between them.

'Hamish, you have to wake up. Hamish!'

31

Daley was removing his walking boots when the door to his glass box flashed open and Symington appeared in the threshold. Her face was flushed with anger, her dark eyes blazing as she slammed the door in her wake and stood before Daley's big desk.

The DCI ignored her dramatic entry and carried on untying his boots.

'Look at me!' Symington demanded.

Daley's head emerged above the desk. He sat back in his chair and surveyed his superior with a neutral expression.

'You disobeyed my direct order, DCI Daley. Not to mention that of the ACC. What the hell did you think you were doing?'

'I was trying to find Hamish,' Daley replied flatly.

'Which, I note, you failed to achieve.'

'Sadly, no, we didn't find him. But we've discovered something of interest. I'm just about to contact the ACC with my report.'

'You'll report it through me!'

'No, I won't, ma'am.'

'What?' Symington looked as though she couldn't believe what she was hearing. 'You'll do what I order you to do. I'll give you one last chance to tell me what happened on that island, what you discovered and what's involved, or I'll have no choice other than to suspend you, Jim.'

'You're going to suspend me?'

'You can bet your life on it. Don't think I'm bothered about your reputation.'

'And what about yours?'

'What?'

'Have you forgotten that you told me the predicament you were in? Have you forgotten what I know about you?'

'This was an order from the Assistant Chief Constable. I just passed it on. You had no right to disobey me regardless of the circumstances.'

Daley said nothing for a few moments, then typed something quickly on the keyboard in front of him.

'What on earth are you doing?'

'I'm backing up a wee theory of mine. You see, I don't think you really wanted me to obey the ACC's orders. I think you knew I wouldn't.'

'Nonsense!'

'You say that, but I have proof to the contrary. You know how much Hamish means to Brian and me. He saved my life when I first came here – Liz's, too. You know me well enough now to realise that I'll do anything to save my friends – anything. And you used that knowledge, Carrie.'

'You've left me no choice, Jim. You've put us all at risk now. The ACC wants to know why you went there against his wishes.'

'Take a look at this.' He pointed at the computer monitor on his desk.

Symington walked round the desk beside him. Daley pressed a button, and her face appeared on the screen. Even she could see the furtive look on her face as she appeared to be typing on a keyboard, staring straight back out of the screen.

'What is this?'

'You should know, you did it.'

'I don't know what you mean.' Symington felt as though she was plummeting through the floor. As though what was happening to her wasn't really happening at all.

'They're clever guys, those techies. They can take over your computer remotely and do things I never thought possible.'

'This is ridiculous. You're like some kind of stalker, Jim.'

'No, I'm not the stalker, Carrie – you are! You told me you didn't intend to arrive in the office until lunchtime, but you were in here before the day shift arrived. The first thing you did was to try to find something on my computer. I wonder what that might have been?'

Symington merely shook her head.

'Then poor Mr Houston is found beaten half to death in his home – which, more crucially, is also his place of work. Somebody was looking for something. The same thing you were looking for. I've spoken to Shaw. I know what you were doing. Because every move, every keystroke was recorded on my PC. But you didn't find the pictures he'd taken of Hamish's abduction. Even he wasn't sure at first what they were. Blurred, but good enough. But I sent them out to the photographic unit. They've managed to enhance them. We know for sure that they took him by force. We know now that they were on the island. What we don't know is what they were doing there. But we can guess it was something to do with our dead men on the plane. And we know what type of RIB they used. It's a big Red Bay job. A custom build, no less. But the man it was made for sold it on, and he was keener on money than receipts, by the looks of things. But we have a solid lead, nonetheless.'

'Oh God. I'm sorry, Jim.'

'So am I. But I knew I couldn't trust you, Carrie. I knew that this Bower would put more pressure on you somehow. What's he done?'

'He has my parents, Jim – my mum and dad!' Carrie Symington flopped down on the chair opposite Daley, burying her head in her hands. 'I didn't know what to do. I was desperate!'

'You should have come to me, Carrie. A man is in the hospital because you didn't. From what I hear, Houston is lucky to be alive. Brian's up there now.' Daley leaned across the desk and grabbed her hand. 'But we can turn this to our advantage. And I promise, we'll save your parents.'

'How? What can we do? He's one step ahead all the time, Jim.'

'He thinks he is.'

Sergeant Shaw's head appeared round the door. 'Sir, I've someone here to see you.' Before he could answer Daley's questioning look, a smart-suited man pushed past him.

'Jim, Chief Superintendent Symington. What a pleasure. I didn't think I'd be seeing you both again so soon.' MI5's Iolo Harris grinned at the police officers. 'Sorry for barging in, but I hear you've been having a bit of trouble.'

'Yes, but I didn't think it was this serious.'

'Oh, but you were wrong, Jim. You were very wrong.'

Terry struggled to pull Hamish along the floor. Sean had been right: the old fisherman had a pulse, but it was weak, and Terry couldn't rouse him.

'You're fucked, boy,' said Fergal weakly. He was now propped up against a banquette, holding the wound, blood pouring between his fingers. 'You can't kill someone like Sean and get away with it. You were dead men before, and now you'll die the worst death possible.'

Terry brandished the gun at the man he'd shot minutes earlier. 'Shut up, or I'll shoot you again! You've made it quite clear I've nothing to lose, so nothing you've got to say now makes any difference to me. Anyway, your man's not dead, he's just out cold.'

'Aye, so you say. He looks pretty fucked to me. Anyway, if he doesn't die, I will. It amounts to the same thing.' He grimaced in pain, sliding down the banquette.

'I'll take my chances.' Terry was panting with the effort of pulling Hamish across the floor. He had no idea how he was going to get him to safety, but he knew he couldn't leave the old man here alone, to die.

'Don't you worry, bonny boy. There's nowhere to go. My pal will be back with the cavalry, so he will. That's him off in the van. You've no idea where you are, even.'

Terry stopped for a moment. He placed Hamish's head gently on the floor. He remembered that Sean had been talking to someone on a mobile phone. He walked across to him. The man was lying just where Terry had left him.

'If you're trying to revive him, it's too late.'

Ignoring Fergal, Terry kneeled over the man he'd battered with the glass ashtray and fumbled about, trying to find his jacket pocket in the gloom.

The right one was empty, and so was the corresponding pocket in his trousers.

As Terry leaned over Sean to try his other pockets for signs of a phone he was suddenly aware of movement. Before he realised what was going on, Sean's hand was round his throat. His face contorted as his grip tightened. 'You wee bastard!' he gasped.

For Terry, the murky world began to spin. He saw stars flash before his eyes as he fought for breath. His head felt as though it might explode. Injured Sean may be, but his grip was like iron.

'You stupid boy,' Sean screamed through gritted teeth. 'Why couldn't you just have stayed behind your desk and left us alone? You're no more than a wean, and I've got to take your life!'

Terry was becoming desperate now. He knew that he was about to pass out, and he realised that he might never open his eyes again. The pistol had been in his pocket, but he wasn't sure it was still there following Sean's unexpected attack. With the very tips of the fingers of his right hand he searched for the weapon, while at the same time a white spark of pain obscured his vision. He was near the end – he could feel it.

Sean was still weak from the blow to the head, but he was a powerful man. He was trying to wriggle free of the weight of the younger man he was slowly strangling. Once he managed that, he would finish the job.

Terry's fingers brushed against the scored handle of the stubby .38-calibre pistol. But just when he thought he had purchase on the weapon, it slipped further down into his pocket. He managed to draw a pitifully wheezed breath through the tight grip on his throat. His last, he thought.

Sean was nearly free now. It was difficult trying to move while still gripping the neck of the young man who'd hit him with the ashtray. He was pushing himself back along the floor with one arm, his head still throbbing. But he'd been fighting on the cobbles since he was a kid. And though his opponent was young, the punches he was directing at Sean's face barely registered. All he had to do was roll free. But in doing so, he would have to let go of Terry's throat for an instant in order to spin on top of him and finish the job.

Terry felt the grip on his throat loosen. He pulled in a gasp of air that rasped in his throat and shrieked like a wild animal.

Sean was on top of him now. With both hands, he regained a grip on Terry's throat. 'Fucking die, you wee bastard!' His sheer fury, the adrenaline, was making him stronger. But just as he felt the life drain from Terry, there was a loud report and he felt as though a truck had hit him in the chest. He flew backwards as though propelled by an unseen hand, the smell of cordite strong in the air.

Terry lay back on the hard floor, gulping for breath. For a few seconds he couldn't move. As the room began to spin, he was aware of a thin sound: a moan. He assumed it came from Sean, but forcing himself up from the floor he saw the man with whom he'd been in a struggle only moments before lying motionless only feet from him. He turned his head towards Fergal, but he was slumped forward, his back still resting on the banquette, legs spread out on the floor before him. For all the world he looked like a drunk, but Terry knew he must be unconscious through loss of blood.

He looked across the room. A sliver of light was showing through a gap in the fire doors. The last man through them hadn't had time to secure them properly. But caught in this chink of light, something was moving.

Coughing and spluttering, feeling as though he'd swallowed

a tennis ball, Terry crawled towards the groans. 'Hamish, are you okay?'

The old man's blue eyes sparkled in the sliver of light. 'I'm too old for this. I shouldna be taking such a cargo o' drink on board at my time o' life. My heid feels as though a horse stamped on it.' He stared at Terry. 'Who are you?'

'Terry, remember? I tried to save you. I'm trying again!'

Hamish looked utterly bewildered. 'The last thing I remember was being out on the boat. My, the sea was like a millpond.' He looked around, squinting in the gloom. 'Man, but it's been some party, right enough. A couple over there in worse shape than me, by the looks o' it.' He nodded to the two men Terry had shot.

'Can you move? We have to get out of here.'

'Why would I not be able tae move? I've been on the go since before your grandfaither was alive, by the look o' things. Gie Annie a shout – she'll get me a taxi. I need tae get tae my bunk.'

'I don't know who Annie is, but she's not calling for any taxis.' Terry was thinking more clearly now. He left Hamish's side and staggered over to where Sean lay. More cautiously than before, he rifled through his pockets, pistol held firmly in one hand. He felt the slim mobile phone and took it out, expecting the device to spring into life when he pressed a button. But squinting at it in the darkness he saw the screen was smashed, no doubt hit by the bullet that had felled its owner. It was useless.

He stumbled across to where Fergal was slumped. Still with the weapon in his hand, he searched the man's pockets. Even in the semi-darkness, Terry could see the deathly pale glow of his skin, though the man was still breathing shallowly. He felt a surge of guilt. Then he remembered his uncle's words.

When you're fighting for your life Jesus isn't taking notes, son. You get a pass.

There was no doubt he'd been fighting for his life. He found a mobile phone in Fergal's pocket. He should have realised. It could only be accessed by face unlock. 'Shit!'

'Here, that's a hell o' a racket. I've a right hangover – do you mind keeping it doon tae a dull roar, son?' said Hamish.

Terry knew time was against him. He made for the bar and cast about the surfaces. Sure enough, just near a hatch he found a phone. He put it to his ear, but it emitted only one long tone. He'd heard that sound before. His mother and father had always struggled to pay the bills, and he knew the sound of a landline that had been cut off.

He hurried back to Hamish and helped the old man to his feet. The old fisherman was unsteady and moaned pitifully, but Terry knew they had to get out of this place. He was sure they could find help.

With Hamish's arm over his shoulder, he pulled the old man along, paying no attention to his muttered protests.

The pair emerged through the fire doors into a bright, warm, sunny day. But as Terry squinted into the sunshine, he didn't see what he expected. Instead of streets and houses, he saw a car park, with green fields all around. A single-track lane rolled from the pub into the hazy distance. Ahead, he could see the ocean, but knowing the lie of the land he was sure it would be no gentle stroll to the beach.

'Ah, shit.'

32

Iolo was sitting beside Carrie Symington looking across Daley's desk. He looked between the chief superintendent and her DCI.

'Bad time, is it?'

'Sorry?' said Daley.

'Come on, man, I can feel the tension in the air. You can cut it with a knife.'

'We've had an, eh, operational disagreement,' said Symington flatly.

Daley took her in for a few moments. There was no doubt that his diminutive boss had hidden resolve. She'd looked like a broken woman a few moments ago, but the appearance of Iolo Harris had been enough for her to regain her composure, the carapace of her rank firmly in place.

'It's always nice to see you, Mr Harris. Though if I remember correctly, you rather went your own way when we last met.' Symington's chin was set firm.

'I am a mere functionary, as you know, a cog in a big government machine, Ms Symington. Like you, I take orders and carry them out to the best of my ability. Limited though that may be, I admit. But they've seen fit to keep me on all this time, so I guess I can't be too bad.' His accent was modulated, but the boy from Port Talbot was still evident.

'Trouble is, your remit and ours are rather different, Iolo,' said Daley.

'We can diverge from time to time in our methods – even in our goals. But we're still on the same side, Jim.'

'May I ask why you're here?' said Symington.

'Your plane that fell from the sky. Well, landed, after a fashion, I think it's fair to say. There's been a small shift in the dynamic of the investigation.'

'You mean we're out on our arse and you're taking over.' Daley shrugged. He knew that events such as this would never be left with a rural CID. Though he'd been expecting a specialised team from Glasgow, not MI5.

'Interesting reasoning, my friend. But you couldn't be more wrong.'

'Wrong?' said Symington.

'Yes, very much so. In fact, though you'll be answerable to a rather altered hierarchy, I want you to take the lead. Be on point, so to speak. Vital, it is.'

Daley smiled mirthlessly. 'You mean we do the dirty work while you plan the moves.'

'You're becoming very cynical, DCI Daley. It's healthy, mind, because you're absolutely right.'

'I'm sure my superiors will have something to say about that,' said Symington.

For the first time since Harris's arrival, Daley detected a hint of desperation in Symington's eyes. Her thought processes weren't hard to follow. Contained within Kinloch police office, the chief superintendent's predicament was relatively safe. But now the Security Service was involved, the likelihood of her association with Bower being revealed was high. Even higher than he thought, as he was just about to discover.

'This Bower character, Carrie . . . I know you've been experiencing "pressure" from him, yes?' Harris said it calmly, as though discussing some trivial matter of procedure.

Symington's mouth opened and closed, her face suddenly pale under her short dark hair.

'How much do you know?' said Daley flatly.

'Well, most, I suppose. You see, we've had Mr Bower in our sights for some time. In fact, we thought we'd have to blow our cover to save you when he paid that unexpected visit to your flat, Carrie. Thankfully, the conversation was reasonably convivial – for what it was.'

'So, you know.' Symington looked utterly broken. 'You had my flat bugged?'

'No, Bower was bugged. We stuck it in his phone – long story. But he's a cunning bastard. He changes his mobiles as often as I have a bath – once a week on a Sunday.' He chuckled. 'And, yes, I know. I know about what Chappell did to you. I know how Bower is trying to leverage you. I know lots of things.'

She looked him straight in the eye. 'Do you know about my parents?'

'Yes, we do.' He reached into his pocket and produced a mobile phone. He pressed the screen and put it to his ear. 'Everything all right, Cranley?' He listened for a few moments, a broad smile spreading across his face. 'Well, as we expected, then. I knew you were the man for the job. Do me a favour and put him on, will you?' Harris turned to Symington. 'Here, this is for you.'

With an unsteady hand she grabbed the phone. 'Hello?' she said, her voice shaking. She listened for a few seconds before shooting up from her chair. 'Dad, you're okay! How's Mum?'

As she talked, the Welshman leaned across the desk and spoke quietly to Daley. 'We'll leave her to it, eh, Jim? Let's go for a stroll in your car park.'

Leaving a tearful Symington speaking to her newly liberated parents on the mobile, Daley and Harris left the glass box and were soon out in the sunshine, Harris taking deep lungfuls of air.

'This is what I miss, you know. In London, I mean. I'm not saying the air in Port Talbot is as fresh as here, mind. But a quick drive to Ogmore and you can open your lungs and breathe.'

'How much do you really know about Carrie?' said Daley.

'Nothing, until a few weeks ago, to be honest. Not until Chappell and Bower came under our scrutiny. Gradually, with surveillance, it became clear your superior has a skeleton in her cupboard. Been tough on her, that's for sure. I won't even tell you the things Chappell put her through. But it sickened me, and not much does these days. He didn't spare many details. We thought it was braggadocio, at first – he was the type of scum who'd get a kick from that. But, no, our analyst told us otherwise. Bastard, he was. He deserved to die in a bloody car park with his throat cut.'

'But she's finished now, surely?' Daley looked at his feet, kicked a loose stone across the yard.

'Jim, if you had any idea how many senior police officers have dirty little secrets, or things to hide, there'd barely be anyone left above the rank of inspector.' He winked at Daley. 'You're just one of them, boyo. If you're willing to keep quiet about it, we'll not be sticking our beaks in.'

Daley looked surprised, and Harris picked up on his expression.

'You're not some daft kid, Jim. You know how the world turns. In any case, she's a bloody victim!'

'That's not how our top brass will look at it. You know that.'

'Bollocks to them, that's what I say. I'm sorry to decry your colleagues, but that's always what's kind of put me off the police force. Too tied up with shit that doesn't matter. They make a big thing about looking after their own, but that rarely happens. Most senior officers would give their eye teeth to bring down a colleague.' He smiled at Daley. 'You had a lucky escape yourself recently.'

Daley shrugged. 'I did.'

'Listen, this is complicated. Right now, Carrie is an asset. Bower thinks he has her where he wants her, and that's to our advantage.'

'But what's it all about? And why are you entrusting us with this investigation?'

'Quite simple, Jim. We all have to tread carefully. You'll be aware of the many climate protesters who've sprung up?'

'Yes, of course I am.'

'Well, it's not all about standing on tube trains, gluing yourself to railings and dodging school. There's what you would call an "extreme wing".'

'I've heard. People like the League of World Saviours?'

'Exactly! You're on the ball, but I knew you would be. You can explain to me how you know about that merry little band in a short while. Meantime, have a look at this.' Harris pulled a photograph from his pocket and handed it to Daley. 'Sorry about the quality, best we could do. You recognise either of those lads?'

Two young men were standing at a bar. They were very close to each other, one holding the other's hand casually as they smiled broadly.

Daley studied their faces for a moment. 'No, can't say I do, Iolo.'

'That's a pity.'

'Why?'

'Because one of them just bought a firearm at a remote location north of here a couple of days ago.'

'How do you know?'

'One of our guys is embedded with the people who sold him it. This lad here' – he pointed to the taller of the two young men in the picture – 'is Desmond Innes. He's been radicalised, if that's the right word. A radicalised climate extremist – who knew? The other lad is a bit of a mystery right now. But our man remembered his face from this picture. However, as your chief super is being bribed by Bower, and this lad bought the gun on your patch, not to mention our dead pilots, I thought it a good tactical move to pay an extended visit.'

'So whatever is going on is going on here?'

'You're out of the way, lots of little nooks and crannies and the like. Put it like this: if I wanted to smuggle things into this country, Kintyre would be high on my list.'

'I suppose so. What are we talking? Obviously firearms – drugs too, maybe?'

'Yeah, a bit of that. But that's not what we're most worried about.'

'Weapons, drugs – what else is there? Surely not human trafficking, not here?'

'Bad as all those things are, this could be worse.'

'Shit.'

'I'll come clean about all that in due course. We have to be careful around the climate brigade.'

'Why so?'

'Orders from on high, Jim. Wouldn't look good for the government to be turning on folk saving the planet.'

'So you use us instead.'

Harris laughed. 'That's the spirit, Jim.'

Daley nodded grimly. 'The price of being out of the way, yet handy for the Atlantic, and a passage into the UK.'

'You hit the nail on the head, man.' Harris took the photograph back from Daley. 'First thing I want to do is find out who this young man is. We've had to be careful asking too many questions around young Desmond here. He's a sharp lad – misguided, of course, but not stupid. Very persuasive, as well, a real convert. Has the passion of one, too. But we're relying on the assumption that this lad isn't quite so sharp.' He prodded the smaller of the two young men in the photograph. 'Finding him is a priority.'

'How do you know he's still in the area?'

'He's waiting for more items to come his way. He's a mule – not a very bright one either, by the sound of things.'

Daley stared at the image. Brian Scott's son was unmistakable.

'You okay, Jim?'

If Daley's smile was forced, Harris didn't notice. 'Yes, just taking it all in, if you know what I mean,' he said.

33

A dark cloud had drifted over the coastline of County Antrim. It was as though someone had turned off an electric fire. There was a sudden chill in the air, and even the seabirds, shrill when Terry and a bemused Hamish had stepped out of the bar, were now quiet under a rapidly darkening sky.

'Not rain. That's all we need,' Terry muttered.

'You'll no' find a train here, young man,' said Hamish, staggering along with his arm over Terry's shoulder.

There was only one road, no more than a lane that led away from their erstwhile prison. It was long and straight but being so close to the sea lacked any kind of cover, not even a stone wall or a bush. Terry had learned from recent mistakes. He wasn't keen to walk into captivity again as he had done on the shore road, so, seeing no other option, he headed for the cliffs, hoping desperately that something – anything – might turn up. One thing was for sure: Hamish was still suffering badly from whatever drug had been administered to the pair of them. He was mumbling deliriously, stumbling badly.

Terry scanned the scene. They were within feet of the cliff's edge, with no apparent place to hide. His plan, if indeed it was a plan, was to creep along the cliff's edge and get as far away from the bar as possible. He shuddered at the memory of shooting two men. He was a killer. It didn't sit well with him.

But what else could he have done?

'Here, how far away is the next watering hole, son? I'm fair parched,' slurred Hamish.

'If you can manage, we'll just walk a wee bit further, Hamish, and then you can have a rest.' Terry looked back the way they had come. The building in which they'd been held was receding, but not quickly enough for his liking.

'I could be doing wae my bunk, and that's the truth.' Hamish tripped, almost taking Terry with him. The younger man managed to prevent the old fisherman from falling, and they both stopped, each breathless with effort.

Terry noticed an old-fashioned signpost about a hundred metres ahead. It was perched on the edge of the cliff, but he saw that a narrow path had been worn on the rough grass towards it by the passage of many feet.

'I think I'm going tae spew,' said Hamish rather unhelpfully.

'Not far now. We'll get a proper seat soon.'

Terry turned back, squinting at the pub. There seemed to be no movement. His heart thudding in his chest, he pulled Hamish along towards the signpost.

Annie was going through the motions. She'd tried to force the thought of her old friend from her mind, but it hadn't worked. There were a few folk in for meals and a couple of stray holidaymakers who'd come for coffee and cake.

'Pint of heavy, please.' The man on the bar stool had long hair dragged back into a ponytail. He was wearing a collarless shirt under a grey waistcoat that had seen much better days.

'Surely,' said Annie with little enthusiasm. 'Can I get you a menu? We have gluten-free and vegetarian.' The chef had asked her to push these options, the least popular dishes on offer.

'Nah, I'm fine. We're obsessed by weight in this country. That's why there are so many fat people about. Wasn't like that when I was a pup.'

'No, you're right there. You want to see some that come in here. But it pays my wages, so I'm no' complaining.'

'You'll know something about the old guy who's missing, yeah?'

Annie stared at this new man at the bar. He'd no right to ask about Hamish – no right at all. He was a stranger. People in Kinloch liked to keep good and bad news to themselves. She noticed that he had ink-stained hands. Gradually the truth dawned on her. 'You're a journalist, aren't you?'

'Well spotted. How did you reach that conclusion?'

Ignoring the question, Annie replied, 'If you think anyone in this bar will talk to you about Hamish, you can think again!' Her raised voice attracted the attention of the customers.

'I'm just in for a drink before I meet someone. Calm down.'

'Oh aye, you just happen tae step in here for a drink, and you a journalist, tae. I've never set eyes on you in my life.'

As she spoke, Alistair McGinn, a large fisherman, arrived at the bar beside the journalist.

'Is there a problem, Annie? I heard raised voices fae oot in the corridor.'

'It's okay, Ally. This *gentleman* was just leaving.'

'Leaving? I haven't had my pint yet. And I'm meeting someone, remember?'

In an extravagant gesture, Annie removed the pint glass

239

from under the font and poured the dark beer into the sink. 'You're barred. Get out!'

'Come on. You can't treat customers like this!'

McGinn edged towards the man with the ponytail and rose to his full height, which was well over six feet. 'If she says you're barred, you're barred.'

The journalist looked him up and down, remaining perched on his stool. 'Who are you, rent-a-twat?'

Before Annie could do anything to stop him, Ally McGinn drew back his fist and swung at the other man's face. It was a glancing blow, but delivered with such power that it sent the victim tumbling backwards off his stool and onto the floor.

'What's going on?' Ian Macmillan, standing in the doorway, looked bemused and angry at once. He turned his gaze on Annie. 'Well?'

'This man's a journalist. He's after stories on Hamish so that he can print them in some rag. Ally was jeest helping me oot.'

Macmillan leaned down and helped Nathan Sidley to his feet. 'I'm sorry about this, Mr Sidley. And I apologise for being late. I had a call to take. Please, take a seat, I'll be with you momentarily.'

Brushing himself down, the journalist spotted a seat at a distant table and wandered over to it, shaking his head.

Macmillan leaned across the bar. 'When do you finish? I want to have a word with you.' His face was stern.

Annie was embarrassed. She noted the dark shadow of extreme displeasure on Macmillan's face, very similar to what she'd seen through the crack in the door when he'd been swearing down the phone in the middle of the night. 'I'm sorry, Mr Macmillan. But we can't allow oor customers tae be bad-mouthed in the press, can we?'

'Mr Sidley is here to see me. How does that fit you? Okay, I hope?'

'Oh, I'm sorry. But he should have said something.'

'So people have to explain themselves when they come in? I don't think so.' Macmillan stared up at Ally McGinn. 'You, get out. If Mr Sidley wants to call the police I won't try to stop him.'

As Macmillan walked away, McGinn shrugged his shoulders at Annie. 'How was I tae know?'

'You'd better get going, Ally. I'll smooth things over with Mr Macmillan. It was my fault.'

The big man left the bar, being careful not to catch the gaze of either Macmillan or the man he'd just knocked off a stool. Meanwhile, Annie made for the table at which her boss and the journalist were now seated.

'Can I get yous anything?'

'I'll have the beer you poured down the sink, please,' Sidley replied.

'Just a coffee for me – flat white. Mr Sidley's drink is on the house. The least we can do.'

Back behind the bar, Annie's hand shook under the beer font as she poured another pint of heavy. She'd been stupid and impulsive – she knew that. But she wasn't going to let some hack write about her old friend and customer. She glanced at Macmillan and Sidley. Whatever they were talking about, they were huddled together conspiratorially.

Hamish was almost in a state of collapse by the time Terry managed to manoeuvre him along the clifftop. From here he could see that the worn path led past the wooden post and over the edge of the cliff.

'You stay here, Hamish.' He helped the mumbling figure to sit down on the rough grass and went to inspect the signpost and what lay on the other side of the cliff.

RSPB Observation Point. Take Care.

Terry looked over the cliff edge. Rough steps had been cut into the rock above a ledge that had been fenced off for birdwatchers. The steps had a handrail, but even so, they were steep and hazardous. Normally, with no head for heights, the young Irishman wouldn't have considered heading down on to the ledge. But he was keen to get out of sight as quickly as possible.

He was still wondering how he'd manoeuvre Hamish down the steps when he realised how much his life had changed in no time at all. He'd been imprisoned, drugged, and forced to shoot – perhaps even to kill – his captors.

With a heavy heart, he rejoined Hamish. He found the fisherman lying on his back staring into the rapidly greying sky.

'Aye, we'll need tae put in at Port Ellen the way the weather is going,' the old man said quite naturally, as though he was standing in the wheelhouse of a fishing boat.

'You think it's going to rain?' Terry asked.

'Aye, mair than rain. A right good summer storm, that's whoot's around the corner. You can tell by the sky and the smell o' the air.'

'Shit, that's all we need.'

'Always a surprise after all this good weather. But the fish jeest love it. So, we're in for a fine catch tomorrow when it's clear.'

'Okay.' Terry wasn't sure if Hamish was still suffering from the sedative, or if the stress of the last few days had rendered him temporarily delirious. He looked up across the mile or so to where the pub still sat in splendid isolation. There was still no sign of movement or approaching vehicles. He felt a twinge of guilt at the fate of his erstwhile captors, before reasoning that he wasn't the guilty party, and all he'd done was save himself and Hamish. 'Right, come on, Hamish. We have to get down below.' He hauled the old man to his feet to the sound of Hamish's protests.

'You're a hell o' a man for being on the go, right enough. Somebody has tae take the tiller.'

'Don't worry about that. We have to get down before this storm starts.'

Though Hamish's mind seemed at sixes and sevens, his meteorological senses were still intact. He nodded in agreement. As they stumbled towards the steps cut in the cliff, Terry felt the first drops of rain on his face. 'Steady now, Hamish. We have to be careful here.'

'Och, I've been going up an' doon steps on boats since before you were on your first wave.'

Walking backwards down the top steps, leading Hamish by the hand above him, Terry felt suddenly vulnerable. Just thinking about the sheer drop down to the hissing sea below was making him feel dizzy. But the stairway was narrow, and they'd never have fitted side by side.

'You'll need tae get a shift on, son. I'm getting soaked up here.' Hamish's left foot was hovering above the first step, as though he wasn't quite sure where to place it.

'Just onc step at a time, Hamish. There's no hurry,' Terry lied.

Hamish managed to negotiate the first part of the descent with relative ease. He now had one foot on the top step, the other on the one below.

'Right, next foot down.'

'I don't need instructions, young man. You mind your ain feet.' Hamish had both feet on the same step now.

'Okay, just a few more to go.' Terry made the mistake of looking down in order to count the steps. He reckoned there were about twenty-five or so until they reached the ledge with its tiny canopy. But he also caught sight of the sea again – so far below a gull was flying beneath them. He felt his stomach churn, and a strange prickling sensation began at his feet and made its way up his leg. 'Who'd be a birdwatcher?' he muttered to himself. Distantly he heard a rumble of thunder. 'Shit!'

'Whoot a tongue you've on you! Like an old fishwife . . .' Hamish didn't get the chance to finish his sentence. He misjudged his next step and toppled down on to Terry, making the younger man stumble backwards and lose his own footing.

Locked in an awkward embrace, the pair tumbled down the narrow staircase, Terry grasping desperately for the handrail as they fell.

34

Daley walked Iolo Harris back into his glass box.

Symington was looking relieved, though there were tears in her eyes. She stood up quickly and rubbed them away when the men came back through the door.

'Right,' said Daley. 'I guess you want to spend some time with the superintendent, Iolo?'

'Well, a few words wouldn't go amiss.' Harris glanced at Symington, who smiled weakly.

'I've got to nip up to the house – for some meds. Mind like a sieve these days.'

'Join the club,' said Iolo. 'It's our age. Senility on the march, that's what my wife says.'

Daley nodded goodbye and strode quickly through the office and out into the car park. Sitting in his car, he pulled out his mobile phone and dialled Brian Scott's number.

'Aye, what's up, big man?' Scott replied after a few rings.

'There's a problem – a big one. I need to talk to you right now.'

'Fire away, Jimmy.'

'No, not on the phone, in person.'

'You sound a bit funny. Are you okay?'

'I'll meet you at your house in ten minutes.'

'Mine? Ella's there, remember. Aye, and Willie, tae.'

'That's just what I was hoping.'

'You've got me beaten here, big man. Is something wrong – no' Liz or the wean, I hope?'

'Just be there.' Daley ended the call abruptly. The picture Harris had produced of Scott's son had taken him aback. And though he trusted Scott with his life, he knew that his old friend had weak spots when it came to friends and family. He'd experienced this before – so many times.

Daley fired up his engine.

Linda Alton, or Delaney as she preferred to be called now her marriage was in trouble, flung open the bar's fire doors and reached for the light switch, bathing the long room in harsh neon light. Fergal was slumped over on the floor, as though he had been resting against one of the banquettes, while Sean lay nearby, a pool of congealed blood to the right side of his motionless body.

'What the fuck!' she swore loudly as she hurried over to Sean. 'Declan, you check Fergal. How the fuck did this happen?' she said to no one in particular. She was surprised when Sean spoke.

'The boy.' He paused gasping for air. 'He hit me with an ashtray – shot Fergal, then me. I'm sorry.' As he rasped the apology, his head rolled to the side.

Linda checked his pulse. It was weak, but it was there. She turned to Declan, who was leaning over Fergal. 'Is he alive?'

The big man shook his head, staring at her wide-eyed, as though he had no idea what to do.

'Right, you listen to me. We leave him here. We'll take Sean in the car, leave him somewhere and call an ambulance. You go through Fergal's pockets and get rid of everything.'

As Declan went to work, Linda's mind was working overtime. On one level, she regretted what had happened to two of her men. But her regret was predicated on nothing more than irritation that things could have gone so badly wrong.

'Right, that's his pockets empty, Linda.'

'Okay, take off his rings, his watch – anything he can be identified by – and let's get out of here.'

'Can't we take Sean to the hospital? It doesn't seem right just dumping him somewhere.'

'Oh aye, good thinking. We'll just wander into A&E and fill out a form or two. Have you forgotten everything we used to do?'

'No! But I've known the man since I was a nipper. Leaving him dying on the street – it's not right.'

'Back then we'd an army behind us. Now we're alone. Where the fuck has Bobby gone?'

Declan shrugged, his focus on Sean's pallid face.

'Get him in the car.'

'How?'

'We'll concentrate really hard and maybe we can move him with the power of the mind. Lift him up, you stupid bastard!'

'I'll be covered in blood, Linda.'

'Aye, so you will. What of it?'

She left Declan to pick up their injured colleague and walked out into the rain. It was falling heavily now, great sheets like billowing smoke against the grey sky and darker sea. She heard Sean groan in pain. At least he was still alive. She'd known him for thirty-odd years and hoped that he'd survive. At least, she reasoned, if he made it to a hospital, he stood a chance. The doctors in Northern Ireland were the world's best for treating gunshot wounds. Then she realised that the Troubles had been over for a long time. The medics who had tended bodies broken by bullets and bombs were probably all retired by now, if not dead themselves. The passage of time was unkind. Your childhood and youth seemed to last for ever. The rest of life seemed to flash by.

But Linda Delaney was not a sentimental woman. She'd left nostalgia and compassion behind a very long time ago.

Though she was getting soaked, Linda squinted through the rain. 'Where are you, you wee bastard?' Terry's face dominated her thoughts. He'd seemed so young and stupid when they'd picked him up on the coast road. Now she wasn't so sure. The men he'd left in the pub were seasoned hands. How could a boy pumped full of morphine have been able to overcome them and escape with the old man?

'That's us ready to go,' said Declan as he closed the back door of the SUV on the unconscious Sean.

She pulled her thoughts away from her missing captives and back to the matter in hand. 'We'll take him to the outskirts of Ballycastle and leave him there. You can phone the ambulance. Toss the phone when you're done.'

'What then?'

'We have to find that pair! We grab them and we finish it. Too much has gone wrong already. Round up the rest of the boys and get them searching. They can't have got far, not from here.'

'No sign of them on the road, Linda.'

'No. That boy might be stupid, but he's not daft enough to get caught the same way twice.' She glanced along the line of the cliffs through the pelting rain. 'But he can't disappear into thin air either.'

They hurried into the SUV and sped off up the single-track road.

Terry wasn't sure how long he'd been unconscious, but he came to with a start, as though emerging from a nightmare. Something heavy was pressing down on him. As his wits returned, he realised that the nightmare had been real, and Hamish was lying on top of him. He managed to wriggle out from under the old man and checked his pulse. Mercifully, his heart was still beating strongly in his chest.

He put his hand to his forehead in desperation. They were both soaked. Though the canopy over the ledge offered some protection against the driving rain, it was blowing into them straight off the sea. He noticed his hand was smeared in blood. Reaching up again to his forehead, more tentatively this time, he found a gash. On further examination, he realised that both elbows were bleeding and a dark stain was spreading across the right knee of his grey trousers. As though by delayed action, his head and limbs began to ache, his body throbbing with pain.

'Hamish, wake up!' He tried to examine the old man. He remembered how Hamish had lost his footing at the top of the stairs and the pair had tumbled down on to the ledge. It was a miracle their fall hadn't taken them over the rail and down on to the rocks far below.

'All the fun o' the fair, eh?' Hamish mumbled.

'What?' Though Terry was relieved that Hamish seemed to be okay, he was mildly irritated that he had apparently suffered no ill effects from the calamity at all. 'How do you feel?'

'I hate a shower,' Hamish replied. 'Gie me a good bath

any day. And I'll tell you something else, this water's bloody cold. Did you no' have the immersion on, Mother?'

'It's not a shower, and I'm definitely not your mother.' Through his pain, Terry could visualise the two men slumped on the floor of the bar. But this time, instead of remorse, he felt a stab of something else. The will to survive.

'We'll need tae get doon below and get oor oilskins. I canna keep the watch soaked tae the skin.'

Though he was talking gibberish, Terry thought Hamish's voice sounded less slurred. Maybe the soaking rain was helping him come to his senses. He hoped so. He needed all the help he could get.

35

Daley was sitting in the Scotts' lounge. Ella was rubbing her hands together, as though she was trying to wash away her woes as tears poured down her face. Meanwhile her husband was pacing about the room.

'The stupid wee shite!' Scott looked at Ella. 'See! This is where that mollycoddling gets us. I should have booted him up the arse like my auld fella!'

'We've been through this,' said Ella between sobs.

'Aye, well, you don't see me oot buying guns fae some bastard, dae you?'

Daley signalled for Brian to calm down. 'You said he was going out – he took your car. Did he say where he was going, Ella?'

'No, Jimmy. Just that he'd have a wee surprise for me when he came back.' She looked at Daley with a pitiful stare. 'I cannae believe my wee boy would be up tae stuff like this.'

'Wee surprise!' said Scott. 'He's likely going to turn up in a Sherman tank, or riding one o' they Scud missiles! He should have taken up that apprenticeship wae my cousin Tommy.'

From somewhere Ella found her fighting spirit. 'He was never cut oot tae be a plumber. He's got a weak stomach –

always has had. Can you picture him wae his arm doon someone's lavvy?'

'Aye, well, he's in deeper shit than that now. He's an arms dealer!'

'Okay, come on now, this isn't doing anyone any good,' said Daley. 'Brian, I want you to go through his stuff, try and find this pistol, okay?'

Scott glanced between Daley and Ella, as though he wasn't sure from whom he should be taking instructions. Eventually, he hurried off up the stairs to Will's room.

'Okay, Ella. He has his mobile, right?'

'Aye, he has, Jimmy.'

'Okay. I want you to do me a favour. But you'll have to sound convincing.'

'What dae you want me tae say? We cannae just hand him over to MI5.' Ella looked horrified.

'Listen, we can make a deal with them. They're not like the police, Ella. It's shades of grey, not black and white. They're after the big boys. Your Will's just a small cog.'

'What kind of deal?'

Daley sat on the edge of his chair. 'He's clearly been influenced by this Desmond guy. He'll be higher up in the organisation. He'll know people that Will doesn't. We have to persuade him to make Des speak to us. I'll deal with MI5. I know the officer in charge. We'll sort something out.'

'Are you sure, Jim?'

'Yes,' said Daley, with more confidence than he felt.

'Okay, I'll try.'

'You'll have to sound as normal as possible – relaxed.'

'That's no' going tae be easy.'

'I know, but still.'

'He loves this boy – like really loves him. Would you dae that tae Lizzie – betray her, I mean?'

'Not a good example,' said Daley with a grin.

Ella smiled at this. 'Okay. My mobile's in my handbag. Can you fetch me it doon fae the table?'

Daley watched as she searched through it. She removed a make-up bag and a harmonica. The latter made Daley raise an eyebrow, but he didn't feel he could ask why she carried such an item around with her. He'd certainly never seen her or Brian play any musical instrument. But you learned something new every day.

At last, Ella produced her mobile phone from the depths of the handbag. She took a few deep breaths.

'Remember, this is the only way we can help him, Ella.'

'Aye, fine I know it, Jimmy.' She touched the screen a couple of times and placed the phone to her ear, waited for a few moments, then shrugged at Daley. 'No reply,' she mouthed to the DCI. But suddenly she straightened in her seat and cleared her throat. 'Hello, son. How are you getting on?'

Daley nodded to her by way of encouragement.

She listened for a while, then spoke again. 'Och, I think I've got a cold coming on. That's why my voice is sounding a bit strange. I was just thinking about making some lunch. When will you be back?' She listened again. 'Where?'

Daley heard the sound of a car pulling up outside and peered through the net curtains.

'Oh right, I'll see you.' She ended the call and turned to Daley. 'That's him outside. He's on about this surprise.'

'Sit tight, Ella. Leave this to me.'

Two things happened at once. The front door swung open, and Brian Scott's feet could be heard thundering down the stairs.

Daley rushed to his feet and made for the hallway, Ella at his heels. They were too late. Scott had a young man in a headlock, while his son was aiming weak punches at his father.

'You said you were okay with this. I hate you, Dad!' Will roared.

'Let him go, Brian,' said Daley.

Reluctantly, Scott released his grip on the man and pushed him away. Des collided with the wall and leaned against it, rubbing his neck and gasping for breath. 'Fuck me, I knew you said your dad was unpredictable, but I didn't expect this, Will,' he gasped, wide-eyed.

'Uncle Jim, stop my dad, please! Arrest him or something!'

'It's not as easy as that, Will.'

'Aye, if there's anybody going tae be arrested, it'll be you, son.' Scott glared at Will.

'Shit,' said Des, and slid down the wall.

Linda Delaney fumed quietly as she mulled over what to do. She had a number of things to achieve in a short space of time. She'd never expected things to run smoothly, but the old man and Terry had complicated everything.

'Where now?' Declan asked from behind the wheel of the SUV. They'd left the injured Sean at a bus stop on the edge of Ballycastle. Making sure the road was quiet, and there were no CCTV cameras about, they'd made him as comfortable as possible before leaving him to his fate. Declan had called for an ambulance on a burner phone, and now he'd stopped the car on a verge to dispose of the device in a river.

'We move the big package tonight. Just me and you.'

'Isn't it risky? I mean the cops will be watching the place, and we've no backup if the boys don't find that pair.'

'You do the driving and the heavy lifting. Leave the cerebral stuff to me, got it?'

She stared at the river as it meandered past. It was still pouring, and what had been barely a flow through the spell of hot weather was rapidly becoming a torrent. Her options were limited, but she still had some. She put the mobile to her ear. 'It's tonight. We need to speed things up.'

Declan watched her. He could hear a man's voice on the other end of the line but couldn't make out what he was saying.

'It's the way it is, like it or loathe it. We knew that we'd have to be adaptable. This is us adapting.' She listened for a few more seconds, then ended the call without ceremony.

'So?'

'So, Dec, you get over to the bar and check out what's going on. How many have we there?'

'Five, I think.'

'Well, make it six. I'll call you when I need you.'

'Where will you be?'

'What are you, my probation officer? Just get on with it. And find them!'

'And if we do, what then?'

The sidelong look Linda gave him was all Declan needed to know.

Daley had persuaded Ella to go out for a while. Reluctantly, she'd taken off in the car, leaving Scott and Daley alone with Will and Des.

Daley had known Will Scott since he was born. In many ways, by build and looks, he was very like his father, though he had his mother's finer features.

Des was taller, thinner, squeezed into a pair of skinny jeans. While Will looked terrified, Des wore an almost detached expression.

'We know about the gun, Will. We know you bought it. We need to know why and from whom,' said Daley.

'Don't say anything, Will.'

'You can shut it!' said Scott. 'How you got my boy intae all this, I'll never understand.'

Des beamed. 'He ain't no boy any more, mister.'

Scott bunched his fists, but a look from Daley kept him in check.

'You realise that purchasing firearms on the black market is a crime? You could go to jail for years, Will,' said Daley.

Will looked at Des.

'You look at Jimmy, son. Never mind him,' said Scott.

'This is a farce,' said Des. 'I don't know who told you about this, but you don't even have the gun. So how can you charge him?'

'It isn't us you have to worry about. And anyway, there's a witness,' said Scott.

'Somebody on the beach?' Will blurted out. 'There was nobody there. I made sure of it.'

'Well, you missed them, Willie.'

'I don't understand.' He looked dumbfounded.

'All you have to know is that there's a witness and they can identify you.'

'It's bollocks, Will. Don't listen.' Des put his hand on Will's knee.

'I'll kick you right in the bollocks if you don't shut up,' said Scott.

'Oh, listen to it. Police brutality – the drama!'

'Do what he says,' said Will.

'Good advice,' Daley observed. 'Will, I need you to tell me where the gun is.' He looked at Des. 'And I need you to tell me what your role in all this is, and who you report to.'

'My role in what?' said Des innocently.

'Buying guns – the money. I want to know everything.'

'I never bought any gun. And I don't know what money you're talking about.'

'What are you saying, Des?' Will looked confused.

'Hey, lover. If you've got yourself in some kind of shit, don't blame me.'

'You gave me that money. You know all about the gun. You organised it all!'

'I think you're delusional, William. A wee bit like when you had the hots for Jed.' He turned to Scott. 'Did you know your son was trying to bed one of his lecturers?'

Before either Daley or Scott could react, Will swung a punch that connected with Des's nose. The crack was sickening.

'You bastard!' Des wailed, blood now pouring down his face.

'Fuck you, Des.' Will looked at his father. 'He gave me the money, the instructions. We were buying the gun for Linda.'

Through the pain of his broken nose, for the first time Des looked frightened. 'Don't say any more!' he shouted.

'You've been using me all this time.'

'Aw, poor Will, always the same. What a shame.' Des turned to Daley, doing his best to wipe away the blood from his nose. 'You saw him – he hit me. I want him arrested.'

Daley grabbed Will's fist before he was able to throw another punch. 'It's time to come clean, Will. Tell me where this gun is.'

Will hung his head.

'Aw, look, he's going to cry,' said Des.

257

'That's it, you're coming wae me.' Scott pulled Des off the couch and marched him to the door. 'If you think my son's got a good right hook, you should try mine.'

'Are you going to let your father do this to me, Will?' There was an edge of desperation in Des's voice as Scott shoved him out the room.

'He can do what he likes as far as I'm concerned. You're a lying bastard!'

Scott kicked the door shut behind them, and Daley edged nearer to his best friend's son. 'You need to tell me where the gun is now, Will.'

'I'm so sorry, Uncle Jim. This isn't how things were meant to be.'

'How were they meant to be?'

'We're trying to save the planet. But things got heavy, you know? I'm kind of caught up in it all, but I don't know what to do.'

'Heavy how?'

'We were down in London – just protesting. These guys – skinheads – they attacked us with baseball bats. I managed to run, but some of my mates were really badly hurt.'

'So the gun was for protection?'

'Yes! No one was going to use it. Linda said it would be a good deterrent.'

'Linda who?' Daley remembered Nathan Sidley mentioning somebody called Linda.

'Linda Alton, she was a temporary lecturer. She's a climate activist.'

'She's also a former terrorist. MI5 have been watching her for some time. Did you know that?' Daley could see by Will's face that he'd had no idea.

'But she wants to save the planet.'

'She wants to do other things, too.' Daley grabbed Will by both hands. 'Your dad and me can sort this. But you have to tell me everything, now.'

'I was waiting for something else.'

'What?'

'I don't know. Des said Linda would only refer to it as "the package".'

'And you have no idea what it was?'

'No, just that there was more stuff to be picked up at the same place where I bought the gun.'

'Which was where?'

'It's a bay on the Firdale road. I can't remember the name, but I can take you there.'

Daley sat back in his chair and sighed. 'You don't need me to tell you how stupid you've been, do you?'

Will lowered his head. 'You don't.'

'So, again, where's the gun?'

'It's in Dad's car. I taped it under the passenger seat.'

'Was that your idea?'

Will nodded.

'I suppose the last place anyone was going to look for it was in a police inspector's car.' Daley smiled.

'That's what I figured.'

'Okay. I'm going to speak to the MI5 officer. You'll have to tell him everything.'

'I don't know that much. Just that Linda would tell Des what to do and he'd tell me. Des has a big bag of cash, too. But that's all I know, honestly.'

'Anything written down – texts, messages, on paper?'

'Nothing written down. We did everything on the phone.'

'And you've got a burner?'

Will reached into his pocket and produced a small, old-fashioned mobile phone. 'Is this what you mean?'

'It probably is, yes.'

'Linda – well, Des – told me that the organisation paid for all the calls, and we were just to use it for climate business.'

'Okay. It's a burner phone. Not registered, no way of tracing the owner, so no way of catching them.'

'Oh.'

'Right, we'd better get going. But remember, you don't owe Des anything. He'd happily see you take the fall for this.'

'Don't worry. I've kind of picked that up.'

Daley stood. 'Trust me, we all live and learn, Will. Every one of us, me included.'

He called the office. Shaw was his usual calm and reassuring self on the other end of the line. 'Get Potts up to Brian's house as quickly as you can, Alasdair.'

'Yes, sir. I'll go and find him right away.'

'And don't let Symington or our guest hear what's going on, eh?'

'Received and understood.'

Daley could almost hear the knowing smile he reckoned would be spread across Shaw's face now. He didn't want Des anywhere near Iolo Harris. Not for the time being, at least.

36

Mercifully, the rain had eased to a fine drizzle. Still, both Terry and Hamish were sodden, perched on the birdwatchers' ledge on the steep cliff. But while Terry – the drug he'd been given now truly worn off – was shivering with cold and shock, Hamish was lying fast asleep, snoring but otherwise untroubled. Terry began to worry about this, but he reasoned that old fishermen were tough. They'd spent a lifetime fighting the elements. He supposed that being wet was something you could become rather accustomed to when you were a seaman.

He thought about his own job. Clearly, he'd have been reported missing by now. Surely whoever was occupying the old farmhouse would be under scrutiny. After all, his boss knew of his destination that day.

This thought cheered him, but the feeling was momentary. Working on the assumption that his erstwhile captors were the same people who had imprisoned Hamish in the old shed before recapturing them both, then the likelihood was that they wouldn't go anywhere near the property again. It would be the first place the police would look.

He thought about the people who had chained an old man in a dilapidated shed. Ironically, though his physical battles had been with the two men he'd left for dead in the pub, it was the woman who scared him most. There was something about her – her cold manner, that soulless expression. But the most frightening thing was her piercing green eyes. When he'd first run into her and the huge guy she was with, he'd noticed it. He should never have been so stupid as to believe they were his rescuers. If sharks had green eyes, they'd be like hers. Why hadn't he trusted his instincts?

Terry thought again of his uncle.

When things are wrong, you'll know, son.

He'd never wondered why that man seemed to know so much about weapons and the dark side of life. He'd been a kid back then – adults always knew everything. But now he was an adult himself, he realised that he had none of the knowledge of the quiet farmer from south of the border. Perhaps he'd been a soldier, though he'd never heard tell of it.

Suddenly Hamish stirred.

'Man, I've got a heid like a burst balloon,' he said, rubbing his temple with one gnarly hand.

'You're awake. Thank the Lord!'

'You can never thank him enough, in my experience, Terry.' Hamish looked around, squinting out over the grey waves. 'I'm assuming our predicament hasna improved any.'

'Not really.'

'Aye, right enough, us perched on a cliff, and all. Mind you, I'd rather be wherever this is than stuck in that shed.'

'What else do you remember?'

Hamish closed his eyes and thought for a moment. 'Noo, I mind o' that woman. The one you sent tae pick me up.'

'That's not really how it happened, Hamish.'

'No, I'm guessing not. Och, she had a look o' Jessie Macfarlane aboot her. I should have known better.'

'Who?'

'A woman I used tae know in Kinloch.'

'An old flame?'

'An auld bitch. She brought me up short aboot my kilt. I was at a wedding, and there's nothing worse than an adverse comment aboot your kilt when nuptials are being celebrated.'

'I'll bear that in mind.' Terry looked the old man up and down. He appeared to have no signs of scrapes, cuts or lumps. Also, now awake, he wasn't shivering, and just seemed at ease, despite being every bit as soaked through as Terry himself.

'I've been thinking I had a right go at the whisky. I'm guessing it was something much less beneficial.'

'We were drugged, Hamish. I'll spare you the details. But . . .'

'Aye, maybe for the best. Whatever they gave me filled my heid wae the most awful nightmares. I can testify tac that.'

Though the last thing Terry wanted to hear about was the product of Hamish's unconscious mind, he reckoned that it was good to keep him talking. It would help him stay awake. 'What were they about?'

'Ach, nothing solid, really. Faces – more kind o' feelings left behind than any firm notions.'

'Sounds mysterious.'

'The workings o' the human mind are a mystery. Scientists can say whoot they like, but they don't really know. I'm telling you, the auld folk knew o' the significance o' dreams. Aye, an' no' jeest dreams, neither. You can have strange feelings when you're wide awake, tae. My auld grandmother – they say she had the sight, you know.'

'The sight?'

'Surely you've heard o' the second sight?'

'Not really, sorry. Should I have done?'

'Quite possibly they call it something different o'er here. I'm always surprised by the different customs on this side o' the North Channel, it being only a few miles away fae Kinloch. It means you can see intae the future. No' all of it, by any means. But you get wee glimpses. It's up tae you how you interpret them, but they've always got something tae say.'

'And what's this sight telling you? Something good, I hope.'

Hamish shook his head. 'No, sadly nothing good tae report.'

'Great!'

'But somehow, whatever blackness there is – aye, and there's plenty o' it – I'm not sure it's shrouding you and me.'

Terry looked out to sea and puzzled over this for a few moments. If their plight wasn't black, he felt sorry for whoever it was Hamish had conjured up in his dreams.

'You wait; the sun will shine on us yet, young man.'

Staring into the grey gloom, Terry thought just about anything else was more likely. This suspicion was confirmed when he heard voices on the breeze. He knew sound carried over water more readily than land. With no little pain, he struggled to his feet and scanned the sea beyond the cliffs. There was nothing new, not even a distant vessel on the horizon. He leaned over, recoiling at the sight of the hard black rocks far below, but there was no sign of anyone on the narrow foreshore.

'I'm hearing voices,' said Hamish.

'Yes, and this time it's not your second sight.' Terry worked through the possibilities as he saw them. Could it be some happy birdwatchers? He thought the weather made that an unlikely prospect. Now the raised voices were clearly coming from above, back on the top of the cliff.

'I'm going to have a look. Sit tight, Hamish.' Terry made his way gingerly up the stone steps he'd fallen down only a short time before. Three steps from the top, he crouched, then craned his neck over the edge of the cliff. Sure enough, about ten men, strung out in a line, were making their way slowly from left to right, some prodding at the ground with sticks, one man with a pair of binoculars.

Terry felt his mouth grow dry, the sheer panic making it hard to swallow. In desperation he'd hoped that the voices belonged to police officers sent to find them. But these were no police officers. They wore jeans, leather jackets, or in some cases no jackets at all, despite the weather. Even from here, Terry could make out tattooed arms, like patterned sleeves on well-muscled arms under T-shirts.

The men were searching for them. And they were getting closer.

Nathan Sidley was in his room in the guesthouse he'd chosen for his mission to Kinloch. Though he liked the comfort and privacy offered by a hotel, he didn't like the many distractions that came with it. Since he was technically freelance, no newspaper was going to pay for his room or cover his bar bill. But, he reassured himself, what he was doing would bring its financial reward soon enough. And the money was guaranteed. Of that he was sure.

He read the message on his phone again. In a way he was surprised. But after a lifetime spent on shifting sands, more unexpected movement didn't faze him.

He pulled his rucksack off the floor. It contained the stuff of a modern journalist's life, even though he was far from being a modern journalist. Yes, mobile phones were handy, and laptops were wonderful tools. But they came with their own problems. He would have hated to be a young reporter these days. No expense account to speak of. No boozy lunches in the pub before rushing off some copy. Instead, eyes on you everywhere you went. In a sense, this brave new world of technology had imprisoned the soul rather than freeing it.

Nathan was an old-fashioned investigative journalist. Fearless, ambitious, exacting in everything he did. He'd been taught by the best, and now he was considered the elder statesman of his craft. Though such was the plight of the newspaper industry – of news-gathering in general – that status didn't come at the handsome price it would once have commanded.

He pulled his Sony Alpha camera from the bag. The battery was showing nearly full. Here was another priceless bit of kit. But the instant results, the immediacy of capturing an image that could be flashed around the world in minutes, didn't compare to the thrill of seeing your work appear magically in the dim red glow of a darkroom. The anticipation, the thrill was all gone, replaced by a tiny screen you had to squint at, and could never hope to appraise properly.

Part of him longed to go back to the days of inky fingers changing typewriter ribbons, querulous photographers with sharp tongues, dodges and dirty deeds, the time and freedom to write, the time and freedom to live. For Nathan Sidley the world had been reduced to unseen pixels that ruled them all: the dominance of the invisible.

On the other hand, he was still hanging on. And whatever happened in the next few hours looked likely to underwrite a happy retirement.

He lay back on the bed, his shoulders still tender from being propelled to the floor by a local yokel. It had been a long time since that last happened. But it hadn't been that far from here – just across the water in Belfast.

Now there was something he definitely didn't miss.

There was a sharp knock at the door of his room. He eased himself off the bed to open it, irritated by the disturbance.

'Who's there?' he asked.

'You're white as a ghost, son,' said Hamish, as Terry appeared back on the ledge.

'Aye, with good reason, too. They're searching for us – about ten of them.'

'Are you sure it's no' the polis?'

'Absolutely sure.'

'Not so good then.' Hamish scowled. 'It's at times like this you wish you had a good pipe o' baccy on the go, right enough.'

'It's at times like this you wish the police would arrive in a helicopter.'

'Fair comment, son.' Hamish took Terry's hand. 'I'd like tae thank you for whoot you tried tae dae for me. You're a fine young lad. And I don't say that often aboot the younger generation, these days.'

'Sounds like a goodbye.'

Hamish looked out to sea. 'Well, maybe it is.'

'What do you mean?'

'I mind I saw this film back in the pictures at Kinloch. Och, must have been the mid-seventies, or thereabouts. Two desperados on the run fae the law; Paul Newman was in it.'

'*Butch Cassidy and the Sundance Kid*?'

'You've got a fine knowledge o' cinema, and no mistake.'

'My dad loves that film.' Terry shrugged. 'Reminds him of his young days, so he says.'

'He must have had an interesting youth.'

'I don't know. He never talks about it. He and my uncle ran about together when they were young. My mother's brother, not his. That's how my folks met – through my uncle.'

'Now there's a thing, right enough.'

'You were talking about the film?'

'Oh aye, that's right. You'll remember the scene on the cliff, you being an aspiring Barry Norman and all.'

'The bit where they jump?' Terry's expression was incredulous.

'Aye, the very scene. Man, but you've a fine heid on you, right enough.'

'Are you really suggesting we jump down there?' He nodded towards the railings.

Hamish looked up at him, his eyes suddenly filled with tears. 'I'm no' going back intae a shed tae be tied up ready for getting my throat cut. If it's a choice between that and a plunge intae the sea, well, the sea wins every time. I've spent my life on it; I might as well die in it tae.'

Though the prospect was grim, common sense told Terry that there was no other way out of their plight. The men searching for them were making their way towards the cliff. They'd surely see the signpost and investigate the viewing platform on which he and Hamish were now huddled. He'd probably killed two of their number. They would kill him – no question. At first, the sheer logic of this calculation surprised him. But he remembered reading about people facing death, the calmness that settled over them when the end was near. He supposed that what he was feeling now was nothing more or less than that. A surrender to the inevitable.

Then he remembered how normal his life had been until this point. He'd been reasonably good at school, though he'd never fancied going to university. A steady position in the civil service was – if he was lucky –a job for life. His last working day had begun like so many others. He got up at seven, showered, dressed, had a cup of coffee and slice of toast, and said goodbye to his parents before heading out for the office.

He hadn't realised then that it would be the last time he'd ever see them. The sudden memory made him gulp back tears.

'Man, but you're deep in your thoughts, son.'

'I'm just thinking how shit this all is, Hamish.'

Hamish nodded sagely. 'My auld skipper used tae have a saying: *Where there's life, there's hope*. I think he was right. And I tell you, I've witnessed a miracle or two in my time.'

'Well, if it's going to happen, it better happen soon.' Terry was convinced he could hear the voices above getting louder.

'So, the first sign o' them at the top o' they stairs, we jump, right?'

'Yes, Hamish, we jump.'

37

Daley was alone with Iolo Harris in his glass box.

'All very mysterious, Jim.'

'I want to make a deal.'

'What?'

'I have information – I know the whereabouts of one of the people you're looking for.'

'I'm sorry – maybe I'm missing the point. But the last time I looked we were sitting in a police office, and you were a detective chief inspector. I've done deals – of course I have – but usually with some grubby criminal in a squalid flat. Not with a police officer in the course of his duty!'

'This is different.'

'Okay. Right, we know that Carrie isn't whiter than white. It's mostly not her fault, but let's say she has a few things in her past that could have changed the trajectory of her career. I get it. If you're worried that I'm going to write reports about all that, don't be.'

Daley sighed. 'It's not about her.'

'Who then? Have you beaten the shit out of another dentist? Because I'm not worried about that either – I'd probably have killed him.'

'You're not interested in justice in the way I am, Iolo. It's the bigger picture for you. This person can help you. But I need a guarantee he'll not be brought down if he does.'

'Wow! It's a right den of vipers you have here, Jim. Fair play, I hadn't expected this. But I'll hear you out, and if I can do anything for you, you have my word that I'll try – *try*, mind.'

'The young lad in the photo you couldn't identify. He's Brian's son.'

Harris looked momentarily confused. 'You mean, as in Brian Scott?'

'Yes.'

'Murkier still, isn't it? I knew you Scottish lads were deep, but this is something else.'

'He helps you, you keep him away from scrutiny, okay? He's been manipulated. All he did was buy a gun.'

'All? With gun crime the way it is now? I don't think that's a minor issue, do you?'

'No, of course not.'

'There're some seriously bad people tied up in this.'

'I know. I think they've got Hamish.'

'Yes, well, we're doing our best there. The PSNI are on it. Though we can't be sure he didn't just sink, can we?'

'I think the photographic evidence speaks against that, don't you?' Daley bit his lip. 'I need you to be straight with me, Iolo.'

'Former Irish terrorists, extreme climate activists ready to take their protests up a few notches – quite a few.'

Daley sighed and lowered his head. 'The worst possible scenario. Fuck.'

'We have an insider. The information is patchy, for reasons I can't go into. But I think they may have Hamish – or had him.'

'Had him? What do you mean?'

'Just what I said. Somehow, he escaped. I'm waiting to hear more.'

'You should have told me earlier!' Daley banged his fist on the desk. 'And where did they *have him*?'

'Across the water.'

'Ireland?'

'Yes, County Antrim. The PSNI have a specialist unit on it.'

Daley felt a mixture of emotions. But one thing troubled him. 'So you've known for a while he didn't just sink. You've had eyes on him, you admit that.'

It was Harris's turn to sigh. 'Yes, we've had eyes on him, of sorts. But I had no idea who he was, or how he came to be in a tight spot. I only realised when I came here. We thought he was just another bad apple.'

'What about your man on the ground? Why can't you get more from him?'

'We think he's been compromised. We haven't heard anything for hours.'

'They've rooted him out, you mean?'

'I honestly don't know.'

'I want you to tell me where it is – Hamish's last known whereabouts.'

'And I want to talk to Brian Scott's son. Deal, is it?'

Annie was in her office at the back of the bar. The longer time passed without hearing any news about Hamish, the worse she felt. It was an all-consuming sadness, the like of which she'd only felt a few times in her life. It was dragging her down.

She'd tried to rationalise things in her mind: Hamish was a good age; he'd had a good life. But these notions always seemed stupid, or callous. Just about everyone she knew who had knowledge of the sea reckoned there was now no hope. The thought forced her spirits down further and further. She'd heard of people with depression – knew some, even. But she'd never thought that any feeling could be so painful. She hadn't felt anything like it for years.

A silver-framed photograph of her late mother took pride of place on her desk. The woman with the monochrome stare felt almost like a stranger now. Both of Annie's parents had died young, when she was only in her twenties. Thirty years – she found it hard to believe. But it was little things that bothered her. She could remember her father's voice, but she struggled to remember her mother's. It seemed perverse.

Annie's aunt – her mother's sister – was still alive. She guessed that, in her mind, she'd replaced her mother's voice with her aunt's, though she couldn't remember them sounding alike when they were together. It was strange how the mind played tricks.

She delved into her bag, fishing out her purse. Annie willed herself to do this as little as possible, but in times of crisis it was always her last resort, a tiny ray of sunshine, albeit tinged with tragedy. With two fingers she pulled out a passport-style photograph of a young couple. Its colour had faded, but his mullet and her feather cut were enough to date the image.

On the back in her youthful, round hand: *Me and Chick '82.*

She stared at him; his face next to hers on the image that was seared on to her heart. He had blue eyes, a square jaw and a big smile. It was that she'd first noticed when they were at school together – the broad, cheeky grin. His hair was auburn like his mother's, thick and wavy. She remembered how it felt running her hands through it.

They'd been to Glasgow for the day, Christmas shopping. Tired of the festive throng, they'd sought sanctuary in a little bar overlooking the Clyde. It was surprisingly quiet, but they'd only had a couple of drinks; the thought of bursting for the loo on the long bus journey back to Kinloch was too much to bear, even then. And for some reason, that hour spent with the young man she loved stood out in her mind as being the happiest moment of her life.

A few days before Christmas, she'd heard the news. Annie had been clearing up after the lunch service. Chick's father, Alec, had appeared in the hotel lobby, ashen-faced, shaking. Now, as Annie stared out from her little office, she could see the spot on the floor where they'd stood on that awful day.

It had been a freak accident in the distillery. He'd been up at the top of the stows – tall whisky barrel stacks, a library of maturing spirit – tapping casks to make sure they were sound, not leaking. The metal frame he'd gripped was rusty. It broke off in his hand, so the inquiry said.

The terror of his last few moments had played across her mind from that day on: the shock as he lost his balance, the horror as he fell; the rush of the hard floor as Chick plummeted to his death.

At the time, both she and his parents had been told he died instantly. A few months later, the man he'd been working with was in the bar with his colleagues. They were celebrating the last day of work before the summer holidays. Annie had just graduated from waitress to barmaid and was busy fussing over empty glasses and full ashtrays. They'd had a few, and she supposed his workmates barely registered her presence when they raised a toast to their dead colleague.

At first, the gesture warmed her heart. But then Willie Tait described how Chick had screamed in agony on the hard floor.

'Poor bastard. By the time I got tae the phone in the wee Excise bothy he'd stopped. He was deid.'

Annie had dropped the tray of empty glasses and remained motionless, unable to move, unable to breathe, unable to come to terms with what she'd just heard; shock, her father had called it.

In less than a year, he was dead too.

Annie swallowed hard as she touched Chick's face on the crumpled old photograph that went everywhere with her. Yes, she'd met other young men; yes, she'd enjoyed their company. But Chick was the only man she'd ever loved. In a way, she'd never stopped mourning for him.

'Annie, a word, please.' Ian Macmillan's voice was low and serious, making her jump.

'Yes, Ian,' she replied with as much lightness as she could muster. 'What can I do for you?'

'Not here. I'd like to speak to you in my office upstairs, please.'

Just at that moment Peter the cellar man lumbered up the stone steps from his workplace in the bowels of the hotel.

'Mind the bar and reception would you, Peter?' ordered Macmillan. 'This way,' he said to Annie before marching off.

Peter gave her a *who knows* shrug as he wiped his hands on his dirty canvas apron, and she followed her boss. She didn't need Macmillan to show her the way. Annie knew every nook and cranny of the building, the creak of every floorboard, the rattle of every lock: the very song of the place.

He went quickly up the winding staircase to the third floor. His office was next to his accommodation suite, just two doors along the corridor from Annie's own room.

He ushered his manager into the office. 'Take a seat.' His tone was still brusque.

'If this is aboot your friend, I can only apologise again. I thought he was a journalist after some scandal story aboot Hamish. You know whoot these folk are like.'

'Did you even take any time to listen before you set your goon on him?'

'Noo, jeest wait a minute. I never telt oor Ally tae touch the man. That was his decision.' Annie decided it was time to fight her own corner. 'In any case, your friend was a cheeky so-and-so. If he'd jeest come in and asked for a drink like everybody else, it would have been fine.'

'So just what did he do that was sufficiently offensive to ensure he ended up on the floor?'

'As I say, he was mouthy.'

'Mouthy?' Macmillan said the word as though he'd never heard it before. 'A man comes in for a drink in my hotel, and because my manager doesn't like the tone of his voice, or the cut of his jib, he ends up being assaulted.' He shook his head. 'It's just not good enough, Annie.'

'It's been a difficult time. You know, wae Hamish missing. The customers are all wound up tight, as you can imagine.'

'No, I can't imagine, Annie!' Macmillan's voice was raised for the first time. 'I know you've worked here for most of your life. And I know for much of that time you've done so without scrutiny.'

'Huh! Nae scrutiny, in Kinloch? You must be kidding!'

'I meant no managerial scrutiny. And that's the problem.'

Annie could feel a knot in her chest. It was the same knot she'd felt the previous year when the hotel was under threat of closure and conversion into luxury flats. She felt as though the ground was slipping away beneath her like shifting sand.

'You can see what I'm trying to do to this place.'

'Aye, tart it up a wee bit. Long before time.'

'No, not just *tart it up a wee bit*.' Macmillan's tone was more conversational now, which raised Annie's spirits. 'Once the rooms are finished, we'll concentrate on the lobby and the dining room.'

Annie nodded enthusiastically. 'That's great! It's been crying out tae be done for long and weary. Mind you, best done after Christmas, I'd say. We've got a lot o' functions booked from the end o' November onwards, Ian.'

Macmillan shook his head. 'Listen, I don't think you're really picking up what I'm trying to say here.'

'You're trying tae improve the hotel. I get it.'

'Yes, that's true.' Annie noticed a slight nervous tic under Macmillan's right eye. She hadn't seen it before. 'But I'm taking the place in a different direction.'

'Oh aye – like wae the meals, an' that. Mair fancy pants. It's the right thing.'

He sighed. 'I want this to be a destination hotel. Where people come to be pampered, eat well, relax. Not just a haven for fishermen and travelling salesmen.'

'They can be a pain in the arse, but the few we have left are jeest aboot all you get in January and February. You'll be glad o' them.'

'No, I won't!' Macmillan banged the desk in front of him with his fist. 'We're going upmarket and it starts here.'

'Okay, whoot is it you want me tae do?'

'Annie, you've been a great friend to the County. I'm more than aware of that. You worked with my grandfather, and that means something to me. But I'm bringing in a new manager. This person has run some top boutique hotels in Canada and the States, is used to web marketing high-end hotel experiences. It's what we need right now.'

Annie stared at him. 'Okay. So I get a new boss. I know that I canna work websites and stuff like that. But there's still a hotel tae run.'

'Annie, I'm sorry. I have to let you go. If it's any consolation, I'm reviewing the entire staff. My new manager wants a fresh start.'

Annie sat back in her chair, open-mouthed.

'I know this is a shock. But this place has to earn money. I've had to sell part of it because of business issues I have elsewhere. The ownership profile will change, as will that of the place itself.'

Annie looked at him with tears brimming her eyes. 'But whoot can I dae? I live here, I eat here, I work here!'

'I'll give you a generous severance package. You'll have three months to vacate your room, to find somewhere else. I'm sorry, but the job's changed. The County Hotel is going to as well.'

Annie raised her jaw proudly. 'So, how much notice dae you want?'

'Listen, under these circumstances, none. I'll give you three months of your salary, plus five thousand pounds as a flat fee, tax paid. But your employment ends with immediate effect. You'll continue to live here free of charge until the three-month period I mentioned is over and you've made other arrangements. I don't think I could be more generous. I'm sorry. It was a purely business decision.'

Annie was about to speak when the phone on Macmillan's desk rang.

'If you'll excuse me.'

'Whoot aboot the bar? Big Peter can't stay there a' day.'

'I've fixed something up for that. Now, I need to take this call.'

Annie felt as though she would pass out as she walked the short distance to her room. She fumbled open the door and fell on her bed sobbing.

38

Terry could hear the voices overhead growing louder on the breeze. They were still some distance away but having risked a hesitant look over the edge of the cliff a few minutes before, he could see they were being methodical. These men knew what they were doing, searching everywhere with a fine toothcomb, the way he'd seen police officers searching on the TV news.

He was thirsty, his throat was dry, and his bones ached from captivity and his battle with Sean. He now felt no remorse whatsoever for shooting both men in the bar that had been their prison. It had been a fight for survival, but one that now looked destined to be lost.

Why had he trapped them here at the very edge of the land? Hamish was in such poor shape and they couldn't have expected such a large search party, but these were poor excuses.

Terry's thoughts became spiritual. He supposed that most people he knew only ever prayed when they were in trouble. Though his mother chided him for his reticence about attending church, he had a true faith. His father had always been a religious man, his mother less so, but they were both regular attendees at the chapel of St Mary and the Holy Saints.

His thoughts were becoming jumbled. One part of his brain was praying, while the other part was considering the jump he and Hamish had planned. They would almost certainly die, though he'd noticed that the tide was coming in; some of the black jagged rocks had disappeared under the crashing waves. But survival was a forlorn hope, and Terry knew it.

Ironically, the sun was shining again. At least he wasn't cold. He raised his head to the heavens, doing his best to pray in a way that could be considered meaningful.

Hamish suddenly sat bolt upright.

'What's wrong?' Terry asked, worried that the old man was having a stroke, or worse. Their predicament was bad enough without a medical emergency.

'We need tae get away fae here. A friend needs me.' Hamish had a faraway look in his eyes. It was as though he was staring blankly out to sea but looking at another place entirely.

'Are you sure you're okay?'

'I'm fine, but there's a tragedy on the cards.'

'Stop being mystical. I know what the tragedy is. These guys are going to look over the edge of the cliff, and if we don't jump they'll kill us.'

'Neither of us is dying today, but that's nae comfort.' Hamish held his head in his hands.

'I wish I shared your confidence.' Terry supposed that stress affected everyone in different ways. Hamish, still cradling his head, was now rocking backwards and forwards, muttering incoherently to himself. Maybe this was his way of coping.

Hamish wailed – a loud, keening sound.

'Shut up! They'll hear you.' The old man fell silent but continued to rock to and fro as Terry held his breath. He could hear shouts, sometimes laughter, on the air, but there was no sense of footsteps rushing to find the source of the wail. Perhaps the cliff and the sea had muffled the noise.

Then something changed.

There was a bang, a crack like the report of a gun. More shouting, the sound of revved engines, a scream, then another shot.

'What on earth is happening now?' said Terry. He quickly realised that he'd said this to himself. Hamish showed no sign of having heard the commotion above, or of halting his rocking.

Crouching, Terry made his way back up the stone steps carved in the cliff wall and raised his head as far above the edge as he dared. There were more men, two vans and an SUV. He saw one individual being struck with a baseball bat as others were herded into the vans, their hands held or secured behind their backs, he couldn't tell.

At first, his heart soared – the police. They were saved! But when he saw one searcher breaking free from his captor and being brought down with a single shot, he realised that whoever these newcomers were, they were most certainly not police officers. At least not like any he'd seen. He'd heard stories of the Troubles, but he was too young to remember all that. His uncle used to sit in the evenings telling tales. At the time they'd been disguised for young ears, but he'd realised much later that stories of poor farmers taking up arms against vainglorious kings were substitutes for his uncle's political credo.

He scuttled back down the steps to where Hamish now stood staring out to sea. 'There's something going on up there, but I'm buggered if I know what it is.'

'Aye. I dare say it'll be the last thing we expect it tae be.' Hamish didn't take his gaze from the distant horizon.

'I wish you'd stop behaving like some weirdo and speak to me, Hamish.' Terry was worried. But Hamish was standing tall now, neither trembling nor looking distressed. In fact, following his wailing and rocking, he looked calm, determined even.

He pointed a thick, gnarled finger out to sea.

'Are you casting a spell, Hamish?'

'Dae you see the stretch of coast yonder?'

Terry screwed up his eyes and looked in the direction Hamish was pointing. 'Aye. What about it?'

'It's the coast o' Kintyre. And it's where I need tae be right this very minute.'

'I think you'll have to wait. We've got a few problems to deal with here first.'

'Problems have a habit o' dealing wae themselves, young man.'

Terry was only half listening. He darted up the steps once more and looked over the cliff edge. His heart sank.

Brian Scott looked on as Iolo Harris led Will into the interview room.

'Come on, Brian. The helicopter is five minutes out. We need to get down to the green.' Daley turned to leave, but Scott lingered. 'Come on!'

'Dae you trust that Welsh bugger, Jimmy? Mind he rolled us o'er on Gairsay.'

'Put it like this, Bri, we don't have many options at the moment, as I'm sure you know. Will has even fewer.'

'He should have a lawyer in there with him – at least one of us.'

'It's what Iolo wants.'

'And what he wants he gets, eh? It's no' like you tae hold your hands up and surrender, big man.'

'I know when I'm out of options, Brian. If that wasn't your son in there, you'd agree.'

'Something doesnae feel right, Jimmy.'

Daley felt the same, though he didn't give the feeling voice. The fact that Brian Scott was experiencing similar reservations was even more disconcerting. They both trusted their guts. Years of being police officers had ensured that. But, Daley realised, it could hardly be any other way, given the circumstances. With Hamish probably in the hands of former terrorists, and Brian's son being questioned by the Security Service, the feeling of dislocation and doubt was inevitable.

'I've told Shaw to make sure that Will goes nowhere. Iolo knows he's in our custody. We've no choice, Brian. We've got to go and find Hamish.'

'That's just it, Jimmy. That bugger should have told us about the auld bloke.'

'It was operational. He didn't know who Hamish was, he just knew they were holding someone.'

'He put Hamish's life in danger. Who knows, he might already be deid.'

'It's being bright and cheery that keeps you going, isn't it?'

'I don't trust these spooks, Jimmy. I never will. But I trust you. Let's go.'

Reluctantly, Scott followed Daley out to the car, leaving his son to be interrogated by an MI5 officer.

39

Carrie Symington fretted in her office, her mobile phone before her on the desk. All her calls were being monitored now in case Bower contacted her. But this arrangement itself made Symington uncomfortable. Despite Iolo Harris's boundless goodwill and bonhomie, she knew he was utterly ruthless when it came to achieving the ends upon which he was set. She knew if his mission's being accomplished involved revealing her past, he wouldn't hesitate.

Worse still, though she reckoned Scott was still on her side, Symington was no longer convinced she had Daley's support. Would the big detective stay loyal to her, if only for his friend's sake?

Harris's head appeared round the door. 'No word, I take it?'

'No, nothing,' Symington replied. 'Should I go back to the hotel? It's maybe where he feels safe.'

Giving her proposal no consideration whatsoever, Iolo shook his head. 'Nah. If he wants you, he'll be in touch on the blower. We're reaching the business end of all this now. He needs you.'

Symington thought of the dead men on the plane. It seemed like weeks ago instead of just a few days.

'Problem?'

'I was just wondering about the men who died on the aircraft. We don't seem to be hearing very much on that subject.'

Iolo grinned. 'Don't worry, I know all we need to know. They were a bit like young Mr Scott through there: daft. It always amazes me how easily led some people are – especially when it comes to causes they think are worthy.'

'Like saving the planet? I'd call that more than just *worthy*.'

'Would you indeed? Well, nice to see you haven't lost your spirit, despite everything.'

Symington caught a barb in this. 'Do you believe in anything apart from the Security Service?'

'Yes, I believe in lots of things. It's what I know that's the problem.'

'Like what?'

'That it only takes a few really shit people to turn good intentions bad. Take these extreme climate protesters, for instance. They want to save the planet, yet they're willing to go to any lengths to do it.'

'You know what they're planning?'

Iolo took a seat. 'They have some very wealthy backers, you know. And in my experience, where there is money there's the opening for greed. Let's just say that if the money men knew how their donations were being used they'd run a mile – fast, too.'

'I know they're in league with former terrorists, so I assume they're looking for weapons – bombs, or at least the capability to make one.'

'Yes. But it's not as simple as that. Bombs we can deal with – we know about them, we can see them. It's things we can't see that are most dangerous.'

Symington shook her head. 'Riddles now?'

'All I can say at this point. But I think we're going to find out for sure very shortly.'

'Did you get this from Will Scott?'

'Yes, and other intelligence we have.'

'How is he?'

'The lad? Oh, I'd say scared shitless.'

'No wonder. It's not every day MI5 come calling.'

'It's not every day you find yourself in the middle of a plot to kill lots of people.'

Symington's blood ran cold. 'That bad?'

'Yes, I'm sad to say it is.'

Daley wasn't keen on helicopters. They looked and felt far too flimsy for his liking. He gazed out of the window to try to take his mind off obsessing about the rotor blades malfunctioning and the fatal downwards plunge. He didn't feel that way about planes, and supposed it was something to do with the more solid reassurance of fixed wings.

He looked across at Scott, who was clearly distracted, no doubt worrying about Will. 'You okay, Bri?'

'Dandy.' Scott's voice was metallic through the headphones.

'We shouldn't be too long. PSNI officers will meet us.'

'Forgive me for no' jumping wae joy.'

'How long?' Daley asked the pilot.

'Roughly five minutes, sir.'

Daley looked back out over the sea. Even though the sun was shining, and the water was blue with little white tips here and there, it still looked forbidding as far as he was concerned. He thought about Hamish and his love for the element. Where was he? Was he still alive? It played to his notions of chance and bad luck. Every time he stared at a

287

dead-eyed corpse, one more victim of the endless churn of violence, he wondered at what point they'd taken the fatal decision that had ended their lives. For a police officer, the very process of building a case was a tale being told. You were assembling the full picture of what took an ordinary person to a mortuary slab.

'Is that the Giant's closet?' said Scott, nodding at his window.

Daley craned over his friend. 'Causeway, Brian.'

'Oh, right. They're almost identical. Fae what I've seen in pictures an' that.'

The pilot cut in. 'Just making our descent now. We'll be landing in three minutes.'

Instinctively, both Daley and Scott checked their safety belts as the aircraft banked to the right. They were flying over a small town nestled around a harbour now, normal people going about their usual business, unaware of the drama that was unfolding all around them.

The buildings dwindled to farmland as their height above the ground decreased. Farm animals, the odd tractor or thicket of trees, stone dykes and fences marking field boundaries, scattered farmhouses.

The helicopter began to slow, coming to a stop hovering over a field.

'I hate it when they dae that,' said Scott. 'You're used tae flying in planes – hey, if one o' them stops in mid-air, you're in the shit, let me tell you.'

The noise in the cabin grew louder as they lowered towards the field. Daley could see police officers in forensic suits, others with automatic weapons. They landed with a bump, and slowly the noise disappeared as the rotors ratcheted to a stop.

The detectives unbuckled their harnesses and exited the aircraft. A PSNI inspector was there to greet them, a sidearm in a holster at his waist.

'You know where you are when you see all these shooters, Jimmy.' Scott shuddered.

'Don't worry, they're on our side.'

'Tell that tae my boy.'

The inspector introduced himself as O'Leary. He led them up a small hill and into a muddy farmyard. There was little sign of life, or the stuff of agriculture. No farm machinery or livestock.

'Been lying empty for four years or so,' said O'Leary. 'I'll take you to where we think they held your man.'

He led them round the side of the building, out of sight of the front door and the rough lane that dropped down on to the main road. Before them a long shed sat at an angle to the main house. It looked as though it could collapse at any moment.

'Here we are.' O'Leary stepped over the remains of a door and into the dank shed. Slits of sunlight entering through gaps in the planking cut through the gloom, but with no door they were able to see reasonably well.

'I'll huff and I'll puff, and I'll blow your hoose doon,' said Scott. 'Isnae exactly Barlinnie. A right gust o' wind and this would be hanging aboot oor ears.'

'Can we pick anything up?' asked Daley.

'No problem. Our forensic lads have been through it all.' He reached into his pocket and produced a small evidence bag, already labelled and tagged. 'Do either of you recognise this?' He handed Daley the bag.

'Shit,' said Scott as Daley turned the bag over in his big hands. 'It's Hamish's briar pipe.'

Daley nodded to O'Leary. 'Yes, I'm pretty sure this belongs to the man we're looking for.'

'Aye, we thought as much. We found a mobile phone, too.'

'I'm no' sure Hamish had a mobile. But what I want tae know is why didn't he just batter his way oot o' here? A ten-year-old could break the walls o' this place doon.'

'Over here.' O'Leary pointed to a severed rope attached to a stake. 'Looks like he was tied up there. We've taken DNA samples from it and other items. We're waiting for your boys to find something of your missing man's to match it with, then we'll know for sure.'

'What other items?' asked Scott.

'A bucket of urine.'

Daley shook his head. The very thought of Hamish tethered in here made him sick to the stomach. 'Tell me about the phone – and why is the door battered in?'

'Ah, that's the better news. The phone belonged to one Terry Johnstone who works for the council in Ballycastle – a trainee assessor. He was sent here to ascertain if the farmhouse was occupied. Folk had seen lights, and you know how easily spooked people can get in the countryside.'

'Especially aroon' here,' said Scott.

'Meaning?' O'Leary cocked his head to one side.

'Northern Ireland. It's no' exactly withoot its problems, eh?'

'Have you never heard of the Good Friday Agreement, Inspector Scott?'

'Aye, I have. I've heard o' the tooth fairy, tae, but it doesnae mean I believe it.'

'I'll have you know that our crime rates are well below those in some parts of Scotland.'

'You'll be right wae Kinloch,' Scott said ruefully. 'Anyway, if it's that safe and quiet how come yous are Mr Glock's best customers?'

Daley intervened before the PSNI inspector decided to shoot the ADI. 'This Terry Johnstone, is he a good lad?'

'By all accounts he is that. Conscientious at work, no criminal record et cetera.'

'From a good family?'

O'Leary hesitated. 'His mother and father are fine folk.'

Daley detected something in the inspector's voice. 'But?'

'His uncle. Lives in the Republic these days. Well, ever since he was released. Joe Dougherty.'

'Released?' said Scott.

'He was an old IRA man. Not the bombing and shooting kind. He dealt with internal affairs, if you take my meaning.'

'An enforcer, you mean,' said Daley.

'I don't think I should comment on that, DCI Daley. It's more complex than you might imagine here.' Deftly, he changed the subject. 'We found Terry's car at the bottom of the lane.'

'But you think he helped Hamish escape?'

'Quite certain of it. The mobile phone belongs to him. There's blood splatter around the door. I'll bet it comes up a match for the lad. We know he was sent to the farmhouse to find out what was going on and happened upon your friend tied up in here.'

'And broke him out.'

'Aye, a brave boy, so he is.'

'Wait. How come they left the car?' said Scott.

'Someone was thinking. My theory is that they were frightened their captors would appear back any minute.

Looks like they took off up into the hills. That's where we lost them.'

'You can surely track them?'

'My name's O'Leary, not Tonto, kemosabe. But we're trying.'

'You'd never get a job wae those guys that chased down Butch Cassidy and the Sundance Kid. Relentless bastards, that mob.' Scott shook his head at the memory.

'Is he for real?' O'Leary asked Daley.

'Unfortunately, yes.'

'What dae you mean *unfortunately*, Jimmy?'

'So what next?'

'We're following the intelligence from the Security Service. We've had reports of an incident about ten miles from here. We've officers heading for the scene now.'

'Connected?'

'Who knows? But it seems unlikely with all that's going on that it wouldn't be. Despite what your inspector over here thinks, County Antrim is a quiet place these days.'

Scott shrugged, unconvinced, while Daley thought. 'We're looking for a RIB – a big one. Red flashes.'

'You'll have your work cut out. They make them just down the coast. Hundreds that match that description.'

Daley leaned in. 'How much have they told you?'

'Who, MI5? Just about the usual.'

'Which is?'

'As little as possible – bugger all apart from the bare bones, in this case.'

'What about an airfield in the vicinity?' Daley cast his mind back to the lines he'd drawn on the map at home. Based on the flight direction of the plane that crash-landed at

Machrie airport, and on observation from those on the ground, plus the time the pathologist reckoned it had been in the air, it could only have come from this area, he reckoned. 'I know it's a long shot.'

'Maybe not as long as you think, DCI Daley.' O'Leary led them out of the gloomy shed and back into the sunshine. They skirted round the side of the farmhouse, Scott cursing at the underfoot conditions. A washing green with overgrown grass and three rusted poles but no clothes line stood to the rear of the building. Further on, the land dipped down on to another field. It was flat, long and straight. 'How's this for your airstrip?'

'Spot on,' said Daley.

'And we've found traces of aircraft fuel and wheel tracks.'

'What's been going on, Jimmy?' said Scott.

'I don't know, Bri. But whatever it was, it started here.'

40

Declan shook his head as he ended the call. 'No reply. What do you think's wrong?'

Linda Delaney was unmoved. 'I can't micro-manage everything. At some point folk have to take responsibility for themselves. Fuck, you would think I was dealing with boy scouts, not the men I used to know. Drive on. I'll tell you where to turn off.'

Declan did as he was told, revving the big diesel engine of the SUV along the narrow single-track road. They passed by rolling hills of fields with cows, sheep and the occasional horse.

'You don't see so many horses these days,' he said by way of making conversation.

'No wonder you're not married, big man. You're a boring bastard. Shut up, I'm thinking.'

Thereafter, Declan decided his best course of action was to carry on in silence, something he hated doing. The big Ulsterman enjoyed driving, but always accompanied by Bruce Springsteen or the Waterboys at full volume. As he slipped into a lay-by to let a tractor pass, he tried to pluck up courage to ask Linda if he could switch on the radio.

It was strange, he thought. Even Sean, a hard man he'd known for three decades, deferred to Linda, and by no means was it his natural state. He'd seen Sean stand up and better some of the toughest men he'd known. Yet this small, middle-aged woman was the boss, there was no doubt of that.

'Slow down and take the next right,' Linda commanded, as though she'd read his mind.

He nearly missed the turn-off. A line of oak trees in full leaf concealed the entrance to the rough lane. But before Linda could chastise him further he steered the large vehicle into the tight opening. Travelling much more slowly now, the SUV was brushed by overhanging branches and stray thickets of bramble while an endless parade of insects, apparently bent on self-destruction, bounced off the windscreen. If this was a farm lane, it was a long one.

They swung round a tight bend and took a steep hill down into a wooded valley. A stream trickled along its dry-looking course and a murder of crows emerged from a tree, no doubt disturbed by the intruders.

The lane swung left this time, suddenly broadening out. The surface improved, too, from hard soil and rough boulders to badly maintained tarmac.

'Honestly, Linda, I don't know where you find these places. I've lived about thirty miles from here for most of my life and I had no idea they existed.'

'I'm sure I could fill this car with the sheer number of things you don't know exist.'

He was tiring of her sharp tongue. He was no wee boy, wet behind the ears. He'd earned his stripes a long time ago, and now he was being treated like the hired help by this slip of a woman.

'What's up with your face?' she asked.

He hesitated, but there was no time like the present. 'If you want to know the truth, I'm pissed off at the way you speak to me, Linda. I'm not one of the wee boys you lecture at your fancy universities across the water. I'd like you to take that into account, if you don't mind.'

'Aye, but you're the big man, right enough.' She sneered at him. 'But keep this in mind, Dec. We're both here doing what's asked of us for the greater good. And I happen to know you're getting a right good bung. But if you don't like me, I'll give you the phone and you can explain that to the men in charge.'

'I thought you were in charge.'

'See, there you go. Another in the long list of things you know nothing about. Take my advice: shut up and do the heavy lifting. That way everyone will be happy.'

He opened his mouth to reply, but Linda interrupted.

'In here.'

They made their way through a set of tall gates that were welcomingly open. They were bordered on each side by palisade fencing topped with razor wire.

'Somebody's not wanting any visitors,' said Declan.

'Aye, that's why they've left the gates open, you halfwit. Stop here. You can move the car in a minute, when we know what's what.'

They were parked in front of a building that looked out of place, somehow. It was as though a large factory unit had landed in the midst of trees, fields and gentle hills. The big warehouse, clad in dark green ridged aluminium, would have looked more at home in an industrial estate than at the end of a farm lane.

'What goes on in here?'

'You're about to find out. But take my advice and let me do the talking.'

Terry and Hamish were in a quandary. The two vans used to mop up those who'd been searching for them at the top of the cliff, including the one who'd been shot, had gone, leaving a single Range Rover. Its two occupants were now making their way slowly but surely towards the cliff edge. As Terry hurried back down the stone steps, he reckoned that they were no more than a few hundred metres away. A fact he imparted to Hamish, who was still looking out to sea.

'So, what do we do?' he finished.

'I've no' seen these men myself,' said Hamish. 'But you've done a fair job o' describing them to me. I canna say I'm over enthusiastic tae make their acquaintance, mind you.'

'We'll need to make our mind up soon.' Terry looked over the side of the fence. The black rocks had disappeared under the tide now, leaving just a few passing glimpses to indicate they were there at all. He wanted to feel confident that if they jumped, perfect swallow dives would find them plunging into a deep pool of cold, clear water, ready to emerge unscathed and safe from their possible tormentors. But he knew that was an unlikely outcome. If they jumped, they'd almost certainly be leaping to their deaths.

'Shot a man, you say?'

'Aye, right in the back as he was trying to run away, Hamish. Just like I told you.'

Hamish closed his eyes.

'Here, this is no time to have a wee nap. It'll be the big sleep soon enough.'

With his eyes still closed, Hamish replied: 'Are you aware o' the saying *My enemy's enemy is my friend*?'

'Hamish, really? Philosophy now? We've got two minutes to decide what to be at, or we'll be joining the dead guy in that van.'

'But you say they shot the poor bugger in the back as he was trying tae escape. If you reason it oot, it makes sense.'

Terry could hear voices now. The men from the Range Rover were near the cliff's edge. He walked over to the fence and threw one leg over it on to the narrow lip of rock.

'You would say the men they rounded up were on the look-out for us, aye?'

'Oh, I don't know. Yes, I suppose so. But it's not like they're the boy scouts, is it? They killed a man in cold blood.' As he said the words, a wave of nausea washed over him at the thought of the men he'd left for dead in the bar.

'You get your leg back o'er here. I think we should take oor chances wae this pair. Anyhow, I've things tae get done – important things.' Hamish's gaze returned to the horizon.

For a brief moment, Terry was poised between heaven and hell. Though he wasn't sure of the direction of either. Jump, and he may survive, the sea breaking his fall. Stay put, and there was every chance he would be shot dead. Yet he was aware that, in each case, the opposite could be true. He swallowed hard. 'So, you're staying here, Hamish?'

'I am that. And I'd strongly advise you tae do likewise. I'd hate tae see your mangled body being carried oot tae sea. Even though, by the way, the tide seems tae be running, you'd likely be washed up on a beach in Kintyre. A fine destination, mind, even for the dead.'

'Great! I always wanted to visit, but I'd kind of hoped to go by ferry.'

But before he could stare back into the crashing waves below, the decision as to whether or not to jump was made for him.

'Oi!' shouted a man from the top of the cliff. He was pointing a pistol down the steps in Terry's direction. 'Get your leg back over that fence, and the pair of you up here before I lose what patience I've left.'

His accent was broad, from the south of Ireland, Terry was sure. Meekly surrendering to his fate, he pulled his right leg back over the fence and looked at the old man he'd tried to save. 'Come on, Hamish. We'd better do as he says.'

'Aye, we've little choice in the matter, and that's a fact.'

'Come on!' the man shouted gruffly.

Terry helped Hamish to his feet, and with the younger man behind, they slowly ascended the stone steps to the top of the cliff.

The big building was scrupulously clean inside, festooned with pipes, coils and large aluminium tanks. The smell of chemicals was strong in the air, making Declan's eyes water. A man in a white hooded suit strode towards them. He was wearing a full-face mask, with a clear visor above a breathing apparatus. He was carrying another two.

'Here, you'd better stick these on.' His voice was muffled as he handed each of them a mask. 'And for fuck's sake don't touch anything, got it?'

Linda nodded. They put on the masks.

Declan felt claustrophobic. He'd never liked masks or helmets. As a child, he'd been taken to the beach with the rest of his class on a school trip. His father, after enduring months of his son's pleas, had relented and bought him a mask and snorkel. This trip was its christening.

But as he swam through the cold seawater, cosseted by its silence, in wonder at the new world just beneath the waves, he drew in a breath through the snorkel, and choked as he inhaled salty seawater. Up to his armpits, he struggled to his feet, coughing, choking, desperately trying to expel the water – the stinging, suffocating water – from his throat.

A group of boys were standing a few feet away. As he gasped for breath, he could hear them laughing, one of their number bent over in two at the hilarity of it all. Duncan Donnelly – Declan could still see his face. Instantly, he knew what had happened. Donnelly had poured a small bucket of water into his snorkel.

This boy had tormented him for months. When he'd told his father about it, instead of a listening ear he got a thick one of his own, as his dad slapped him and told him to stand up for himself.

Despite his shaking limbs and streaming eyes, he'd had enough. Declan waded over to where Donnelly was still laughing uproariously, caught him by the back of the neck and forced his head under the water.

At first the other boys kept laughing. But as Donnelly started to panic, splashing his arms in a frantic attempt to free himself from Declan's grip and draw a much-needed breath, they all fell silent.

It took two teachers to pull him off the half-drowned boy.

When Declan told his father what had happened, and that the headmaster wanted to see him, he patted his son on the head and took him for a fish supper.

As the mask clouded with his breath, he remembered it all.

'Come on, you!' said Linda.

They followed the man in the white suit into another room. When they were all safely inside, he slammed a thick steel door and pulled the mask off his face.

The room was covered in sheets of brushed aluminium, if anything cleaner than the bigger space they'd just left.

As Declan removed his mask, he was thankful that it smelled better here.

On a pallet sat two large canisters that looked roughly like those attached to caravans, supplying gas for cooking and heating. They were dark green in colour, and each had a large gauge at the top, held in place by thick steel bolts, from which two tubes protruded from a larger gauge that was welded between the canisters. About three feet from the gas bottles, the tubes were co-joined, opening out into a large funnel-shaped apparatus to which were attached the same thick steel bolts.

'What the fuck is that?' asked Declan.

The man in the suit looked at Linda. 'You mean to say he doesn't know?' Free of the mask, he had a cultured English accent.

'It's a need-to-know basis in my world.' Linda was her usual brusque self.

'Well, I need to know now,' said Declan, again irritated by her attitude towards him.

'Go ahead, tell him,' she said with a sigh.

'These bottles contain the constituent chemicals of sarin gas. Once they're mixed and out in the air, you'll wish you were somewhere else.'

Declan looked at him. 'So what happens?'

'Your chest tightens, you can't breathe, and you shit yourself just before you drown in your own bodily fluids, okay?'

Linda laughed. 'You asked, now you know, Dec. Climate action just got serious, eh?'

As he stared at the two gas bottles and then back at Linda, Declan was transported back to those cold waves on that dull day, many years before.

41

Symington read the text message again. She was alone in her office, her hand trembling.

Meet me here in two hours. The simple instruction was followed by a set of co-ordinates.

She placed her phone on the table and keyed the figures Bower had sent her in to the computer on her desk. She bit her lip as the numbers were transformed into a map. It looked as though he wanted to meet her at a small bay on the north-eastern side of the peninsula.

She sat back in her chair, looking absently at a dark crack that meandered across the flaking paint of her office ceiling. With force budgets straining at every seam, office decor wasn't a high priority. She made a mental note to bring this up at a meeting, then wondered why on earth such a ridiculous notion should enter her head at this time.

'Off somewhere nice?' Iolo Harris's head appeared through the doorway unannounced.

'Sorry?' It took Symington a few moments to work out what he meant before the penny dropped. 'So you've cloned my phone and computer?'

'It's a tough time for you, Carrie. Fair play, we didn't want you being put under pressure without us knowing.'

'On whose authority?' Her face was red with fury. She was a senior officer in Police Scotland. They had no right!

'On my authority.'

As she stared at Harris, gone was the genial smile, the wink, the friendly nod of the head. No, here was the real man, she reckoned. At least the man he was at work. Everything done for a reason. No cost too great when it came to protecting the nation. The thought seemed to come from nowhere, but it was as though his blank stare had spoken to her.

Harris's smile suddenly returned. If his mask had slipped, it was only for a brief moment. 'It'll be nice to get out of the office. Feeling a bit cooped up in here, to be honest.'

'What do you want me to do?'

'You go and meet him. What else would you do?'

Symington considered this. 'He must know I know he can't use my parents against me as leverage any more. He'll smell a rat.'

'What makes you think that? We put a little pressure on the scum that were holding them, that's all. As far as he's concerned, they're still in captivity, and you're still desperate to save them. He'd have run a mile if he knew they'd been freed.'

Something didn't make sense. The thought had grown increasingly loud in her head as the relief at her parents' safety had changed into something else. She decided it was time to give it voice. 'How did you find them?'

'Sorry?'

'My mum and dad. How did you know where they were being held?'

'I'm a spook, Carrie. I do this stuff every day. There're quite a few of us, you know.'

'So you're working on information from somebody on the inside?'

'Yeah, that's one of our techniques. But if you don't mind, I'm not really keen to outline our operational approach to this or anything else right now. I hope you understand.'

'Yes. Yes, of course.' She hesitated. 'But one thing troubles me.'

'What's that?'

'You must have known what Bower was planning – given you have all this intelligence, I mean.'

Harris shrugged. 'What if we did?'

'He murdered Chappell!'

'Yes, so it would appear. I'd have thought you'd be the last person mourning his loss, to be honest.'

'I believe in justice – for everyone. That's why I'm a police officer. I think you work in a very different way.'

'No doubt about it, superintendent, our working lives are very different. But we have similar concerns, I think.'

'I don't think so at all. I couldn't live with myself knowing I'd let a man die. No matter what kind of person he was.'

Iolo Harris closed the door and took the seat opposite her. 'But you're willing to cover up a miscarriage of justice for years to save your career. I think that's the idea, isn't it?' Again, the cold, blank stare.

Symington held her head high. 'I'm not going to do that for much longer. Once this is all over, I'm going to take it to the bosses.'

'I'm not sure they'll thank you for that, Carrie.'

'Why wouldn't they? I'm just being honest. After all, like you say, a miscarriage of justice will be addressed. A right will be wronged.'

'And they'll have to admit that one of their bright young things lived a lie for a decade and a half. A boy lying dead, while you were doing everything you could to cover your tracks and climb the greasy pole.'

She stared at him for a few moments. 'Do you know what that's been like? Do you know how I feel every time I look at myself in the mirror?'

'Yeah, I've an idea. Not pleasant, I shouldn't think. All that braid, those shiny buttons. It must look rather tainted from where you're standing.'

'Exactly. I was young. I made a mistake. I didn't get drunk on purpose, and the accident wasn't my fault.'

'Yet here we are. You and your shiny buttons, and me with all my – well, my methods. The world is based on reality, on pragmatism, not overblown ideals. That's for the nursery. I happen to think you'll become a very good senior officer one day – one of the movers and shakers. Why? *Because* you've been through the mill, not despite it. And in any case, what would your dear old mum and dad think when they found out how little Carrie got to where she is?'

There it was, her weak point. 'You know how things work, Iolo. Something like this . . . when I come clean, as you say, it won't reflect well on Police Scotland. They'll not make a big fuss. I've thought about it a lot over the years. The most likely scenario is that I'll be quietly sacked, lose my pension and find some kind of peace.'

'You're forgetting how many leaks there are. Especially in your profession.'

'I'm sure it will be in their interest to keep a lid on it.'

'Maybe. But so many other people know, don't they?'

'Who?' As she said it, she knew the answer. 'Why would

you do that?'

Harris shrugged. 'I don't know what you mean. Now, let's have a chat about this little jaunt to the beach. I have young Desmond to interview.'

'We can't hold him for ever. You'll need to decide what you're going to do with him soon – and Brian's son.'

'As we've been discussing, in a roundabout way, I can do what I like when the safety of the country is at stake. Forget your protocols, Carrie.' He looked at his watch. Though it was clearly an expensive one, she noticed he kept its face under his wrist. It was a classic sign of someone with a military background. 'I'll see you in half an hour. Once I've put the shits up this lad.'

'What did Jim say?'

'I've done a deal with young Will Scott. That's all he cares about, I think.'

Iolo Harris left the room, leaving Carrie Symington with the bitter taste of bile in her mouth. Of course, he was right. Justice was never really done; it only had to be seen to be done. The wickedest in society rarely saw the inside of a cell. They just cut a deal.

Annie was alone in her room on the top floor of the County Hotel. She could hear the familiar buzz and clatter, the sound she'd known for so many years, the heartbeat of the place. Now, though, it seemed foreign – alien, almost. It was like waking up on the couch in a stranger's home after a party. Though they were polite, offered you a cup of tea and a slice of toast, you could tell they just wanted you to leave. The booze had worn off into a hangover, and the world looked a very different place.

For Annie, this building, this hotel that had been her life, felt like that now. The good times were over – it was time to go.

She knew that finding another job and a place to live were priorities. But something in her wanted to be alone, shuttered against the world, not out announcing to all and sundry that the job she'd been so proud of had been lost.

General Manager.

The brass badge was on her nightstand. When Macmillan had first given it to her the pride she'd felt was like walking on air. In many ways, she'd been doing that job for years, albeit with little credit or remuneration. But she'd had respect, from her customers, her staff and her employers. When something went wrong, Annie fixed it. If ideas were required in order to bring in more guests, she came up with them. When somebody needed a shoulder to cry on, Annie was there for everyone – and there had been many in such need during her time in this place. She was a surrogate mother and a confessor rolled into one. And she never judged.

But who would be there for her now her life had collapsed around her ears?

The truth was, she knew how things would pan out. First of all, her absence would be commented upon. Then word would filter out across the town.

Wait till you hear this.

She knew how things worked in Kinloch. How the speculation would start.

Noo, I'm no' saying for sure, because I've always liked the lassie. But, apparently, she's had her fingers in the till for years. This Canadian chap was too sharp for her. Would you believe it? Butter wouldna melt in her mooth.

Oh yes, Annie could hear them all.

Of course, there'd be a loyal element. Her friends would rally round, but even they would be susceptible to rumours and gossip. The doubt would always be there.

I hear the polis are looking intae it. No wonder she kept in wae thon big Daley and Scott.

She tried to think of those who wouldn't judge her, those who'd always be in her corner, no matter what. But the list was a short one.

One face came to mind again and again. Hamish. He'd have taken up the cudgels with anyone to defend her. He'd done it before. And in a place where the old man held such sway, had earned so much respect, folk would change their minds, think twice before they spoke ill of her. Though Hamish was too old to battle on the cobbles, there were plenty who'd do it for him by proxy without a thought.

Then she thought how selfish she was being, for the man she'd known all her life – a replacement father in many ways – was gone. In that moment, Annie knew he was never coming back. She could feel his loss in her heart, deep, deep down. Despite losing her job and her home, this alone left a gaping hole in her life.

She pulled a battered shoebox from under the bed. It contained bundles of old photographs, memories frozen in fading colour or monochrome. Her life, all neatly bound in thick elastic bands and yellow Kodak wallets.

Yes, Annie had images on her mobile phone, but they weren't the same. Somehow, they were throwaway, disposable. They weren't the great people and the big moments, not the folk who really mattered to her.

There were her mother and father on their wedding day, black and white smiles. They were standing at the head of the dining room of this very hotel, under the large stained-glass panes of the window that beamed a golden light into the big room when the sun shone or shed a little colour on the dullest winter day. One of her first jobs in the hotel had been to stand on an ancient set of stepladders and wipe the window clean of nicotine with old newspaper drenched in vinegar. She smiled at the thought.

Then a ceilidh back in the day. She laughed at her spiral perm, she cried at the sight of Chick holding her fondly as they danced under the lights of the mobile disco. Something there for everyone of all ages: from The Jam to Jim Reeves, a big band to a wailing folk singer.

It looked so quaint, old-fashioned now. But those were golden days, happy times.

Then a picture of her, arms outstretched, on the first day she'd been left in charge of the bar. It was a Polaroid image: how long had it been since she'd miraculously appeared in full colour a few moments after the picture had been taken? She honestly couldn't remember. But it had been her little kingdom from that day until Ian Macmillan had taken it away.

Annie shuffled through the photographs in no particular order, setting them free from their elastic bonds. As she did so, one fell from her hand, and landed face down on the floor.

There was Hamish, his big orange kipper tie and the kilt that hung too low, hunkering about his thin, knobbly knees. It had been taken only a few years ago.

Now it was time for Annie to sob. It felt as though her life was at an end, as though everything had been taken from her. She'd lost her parents, lost the only man she'd ever loved so many years ago that it hardly seemed like her life any more, more like a movie, or a sad story she'd read. She'd been young then. It was easier to bounce back when you were young. What place was there for a fifty-something woman who'd only ever worked in one place, doing one thing?

All the hotels had cut down on staff, and in some cases closed altogether. In any case, they had their own employees, some of whom, like her, had worked in the same place for years.

The County Hotel and its customers had been her family, been her life.

Now there was nothing left.

42

The long bar was illuminated by bright LED lights now. A body had been removed. Daley surveyed the scene with a forensic eye, looking for anything that might point to Hamish, or the young man who'd selflessly rescued him – or tried to.

Up-ended tables, slathers of dark, dry blood pooled on the floor, spent bullet cases, all now being dealt with expertly by the PSNI forensic team. They recorded, bagged, brushed and photographed everything. He'd seen the process a thousand times before, but with each year more was added, further scientific advances augmenting their investigative toolbox. But still murderers walked free, the taking of lives unpunished. Still people grieved, still the dark pall of tragedy hung over the households of bereaved families. Daley knew that whatever technical advances were made in the fight against crime, this would always be the case.

Inspector O'Leary was talking to the crime scene manager. Their conversation was brief, and when it was over the man from the PSNI approached Daley.

'One body, but too much blood for the one shooting. I think we have more than one victim here. Look at the blood over there.' O'Leary pointed to a great dark pool in the middle of the floor.

'But your overall impression?'

'One of two things: either our brave boys managed to overcome the folk guarding them, or there's a third party involved. Certainly, they tell me that there are signs of a pitched battle outside, a few hundred metres from here. Blood splattered on the grass, shell casings, the lot.'

'So you think that the people holding Hamish and the young lad were intercepted by a rival gang, or something?'

'Yes, that's the idea – unless your Hamish has advanced defence skills. We know that young Terry wouldn't say boo to a goose.'

'Can I have a look outside?'

'Be my guest. Just avoid the places our SOCO teams are working and you'll be fine.'

Daley smiled. 'I do have a grasp of the technicalities involved, inspector.'

'I'm more worried about Inspector Scott. He nearly walked right over some tyre tracks. Whoever was here left in a hurry – maybe three or four vehicles. We're not sure, but we'll have answers soon.'

Daley left the bar and wandered out into the sunlight. The ground was wet, a testament to the heavy rainstorm he'd been told had hit this place only a few hours before.

A wide vista opened out before him. They were about half a mile from the cliffs. Across the North Channel, he could see the loom of the Kintyre peninsula. Home – or so he thought of it now. It was strange to be in a place only a few short miles from where he lived and worked that was so familiar and unfamiliar at the same time. The old RUC had recruited from the Glasgow police when he was a young cop. The money was good, but the risks had been high – still were, in some cases, he supposed. But some had taken the plunge.

'Owned by a shell company based offshore.' Brian Scott's voice sounded behind him.

'What, the bar?'

'Aye. They're looking intae it. It'll be one o' they Russian doll affairs. A doll within a doll within a doll type o' caper. You know the score, Jimmy.'

'Yes, I know what you mean.'

'Hard to think who'd come all the way oot here for a pint, eh?'

'I suppose sightseers, that type of thing.' Daley was looking at a long, very narrow path that seemed to lead from the pub to a point on the cliff. It wasn't of purposeful design, rather the outcome of a large number of feet over a period of time. 'Come on, Brian, let's take a wander.'

Skirting the SOCO teams, Daley and Scott ended back on this path. No grass grew on the narrow way, so clearly the route was a popular one – but why? Daley wondered where it would take them.

'They reckon that some other mob's got Hamish. I cannae see that, can you?'

'Hard to say, Brian. Something serious happened, that's for sure.'

'What happened tae good old fighting back? The auld fella has a lot o' spirit. I wouldn't put anything past him.'

'Yeah,' said Daley with little enthusiasm.

They were getting nearer to the cliff's edge. 'What's that?' Scott asked, pointing ahead.

'Looks like a signpost of some kind. We'll have a look.'

It soon became apparent that they'd reached a birdwatching station on the cliff. Daley looked over the edge at a set of railed-off steps cut into the rock face that led down to a ledge

313

guarded by a fence and covered by a narrow, and probably inadequate, canopy.

The rain had made the dark stone even darker, but it was drying in patches under the warm sun. 'Is that a footprint, Brian?'

Scott looked over the edge of the cliff down on to the steps. 'Could be, Jimmy. It'll no' last long in the heat o' this sunshine.'

'I'll go down and take a picture on my phone. Go and grab some of the SOCO boys, will you? They'll just have to eliminate my footprints. I want to catch this.'

As Scott made his way back towards the bar, Daley took to the steps. He had no head for heights, and as he was keen not to destroy any possible evidence left behind, he was walking at the very edge of the steps, almost hugging the handrail. The drop was sheer and dizzying, with gulls floating on the breeze calling loudly, a sound that echoed from the cliff face. Below, the tips of black rocks could be seen as the wash of waves receded, only to be quickly covered again by the next in line. The sheer drop made him think of Hamish. Hunted, scared, having gone through goodness knows what in the days since his disappearance, could he have been so desperate that jumping was preferable to being recaptured?

Daley's thoughts on this were brief. He'd no idea what had really transpired. Again, it was a gut feeling. But his reasoning did nothing to quell the sense of trepidation.

There it was, just about four steps above the platform, the distinct impression of the sole of a boot. Daley used the camera on his phone to take a close-up, detailed image. As he edged down on to the platform itself, he could make out two or three such prints, still wet against the dry stone, but evaporating quickly in the heat. He repeated the process, carefully taking several images of them all.

He knelt down to examine the fading footprints more quickly. Two were of a stout, ridged sole, the other flat, with no discernible grips to be seen. Most likely a dress shoe, he reckoned.

As Scott appeared with a couple of SOCO officers, Daley pictured Hamish. He always wore what he called sea boots – wellington boots with stout soles cut down to just above the ankle. Though Daley had never examined Hamish's footwear closely, he could see that one of the sets of prints would easily match such a profile.

As he made his way back up the steps and left the SOCO team to their business, his mind worked overtime. He could see the bar in the distance across the flat clifftop.

'What's up, big man? You look as though you're miles away,' said Scott.

'I think they've got it wrong.'

'Who?'

'The local boys. I think Hamish and this Terry did escape. I think they hid down there. But what happened after that I don't know. I'm sure Hamish was here, Brian.'

'It's possible. But why head tae a cliff?'

'Okay, maybe they're injured, or one of them is, at least. They don't want to hit that road – it's a single track, too dangerous. Anyway, it's what anyone looking for them would expect. Anyone could come down it, and the likelihood is they wouldn't be friendly. Look about. It's as flat as a pancake. If you were trying to hide, this is just about the only place.'

'Bit desperate, is it no'?'

'You saw the aftermath of what happened back at the pub. They'd be scared, that's for sure.'

'No blood on those steps, is there?'

'No, but that's a good sign. Mind you, the rain could have washed it away.'

'If you're right, Jimmy – if – then who's got them now?'

Daley looked across the North Channel. 'That's a good question, Brian.' He cast his eyes back down to the crashing waves below.

'Nah, you don't think he'd have done that, Jimmy? Don't even think it.'

Daley shrugged. 'It's the devil and the deep blue sea, Brian.'

Scott looked down. He glimpsed the dark, unforgiving rocks. 'It's no' the deep blue sea I'd be worried aboot.'

Hamish and Terry had been blindfolded and their hands tied before being taken in the Range Rover across rough, rocky ground. Even though they couldn't see, the jostling and complaints from the two men in the front seats made it obvious that this was no metalled road.

Hamish leaned his head against the window, a feeling of utter despair in his soul. But that despair wasn't a product of his current predicament. He felt something wrong; he could sense it, almost taste the fear.

The old fisherman couldn't count the times in his life he'd experienced this sensation. Yes, he played to the crowd with his homespun seer routine. But that was all a charade. This emotion, feeling – whatever it was – was real, genuine. He'd felt it first on the day his father had died. It was a deep, heartfelt sorrow that ate away at his gut, at his soul. Now he was blindfolded, the dreams he'd had since he'd been spirited away from his boat played across his mind's eye like a horror movie. Fleeting glimpses of blank faces under the waves, choking, writing souls at their sides. Yet all the time, the meaning – the root – of what he was experiencing remained just out of reach. But he knew he had to get home as quickly as he could.

That feeling shouted more loudly now than it had on the cliff ledge. He may be in danger, but danger seemed everywhere, and he wasn't sure he was in more peril than anyone else. One voice called out to him, but despite his best efforts he couldn't place it. It was like being in a crowd of people and seeing someone he'd once known. Yes, they were familiar, but he couldn't think who they were, couldn't place the face.

The SUV rumbled to a stop. He was pulled from the car by rough hands, the only thing that stopped him falling flat on his face. He heard Terry yelp in pain.

'Are you all right, son?' he shouted, but there was no reply. No sense that Terry had heard him.

Hamish was jostled along, his hands still bound, the blindfold tight across his eyes. But he could see flashes of the bright sun. Mud cloyed at his boots as he stumbled on.

A door opened, then slammed shut. He was inside now, the rush of the air and the sounds of the countryside muted. He was pushed forward, landing on a couch, or a bed, he wasn't sure.

'Just you stay put.' The man's voice was gruff. From behind, he pulled the blindfold from Hamish's face, and then Hamish heard his footsteps retreat and a door close, a key turning in a lock.

He'd landed awkwardly, and it wasn't easy, using only his legs and shoulders to move, to find a comfortable seated position. Yes, he was on a sofa. It was poorly sprung and uncomfortable. Old, like himself, he reckoned.

He managed to get his breath back and sat silently. A yelling crow, the engine of an aircraft high above, the rustle of wind in the trees, could be heard outside. No ticking clock, no crackling flames, no voices through the wall. The room had a fireplace, a table and an old armchair, all backed by some dark wooden cupboards.

Hamish leaned back into the couch. His legs, back and head ached, but his mind was more troubled. He felt old and tired, and resigned to his fate, whatever that was. He tried to think of something – anything – to silence the voices in his head, but the cries only grew louder.

He thought of his home, his mother, Hamish his cat, his old skipper Sandy Hoynes, the warmth of a sip of whisky. But still he couldn't banish the gnawing ache of sorrow he felt. He thought of the people back home, all those who'd be worried by his absence. Maybe they'd given up, assumed he'd happened upon some misfortune at sea and perished. It would be nothing new for the people of Kinloch to mourn seafarers missing from their community. Souls torn from the world, gone as though they'd never been. It was a feeling common in fishing communities everywhere, he was quite sure.

He thought of places where he was happiest. He gulped, and cried out, for in that instant he finally placed that face in the crowd. It was one he knew well.

Hamish barely recognised the sound that came from his own throat, but he heard the desperation in the ear-splitting scream, a call from the very darkest place.

43

Symington had driven to the bay in her own car. Two unmarked vehicles carrying Iolo Harris and armed police officers had gone on ahead, driven past her destination, and were now – she hoped – deployed nearby to make sure the superintendent came to no harm.

It was a beautiful, warm summer afternoon. The sky was a flawless blue, almost matching the sea, which was calm as a millpond. Symington knew this was where Will Scott had purchased the pistol. Clearly, whoever Bower was working with had chosen this venue because of its seclusion. The beach was hidden from the road and closed off at both ends by rocky headlands about seven hundred and fifty metres apart. In effect, once on the beach, unless you could get back to your car and make your escape by road, you were trapped.

Though Symington trusted her men and knew that Iolo had more than enough experience to take operational charge, she wished Jim Daley and Brian Scott were here, not in County Antrim.

But, Symington reasoned, she'd met Bower before in much less secure circumstances. She knew what to expect, but now she had the upper hand. Her parents were safe, and she had a small army ready to come to her aid, if necessary.

There was no sign of Bower. But she was a few minutes early, so she decided to sit on the warm sand and breathe in the sea air in an effort to stay calm. After all, it was in a situation like this that he'd surprised her before on the beach outside Machrie. This time, though, she had no wine to steady her nerves.

Symington tried to rationalise what was happening. That her parents were safe was good, though she still wasn't quite sure just how Harris had managed to locate them so quickly. Come to that, she worried that Police Scotland seemed to have been all but cut out of the loop and Harris given a free hand to solve the mystery of the crash-landing plane as well as dealing with Will Scott and his boyfriend Des. He was in charge, not her, not Daley. Added to the involvement of Bower, and Harris's casual approach to the murder of Chappell, it all made her feel uneasy.

She looked at her watch, a Tudor 1926. It had been a present from her parents the previous Christmas – too generous. The white dial and blue hands showed that Bower was now late. She sighed, desperately hoping that the presence of Harris and her officers hadn't scared him off. She knew he was no fool. Wicked, yes. Stupid, no; definitely, he was not that.

Suddenly, movement from behind, voices. Symington got to her feet and looked to her left, the direction from which the commotion was coming. Four young people, two men and two women, had appeared at the far end of the beach. They were dressed in T-shirts and shorts, their skin tanned by the long spell of fine weather. As she watched, one of the women removed her T-shirt to reveal a bikini top, while one of the men spread a large blanket on the sand. They were laughing, chatting, having fun: the joy of being young on a beautiful day. For a moment, Symington felt a twinge of jealousy. No, she wasn't old, but her youth had been spent on long shifts, overtime, or studying to pass exams to further her career.

Though she couldn't wear an earpiece – Bower would have spotted it – she could speak to Harris via a tiny microphone hidden just under the collar of her shirt. She was in civvies, and very conscious of the clash of her smart trouser suit against the beachwear of those with whom she now shared this stretch of sand. But they hadn't paid her much attention, and seemed too caught up in their day out to be interested in the woman in the plum-coloured jacket and trousers further along the beach. Even so, as she angled her head towards her collar, she tried to make her one-sided conversation with Harris as subtle as possible.

'He won't come with these kids here. Trust me, I know him now. He'll have been banking on an empty beach, I'm certain of it.'

The prearranged signal to abandon was a single shot in the air. It would be nothing unusual to hear someone taking aim at a seabird, or some other poor creature, therefore unlikely to attract much attention. But, as she waited, no sound came.

Along the beach, beer had been produced from a cool box. The noise level increased as cans hissed open and music thudded from a big speaker. It had a steady, heavy pulse. Soon Symington could feel her heart beating in time.

'Excuse me, dear. I wonder if you can help me?' The voice came from over her shoulder, startling her. She turned to face an old woman wearing a bright floral print dress and a battered straw sunhat. 'Oh, I'm sorry to alarm you, but it's my dog.' The woman looked on the verge of tears. 'He's stuck in some wire. I'm afraid he's hurt himself.'

Symington looked round. She thought of directing the old lady to the young people up the beach, but with their party now in full swing, and this elderly lady clearly distressed, she felt obliged to help if she could. Anyway, she loved dogs, and couldn't bear the thought of an animal in pain. With all these people about, she was certain now that Bower wouldn't appear anyway. It was a relief, in a way.

'Yes, of course. Where is he?'

'Oh, thank you, dear. I was taking a short cut through those bushes down on to the beach. It was a little path last year. Dougal just ran on, you see. I'm sure he remembered the place. But someone's put up a small fence, and he got tangled in it. Barbed wire – it should be banned!'

'I'll help you rescue your dog, don't worry,' said Symington, loudly enough to be sure that Harris would pick up her voice on the mic.

'Thank you, I'm so grateful. I'm Carole, by the way.' The old woman held out a wrinkled hand for Symington to shake.

'Carrie. I'm pleased to meet you. Now, where is he?'

Carole led the way off the beach towards some patches of thorn bushes. A sandy path bisected them. 'Just over here,' she said over her shoulder.

They were out of sight of the beach when Symington heard the sharp report of a gun. As she turned to look back, she suddenly felt a sharp pain in her head and the sun wobbled in the sky. Then everything was dark.

44

Nathan Sidley wasn't happy. He worked alone; it was his unwritten rule. The bulky photographer who'd been foisted upon him was taciturn, surly even. Nathan had been taking his own pictures for forty years, back to the days when you had to know what you were doing in order to capture a decent image. These days it was point and shoot. A child could do it. Of course there were still some honest, talented professional snappers left in the business. But like proper journalists, they were becoming thinner on the ground as the exigencies enforced by declining newspaper sales hit hard. His editor was twenty-nine and was much happier with a balance sheet than reams of copy.

As Sidley tied his ponytail back in place, he glanced at the man driving the Land Rover. He'd been in his company for a couple of hours, and apart from a handshake and introducing himself as Ronnie, he'd barely said a word. Sidley hated people like that; his business was talking to people. Silence was the enemy of investigative journalism.

'How long have you been in this game, Ronnie?'

'About ten years.'

Sidley tried again. 'You must be a Londoner, eh?'

'Nah, I'm from Essex, mate. I'm not a big fan of the "big smoke".'

He was getting somewhere. 'Oh, why not? I've lived there for years now. Love the place. Though it's changed more in thirty years than just about anywhere I know.'

There was no response to this, merely a nod and a muted grunt.

It was time to get to the nub of the matter. 'So, tell me something, Ronnie. Why are you here? I haven't had a photographer with me since the *Morning Post* was still on the go.'

Ronnie shrugged. 'Boss says I'm to get the best angle on this. He wants drama.'

'That little shit wouldn't know drama if it bit him in the arse. Anyway, I can do that. No offence, like.'

'I'm just doing what I'm told, mate.'

Sidley sat back in his seat, looking absently at the fields and hills of Kintyre flashing past. He remembered the old days. He'd have been in a pub by now – long before now. The great characters he'd worked with over the years flashed before his mind's eye in a cheerful parade. They'd laughed, they'd argued, sometimes fought – mostly over women – but they'd got the job done. Sidley thought of the thin tabloids that newspapers had become. There were more academic qualifications in the quiet newsrooms now than there had ever been, but regardless of media and communication degrees the standard of journalism was pitiful. Kids these days couldn't write without spell and grammar checks, and even then they produced pallid, boring prose, frequently riddled with errors.

I want it to sparkle, son, not gutter like a fucked candle.

He remembered his first editor at the *Liverpool Echo* with a smile. He'd learned so much in three short years. The experience had set him up for life as a working journalist. He'd learned his trade with men and women who could smell, taste and feel a story. The angle of a head, a hurried reply or a furtive look: little signs that led to big news. Sidley reckoned that the journalists of his era would have made better detectives than some of the plodding, lazy, corrupt bastards who had tried to make his life difficult back in the seventies and eighties. Sadly, though, the process had been turned on its head. Now police forces were full of bright young things, and newspapers – or what was left of them – populated by dull-eyed keyboard warriors, happier ranting on social media than producing cogent, readable copy.

'So, tell me again. They've had a tip, am I right?'

'Sort of, I think.'

'What kind of *sort of*?'

'Like we've to go to this place and stay put until you get a call.'

'Blaan, you said.'

'Yeah, that's it. Funny, eh?'

'Funny? How so?'

'You know, the names.'

Sidley stared at the man with the thick neck and bulging biceps. 'I suppose so. You been about a bit, then?'

Ronnie shrugged. 'Here and there, mate.'

It was like pulling teeth. Sidley decided to give up. Ronnie was on the inside, staff, so he said. Nathan was the freelancer. He'd hung about in old buildings, cafés, parks, pubs, palaces, brothels, warehouses, offices, houses, all manner of places, waiting for a story or a lead. This was no different.

But Sidley now realised something he'd suspected since arriving at Kinloch. The man beside him had only confirmed those suspicions. It was amazing how careful, how rehearsed, some people could be. But in his experience they rarely got it exactly right – there was always a chink in the armour, a tell-tale mistake.

Doesn't take long to smell a wrong 'un, son.

It was his old editor again.

Nathan Sidley sat back and watched the world go by. He would let this string out as far as his nerve would allow. But he knew that he couldn't do it alone.

Annie couldn't remember the last time she'd taken a walk around Kinloch. Yes, she would go here and there, running errands for the hotel, but a proper meander through the streets she knew so well was something she rarely did.

Walking out of the County Hotel had been hard. She'd done her best to avoid speaking to anyone, but when a young waitress ran after her to ask if she knew where the freshly laundered napkins were, she had to fight back the tears and mutter something about being busy, before rushing out through the big front door. She made a mental note to go back via the entrance from the car park. It was much quieter.

Deliberately, she had walked straight past the bar, the cubbyhole that was now her former office, and the reception desk, without even a glance. She heard a murmur of voices through the serving hatch but could guess that the main topic of conversation would be Hamish's continued absence. Unless Macmillan had said something, it was unlikely that anyone knew she'd been sacked. That, plus the fact that she was still living in the hotel, would hold back the gossips for a while, but she knew it would only be a temporary reprieve.

She walked up Long Road, past a café, greengrocers, newsagents, toyshop, and a little boutique selling homemade candles and fancy goods. People waved and tooted their car horns. Tommy Jackson, a builder and long-term patron at the County, shouted a cheery hello. Sadie Meenan stopped to ask her if there was any news about Hamish, then rushed off about her business with a sad shake of her head. The clock on the Big Kirk's tower was, as usual, wrong. The distillery hidden at the end of a narrow lane belched out the odours of its trade; the little bakery at the end of the road smelled of fresh hot rolls as the sweet, familiar scent of alcohol drifted from pubs along the way.

On her walk, Annie passed her old school, the house where her mother had been brought up, an old sweetie shop she'd used to run into as a child, and the little bar on the edge of the loch that was now a launderette. The swing park, the houses, the seawall: it was all as it had ever been – in her mind, at least.

Everything was the same; everyone was friendly. She saw old school friends, elderly customers and her mother's cousin. She breathed in the strong tang of the sea, and tarried a while near the harbour, watching the fishermen go about their business. She knew them all, and spotting her some waved or called out a warm, friendly greeting.

But there was a space by the quay where Hamish's old lobster boat should be. Though there were no hard and fast rules as to where boats could tie up, the other fishermen had left this space free out of respect for the man who, no doubt, had helped every one of them in one way or another over the years. She had to swallow back the tears. The loss of the old fisherman weighed down on everyone, for they were all sure that he was gone, and gone for good. Folk just didn't disappear at sea and miraculously appear again. They all knew it, though none were willing to give the notion voice. Everyone felt the loss, Annie most keenly of all.

She walked on, past the old Mission to Seamen at the head of the pier. Where once fishermen had gathered with cups of tea and bowls of soup, now council workers toiled at their desks. She looked in the window of the shop that had replaced Woolworths, remembering in her youth buying the latest hit single, or a bag of pick-and-mix.

It was all so warm, so familiar – it was home, her home. The thought that these cheery greetings and happy waves could quickly turn into glances of suspicion, furtive conversations behind raised hands, or simply blank stares, was heartbreaking. Annie knew this town as well as anyone else. The good outweighed the bad by a large margin, but still, as it did everywhere else, the worst side of human nature lurked even here, ready to raise an ugly head.

She stood in Main Street and looked up and down. What a lovely wee town, she thought, before turning on her heel and pushing open the door to the chemist's.

45

Scott was smoking, staring out across the blue stretch of sea to where Kintyre shimmered in the heat haze and worrying about his son. Iolo Harris would have the boy for breakfast, of that he was sure. But he hoped that, whatever Harris had concocted, it would save Willie from prosecution. His family were no strangers to Her Majesty's Pleasure. He'd chosen a different path and had never regretted it.

He thought back on the long hours spent away from his children as they'd grown up. The life of a police officer was like that, especially a detective's. The job ruled you rather than the reverse. Missed birthdays, curtailed holidays, a general absence when it came to simple things like school sports or concerts, opening Christmas presents, or so many other family events that he should have attended.

Daddy's got to go back to work.

He shook his head with regret as he took one last draw at his cigarette.

For all his faults, Scott was a practical man. He'd plead, coerce – do anything he could to keep his son out of jail. Over the years he'd seen the lowest of the low walk free from court. He was damned if Willie – despite his stupidity – would be one of the unlucky ones. Besides, the academic, bookish, thoughtful boy would be eaten up in prison. He shuddered at the thought, though he still had old pals from his youth who might do him a favour on the inside.

'Don't tell me, you're thinking of Will,' said Daley, always able to tell what was troubling his old friend.

'Aye, and you'd be the same wae your Jamie. I'm telling you, weans break your heart near every day, big man.'

'Well, you'll have the chance to see him shortly.'

'Eh? We're on the trail o' Hamish, aren't we? I'm beginning tae think he might be okay.'

'We're surplus to requirements, Brian. Recalled to life, as it were.'

'What?'

'*A Tale of Two Cities*, or in this case, a tale of two police forces.'

'You've always been a hell o' a man for talking in riddles, Jimmy.'

'We're going home. PSNI are taking us back in the chopper in half an hour.'

'And what aboot the auld fella?'

Daley shrugged. 'Your guess is as good as mine. I can't work out whether they just want to get on with it over here without our input, or the order came from back home. O'Leary doesn't know.'

'Aye, and pigs might fly.'

Daley laughed. 'Pigs will be flying all the way back to Kinloch very shortly.'

'You seem quite happy aboot it, Jimmy. I have tae say, I'm surprised.'

'We'll only get in the way, Brian. It may be just a few miles across to Kinloch, but we're worlds apart. This mob know what they're doing, and there's no doubt things have got heavy – heavier than we're used to.'

'Huh! Gie them James Machie tae deal wae, then they'll know all aboot it.'

'Unlikely, wouldn't you say?'

'Aye, true. But how did Hamish get himself intae this? I cannae work it oot.'

'I think we'll find out soon, one way or the other.'

'That doesnae sound too hopeful, Jimmy.'

'You've seen what went on here, Bri. Whatever is going on, these folk aren't messing about.'

'No, that's for sure. But there's mair hope now than when we got here, eh?'

'Well, we know – or we think we know – he was alive today.'

'That's it, just you cheer me up, you grim bastard.'

'At least you'll be able to find out what Iolo's up to with Will.'

'And I'll have tae tell Ella.'

'The fun never ends.'

Scott stamped his cigarette out on the grass.

'Pick that up or they'll likely make us swim home.'

Scott groaned as he bent forward. 'I remember my faither making noises like that. I think I'm getting auld, Jimmy.'

'We all are, Brian. We all are.'

They were bumping back along the rough track now, this time in an ancient Luton Transit van. Declan was at the wheel, and every bump and rattle sent his heart to his mouth.

They'd used a forklift to hoist the pallet that held the two deadly gas canisters he'd been shown in the big lab. Though he'd been scared many times in his life, the thought of slowly choking to death as his nervous system shut down was the most terrifying prospect he could imagine. Beside him, though, Linda looked as if she didn't have a care in the world.

'Could you not have found a van with some kind of suspension on it?' he complained as they hit yet another pothole.

'I'm beginning to think you're a bit of an old woman, Declan, do you know that?'

'I just don't want to die. I'll be honest with you, Linda, I am shit scared.'

'The bottles are shrink-wrapped to the pallet. They're safe as houses.'

'Aye, until one of them leaks.'

'You're not getting this, are you? It wouldn't matter if one of them did leak; the gases have to mix to be effective.'

'What if they both leak?'

'By fuck, you're like a wean. They won't! And the reason we're in this jalopy is because it's clean, perfectly serviceable, and it doesn't stand out. You of all people should realise that.'

'But you haven't told me where we're going.'

'We're going to the old slipway.'

'You mean we're taking this shit out on a boat?'

'No, I just want to take a picture of the gas bottles by the sea for Instagram.'

'See, this is what I mean about you no' giving me any respect, Linda.'

'Earn it, then.'

'What if we get caught?'

She smiled. 'Aye, what if?'

The PSNI helicopter landed on the broad expanse of grass before the loch. Daley and Scott ducked under the rotors and headed back to Kinloch police office. It didn't take Scott long to find his son, who, to his dismay, was languishing in a cell.

Will's face was pale and drawn as he supped the coffee brought to him by his father. They sat together in the small office canteen.

'So, what's the scoop?' said Scott.

'What?'

'What does Harris want?'

Will leaned back in his chair, looking utterly miserable. 'I'm to be the lure – like a worm on a hook.'

'A worm?'

'Like fishermen, Dad.'

'Aye, I get that bit. But a lure for what?'

'They have intelligence, or whatever. Something is going to be handed over by the same guys who sold me the gun. Something important, I don't know.'

'Handed tae who?'

'To me! You're not very good at this, Dad. What have you been doing all these years, bringing coffee?'

'Oh, don't get cute wae me, son. I didn't head off tae some beach tae buy firearms.'

'Firearm, singular!'

'One, two – it doesnae matter, Willie. You've broken the law, son. You'd have gone down for it if Jimmy hadn't spoken tae Harris. Aye, and don't forget it.'

'I only did it as a favour to Des. Now I'm Mr Big!'

'Right, listen tae me. They're going tae spring this mob – both sides. Whatever you've tae pick up, it must be big news.'

'I have no idea. Mr Harris talks in riddles.'

'Aye, that's true.'

The door crashed open and Daley hurried towards them.

'What now, Jimmy?'

'It's Carrie. Bower got her.'

'Eh? Last time I heard she was meeting him on that beach wae half o' Police Scotland hiding in the bushes.'

'That's not how it worked out, Bri. Come on, Iolo wants to see us.'

Will stared, open-mouthed. 'Can I ask a question?'

'Aye, but make it quick, son.'

'Do any of you know what you're doing?'

'Fair point,' said Daley.

46

Hamish must have dozed off, for when he opened his eyes he was lying on the couch on his side. He was tired. The whole experience had been a traumatic one, and he saw no likelihood that that was about to change any time soon.

He looked over to the fireplace. In front of an old iron grate sat a wire mesh fireguard. It looked in poor repair, with parts of the frame missing and the mesh sticking out at odd angles.

Hamish twisted a finger to touch the rope bonds around his wrists. He managed to struggle to his feet by leaning on one elbow and propelling himself forward in the hope that he'd manage to stay upright. Thankfully, after a stagger forward, he did so. He made his way to the fireplace and, deciding which part of the fireguard looked best suited for purpose, turned his back on it and tried to position the rope against the sharp edge of the exposed mesh.

The first movement of his hands was agony. He'd miscalculated, and the ends of the wire cut into the flesh of his hand. He bit down hard on his lip to stop himself from crying out in pain.

'Aye, if at first you don't succeed,' he whispered to himself, remembering Robert the Bruce in the cave with the spider. More carefully this time, he considered the fireguard and, turning round, placed his bound wrists more carefully on the sharp mesh.

It took another few pinpricks of pain before he was satisfied that the rope was now in contact with the rough edge of the fireguard. He tried to twist round in order to have a look, but his old frame wasn't supple enough, though he could see drips of blood on the pale tiled hearth below.

Slowly, he began to move his arms up and down. He could feel the wire mesh biting into the rope. It might take a while, but he had to try.

Hamish's heart was still heavy. Though he should have had more concern for himself, the fear that drove him on to break his bonds was for someone else entirely.

'Ah, come on, you bugger.' The oath was whispered, but genuine. He had to free himself, to escape this place. He was desperate to get home in order to prevent a tragedy.

He worked the rope against the mesh until he felt the agony of cramp in his shoulder. Gasping at the pain, he staggered forward and landed awkwardly on the couch. The world spun for a few moments, but soon the cramp subsided, and he was able to push himself once more into a seated position by using his elbows. He leaned back, breathing heavily, frantically trying to muster enough strength to have another go.

He remembered now how they'd sedated him. He could see the woman's face as he slipped into unconsciousness. Hamish hadn't liked her from the moment they'd met. There was something about her eyes that made him instantly uneasy. And as was often the case, he'd been right.

With all the strength he could muster, he forced himself back to his feet and stumbled across to the grate. Being careful not to cut himself again, eventually he felt the mesh start to bite into the rope again. It wasn't thick; he could feel that with the tip of his finger.

Undaunted, but with his legs trembling, Hamish tried again.

As he worked his arms, he tried to think of something that would take his mind off the ache in his shoulders. He remembered his mother's Sunday roast. Beef was her favourite, a treat, as most of the time they ate fish. Her roast potatoes tasted like none he'd had before or since.

He remembered the first time his father had taken him out on the boat. The smell of the sea and the rolling slow swell felt like freedom, felt like the future – his future. No longer would he be a land-bound creature; he had the oceans to explore, just like the pictures he'd seen in books and the plays he'd heard on the wireless.

The old man longed to be free. But it wasn't just that longing that drove him on, but something much more urgent and compelling.

He could feel the ache spread across his shoulders. His hand stung where he'd cut it. But still he fought against the rope.

Then, in a flash, it was as though a dam had broken. The pressure on his wrists had eased. Desperately, he tried to pull his hands completely free. Not quite. He wasn't there yet.

With renewed fervour he went about his business. Just when he thought he could no longer remain standing, it happened. His hands flew apart. He staggered forward, propelled by the sheer effort of it all.

He examined the cut on his right hand. It was deeper than he'd thought. Already dark blood was congealing against his leathery skin. But he wasn't worried about that now. Instead he, looked across to the sash window. If he could open it, he would be able to escape this godforsaken place.

He unwound the remaining rope from his wrists and tried to catch his breath. His shoulders still throbbed, but something stronger drove him on. He was just about to make his way to the window when his heart sank. A key sounded in the door. It swung open.

Nathan Sidley was standing in a car park on the edge of Blaan. The coast of Ireland shimmered in the haze. A few metres away, his photographer was busy on the phone. Sidley noticed how straight-backed he was. In his experience, people of Ronnie's profession were used to huddling under hedges against the rain, or standing for hours in the blazing sun waiting for a single chance at a shot, seen but unseen. This guy stuck out like a sore thumb. Also, the brave men and women who exposed themselves to terror, war and conflict to get the best pictures possible didn't stride boldly forward: they crouched in fear of their lives. Sidley had the feeling Ronnie would march into battle – literally.

He sat on a fence, pretending to be enjoying the sunshine but quietly studying Ronnie from behind his sunglasses. The edge of a Union Jack tattoo was showing just under the right sleeve of the man's T-shirt, accentuated by the bulge of his biceps. Nothing about Ronnie spoke of newspapers, but it did speak of something else: the military.

But why would his editor send him a soldier? Sidley decided to find out. He scrolled down the contacts list on his phone until he came to *Arsehole*. It displayed little respect for his boss, but the kid didn't deserve any. His job wasn't to produce the best newspaper possible, it was to count paperclips, make people redundant and come up with ever more pointless cost-saving ideas. When Sidley was a young reporter, he'd been paid every week. Not much, admittedly, but enough to live on, buy some fags and a few pints to keep him going. Nowadays pallid interns sat at computer screens, headphones plugged into their skulls, writing copy he'd have been booted out of the office for forty years ago. But it was hard to blame them. Without even the courtesy of the bus fare home, what was there to motivate them?

'Timothy, how the devil are you?' Sidley's Scouse drawl was at its most pronounced. He was being sarcastic, and he knew that his editor would know it, but there was no better accent to hide sarcasm behind than his native Liverpudlian.

'Nathan, how can I help you? Hope this story of yours is going well. You're investing a lot of your time and our money in it.'

'I'm getting there. Just wanted to ask you a quick question. I know what a busy life you have.'

'Yes, damn right. Ask away, but be quick about it.'

Sidley bridled at the editor's dismissive manner, but rather than deploy his sharp tongue he reasoned that it was best to get on with it. 'Ronnie. How well do you know him?'

'Ronnie who?'

'You know, the top-class photographer you've sent me to add some drama to the piece.'

'Ah, yes. Ronnie.' Suddenly, his editor was hesitant. 'I must confess, I don't know a great deal about him.'

'No shit. My problem is, he seems to know a great deal more than me.'

'Oh, how so?'

'Well, he tells me that the office had a tip that something was kicking off down here. I'm standing in a car park in the middle of nowhere waiting for this something to happen. He's on the blower, I assumed to you.'

'Clearly not.'

'Well, since you appointed him, I suppose you know best what he's doing. But I'd have been happier if you'd told me what leads you had, not the snapper.'

'I didn't appoint him. It came from upstairs, as a matter of fact.'

'And what about this information?'

'I presume from the same source.'

'Upstairs?'

'Yes.'

'Tell me, Tim, old chap. In this case, what is "upstairs" the euphemism for? Is it the editor-in-chief? The owner?'

Again, Timothy's reply was hesitant. 'I'm not sure, to be honest.'

'So you've sent me a guy you don't know, who seems to be in possession of facts neither of us is party to?'

'It is what it is.'

'But what is it? Where are his tips coming from?'

'Ask him.'

'You're a fabulous editor, Tim.'

'I'm sure you don't mean that, Nathan. But just get the job done, there's a good man.'

'Oh yeah, I'll get the job done. But maybe it won't be the job "upstairs" want.' Sidley ended the call before his editor could make further comment. In any case, it was obvious he was nothing more than a flunkey. Though it was still unclear who had sent Ronnie the photographer, Sidley reckoned he knew where he'd come from. He hated being played, but, in his experience, there was always something behind it – sometimes something more interesting than the main event. But how did he get to whatever it was?

He dialled a number on the screen and put the phone to his ear.

'DCI Daley, please.'

47

Jim Daley wasn't sure he'd ever seen Scott so angry, and for once, he shared the sentiment.

'How could you just lose her? You should have had men at both ends o' the beach. Aye, and you should have waited for me an' Jimmy tae get back. You've no right taking operational command o' police officers.'

'Oh, I think your chief constable would have something to say about that,' said Iolo Harris.

'Aye, he's a real star and all.'

'I'll pass that on.'

'And we can't trace her?' Daley asked.

'No. Her phone was found just along the road.'

'You should have had roadblocks on either side', Scott went on. 'Once this bastard Bower made contact, you should have closed the net on him.'

Daley looked at Harris. There was a confidence about the man he didn't like. He seemed in no way alarmed by the fact that a chief superintendent had been effectively kidnapped. 'There's something you're not telling us, isn't there?'

'Like what?'

'Men like you don't make basic mistakes. Remember, we've worked together before.'

'But clearly I made an arse of this, Jim. Certainly according to your faithful assistant here.'

'Well, what about my boy?' Scott demanded.

'Having interviewed them both, I'm pleased to say that young Will is an honest, steady young man. The same, I'm afraid, can't be said for his boyfriend. A real zealot, and slippery with it.'

Sergeant Shaw's head appeared round the door. 'It's Nathan Sidley to speak to you, sir. It sounds quite urgent.'

'Excuse me, please,' said Daley. But as he left the glass box, he was sure he detected a puzzled look on Harris's face.

In Shaw's domain, the bar office, he picked up the phone. 'Nathan, what's up?'

'I'm wondering, did you ever identify our other man in the plane?'

'No, but since we've lost operational control, I might not have been told.'

'So the spooks are in charge?'

'Don't quote me on that.'

'It makes sense.'

'How so?'

'I've been assigned a photographer. He's not like any I've seen before, and I've seen hundreds of them. I'm going to make a few calls, but I'm sure nobody will know him.'

'In what way is he different?'

'He's military. It's written all over him.'

It was Daley's turn to be puzzled. 'But why would your paper send a soldier?'

'Maybe they didn't have a choice. But in any case, not only is this lad built like a brick shithouse, he knows things I don't. We're down in' – he hesitated over the name – 'Blaan?'

'What for?'

'He's waiting for a call.'

'From who?'

'I thought you might know.'

'I don't.' Daley thought for a moment. 'Listen, leave this with me. I'll speak to our friend from the Security Service here. But keep in touch.'

'I will, but I want to be kept in the loop, Daley. I've got a living to make too, you know.'

Annie put down the phone after a brief conversation with the harbour master. Still no word of Hamish, but she'd known that in her heart before she dialled.

She lay back on her bed and thought about him. The slanting eyes, the ever-present Breton cap. His broad grin and his leathery face were things she'd taken for granted.

Now they were gone, and so was her job – her home.

She was past tears now. She still felt the ache in her heart, but her mood was one of beaten resignation. There was nothing she could do to bring the old man back, and she wasn't sure she had the spirit to start again with a new job and a new home.

People were strange – rarely how they appeared. Not when you got to know them, at least. She could never have dismissed someone the way Macmillan had her. And yet, when he'd first arrived, she'd thought him the saviour of not just her job but the old hotel itself. Now he was her nemesis.

Annie preferred gin to vodka, but the big bottle was the first thing she'd laid her hands on in the hotel's spirit store. It was locked, but she'd always left a spare key tucked away on the narrow windowsill across the corridor. There was nothing worse on a busy night of thirsty drinkers than being unable to open the door to where they kept the spirits because you couldn't find the key.

Annie poured a large measure of the clear spirit into the cracked mug by her bed and stared into space.

Ronnie finished his call and walked across to where Sidley was still perched on the fence.

'Okay, I know where we're off to now.'

'You do? I think you should forget photography and get into journalism, pal. You're obviously better at it than me.'

'Just a tip-off, mate. That's probably why they sent me.'

'So, what can we expect, then?'

'A hike – well, for a good part of the way.' Ronnie flourished his phone under Sidley's face, shading it from the sun with his other hand. 'We can drive up to this point, maybe a bit further. But when we get to the end of this track near the top of the hill, we'll have to go on foot – we're heading for this bit here, see?'

Sidley studied the map. He could see that the route Ronnie had indicated would culminate in a very steep hill down to a beach. 'So, we're just having a day out on the sand. Brilliant!'

'Nah, *here*,' said Ronnie, pointing to a featureless spot on the map.

'That's a field.'

'There's actually some kind of building there. It was built for a tidal energy project that failed before it started.'

'You're a mine of information, Ronnie. Anyway, what about it?'

'That's it. This is where it kicks off.'

'What kicks off?'

The photographer shrugged. 'Whatever it is you've been chasing up.'

Sidley laughed. 'So you know where but not why?'

'In a nutshell, mate.'

Sidley knew what he'd been told earlier in the day. Everything matched up nicely. He knew why, and Ronnie knew where. It was classic. But for the time being he'd play along. After all, it wasn't what you found, it was what you wrote about it that was important.

They jumped back in the car, and after a mile or so down a single-track road they turned on to a forestry track.

48

'I'll do it,' said Will, much to his father's displeasure.

'No you'll no,' he replied angrily.

'Now, now, lads, play fair. Will here knows that he's doing his duty for his country. He's made a mistake; now he wants to atone for it. I'd be proud if he was my son.' Harris looked pleased with himself.

'Oh aye?' said Scott. 'But he's 'no' got much o' a choice, has he?'

'Yes, he has. He can do this, or he can do time for purchasing an illegal firearm.'

'You're a twisted bastard. I discovered that on Gairsay, and now this.'

'You surely don't condone rogue terrorists running about the place selling goodness knows what to the lunatic fringe of the climate brigade, do you?'

'No, I don't. But I don't want my son in the middle o' it neither.'

'Dad, shut up, will you? I've agreed what I'll do. If it means I stay out of prison, it's worth it.'

'And he'll be well looked after, you have my word.'

'Like Chief Superintendent Symington? Aye, I've nae worries then.'

'I'm bringing in my own men.'

'It wisnae oor fault Bower grabbed her right under your nose. It was yours!'

'She didn't follow the plan! Off she went into the undergrowth. What did you want me to do?'

Scott was about to give a graphic description of what Harris should do when Daley appeared through the door.

'You want tae hear this, big man. Tell him, Willie,' said Scott.

'I'll brief DCI Daley, if you don't mind, DI Scott. Now, if you could give us the room, please.'

Daley nodded at Scott, and reluctantly he and Will left the glass box.

'Okay, what's happening, then?'

'We have a location. Young Will Scott is going to be at the handover.'

'What about this Linda woman?'

'She seems happy with the arrangement.' Harris shrugged. 'Wily bugger, she is. She wanted the lad Des, but no way.'

'Why Will? He's just a boy?'

'He wasn't her first choice. Des had a text from her when you were off gallivanting around County Antrim.' Harris adopted a mock-sad expression. 'Bit sick, he is. Can't keep a thing down, poor bugger.'

'Oh aye. You mean you're holding a gun charge over Will and he's more malleable.'

'Now, what is it that guy used to say? *You may think that, but I couldn't possibly comment*.'

'It didn't end well for him, as I recall.'

'No, but that was fiction. There's a difference.'

'Are you sure?'

Harris stared at Daley for a few moments. 'What do you mean?'

'Just opening my mouth, really.' He smiled.

'Well, in any case, nothing for you to worry about, really. My men will be here soon. Special forces. The operation won't require any police input.'

'Nothing to worry about then. What about Carrie?'

'Now, though I can't say too much, I think she's going to be okay. She's their insurance, you see.'

'Whose insurance?'

'That is yet to become clear, but who wants to kill a senior police officer? Come on, Jim.'

'And when does this all begin, if you don't mind me asking?'

Harris looked at his watch. 'In about two hours from now. Anyway, if you'll excuse me, I have a lot on.'

'Make sure Carrie and Will are safe, Iolo.'

'Top of my list, Jim. I'll see you in that hotel for a pint when it's all over.'

Daley watched the MI5 man leave his office and pulled the mobile phone from his pocket. He read the text and went off in search of Brian Scott.

The man who stood before Hamish was in his sixties, hefty, with wisps of red hair turning grey over a balding crown and the big rough hands of a farmer. He was holding a pistol in one of them. The man looked as at home with it as he would with a shovel, Hamish thought.

'Aye, but you're a game auld fella, right enough.' His voice was like gravel and from the very south of rural Ireland. 'Get yourself parked on a chair, so.'

Hamish limped back over to the couch. It was a strange feeling. He'd been through so much but had never been sure he'd come out safely at the other end of it all. The prescience for which he was famous had let him down. But the fear in his breast wasn't for his fate, but that of another.

'You're a fisherman, I'm told. Hamish is the name, am I right?'

'I am that. And what do I call you? I'd prefer to be on nodding terms wae the man who's sending me tae meet my maker.'

'Och, since you're Hamish I'll be Sheamus; is it not the same name?'

'Isn't that the irony. Despatched by a man wae my own name. No' many Hamishes but Sheamuses tae the dozen.'

'Not as many as once there was, and that's the truth.' Sheamus narrowed his eyes, as though observing Hamish carefully. 'From across in Kintyre, they say.'

'You mean young Terry says. I'm telling you, you better no' have laid a finger on that fine young man. My end might be in this room, but I'll make damn sure my spirit follows you tae your dying day – aye, and beyond.' He jutted out his chin defiantly. In truth, though, he was exhausted, troubled and ready for his end.

'You're a brave man into the bargain. I've met a good few, but none that were fishermen.'

'You canna have met many fishermen, that's all I can say. For every wave has danger at its soul – aye, and so do no waves at all, as I've jeest found oot.'

Sheamus grinned at this. 'I'm not a man of the sea. I've managed to find sufficient trouble on land over the years, so I have.'

'And you carry it wae you, if you don't mind me saying.'

This comment made Sheamus laugh heartily. 'You'll be a whiskey man, I reckon.'

'I've been known tae enjoy a dram. And if you have one tae hand, now's the time tae say. For I can think o' no better moment.'

Sheamus let the gun down at his side, but still kept it firmly gripped in his big paw. He made his way to a cupboard from which he produced a bottle of Jameson and two small glasses.

'If I'd known that was there I wouldna have bothered trying tae escape. They don't call it the water o' life for nothing, even if yous canna spell it right.'

'I wouldn't worry, Hamish. Sure, it has the same effect, with or without an *e*.' He laid the glasses down on a small table, pulled out the cork with his teeth and poured two large measures.

'For a killer you've got a fine pouring hand.'

'I could never bear those miserable buggers that dribbled the stuff in. Is it not just enough tae make your lips tingle, and no more?'

'I can forgive a man a great many things, but being parsimonious wae a dram isna one o' them.'

Sheamus handed his captive a glass. 'To those of us who are about to die, we salute you!' He put his glass to his mouth and drained it in one swallow.

'Aye, you've a fair drouth, right enough. But tae continue the metaphor, when in Rome dae as the Romans dae.' Hamish followed Sheamus's lead and emptied his glass.

'You'll be a Protestant, I wager?'

'I am, but I dare say the church has given up on me, for I've no' been through the doors o' one since I lost my mother.'

Sheamus took a chair, the pistol now on the table. 'Never a worse day, and that's for sure. I remember lowering my own mother down. I've never cried for anyone else, but I wept buckets for her.'

351

'The priest would be a comfort, mind you.'

'I gave him his marching orders when he said that my auld mammy might languish in purgatory because she'd stolen food tae feed us weans when we were no higher than boots.'

'Doesna sound much like a man o' God tae me. The Reverend McNee buried my mother. Mind you, I'm no' sure who was the drunker, me or him. But better that than this purgatory nonsense.'

Sheamus walked the bottle back to Hamish. 'You'll be having another?'

'I don't feel as though it would be polite to refuse.'

They drank in silence for a while. Then Sheamus spoke. 'Well, I suppose we'd better be getting on with it.'

Hamish's face betrayed no emotion as Sheamus reached for the gun.

49

Symington had still been blindfolded when the car she'd been bundled into came to a halt. Without a word, she'd been manhandled into a large space and thrust into a chair; she could guess the size of the building by the echo of men's voices. Though most of their journey had appeared to be off-road, this place didn't give her the sense of anything agricultural. There was no smell of dung, of cattle or sheep. In fact, without her vision all she could detect was a musty, unlived-in odour, tinged with the hint of oily machinery.

The voices came from what must have been the far end of the building. Bower's low estuary drawl was foremost among them, though she couldn't make out what he was saying.

Footsteps echoed towards her. Hands grabbed her head, forcing her chin up, and the blindfold was pulled roughly from her eyes. As Symington blinked into the light, she saw she was in what could have easily been a cowshed, but clearly hadn't ever been used as such. A slick, clean concrete floor ran from one end to the other, and the walls were of steel construction. In the rafters half a dozen striplights hung from the ceiling, one blinking intermittently. She was sitting on a plastic chair – the only one in the place, as far as she could see – while the man who'd removed her blindfold stood silently beside her. Bower and another man she didn't know stood at the other end of the long building. Apart from that, the place was empty.

She looked at the man who towered above her. He was staring straight ahead, his face blank. Symington quickly decided that she'd get nothing from him.

'They'll be looking for me right now!' she shouted, her voice echoing in the cavernous space.

Bower turned from his conversation and smiled. 'Yeah, so what? They're not going to find you out here, are they?'

Not for the first time, Symington felt a chill in her heart. She'd been knocked unconscious by a well-aimed blow to her neck and had slowly regained her senses during the journey. Though she'd asked where she was being taken, nobody had replied. And she was sure Bower hadn't been in the car. But he was here now.

She chewed her lip as he walked slowly towards her, an automatic weapon slung casually over one shoulder.

'I hope you're comfortable, Carrie?' he said, with little attempt to hide the fact that he didn't care whether she was comfortable or not.

'I'm thirsty,' she replied, staring into his face.

Bower nodded to the man standing behind her, who strode away without a word.

'I want to know what you're going to do with me.'

'You do? I want to know why you can't find a decent pub without screaming kids in it any more. Nobody ever tells me.'

'I'll ask you again, what are you going to do with me?'

Bower grinned. 'You're my little get out of jail card, aren't you?'

Carrie searched his face, and though he was hard to read, she was sure she could detect a lie.

'You're smarter than I thought, mind you.'

'Why?'

'You managed to find those parents of yours. That was clever.'

Though he said the words, something about his manner made her think that the freeing of her mother and father had come as no surprise. Or was she just carried away with the police officer's instinct that Daley and Scott always banged on about?

Bower hunkered down on his knees, his face now level with hers. 'I don't really know how things are going to go here, Carrie. But you'll have to play your part, right?'

'What part?'

Bower nodded to the middle of the floor. 'That's where you'll be sitting.'

'What for?'

He laughed. 'Just so I know where you are, that's what for.'

'You're not making sense.'

'Okay, I'll tell you all you need to know. I'm – well, these nice gentlemen and I – are expecting a package. It's going to be delivered here soon.'

'And what do you want me to do?'

'I want you to sit and look pretty.'

'What is this package?'

'Are you sure you want to know?'

'Yes. I wouldn't have asked otherwise.'

'Okay.' He leaned his head closer into hers. 'It's sarin gas.'

Symington felt her mouth dry instantly. She'd been on an anti-terror course six months ago. The purpose had been to analyse the most likely methods potential terrorists would use against members of the public. Sarin gas was one of the favourites: its effects were devastating. 'You have no idea what you're getting yourself into.'

'I know exactly what I'm getting myself into. If you mean the gas, that is. They tell me you lose control of your organs. Can't breathe, that type of thing.' He grinned. 'Best bit is that you remain conscious until it's too late. You know, before you fall over and die, choking and suchlike. Nasty way to go, but so effective.'

Before Symington could say any more, the man who'd removed her blindfold reappeared carrying a bottle of water.

'I'd be careful of how much you drink, girl. You might just end up drowning in it before the day's out.' He laughed as he stood up and beckoned the other man to join him with a nod of his head. Looking over his shoulder, he spoke to Symington again. 'And don't think of any heroics. The man over there, he's a bloody good shot.'

Symington looked across to the end of the building. Hidden in the shadows, a figure in black fatigues, his face obscured by a balaclava, had a sniper's rifle pointed at her. When Symington looked down, she saw a bright red dot play across her chest.

Declan Louth couldn't remember his grandfather. He had a faded photograph of a painfully thin man with a drooping moustache and grey hair holding him as a baby, but he had absolutely no memory of him.

His grandfather had been a member of the Provisional IRA. He'd starved himself to death in a fetid cell in the Maze prison. But unlike most grandsons who had never seen or couldn't remember their grandfathers, Declan had been handed a manual for life, written on various scraps of paper, old notebooks and prison jotters. The old man had whiled away his last few months of life making sure his son knew who he was and where he came from. And why, instead of being a grandfather to his sons, he'd taken his own life to advance the cause that had dominated it.

There were many passages that Declan could readily bring to mind.

A man has to believe in something. No price is too high for freedom. Live your life with honour and learn. Be the best man you can for the struggle ahead.

All these lessons for life were etched in his mind: heartfelt words, from a man who – rightly or wrongly – brought about his own end with calm determination.

But of all the signposts in the manual of life he'd inherited, one stood out.

Don't get caught alive. Don't make the mistake I made. Don't let them win.

As he sat in the cabin of the fishing boat with Linda Delaney, he went through this advice over and over again. Declan wondered how his grandfather would have dealt with a woman who treated him with such contempt and arrogance. He was quite sure she'd have had a bullet in the back of the head by now. But he wasn't the man to do such a thing, though he'd have dearly liked to pull the trigger.

But these were different days. The men of that generation were mainly either dead or old and bitter. Some of them were politicians: suits and ties had replaced balaclavas and military fatigues; their bullets were now words and schemes. Others withered away in retirement homes, or as little more than a burden to their families. But still they dreamed their dreams or cursed their luck.

But Declan had always known that wasn't the life for him, although he'd stayed true to the cause, had always done what he could. If it meant tolerating Linda Delaney, then that was the way it was. Still, he'd agreed with those who thought her many years spent in England made her untrustworthy. When she'd come to them, the hard core of Republicans still willing to do what had to be done to make a difference, many had been sceptical. He remembered how Sean had bridled at the thought of doing business with kids from colleges across the water.

'I'd like to know what's in it for you?' Declan had heard the man he'd left bleeding at a bus stop say.

'It's not what's in it for me, it's what's in it for *us*,' Linda had replied with the cool persuasion that was her trademark.

Declan was supposed to be her minder. Not just for protection, but, as Sean had said, 'to keep the bitch honest'. *If you think she's at it, don't hesitate.*

In some ways, he wished he'd ended it all before it began. The men in the plane were bad enough. That had been Sean's warning to those he thought could betray them. Nothing stood out like the British military, not to those who knew them. Even if they did come bearing fancy gifts. That had all been a mistake, according to Linda. But they hadn't been infiltrated and all was well.

But Declan had had his doubts.

Now he was heading across the short distance of the North Channel to sell a wicked thing to stupid kids that Linda had manipulated for their, or more likely her, own ends. The greed for gold, at any rate. It didn't sit easily with him.

'Where are you off to?' she said, with that grating air of authority she had.

'I'm going to get some fresh air, if you don't mind.' Declan didn't wait for the reply but stepped out on to the deck of the fishing boat and leaned against a rail.

The sun was lower in the sky now, but it would be a few hours yet before the short night descended. The water was calm – barely a wave. And the birds that would normally follow a vessel like this in a squawking frenzy were nowhere to be seen. It was as though they sensed what this harmless-looking fishing boat carried. And knew it was evil.

They were about halfway between County Antrim and the Kintyre peninsula now. The scene before him was beautiful: slow waves tipped with shades of green, red and purple, the gentle lap of water against the bow as the fishing boat rumbled along on an empty, silken sea. It was all so at odds with what he knew to be their purpose.

He'd Googled sarin gas. He knew just what it could do. Though he had no qualms about taking a life in a just cause, the thought that those dedicated to saving the planet were planning to do so by killing others didn't seem real, and it gave him pause. In addition, he was pretty sure that Linda had cheated and lied in order to get the hugely over-inflated sum of money they were charging for this *super weapon*. Even a few old pistols and other bits and pieces that should have remained in the ground where they'd been buried long ago had been sold at an obscene price.

Yes, the money was good – fabulous, in fact. From rich kids with access to wealth he could only dream about. But still, Declan felt something was wrong.

Trust your instincts, son. And if you fail, take as many with you as you can.

This mantra played over and over in his head as the boat sailed on towards Kintyre.

50

Daley and Scott were waiting outside Kinloch Car Hire. It was well past close of business for the day, but Daley had called the owner, who was only too pleased to open up for the local police. He also knew they'd pay top dollar, so that was another incentive.

'You'll need tae run this past me again, Jimmy,' said Scott. 'It's mair complicated than the last phone they gave me. I'd only just learned how tae work that when they gave me another one.'

'I know where Symington is. Well, I think I do.'

'Aye, I got that bit, I'm no' a halfwit!'

'Though you still think that your ancestors were kept busy running away from dinosaurs.'

'Have you no' beaten me o'er the head wae that enough? You're relentless, man.'

'I've just got a feeling that Hamish and Carrie are there – or could be.'

'I don't follow you, big man. The gaffer, aye, I can see it. But Hamish, how do you work that oot?'

'It's the Irish connection. Think about it, Brian. Will's off to a remote location nobody knows about. It's the nearest place on the peninsula to County Antrim.'

'You're still making connections I don't understand, Jimmy.'

Daley was about to reply, but he realised that he was far from sure he was right either. Maybe the thought of finding Symington made sense. But Hamish – well, that was a leap in the dark.

A black BMW drew up to the kerb beside them.

'Gentlemen, now what can I do for you?' Arthur Cook was a dapper man with a neatly trimmed beard. He stepped out of the car in chinos and a red sweater. 'You'll have to excuse the attire. It being a Friday night, I was just heading out for a pint.'

'Glad we caught you then,' said Daley.

Cook used his key to open a large roller-shutter door then typed a number into the alarm system. Overhead lights flickered into action to reveal half a dozen sparklingly clean cars and SUVs.

'Now, here we are. I've more out the back in the yard – the older models. What was it you were after?'

Daley took in the selection of vehicles on display. 'Well, something more practical, to be honest.'

'Practical?'

'Yes, like a Land Rover, for instance. We're going across rough terrain.'

'Oh, I see.' Cook stepped right in front of a gleaming SUV as though he was trying to render it invisible, but Scott pointed straight at it.

'That thing would dae, eh?'

'Oh no, definitely not.' Cook shook his head vigorously, lips pursed together. 'They make all kinds of promises with these off-road cars, but they don't match up to the reality. A wee bit of rough ground, and one of you would be out pushing in no time.'

'Remind me no' tae buy one o' them.'

'Do you have anything suitable?' asked Daley.

Cook rubbed his chin. 'This way, gents.'

The two policemen followed Cook through to the back of the garage. He unlocked a large padlock and used an oversized key to turn a deadlock, opening a robust door.

'Now, I got this in a couple of weeks ago. I bought it as a favour for an old friend. I'll sell it up the road, hopefully get my money back. But if you can't do something for your friends, what can you do?'

A grey Land Rover Defender was sitting in the yard, alongside two Transit vans and a Honda saloon. All had seen better days.

'I buy and sell a bit still. It's how I started out.' Cook looked pleased with himself, as though he was saying *look how well I've done*. 'My friend used to do a lot of work on farms – hence the Land Rover. All that's died out now. Aluminium is king, so they tell me.'

Scott examined the Land Rover. Painted on the side was the legend *Kinloch Tiles & Plasterers. If you want to get plastered, you know where to find us.* Scott stared at the cheery wording with distaste. 'We'll look like a right pair o' chookies in this, big man. Have you no' got something else?'

Cook shrugged his shoulders. 'I'm sorry, gentlemen. Not a lot of call for this sort of thing. I'm mainly into cars and vans.' He thought for a moment. 'Don't you have a couple of Land Rovers at the station?'

'One's out of commission and the other is in use.' Daley eyed the Land Rover. 'Is it sound?'

'Oh yes. I've just had it checked over with a view to punting it. It's in top nick.'

'Okay, we'll take it. You'll understand that we're in a bit of a hurry, so we'll sort out the paperwork later, if that's fine with you?'

'Well, what about insurance and the like?' Cook clearly wasn't keen on letting someone drive away without leaving a signature.'

'Insurance?' said Scott. 'Here's a fiver. That should cover the cost o' the bloody thing.'

Daley produced a chit from his pocket. 'Just sign this, Mr Cook. It covers everything.'

As Cook was opening the big gates that led on to the road, Daley wrestled with the gears, the crunching sound making Scott wince.

'You're too used tae those fancy motors you drive now. Are you sure you don't want me tae drive?'

A parade of incidents passed before Daley's mind. Brian Scott drove everywhere at just about the same speed – fast. Sitting alongside him in the passenger seat was like a thrill-ride at an amusement park. 'I'll be fine.'

The old Land Rover puttered and rattled. 'I'm no' sure we'll get oot o' Kinloch in this jalopy. How come we didnae take one of oor own motors?'

'Because they're white with big stripes and *Police* brandished everywhere.'

'You never said we were going on the fly.'

'We're observing, Brian.'

'Aye, observing me pushing this heap o' junk oot o' a ditch.'

'You're always so negative.'

'Huh, listen tae Pollyanna here.'

'That's a surprise. Where did you get that?'

'Nae idea. I've heard folk saying it. This Pollyanna lassie

must be a right optimistic soul. Anyway, it's no' as though we won't stick oot like a sore thumb in this bugger.'

'Nobody will turn a hair. Remember we're under orders not to have anything to do with this.'

'It's okay, we just look like Del Boy and Rodney. And mind my son's wae that Welsh idiot.'

'He's lots of things, Brian, but an idiot isn't one of them.'

Old Mr Anderson was out for his evening constitutional when he saw them drive past.

If you want to get plastered, you know where to find us.

Reading the message on the passing vehicle gave him a drouth, and he resolved – despite doctor's orders – to stop in at the first bar he came to for a pint.

Nathan Sidley's feet were sore, and the sweat was pouring down his face. 'How long now?'

Ronnie looked at his phone. 'I'd say less than half a mile. And it's all downhill.'

Sidley eyed his new companion. 'For a photographer you're good at orienteering.'

'I was in the Scouts, wasn't I?'

'They taught you well.'

They were walking through a thicket of old trees, hanging with moss. A stream trickled by. The place had an earthy smell and a timeless feel. Sidley wondered how many feet had trodden on this ground. Not many, he reasoned.

Soon they left the shade of the trees, and though the sun was much lower in the sky now, he could clearly see a wide valley below. Nestled beneath gentle, rolling hills, a silvery burn twisted and sparkled its way to the sea. Just at the point a tiny estuary opened out, Sidley could discern a reasonably large building. It was too big to be a barn. A path ran from it to the bay, where a small jetty had been constructed. Though it was far below, it was clear that this was their destination.

'Shit!' Ronnie exclaimed as a deer darted in front of them and vanished into the thicket.

'You're a bit jumpy, lad,' said Sidley.

'I don't trust the countryside, mate. Too many things you don't expect.'

Sidley mulled this over. Big lad like you isn't frightened by a deer, surely? But you're expecting something, he thought.

Taking to a grassy field, the pair began their descent into the valley towards the building with the jetty.

'We'll need to keep our eyes open here,' said Ronnie.

'What for?'

'Well, we don't want anyone to see us, do we?'

Sidley gave him a knowing look. 'Of course not. Since you seem to be the expert, I'll just follow you, eh?'

'Stop!' said Ronnie, crouching into the long grass.

Doing likewise, Sidley kneeled beside his photographer. 'What is it?' he whispered.

'Look, across there.'

Sidley followed the line of Ronnie's pointed finger. Sure enough, down the hillside at the opposite side of the valley, dark-clad figures had fanned out across the hill and, like them, were heading down towards the building by the beach.

'They're not exactly camouflaged, are they?' said Sidley.

'Not from up here, no. But the way they're coming down that hill, nobody will see them from below.'

'Who are they, do you think?'

'No idea, mate. We're just following the tip-off, aren't we?'

Sidley knew that the appearance of the crouching figures

on the hill opposite came as no surprise to Ronnie. 'Aren't you going to grab a couple of shots?'

'What?'

The journalist stared ahead. Ronnie hadn't even the slightest instincts of a newspaper photographer. But if he was right, the cameraman could well be leading him to one of the biggest scoops of his career.

Then, in the golden light of the fading day, a fishing boat appeared round the headland that rose above the grey building. Sidley looked on as it made for the short jetty that thrust out into the small bay. When he looked across the valley, the group of dark figures was much less visible now, as they crouched motionless in the grass.

51

'You'll forgive me for my behaviour back there,' said the Irishman. The older men had two younger companions on the big RIB. Terry, dressed in a fluorescent jacket, sat beside his uncle, while one of the men who had snatched Hamish and Terry from the clifftop in County Antrim was at the controls of the vessel that had ferried them so quickly across the North Channel.

'Aye, I forgive you,' said Hamish. 'You had tae be sure I was who I said I was. I understand that.'

Their progress had slowed now; the RIB's trim lowered into the calm water as they slipped into the channel that led between the island and Kinloch. Hamish should have felt his heart soar, but instead he felt a growing fear in his heart.

'Are you all right?' said Terry.

'No, I canna say I am, young man. But I owe you and your uncle my life. Though he's a got a bit mair resources aboot him when it comes tae the rescuing department, right enough.'

'This lad here is better doing what he's at. The time for war is over. Though I know there are a good few who think differently.' The Irishman stared ahead as though he was looking into the future.

'When I went to work the other day I had no idea what I was walking into,' said Terry.

'That's the way of the world, nephew. You never know what's around the corner. Be aware of that and be prepared for an assortment of difficulties in life.'

'You clearly are. How did you know about me and Hamish?'

'Ireland may be divided, son, but it's a small place. And people like me enjoy nothing more than hearing about what our erstwhile comrades in arms are up to. I heard things were afoot, and when your ma called me, sure, that was enough.'

Terry looked up at his uncle. 'I'd never have got out of that bar alive if I hadn't remembered what you taught me.'

'That's the way it should be; the old pass their wisdom to the young. I'm for sitting beside the fireside with a good whiskey in my fist now. My days of making a mark on the world are over – for good or ill.'

'You did us proud. I hope tae make your acquaintance again some day,' said Hamish.

'I've no' seen the last of you, for sure. Though I think you've a few sorrows to overcome before we meet again. Oh, by the way, I'm Joe – Joe Dougherty. Though I quite fancy Sheamus as a name, right enough.'

'Aye, I had a notion it was a nom de plume.' The old Kinloch fisherman stared at the twin piers and the pontoons of the familiar harbour, rapidly drawing closer. 'That's us almost there. I hope tae see you both again. I owe you a great deal.'

'You'll forgive us for no' hanging about. I need tae get this young man back home. The guards will be wanting tae talk to him, but you know fine what to say, Terry.'

'I do so.'

The RIB drew up at the pontoon, the man at the helm guiding her expertly into an empty berth.

'May God go with you, Hamish.' Joe grabbed his hand and shook it enthusiastically. 'I wish you the very best from across the water. As a son of the soil to one of the seas.'

'I thank you both again, from the bottom of my heart.' Hamish took Terry's hand. 'You've saved my life, the pair of you. And I'll no' forget it. I hope you and your uncle will make the trip to see me.'

Terry nodded. 'We will.'

'Now, gentlemen, if you'll forgive me, I have somewhere to be. Aye, an' in a hurry, tae.'

Hamish stepped on to the wooden pontoon and scurried up to the road, as the RIB's engines fired up and the vessel swung away.

'Hamish, it's yourself!' said fellow fisherman Adam Robertson. 'Everyone thought you were deid!'

'Aye, and I damn near was. You'll have the van wae you, Adam?'

'Aye, I have. Where are you for?'

'The County, quick as you can, son.'

'You're a hell o' a man for the drams, Hamish, right enough. But I dare say you've a tale or two tae tell.'

'You could say that. Now, if you don't mind, there's something I need tae be at.'

The old Land Rover bumped along a farm track, then into a field.

'How do you know where you're going, Jimmy?' said Scott.

'I studied the map, how else?'

'So that wisnae auld Galbraith the farmer you phoned a mile or so back, then?'

'It's always good to take advantage of local knowledge, Bri.

369

It's the first thing they drummed into us at the college. This way is a shortcut.'

'The first thing they drummed intae me was a hundred trips roon the parade square at four in the morning in my best uniform. Ach, it had been a good wee night in that pub in Kincardine; I lost track o' time. It was up a stair. Do you remember it, Jimmy?'

'I think I went there once.'

Scott stared out of the window. 'I wish oor Willie had joined up. He might no' be in the predicament he's in noo.'

'Oh yes, just the job if you want to stay safe. How many times have you been shot?'

'Aye, fair point, big man.'

Scott's mobile rang. He picked it out of his pocket and looked at Daley. 'It's the office. How much dae you bet it's some ACC that's got news o' what we're up tae?'

'Answer it!' said Daley impatiently.

Scott put the phone to his ear. 'Aye, okay. Right – you're kidding! No way! I cannae believe it. Fantastic!' He put the phone down and shook his head. 'That's just brilliant!' He battered the dashboard with his hand, a large grin spread across his face.

'Do you mind telling me what's so fantastic? Have you won the lottery?'

'It's great, big man.'

'Tell me!'

'It's Hamish. Adam Robertson – you know, the clam fisherman – left him off at the County. He raced in like a whippet, apparently. Adam just appeared at the office. He thought he should let us know. Shaw's just heading down tae speak to Hamish now.'

'Wow! I can't believe it myself.'

'You thought he was gone tae, didn't you, Jimmy?'

'What else was there to think?'

'Right, we just need tae save my boy and find oot what's going on and everything in the garden is rosy.'

Daley smiled as they bumped along the field. But unlike Scott, he wasn't experiencing any kind of euphoria, just the dread of bitter experience.

52

The skipper of the fishing boat drew alongside the short jetty, the boat kissing the tyre fenders with the slightest bump. A younger crew member jumped lithely from the boat and secured the vessel fore and aft to small bollards.

Linda was at the taffrail, as though sitting in judgement over the entire operation. She was observing everything as the pallet carrying the gas canisters was winched out of the hold with a block and tackle affair powered by a noisy motor.

Declan looked on, his heart in his mouth. 'I hope they know what they're doing,' he said to nobody in particular.

'You're right to worry. We've worked with our fair share of idiots in the last couple of days.'

He studied her calm expression. 'Don't you care?'

'Care about what?'

'What this stuff is going to do.'

She shrugged. 'I make money, you make money, and we disrupt the state. What's there to care about?'

Declan shook his head. 'It's wicked, that's what it is.'

'And guns and bombs aren't?'

'That's a long time ago now. Times change, you must realise that.'

The pallet was now directly above their heads as the motor squealed.

'You've got to decide what you want from your life, Declan. I think you might be better with those appeasers up the hill in Stormont.'

'So why did you pick me for this?'

'You're big and you generally don't complain.'

'Easily cowed, you mean?'

'Aye, something like that.' She turned to face him. 'Do you want to do this or not? If not, you won't get one penny, I'll see to that.'

A quick fantasy passed across his mind. He was picking Linda up and throwing her overboard. Enjoying the panic in her eyes as she fell between the boat and the lapping waves. But in reality he nodded a silent acquiescence. He was finding it harder to hide his dislike for her. Here was a woman who treated enemies and friends alike, all with casual disregard. He wondered if she actually believed in anything but herself.

'Okay, that's it down. Get the trolley and off you go.'

'Trolley?'

'Aye. How else do you think you're going to get that pallet up to that building, levitation?'

'Me?'

'Aye, you. Did you think I was going to take it?'

'I thought you'd be coming along, at least.'

'I'm the brains behind this show. You're the brawn. Anyway, our boys are in there with a hostage, just to make sure everything goes just so. When I say *our* boys, you know what I mean.'

'I'm totally confused by all this. I don't know my arse from my elbow. So you're expecting trouble, is that what you're saying?'

'I always expect the worst. It's good to have some leverage.'

'So, what have I to do?'

'Go up there with the kit. Our men are ready. One of my young climate guys will be there, keen as mustard, with a big bag of money. Get it, count it, and get back here. You get back aboard, and we're done. How difficult is that?'

Declan nodded. 'Right, easy as that, then.' He looked sceptical. 'But why does this lad not just come down here and give us the dosh?'

'Because that's the way we're doing it, right? Do you think I'm giving these wee lads and the idiots that back them any sniff of the cash?' A steel trolley with a long handle was now being winched on to the jetty. 'You jump down there, they'll get the pallet aboard, and away you go. It's not as though it's a long pull. Just get on with it for fuck's sake.' Linda turned to go back below.

'You'd better be waiting for me.'

'Okay, I'll just let you get lifted. Who needs money, anyhow? It's not as though you know about my part in this, is it? Get some wits about you, man.'

Decal watched her take the narrow steps to the cabin below. Carefully, he scaled the fishing boat's side and landed on the jetty just as the shrink-wrapped pallet was being winched on to the metal trolley.

Iolo Harris was looking through a pair of binoculars at the activity on the boat. 'Bingo, now we're good to go.' He reached for the phone in his pocket and typed out a message.

'Who are you texting?' said Will.

'When that becomes your business, I'll tell you. Just you stick to the plan.'

Will felt his legs shaking. He'd been bored with life at university. The endless studying, tedious lectures – it all seemed so pointless. In any case, where was he going to get a job when he graduated? He'd heard of so many over-qualified former students working in McDonald's, it was frightening. But then he'd met Des. What he wouldn't give to go back and do it all over again.

He knew he should be confident. He was surrounded by well-drilled soldiers – special forces – who were armed to the teeth. But something was nagging at him.

'This *package*, it's disgusting. It kills people.'

'So do guns, but you bought one of them no bother.' Harris put his hand on Will's shoulder. 'These are the type of people you've been dealing with, boy. Look at it this way, you've got a get-out-of-jail-free card. Desmond won't be so lucky.'

'What about Linda?'

'Leave Linda to me.' He picked up a large holdall and handed it to Will. 'Now, be a good boy and take this down the hill. You don't have to worry – we've got your back.'

'What, you mean now?'

'No time like the present, bach. Off you go. A man will meet you at the wicket door at the back of the building.'

'What's a wicket door?'

'A small door in a big door. Man, what do they teach you at university these days?'

'I'm not studying doors.'

'Got your father's wit, then? Good. Now get going.'

'And what happens when I hand over the money?'

'You do as they ask. They'll all think they're home and hosed. When they start to leave, we'll be in there. Anyway, we can hear everything. You're wearing a wire, remember?'

'I remember. What if they search me?'

'This isn't *The Sopranos*. It just looks like a watch. Come on – lights, camera, action! There's a good lad.'

Holdall in hand, Will stepped out of the shadows and made his way down the hill.

53

The bar was quiet, only a couple of strangers having a meal at a table near the back of the room when Hamish rushed in. He knew the girl behind the bar by sight but couldn't remember her name.

'Where's Annie?' The words tumbled out. He was short of breath with worry and the dash from the pier.

'Hamish! It's you!'

'Aye, it's me – where's Annie?'

The girl shrugged. 'She's been off for a couple of days – ill, I think.'

Hamish shook his head. 'Aye, I knew fine there was something up.'

'She was worried about you – really worried. We all were!'

'Is she in her room upstairs?' Hamish knew there'd be obstacles, but he had neither the time nor the inclination to face them.

'I'm not sure Mr Macmillan likes people going up to the staff quarters. Hold on, I'll phone her room and get her to come down. I know she'll be pleased to see you.'

The barmaid dialled Annie's extension number and let it ring for a few moments. 'No reply. She must be away oot.'

'I'm going up.' Hamish was making for the lobby when Ian Macmillan appeared in the doorway.

'I thought it was you! Recognised the voice.'

'Aye, it's me, Mr Macmillan. You'll no' mind if I take the stairs to Annie's room. I hear she's not been well.'

Macmillan's expression changed. 'It's been a difficult few days, you know.'

'In whoot way?'

'You know, with you being gone and all. Some things have happened.' He shrugged.

'You're talking in riddles, man. Come oot wae it!'

'Annie and I – the hotel – well, we've parted ways.'

The barmaid gasped, her hand to her mouth.

'Whoot dae you mean, *parted ways*?'

'Well, I'm looking for a different style of management. I have to bring this place into the twenty-first century. We have plans, and I needed someone new. I'm not too sure Annie would have enjoyed working in a different environment.'

'So you fired her? Man, she must be fair shattered. This isn't jeest her work, it's her home – her life!'

'She's not too old; she'll find something else. It's not as though she's looking for a blue-chip placement now, is it?'

'Wae all the culinary experimentations going on here, I widna be in the least surprised if yous started serving up blue chips.'

The barmaid pushed her way past them.

'Patsy, where are you going?' said Macmillan.

'Hame! Aye, an' here's your towel.' She threw it in his face. 'You can stick your job up your arse!' She stormed out, high heels clicking on the stone floor of the foyer.

'You see, this is the kind of thing I wanted to avoid.' Macmillan was holding the towel as though it was a foreign object.

'I'm no' really bothered whoot you were wanting, Mr Macmillan. Now, if you'll excuse me, I'm away up tae see Annie.'

'I can't let you do that, Hamish. Staff quarters are out of bounds for customers. You've clearly been through a lot. You've got blood on your hands and face. You look shattered. My advice would be to go home, get a bath and a rest. I'll tell Annie you're looking for her.'

'Ach, you're havering, man. Get oot my way!' Hamish pushed Macmillan, who staggered backwards a few steps before falling flat on his backside.

The front door of the hotel swung open, and Sergeant Shaw strode in just as Macmillan caught Hamish's leg as he was stepping over him to get to the stairwell.

'What on earth is going on? Hamish, everyone's been so worried about you. Where on earth have you been?'

'It's a hell o' a long story, and I've no' got the time to fill you in right this minute. But it's fair tae say I need tae see Annie. I'm feart that something terrible has happened.'

Macmillan scrambled to his feet and brushed himself down. 'Listen, officer, I don't know what Hamish here has been through. And I'm willing to overlook the fact that he's just assaulted me. But he wants to go to the staff quarters, and they're out of bounds to the customers. End of story.'

'Son, will you listen tae me? I feel something. Dae you know whoot I mean?'

Shaw looked between the two men: the smartly dressed, if flustered, businessman, and Hamish, who looked bloody, battered and frantic. 'I don't think it will do any harm for Hamish to check in on Annie. After all, they're good friends.'

'So you make the rules in my hotel now, officer?'

'I think on this occasion it's advisable. Now let's go and check Annie is okay.'

Macmillan shrugged. 'You guys don't do things the way they do at home, that's for sure.'

But neither Hamish nor Shaw was listening to him. With the old fisherman taking two stairs at a time, the policeman behind, they made their way up to the third floor of the County Hotel.

Daley and Scott were within sight of a building near the shore when Scott called out.

'It's Willie! Look, heading down the hill. He's carrying something.'

'Are you sure it's him?'

'I think I know my own son when I see him, Jimmy.'

'Okay, we walk from here.' Daley parked the Land Rover just behind a mound beside the river. It didn't completely mask the vehicle, but he was hoping that everyone's attention would be elsewhere. 'We'll follow the river. We can crouch under the bank. But we're going to get our feet wet, Brian.'

'At least we'll no' be eaten by a shark this time.'

'Maybe a gentle mauling by a trout. Come on!'

'And what are we supposed to do when we get there, Jimmy? We couldn't even draw weapons.'

'Iolo's here with half the SAS, or whatever they are; I think we'll be okay. Anyway, I'm not sure that guns will be needed, somehow.'

'There you go.' Scott was puffing with the effort of slithering over the slick rocks at the side of the river. 'All this mystery,

I don't know where you get it. You read too many o' they books, I've always said it.'

'Just keep going, Bri.'

Nathan Sidley and Ronnie had also made their way down towards the big shed. The older man was feeling every year of his age, while Ronnie, fit and agile, leapt over fences and scaled small hills as though they weren't there, despite carrying heavy photographic equipment.

'Right, we'll stay here behind these bushes and let everyone get into place. You okay?' he asked.

'Sound as last Tuesday, lad.' Sidley was trying hard to catch his breath. He glanced towards the jetty. 'Look, someone's coming. What the fuck is that?'

Up the path appeared a man dragging a small, four-wheeled trolley. On top of it, secured by guy ropes, sat an object obscured by thick plastic shrink-wrap.

'That's the goods, and this is the handover. Our tips were right.'

'Yeah, that's fine, Ronnie, but did they tell you what these *goods* are? That could be a dirty bomb for all we know. And again, why are you getting these tips, not me?'

'Don't worry about that, mate. We get inside that building, you write your piece, and I'll take some pictures. It'll be amazing.'

'And what about the good guys on the other side of the hill?'

'That's the beauty of it. We'll see criminals at work and then being brought to book. You can't get a better story than that now, can you?'

'You're very sure about all this. Too sure for my liking.'

Ronnie looked into Sidley's eyes. 'If you don't want to do it, I dare say I can manage a few words, you know what I mean?'

There it was. For the first time Sidley knew where he stood. He was here, but any old hack would have done. 'So, tell me your plan then?'

'We wait here until your man with the trolley gets inside.'

'Then what, storm the place?'

'There's a fire escape round the other side of the building up a few stairs. We go in there.'

'Okay, just break down the fire door – nobody will notice that.'

'I'm informed that it's open. Place has been lying empty for five years. Things get broken, you know what I mean?'

'Not really, but I think I'm beginning to understand.'

'Ain't you the smart one. We hang on. He's not far away now.'

The big man pulling the trolley was only metres from the building.

54

Doing as he was told, Will approached the door within a door. The steel construction was bigger than it looked from further up the hill. For a moment, he was reminded of the lessons in perspective he'd learned in art classes at school.

Forcing himself to focus, he stood at the door and lifted his hand to knock. His heart leapt and he took two steps backwards when it opened to reveal a tall man with dark hair, entirely dressed in black.

He stared at Will, looking him up and down, then at the holdall.

'Couldn't they find anybody younger?' he said sarcastically.

Will shrugged. 'I'm just doing what I'm told.'

'Good lad. Right, come with me. Our man's outside.'

Will was ushered through the small door and along a dark corridor. His minder pushed open another steel door and suddenly a huge space opened out before him. At one end he could see dark figures under dim striplights, while almost in the centre of the floor someone was sitting on a chair, her mouth obscured by grey duct tape. As Will was led forward he realised that it was Chief Superintendent Symington. Her wide-eyed stare unsettled him as he approached. Whether she was trying to warn him, or was just scared, he couldn't tell. But he decided not to acknowledge her just in case it aroused suspicion. His heart went out to her, though; she looked so vulnerable and scared.

'Right, you stand here.'

Will did as he was told.

He could hear a clanking sound, metal on metal, the whir of an electric engine. Suddenly, bright light started to appear from the other end of the room: the flash of the evening sun on the sea beyond. Through a huge roller-shutter door came a man dragging a steel trolley behind him, the kind Will had seen in supermarkets. His frame was a dark silhouette against the lowering sun. To Will, it looked like a contrived stage display by a big-name rock band, but this was no night out with beers and friends. He stared as the man paced over the floor. It was clear that more men dressed in black were directing this newcomer towards him.

Will felt his palm sweaty on the handle of the holdall.

Sidley looked on as the big door began to rattle back down. Ronnie had described how they would be hidden in a shadowy recess at the top of internal fire escape stairs. There was little doubt that his informant was nothing if not meticulous. He wondered why a fire escape would be constructed this way, but reasoned that it must have had something to do with the manufacturing process for which the building had been intended. He watched as the big roller-shutter clanked to a halt about two feet off the ground, leaving a gap.

'Okay,' said Ronnie. 'Go for it!' The pair scurried from behind the thorn bush and made for the far side of the building.

Sidley's mouth was bone-dry as they passed by the gap left between the ground and the roller-shutter door. But soon they turned the corner, and, as Ronnie had predicted, there was an external steel staircase that led up to a fire door about halfway up the building.

'Right again, Ronnie. I should have had you with me before now. Would have saved a lot of legwork.'

Ignoring this, Ronnie held out his hand. They halted at the bottom of the staircase.

'What's up? You hearing something?' said Sidley.

'No, I'm just making sure that nobody's seen us.'

After a few moments, it was clear they hadn't been followed.

'Right. Come on, mate.' Ronnie took off up the steel steps.

Daley craned his head above the raised riverbank. The dry summer had reduced the flow of water to a trickle, but he could imagine the bloated river frothing to the sea in winter and spring. To his left, he could make out the rigging of a vessel. An oblong radar rotated slowly above a mast, but a small hill blocked his view of the superstructure. Good, he thought. That means they can't see us either.

'Right, what now, big man?' said Scott.

'We'll stay here for a moment. When we're sure the coast's clear we can get up to that door and take a gander.' He looked at his companion, whose expression was tired and worn. 'It's okay, Bri. Remember, Harris is about somewhere. We're not the magnificent two this time.'

'If it wisnae for the fact that my boy's in there I'd be mair relaxed, Jimmy.'

'It's okay, I hear you.' As Daley peered over the riverbank again, he felt the phone vibrate in his pocket. He pulled it out and looked at the screen.

'Shaw?' asked Scott.

'No, Liz. I've been waiting for a call for days. She chooses now.'

Scott shrugged. 'The mysteries o' the human mind, eh?'

'My wife's mind has always been a mystery to me.'

'Join the club.'

They waited.

55

Declan looked round the big space. He saw men with guns, a young man with a large bag at the other end of the building, and between them a figure tied to chair.

'Who the fuck is that?' he said.

'It's our leverage.'

Despite Linda's assurances, he wasn't sure whose side these armed men were on. She said they were in her control, but this man's English accent grated, and his instincts told him that something wasn't right. He looked back at the man who'd met him at the door. 'What now?'

'We take it where we can all see properly and strip off this bloody plastic.'

'Why don't we do it here? Are you sure?'

Bower shrugged. 'Yes, I'm sure. Even this idiot isn't going to buy something he can't see.' He leaned in to Declan's ear. 'It's kid gloves with this lot, or didn't she tell you that?'

Declan pulled the trolley to the middle of the floor as requested, a few feet from the woman trussed in the chair.

'Who's she?'

'Local police boss. Our insurance, like I said.'

'Fuck's sake! Nobody told me the police were involved!'

'Don't worry, mate. They're tied to a chair.'

The Irishman looked over at the thin young man with the

bag. 'I hope the money's all there, for your sake.'

'Relax,' said Bower. 'What do you want to do, count it?'

'As a matter of fact, aye, I do.'

Bower shook his head. 'It's all there, trust me.'

'So, you won't mind if I check.'

Bower shrugged. 'Okay, okay.' He pointed to one of his men. 'You, come on, get this plastic off here while this paddy counts his money.'

Declan glared at Bower as the man got to work on the shrink-wrap with a knife.

'You'd better tell him to watch what he's doing,' he said. 'Trust me, you don't want to damage that.'

Will looked on as the scene played out before him. His eyes flicked between the man working at the plastic and Symington's desperate gaze. The whole thing had taken on a dream-like quality. He supposed it was the mind's way of coping with stress. The thought of what was being slowly revealed on the trolley was too much for him to take in.

Slowly, Bower approached him and held out his hands. He was saying something, but to Will the words were just a jumble. He was conscious of hefting the holdall and handing it over.

As though speeding up on a roundabout, Will's world began to swim. He could feel his heart racing in his chest, and his face prickling with heat. He looked up into the metal rafters. The striplights were dancing round his head. He felt his legs give way beneath him just before his world turned black.

Declan looked at the youth as he collapsed. 'What's up with him? I thought he wanted to see the goods?'

Bower's expression was dark and mocking. 'Get him back on his feet.' He gestured to one of his men.

Declan sat on the edge of the trolley as the man above him continued to work away with his knife. He opened the bag. It was as Linda had said: hundred-dollar US bills neatly wrapped in two-thousand-dollar bundles. He didn't have the time to count each note; he was desperate to leave this place. But she'd told him to tally the bundles.

He looked across to where the young man who'd had the money was now being dragged to his feet, encouraged to regain full consciousness by less than gentle slaps to the face.

'Come on, paddy, you can count, can't you? You know, one, two three . . .' Bower's voice was mocking. 'We haven't got all bloody night.'

For Declan, a number of things happened at once.

A flash of light caught his eye, high above on the wall of the building. He heard a distant bang that echoed in the big space, and there were shouts and the urgent tramp of feet as a smoke bomb exploded and began to fill the space with choking fumes.

Coughing, he looked up to see figures appearing from the gloom at the rear of the building. They were carrying automatic weapons and wearing gas masks. He'd been set up. His worst fears were justified.

Don't get caught. Make sure you take them with you.

In a split second, Declan's grandfather's words echoed in his head. He stood up, scattering bundles of hundred-dollar bills to the floor. The man who had been cutting at the plastic wrapping thrust the knife he was holding in Declan's direction, but the Irishman was an old hand when it came to knife fights. He caught his attacker with a side-handed crack to the windpipe, and the man staggered backwards, falling from the trolley.

Desperately, Declan reached out. Quickly, one after the other, he turned on the gas from each bottle and then the big black regulator welded between the canisters.

The first shot hit him in the shoulder, the next in the chest. They spun him round like a rag doll. He collapsed on to the pallet, his life draining away in a burgeoning red tide.

As he died, the gases mixed together and began pouring out with a loud hiss.

56

Hearing the commotion, Daley and Scott raced to the gap in the big roller-shutter door. Looking under it they saw a scene of chaos. One body was lying on the floor beside the trolley they'd seen being brought into the building only minutes before, while a few feet away another man was struggling to his feet, coughing and spluttering. He was quickly apprehended by two men wearing gas masks and dragged away.

The billowing smoke further confused the situation, just as was intended. Dark-clad men in their shiny black masks looked like skittering insects as they fanned out across the floor grabbing choking, confused adversaries.

'Where's Willie?' shouted Scott, scanning the place for any sign of his son.

'I don't know, but that's Carrie on the chair, I'm sure of it.'

'Come on – we go in, Jimmy!' Scott bent to duck under the door, and saw, through the smoke, a figure crawling on all fours towards them like a scuttling animal. 'Hey, get oot here!' Scott caught his son by the shoulders and yanked him bodily out of the building.

'Are you okay, lad?' Daley checked the boy over for any injuries.

'We have to get away from here as quickly as we can!' Will tried to run, but his father pulled him back.

'Hang on. We have tae get Carrie oot o' there!'

Will was breathless with panic. 'It's sarin gas. He . . . he turned it on!'

'What?' said Daley.

'The Irish guy, he turned on the gas before they shot him. I saw it – I don't know if anyone else did.' Will fought desperately to free himself from his father's grip.

Daley was under the door in a flash.

'Jimmy!' Scott shouted. 'Get back! You've nae chance in there!'

But Daley's crouching shape disappeared into the smoky chaos. Men were shouting, there was a piercing scream, and then the clattering of boots on concrete.

'I cannae let him dae this on his own.' Scott ducked under the door in pursuit of Daley.

'Dad! Don't be stupid!' Will's call was in vain. He watched as his father ran through the smoke towards the chair to which Symington was tied. She had been trying desperately to push the chair back with the tips of her toes, but the thick duct tape had her ankles bound so tightly to the chair legs that there was little she could do.

Scott could hear a loud hissing when he arrived at Daley's side. The big detective was struggling to free Symington.

'Just pull her out on the chair!' Scott had the collar of his jacket over his face and nose in a desperate attempt to save himself from the gas. But, he noted, Daley hadn't taken any such precaution, and Symington couldn't. Daley's eyes were streaming and he was coughing incessantly, while streaks of black mascara ran down Symington's face and on to the duct tape round her mouth.

Daley nodded to Scott. Together, they grabbed the back

of the chair and frantically hauled it and Symington towards the door.

In front of them, the operation continued. Daley looked up for a split second. Through the smoke, he was sure he saw Iolo Harris. He was standing at the very back of the room, stock-still, like an apparition, no mask, his arms casually folded. From above, something flashed repeatedly, like lightning in a storm. But both Scott and Daley had only one thought in mind as they ducked into the gap between door and floor. It was clear they'd have to free Carrie from the chair, as it wouldn't fit through the gap, even now she was upended on her back. She looked from one to the other, sheer panic in her eyes.

Scott produced the big penknife from his pocket. He slashed first at the bonds on her arms, then her ankles, and even though he heard her muted yelp as he accidentally nicked her leg in his desperate haste, he carried on.

As Scott pared away the duct tape, Daley was tugging handfuls of it from the chair and from Symington's mouth. Will looked on in horror, desperate to help, but not knowing what to do.

'Right, that's her!' shouted Scott. He and Daley pulled Symington free of the chair and through the gap, and the four of them staggered down towards the riverbank. Will jumped over the edge first, closely followed by Daley. Scott helped Carrie over the bank and into Daley's arms, then leapt down after them. At last all four sat on the dry sand and shingle of the riverbed, gasping for breath, coughing and choking.

Symington's voice sounded hoarse between her coughs. 'Help me!'

The three men looked at her as she struggled to breathe.

'Fuck. She's had it, Jimmy.'

Glaring at Scott, Daley leaned over his stricken boss. 'Carrie, are you okay? Just try to breathe.' He held her hand, smiling into her face.

'It's the gas,' said Will. 'She was the closest for the longest time. She's dying!'

'Poor soul,' said Brian Scott.

'Would you all shut up!' said Symington, at last mustering enough breath to talk. 'Do you really think any of us would be alive if that was sarin gas?'

'Eh?' said Scott.

'What do you mean?' said Daley.

'We'd all be choking to death by now – every one of us. Don't be ridiculous.'

Daley thought for a moment. Of course she was right. Sarin gas was deadly, even from the briefest exposure. He looked to his left. There was no sign of the masts or radar he'd spotted sprouting from the boat earlier.

A short burst of gunfire sounded from the building, then everything fell silent.

'Maybe we're deid,' said Scott. 'You see that on the telly, souls that hang aboot, just no' realising they're broon breid.'

'Shut up, Brian,' said Daley, shaking his head. He stood. There was no vessel tied up at the jetty, nor any sign of it on the red ribbon of sea illuminated by the sun as it began to set in a glorious panoply of colour.

'Okay, we leave this to Harris – for now. Let's get back to the Land Rover.'

'For now? I never want tae see the bastard again,' said Scott.

Daley stared back at the gap under the door, where wisps of smoke were now billowing into the fading light. 'Oh, we'll be seeing him again, trust me.'

57

Hamish sat in the bar of the County Hotel, a large glass of whisky in his hand. He was staring blankly into space as police officers spoke into radios and paramedics packed away their equipment. A few feet away, Ian Macmillan was perched on the edge of a chair, head bowed.

The big front doors of the hotel were shut tight against the world. Everything looked so familiar, but nothing was the same. The blue lights on the till shone brightly in the subdued light; a tap dripped into a steel sink below the bar. Beer fonts stood sentry along its length, as though protecting the array of spirits marching along the gantry.

But one spirit was gone for good.

Hamish had only caught sight of her briefly. Her face was white – alabaster against the dark sheets. He could see she was wearing the red dress she wore to funerals. Annie had always hated black.

As Shaw pulled him away, he had remembered the dream that had so troubled him while captive in the musty old shed. The blood-soaked faces in the crimson sea all around, Annie sinking into it, her expression seeming to convey all the sadness in the world.

He'd been right, and he hated himself.

Hamish looked up at the bar, almost expecting to see her standing there, ready to chide him for something or other. His rheumy gaze settled on the corkboard where photographs of customers jostled for position. There they were, the pair of them. He was wearing his terrible kilt and the kipper tie, while Annie was wearing the dress she'd chosen as her shroud.

Hamish cried out. He threw the glass to the floor, the whisky it had contained leaving a dark stain on the red carpet. The old man held his head in his hands and sobbed.

Sergeant Shaw made his way over to comfort him.

'I know how you must be feeling. But you can't blame yourself.'

'I can so! I knew. I saw it. I did nothing.'

'But there was nothing you could do. You weren't free to help her.'

'Yes. In any case, nobody knew she'd do this. How could we?' Macmillan's voice sounded from the back of the bar.

Hamish stared across at him. He raised a bony finger at the proprietor of the County Hotel. 'You killed her – aye, as sure as sticking a knife through her heart by your own hand. This place was her home, the people who frequent it her family. You took it away for no other reason than your greed for gold. I tell you, Ian Macmillan, I curse you, curse you from the darkest place in my soul. Rot in hell!'

Macmillan shook his head. 'Listen, buddy, I know you're upset – we all are. But nobody knows what's going on in someone else's mind. For all you know it was you who caused her to feel the way she did. You disappeared. Where did you go, old man?'

Shaw turned to Macmillan. 'Sir, that's none of your business. And I'd thank you to be quiet, if you would.'

'I'll quieten the bastard!' Hamish shot from his seat, and in two long strides was standing over Macmillan. The proprietor made to square up to the older man, but Hamish locked his rough hands round Macmillan's throat, a look of sheer hatred in his eyes.

Shaw forced himself between them. 'Come on, Hamish! Don't make things worse than they are. Let go. This isn't what Annie would have wanted!'

It was as though the old fisherman's strength ebbed away like a spring tide. His last reserves of energy, following his ordeal and now the suicide of his best friend, had reached their limit. He lost his grip on Macmillan's neck, and had it not been for the strong arms of Shaw would have collapsed on to the floor.

'Paramedic, here, please!' shouted the sergeant as he cradled the old man's thin frame in the bar of the County Hotel.

When Daley arrived back at Kinloch police office with Symington and the Scotts, he was surprised not to see Shaw in the bar office. He took Symington to the family room, where she stretched out on the couch.

'You're for the hospital, Carrie,' he said quietly.

'I'm for a new job, Jim. I can't live this lie any more.'

'This isn't the time. Go and get checked over while I try to make sense of this. I'll get someone to drive you.'

'The whole thing's wrong. I don't understand it either.'

Daley brought her a glass of water from the machine in the corner of the room. 'You'll need to get that cut seen to. Will you be okay for a few minutes?'

'Yes, I'll be fine. I'm not a porcelain doll, you know.'

She smiled weakly, putting the cup of water to her lips with trembling hands.

Heading for his glass box, Daley met Scott in the corridor. He saw tears in his old friend's eyes. 'Listen, Brian, Will's safe. We'll all need to get checked over just in case, but he looks fine to me. It's finished.'

Scott gulped back his tears. 'It's no' that, Jimmy.' He looked up at Daley helplessly.

Daley's chest tightened. 'It's not Liz – young James?'

'No.' Scott swallowed again. 'It's Annie.'

'Annie? What's up with her? I thought she'd be delighted to see Hamish again.'

'She's deid, Jim. Took her own life – an overdose. They found her when we were away.'

Daley took time to absorb this information. 'Annie? But she's one of the happiest people I know. Never changes.'

Scott shrugged. 'Dae you ever really know anyone, big man? Apparently that Macmillan fired her. I don't know. We'll find out mair tomorrow.' He wiped a tear from his eye. 'I need tae get my boy tae the hospital. Aye, and go and get Ella, as well. You don't mind, dae you? Shaw's dealing wae things doon at the County.'

'Can you drive Carrie up there, too?'

'Aye, of course, Jimmy. Is she okay?'

'Shocked more than anything else.'

'I'm kinda shocked myself.'

'I know. Annie was a good woman.'

'Aye, she was a fine lassie. You remember when we first arrived? Made us welcome here when nobody else was so keen, eh?'

'She did.' Thinking of Annie's bright smile behind the bar,

Daley could feel tears welling in his own eyes. 'You be off up the road and get Will and Carrie to the hospital. I'll see you there.'

'Aye, will do, sir.' Scott walked away with his head low.

Daley couldn't remember Brian Scott ever calling him sir. It sounded so strange coming from the man he'd known for so long. But life was strange. Hamish had survived, but Annie was dead. Daley had seen so much death in his life – far too much. He always tried not to think of the people he'd known and lost, but now Annie would join the list of ghosts who followed him every day.

Daley knew he should go to the hospital, but he'd a lot to think about. He flung himself into the chair behind his desk. He thought of the plane and its gruesome cargo, the disappearance of Hamish, and Carrie Symington's plight; but somehow nothing made any sense.

Iolo Harris's ghostly figure, standing still and calm in the smoke and chaos, passed before his mind's eye.

The mobile buzzed in his pocket. He was surprised to see Nathan Sidley's number on the screen.

'DCI Daley, I hope you're safe and well.' Sidley's Liverpudlian accent was loud over the phone.

'I am – we are. You?'

'Yeah, I'm sound, thanks. Listen, can you spare me a few moments of your time?'

'Sure. I'm in the office.'

'Maybe at the guest house – away from prying eyes, if you know what I mean?'

'Yes, I know where you are. I'll be down in ten.'

58

Sidley was typing furiously on his laptop. He had already sent the first part of the story to the newspaper when Daley's knock sounded on his door. He was reluctant to stop, but what he had to say to the DCI wouldn't take long, and he would spend the rest of the night writing up the biggest story of his career. And, he reasoned as he closed his laptop, this one could have a long tail.

The big detective's frame filled the doorway.

'Come on in, Jim. Thanks for taking the time to have a chat.'

'Always happy to help the press, Nathan,' said Daley with only a hint of sarcasm.

'I know you're a busy man, so I'll get to the point. I've some information for you.'

'Oh yes? I'm always pleased when information flows in this direction between journalists and us police officers. Too often it's the other way round.'

'Ha! You're a smart man, Jim.' Sidley pulled out a chair for Daley and took a seat on the end of his bed. 'You know, in my business, people lie to me all the time. Must be the same for you, I reckon.'

'More often than not.'

'I have the identity of your second man on the plane. One

Eddie North, ex-para, he was. Served for five years and left under a cloud.'

'How did you find that out? We couldn't.'

'Tip-off from a reliable source. That's all I can say, really.'

'But you know more, right?'

'I don't *know*, but I can have a guess.'

'Okay, I'm all ears,' said Daley, sitting back in his chair.

'The tech on that plane – no terrorist group could get their hands on kit like that.'

'Yes, I thought that, too.'

'I worked for a long time in Ireland, Jim. I've seen all sorts of undercover stuff – yeah, and I've seen lots of it go wrong.'

'What are you saying?'

'Your men on the plane, same suits, right.'

'Yes.'

'It's an old signature of an IRA cell. Deliver the bodies of undercover units back to the army dressed that way. It was saying *we know who you are*. They sent them back in civvies because as far as they were concerned they were spies, not military combatants.'

'But why? It's all but over across there.'

'You think? The man who died back in that place earlier was Declan Louth, a very high-ranking member of a dissident Republican group. Man fighting for his life in a hospital in Belfast, Sean Dolan, was much the same, maybe even higher in the pecking order. Both very dangerous men. Both part of this thing – whatever it was. Now they're both, well, out of the picture, or as good as.'

'Back to the pair in the plane, you think they were under-cover army, or something?'

Sidley shrugged. 'Or another agency?'

'MI5?'

'Why not, eh?'

'But why? The men died.'

'It's the lure before the catch, Jim. You let the enemy think they've got the better of you just to lure them in. Or to make someone look, you know, trustworthy.'

'Linda Delaney?'

'Could be.' He shrugged.

'But sacrificing men? I can't see it.'

'That's what soldiers do, Jim, they die. You don't buy all this crap about your country protecting their soldiers, do you? If it suits the bigger picture, you're expendable.'

Daley blanched. 'Seems like a lot of effort for the scalps of a few terrorists.'

'It does. But the Good Friday Agreement, Jim: we can't be seen to be knocking off suspected dissidents, can we, now? It's illegal.'

'It's depressing.'

'You can have a think. But there're conclusions to be drawn.' He smiled. 'Have a read of the paper the next couple of days. It might help.'

'I will.'

'And don't forget your old pals if you come up with something, will you?'

'No, I won't.' Daley stood up and shook the journalist's hand.

Sidley stared into his eyes. 'Sometimes, if you want to make a real difference, you have to play as dirty as the rest, Jim. But you know that.' He paused. 'Oh, and by the way, do you know anything about an ex-Met cop called Bower?'

'Why?'

'Declan Louth wasn't the only man to come out of that place dead. We don't have confirmation, but Bower was shot when pulling a gun on one of our brave boys. Just thought you might be interested.' Sidley gazed at him. 'Jim, ask yourself who lost nothing from this – gained, maybe.'

'Linda Delaney?'

'Yes, but she wasn't alone.' He laughed. 'They say all life is a stage, DCI Daley. But stages are carefully dressed. It all adds to the make-believe. You need space away from prying eyes to plan and rehearse something worthwhile, don't you?' He paused, as though debating whether or not to say more. He did. 'Why was your boss there – and was she a hostage or a witness? I can only report what I saw – what my friend Ronnie captured on his phone. He was handy, by the way. His phone's ringing out now. I've asked the question about the gas. The answer was vague; they'd infiltrated the production process at source, apparently. In any case, it's had a D notice slapped on. This is a great story as it is – probably the best of my career. But there's more – so much more.'

'And you won't stop digging?'

'Ha! Time's not on my side, Jim. I've done that much digging my hands are worn to the bone. Time for the new generation to take up the cudgels, I think.'

'Shame. Good luck, Nathan.' Daley nodded and left Sidley to his story. But if anything, he was more confused than ever.

The headlines over the next few days were spectacular. Sidley's piece was quoted on social media and syndicated across the world. The hard-bitten journalist was all over television and radio. But not once did Sidley hint at the suspicions he'd discussed with Daley.

The detective brought a tabloid headline up on the PC screen. The general consensus was that the hardworking men and women of the Security Service had foiled a plot most foul, hatched between extreme climate activists and dissident Republican terrorists. Their intention had been to strike at the heart of the British state with a terror weapon so wicked that hundreds could have died.

As it was, potential terror cells had been uncovered, and the climate movement, shocked by the revelations, sent reeling. Public opinion turned on a sixpence and support for those trying to save the planet began to wane.

There was no mention of the fact that the 'wicked' terror weapon had been nothing more than two canisters of CO_2. And, as far as Daley could ascertain, Linda Delaney had vanished, walking free from the events she had clearly masterminded – from both sides.

But it wasn't the tumble of words that caught Daley's eye, but one screengrab. It had been captured on the footage filmed by Sidley's photographer, Ronnie. As security personnel fanned out across the floor towards the canisters – the corpse of Declan Louth pixelated out of view for decency's sake – there, through the shadows and the smoke, stood a man without a gas mask, arms folded. It was an echo of the image etched in Daley's own memory, albeit from another perspective. The sight of Iolo Harris had troubled him then, and it did now.

He picked up the phone. One person was the key to this, and she was nowhere to be found. It was a long shot, but Daley had to try. 'Can I be connected to the chief constable's office, please? It's DCI Daley from Kinloch.'

59

The weather had turned. The bright, hot summer had been replaced by a leaden sky. Though it was dry, rain wasn't far away. Daley shivered. The scene felt eerily familiar, but he couldn't think why. Perhaps it was just the emotion of it all.

He looked at the large group of people gathered round the graveside. Hamish was huddled into a seafarer's black pea jacket. He looked old and frail, the garment seeming to draw what little light there was from the grey sky, though the badly knotted red tie he wore as a tribute to Annie added a little colour. Daley knew his heart was stifling sore.

Daley watched as Ella wiped away a dark mote from Scott's collar, blown there by the stiff breeze off the loch. Scott stared into his wife's blue eyes, almost hidden by the dark veil of her hat. She stroked his hair affectionately, knowing very well how much her husband was hurting. She whispered something in his ear, and he returned a weak smile.

Carrie Symington was in full uniform, and for a moment a shimmering shaft of sunlight caught the silver braid of her cap before it was gone. She stood stiffly, her arms at her side, ceremonial white gloves on her hands. Daley thought how small she looked, almost as though her spirit had been crushed. He tried to put himself in her shoes; after all, his own career hadn't been plain sailing. But he didn't envy the hard choices he knew she faced. In any event, he had resolved to keep her secrets, and he was sure that Iolo Harris would do likewise. He could see her eyes were brimming with tears.

Liz squeezed his hand and looked up at him with her hypnotic gaze. He could see how beautiful she was, but his heart no longer leapt in his chest at the mere sight of her. He'd fought to get that feeling back, but he knew it wasn't something that could be conjured up by wishing. He thought of his son and squeezed her hand in return. But he feared the little boy was all that remained between them.

The coffin was poised above the gaping hole on two stout planks of wood, red winding cords sprouting from gleaming brass handles round its sides. Daley shivered again. Again, somehow, this was all too familiar. Death had walked with him for so long, and since his own illness it had never seemed closer. The sombre setting of the graveyard and its silent mourners did nothing to banish the feeling. He saw the wind tug at the white hair of Kinloch's undertaker as he handed out small cards bordered in funeral black.

The minister's dark robes billowed in the wind as he called the men and women of Kinloch together to say a last farewell to one of their own. His voice was strong, and it modulated round the silent stones of the graveyard, its echo on the lips of all those gathered. Jim Daley lowered his head as he joined them all in prayer.

The solemn ceremony over, the mourners straggled back to their cars.

'Are you ready, Jimmy?' said Scott.

'Here, Brian.' Daley fished his car keys from his pocket.

'Can you or Liz drive back? I need to clear my head. I want to walk.'

'Aye, okay, big man. I'll see you back at the hotel.'

'It'll be odd. Her not being there, I mean.'

'It sure will, Jimmy.' Scott patted his friend's shoulder and walked off to where Ella and Liz were standing beside Daley's SUV.

Daley angled his head towards the sky and breathed in the salt air. It was good to be alive. There was no place that confirmed that like a cemetery. With most people in a slow procession of cars back to Kinloch, Daley spotted a figure standing over a grave in the distance, in the older part of the cemetery. He walked over.

'Hamish, how are you holding up?'

'Mr Daley – Jim. Aye, no' too bad. Though, in truth, I don't think the whole thing's sunk in yet.'

'No, I understand what you mean.' Daley looked at the weathered gravestone at which Hamish was staring. 'Somebody you knew?'

The old man smiled. 'Aye, I knew him well. My old skipper, Sandy Hoynes. A finer man never sailed the seas, and that's a fact.'

'I see the boat engraved on the stone.'

'Aye, they say it's a birlinn – you know, the old ships of Argyll. But in reality, for all their similarities, this represents something far older – a dragon ship.'

'Vikings?'

'Aye, jeest so – for Sandy had a right notion aboot them in his latter years. I never really worked out why. But the tales he could tell . . . well, they'd have kept you entertained, for sure.'

'Do you always come to visit him when you're here?'

'I dae that. Och, I'm no' one for raking aboot the graveyard at Easter or Christmas or the like. But now I'm here, I want to pay my respects to Sandy, aye and tae the others I've known, including my ain dear mother and faither. Heaven knows, I'll be joining them all soon enough. When you get tae my age, you feel the pull o' this place, and no mistake.'

'You don't have to be your age. Come on, we'll stroll back to the hotel, eh? It's going to rain soon.'

Hamish lifted his face to the sky, sniffing the air like a dog. 'Aye, I do believe you're right, Mr Daley. But it'll no' be the hotel for me. I canna set foot in the place. No' since . . . well, you know.'

'I don't think you should be alone – not grieving like this.'

'I have a fine bottle o' malt jeest sitting there at hame. Fair pleading tae be drunk, it is.'

Daley looked across as the gravediggers went about the task of attending to Annie's last resting place. 'Have you enough whisky for a friend?'

'Aye, I sure have. You're mair than welcome. Though mind and watch oot for Hamish.'

'Don't worry, I'll be giving your cat a wide berth.'

They made their way out of the cemetery in silence, but just as they reached the big gates Hamish spoke. 'I've been thinking. By rights, it should be me that was being laid tae rest back there.'

'It wasn't. But I could wish we weren't here at all, Hamish.'

'True, very true.' He looked Daley in the eye. 'Dae you think you'll ever get to the bottom o' it – what happened, I mean? Och, I've read the newspapers, but I never believe half o' whoot I read.'

'I hope we can get to the truth somehow.'

408

'Aye, any other truth but this.' The old fishermen gazed across to where the workmen had just finished laying the soil over Annie's coffin. 'Goodbye, lassie. I'll miss you.'

Brian Scott hadn't tarried at the funeral tea. He felt uncomfortable in the County Hotel. It appeared that Annie had told no one of her dismissal, and Ian Macmillan was keen that it stayed that way. So her family had unwittingly chosen the hotel for the reception, traditional in a place where friends and family gathered to celebrate the life and times of the recently deceased.

Scott brought Ella and Liz drinks from the bar.

'I've no idea where Jim's got to,' said Liz.

'I saw him wae Hamish. Likely gone tae see the auld man's okay. He'll no' set foot in here,' said Scott.

'Oh, but he's like the wallpaper in this place.' Liz looked surprised.

'It's a long story,' said Ella. 'Maybe no' the best time tae go intae detail. I'm sure your Jim will keep you right later.'

'Mysterious. I go away for a couple of weeks and all sorts of things happen. Typical. Though I feel so sorry for Annie,' she added hurriedly.

'You mind if I go back tae the office for a while, Ella? I've a few loose ends tae tie up.'

'Just move your bed in and you should be fine. Aye, off you go. I'll see you at hame.' Ella looked at Liz and raised her eyes heavenward.

'Jim's the same. The bloody job is his mistress.'

Scott glanced at Ella, who suppressed a smile.

Scott said goodbye to the members of Annie's family he knew and was soon glad to be out of the place. He'd never liked funerals and had found this one particularly upsetting. He'd been fond of Annie, and like everyone else was shocked that she'd taken her own life.

Will was away for the day meeting a friend who'd travelled to Kinloch to take his mind off the trauma he'd been through and his break-up with Des, and Scott stood in the hall and listened to the silence for a moment or two. The old wall clock that had belonged to Ella's father was ticking loudly in the lounge, but that apart all was silent.

He sighed to himself then took the stairs two at a time. In his and Ella's bedroom he opened the wardrobe. The smell of clothes, leather and varnish hit him as he leaned in, and from amongst a pile of shoes he removed a box. It was taped shut, but he sliced it quickly open with his keys, his hands shaking.

He reached inside, his fingers making passage past old bank statements, insurance policies and the like. But soon he gripped something cold and smooth.

Scott pulled the whisky bottle from the box, held it in front of his face and stared at it for a moment. The golden liquid inside distorted the room, making the wardrobe bulge in the middle.

He was breathing heavily now, the bottle still held in mid-air.

Scott cracked it open and put it to his lips. At first the spirit tasted strange on his tongue, burning, almost corrosive, and the smell of the spirit almost made him retch. But after a couple of gulps he felt its cosseting warmth slip down his gullet and ease his troubled mind.

He lay back on the bed. Soon his mind was as distorted as the wardrobe had appeared through the glass of the bottle.

Scott closed his eyes. The guilt would follow, the fear would come later. For now, he felt safe in the arms of alcohol, protected from a hard, unforgiving world.

60

Three months later

September had been a cold month, its storms of wind and rain presaging winter before its time. But for the men and women of Kinloch police office, life had been reasonably quiet.

Nothing much had been seen of Chief Superintendent Symington. Daley had called her on a number of occasions to discuss operational matters. She had been pleasant and businesslike, but he had detected a distinct distance.

He was busy writing up a case about minor drug misuse when the email notification on his phone pinged into life. Wearily, he reached across the desk for the mobile and brought up the message.

With the agreement of the chief constable, he'd issued a description of Linda Delaney across the continent via Interpol. He'd justified this by stating his suspicion that she had been involved in the kidnapping of Hamish. Indeed, the old man's recollections of the incident pointed to her complicity, as he had described her to a tee.

The email, which he scanned quickly, had an attachment. Daley opened it up, and three images filled the screen. The woman was tanned, her dark, almost black hair swept back in a ponytail. According to the email she was enjoying drinks with a young man on a Turkish beach.

He opened a drawer in his desk and after a short search produced a file. One of the photographs contained within was of Linda Delaney. He compared it to those he'd just been sent. There was little doubt this was the same woman, her only disguise being the dying of her hair.

Daley thought for a moment. He flicked through other documents in the file and found what he was looking for: a newspaper clipping from three weeks before.

Iolo Harris to be MI5's new Deputy Director was the bold headline on page five of the *Sunday Times*. Daley didn't need to read the piece: he knew it off by heart. It was the tale of a man with a long and unblemished record of working for the Security Service, notably bringing to book dangerous terrorists and climate extremists. It sounded as though his heroic actions had saved the lives of many innocent people.

Daley stared at the article for a while, then at the image of Linda Delaney. He thought of Will, the torments that Hamish had suffered, the problems that still bedevilled Carrie Symington. He thought, too, of Annie. If Hamish hadn't disappeared, would she still be alive? He could never know for certain, but his heart told him the truth.

He held the mobile in his hand and scrolled down his contacts. Hamish's words as they left the cemetery on the day of Annie's funeral were echoing in his mind.

'Jim Daley. Good to hear from you.' Nathan Sidley's voice was bright over the phone.

'I see you all the time, these days. You're quite the celebrity – awards and all sorts.'

'More importantly, a big bag of money, Jim. Retirement beckons.'

'Maybe time for one last story?'

Sidley was quiet for a few moments. 'Would this be something you can't follow up yourself by any chance? Something that maybe those in the halls of power may frown upon?'

'I'm just searching for the facts, Nathan. I'm looking for any other truth I can find. But, well, sometimes it's not that easy for a man in my position. Do you have a pen?'

'Right in my hand, Jim.'

Daley read the address in Turkey straight from the email he'd just received. 'I know how well you protect your sources, Nathan.'

'It's been my watchword throughout my career. You need have no worries on that score. But this address – do you have any more information?'

'Two words: Linda Delaney.'

There was a short silence on the other end of the phone. 'Received and understood. I'll get on with it right now.' He chuckled. 'Well done, lad. This will be the biggest thing I've ever done.'

'If she talks.'

'She'll talk. She's cornered, and she'll need more money. And remember, I know her of old.'

Daley ended the call and looked at the article from the *Sunday Times* once more. 'Enjoy your new job, Iolo,' he said with a smile.

Epilogue

Four days later

Scott had taken some time off – feeling unwell, which was unusual. Though everyone got sick from time to time, Daley had seen signs that he'd feared for a while. Though his old friend had been very discreet, there was little that could be done about bloodshot eyes, or the hint of stale whisky on the breath. But so long as Scott continued to function well as a police officer – and there were no signs to the contrary – all Daley could do was maintain a watching brief. He was determined that his old friend wouldn't plummet into the depths of despair again.

He'd just turned in to the cemetery car park, the radio, as ever, on for company, when he heard the news coming on. Having had little time to catch up with what was happening in the world that day, he decided to listen before going about his business.

Nathan Sidley, the journalist who exposed the sarin terror threat earlier this summer, has been found dead in Turkey. He was sixty-five years old and was believed to have been holidaying in the country. The cause of death appears to be a heart attack. Turkish police say there are no suspicious circumstances.

Sidley was an award-winning investigative journalist who,

after beginning his career at the Liverpool Echo, *worked for many newspapers during the Troubles in Northern Ireland before turning his attention to climate issues. He leaves behind a son from his marriage to his late wife Anthea.*

Daley stared into space for a moment. He felt empty, angry and confused all at the same time.

No suspicious circumstances. That would be the accepted wisdom. But Daley knew there was a real truth – another truth.

He turned off the radio and walked down narrow paths between sombre headstones, feeling as if in the midst of a terrible nightmare. He could see one recently wrought grave piled with faded flowers, some petals fluttering away on the breeze like the soul they commemorated. Eventually, he came to Annie's last resting place. Grass had grown over her grave now, knitting together the turf under which she lay. It was almost as though she was now sewn into the earth for eternity. He thought that *Loved by all*, etched into the small red granite headstone, was the perfect epitaph.

Daley removed something from his pocket and held it out in both hands. The polished brass plate twinkled in the watery sunshine. The wording was simple: *County Hotel: General Manager.*

The big policeman knelt beside the stone and, using a loose pebble, dug a small divot under it in the black earth. He placed the name tag there, covering it over with the soil he'd removed.

'Farewell, Annie. God bless you.'

Daley prayed silently for a moment before walking away, back to a world that was suddenly darker than even he had ever imagined.

Notes

I wanted this book to shine a light on the close proximity of County Antrim to the Kintyre peninsula. Trade and cultural exchange have taken place across the few short miles of the North Channel for centuries.

Campbeltown has more in common with Ballycastle, in my opinion, than it does with the other towns in Argyll. You just have to visit these places to recognise this connection. The comparisons are there for all to see.

Even the accent isn't a million miles away. Our lovely neighbour Mary Anderson is a native of Ballycastle. I hear her speak words and sayings I last heard from my granny, who hailed from Machrihanish.

As I write, there are airy plans afoot for tunnels or bridges between Scotland and County Antrim. But the sea has always been the real highway. A few years ago, there was a seasonal ferry between Campbeltown and Ballycastle. Once again, the people on both sides of the North Channel found the common ground that has always been there.

Perhaps the politicians who brought the service to an end should consider reinstating it. After all, despite what Brian Scott may think, sailing is the easiest and most practical way to connect us to our kin across the water.

Acknowledgements

As always to my dear wife Fiona for enduring the endless, thunderous clatter of computer keys during the long days of lockdown. Not forgetting felines Susie and Bertie (Cat Bonnington). Much gratitude to my friend in letters Douglas Skelton, with whom I've had many laughs, albeit remotely. You must buy his books.

As I write, my thoughts go out to all those for whom this terrible time has been very dark indeed. God bless you all. To all those who have worked so hard to keep us safe and well, and mend our broken bodies, I salute you. Plaudits are all very well, but proper reward is equally important. This should happen.

To my editors Nancy Webber and Alison Rae, profound thanks. It's been a busy time. Also, to Hugh Andrew and all at Polygon for keeping the show on the road in unprecedented times. A special mention for Lucy Mertekis – it's been a blast! All the best for the future.

Thanks, too, to my fabulous narrator and old friend David Monteath, truly the king of narration. A massive thank-you to my tireless agent Jo Bell of Bell Lomax Moreton. So many great things in prospect, and such good cheer; I am in your debt (gin).

To readers old and new. I've been deeply touched by those

who have contacted me to say how my books have helped them through these strange and vexing times. I'm delighted to have been even a small comfort.

To our friends and neighbours for their help and support. And, as always to the people of Kintyre, without whom . . .

D.A.M.
Gartocharn
May 2021

The DCI Daley thriller series

Book 1: *Whisky from Small Glasses*
DCI Jim Daley is sent from the city to investigate a murder after the body of a woman is washed up on an idyllic beach on the west coast of Scotland. Far away from urban resources, he finds himself a stranger in a close-knit community.

Book 2: *The Last Witness*
James Machie was a man with a genius for violence, his criminal empire spreading beyond Glasgow into the UK and mainland Europe. Fortunately, Machie is dead, assassinated in the back of a prison ambulance following his trial and conviction. But now, five years later, he is apparently back from the grave, set on avenging himself on those who brought him down.

Book 3: *Dark Suits and Sad Songs*
When a senior Edinburgh civil servant spectacularly takes his own life in Kinloch harbour, DCI Jim Daley comes face to face with the murky world of politics. To add to his woes, two local drug dealers lie dead, ritually assassinated. It's clear that dark forces are at work in the town.

Book 4: *The Rat Stone Serenade*
It's December, and the Shannon family are heading to their clifftop mansion near Kinloch for their AGM. Shannon International, one

of the world's biggest private companies, has brought untold wealth and privilege to the family. However, a century ago, Archibald Shannon stole the land upon which he built their home – and his descendants have been cursed ever since.

Book 5: *The Well of the Winds*
As World War Two nears its end, a man is stabbed to death on the Kinloch shoreline, in the shadow of the great warships in the harbour. When DCI Daley comes into possession of a journal written by his wartime predecessor in Kinloch, he soon realises that he must solve a murder from the past to uncover the shocking events of the present.

Book 6: *The Relentless Tide*
When Professor Francombe and her team of archaeologists find the remains of three women on a remote Kintyre hillside – a site rumoured to have been the base of Viking warlord Somerled – their delight soon turns to horror when they realise the women tragically met their end only two decades ago.

It soon becomes clear that these are the three missing victims of the 'Midweek Murderer', a serial killer who was at work in Glasgow in the early 1990s. DCI Jim Daley now has the chance to put things right – to confront a nightmare from his past and solve a crime he failed to as a young detective.

Book 7: *A Breath on Dying Embers*
When the luxury cruiser *Great Britain* berths in Kinloch harbour, the pressure mounts on DCI Jim Daley. The high-powered international delegates on board are touring the country, golfing and sightseeing, as part of a UK government trade mission. But within hours, one of the crew members vanishes and a local birdwatcher has disappeared.

Book 8: *Jeremiah's Bell*
Teenager Alison Doig disappeared from Kinloch over thirty years ago under mysterious circumstances. Her reclusive family still live in a remote part of the Kintyre peninsula, amidst rumours of wrecking, smuggling and barbaric cruelty.

Now rich American hotelier Alice Wenger has arrived in town, determined to punish those who made her suffer in the past. But someone has vowed to keep hidden sins concealed for ever.

Short Stories and Tales from Kinloch

One Last Dram Before Midnight: The Complete Collected DCI Daley Short Stories

Published together for the first time in one not-to-be-missed volume are all Denzil Meyrick's short stories. Discover how DCI Daley and DS Scott first met on the mean streets of Glasgow in two prequels that shed light on their earlier lives. Join Hamish and his old mentor, skipper Sandy Hoynes, as they become embroiled with some Russian fishermen and an illicit whisky plot. And in present-day Kinloch Daley and Scott investigate ghosts from the past, search for a silent missing man, and follow the trail of an elusive historical necklace.

Dalintober Moon: A DCI Daley Story

When a body is found in a whisky barrel buried on Dalintober beach, it appears that a notorious local crime, committed over a century ago, has finally been solved. However, the legacy of murder still resonates within the community, and the tortured screams of a man who died long ago still echo across Kinloch.

Two One Three: A Constable Jim Daley Short Story

Glasgow, 1986. Only a few months into his new job, Constable Jim